sirensong

Also by Jenna Black

glimmerglass
shadowspell

sirensong

jenna black

 St. Martin's Griffin ≈ New York

SIRENSONG. Copyright © 2011 by Jenna Black. All rights reserved. Printed in the United States of America. For information, address St. Martin's Press, 175 Fifth Avenue, New York, N.Y. 10010.

www.stmartins.com

Library of Congress Cataloging-in-Publication Data

Black, Jenna.
  Sirensong : a faeriewalker novel / Jenna Black.—1st ed.
      p. cm.—(Faeriewalker ; bk. 3)
  ISBN 978-0-312-57595-3
  1. Teenage girls—Fiction. 2. Magic—Fiction. I. Title.
PS3602.L288S56 2011
813'.6—dc22
                                                    2011008087

First Edition: July 2011

10 9 8 7 6 5 4 3 2 1

To Sibyl, who helped me learn some of the lessons Dana had to learn in this book, but without any death or dismemberment.

acknowledgments

My thanks to the many great people at St. Martin's, especially my editor, Jennifer Weis, and her assistant, Mollie Traver. Thanks to my agent, Miriam Kriss, who dropped everything to read this manuscript overnight when I got horribly stuck. Not only that, she even managed to get me unstuck! My thanks also to my husband, Dan, who is my first reader for all my books and gets to share in the joys of the deadline crunch. And lastly, thanks to the Deadline Dames, who are always there for me when I need some words of encouragement. You rock!

chapter one

I hate politics. Too bad my father is a big-deal Fae politician, hoping to get bigger. Also too bad that I'd run away from home to escape my alcoholic mother and live with my father in hopes of a more normal life, because what I'd gotten was a heaping helping of anything-but-normal, with a side order of mortal danger. Which is how I found myself dressed in an insanely expensive midnight-blue evening dress—wearing *heels,* no less—and being escorted by my tux-clad father to a fancy state dinner I wanted no part of.

The dinner was at the Consul's mansion. My dad and I joined the glittering cream of Avalon high society, waiting in line between the velvet ropes as a pair of Knights controlled traffic and checked invitations. I'd never been to an event anywhere near as formal as this before, and I wouldn't have been at this one if my dad hadn't insisted.

When I came to Avalon, the only place where the mortal world and Faerie intersect, I already knew my father was some kind of big-deal Fae. What I *didn't* know was all the zillions of ways his status would affect my life. Or that he would try to use me as a pawn in his political chess game. You see, in a little more than a year, the current human Consul—the most powerful person in Avalon, kind of like a president, but not really—was going to have to step down in favor of a Fae. The Consulship changes hands between humans and Fae every ten years, and my dad was bound and determined to be the next Consul of Avalon.

Another thing I'd had no clue about before I'd blundered into Avalon was that every once in a while, when a really powerful Fae—like, say, my father—had a child with a human, that child was . . . special. A Faeriewalker, someone with enough Fae blood to travel into Faerie and enough mortal blood to travel into the mortal world. But here's the kicker: not only can Faeriewalkers travel freely in both worlds, they can bring magic into the mortal world and technology into Faerie.

Yup, you guessed it: I'm a Faeriewalker. A rare breed, seeing as the last one before me died almost a century ago. And because of my unique abilities, I became a political asset, which was why my dad was dragging me along to this event when I'd have preferred to stay home and scrounge something from the fridge. Everyone in freakin' Avalon knew about me, knew I was a Faeriewalker, but Dad had to trot me out to the dinner and show me off, remind everyone that I was his daughter and that if he became Consul, he'd use me to Avalon's advantage. Never mind that I wasn't going to let him "use" me for anything, and he knew it.

"Try not to scowl quite so fiercely, Dana," he said to me in a dry undertone as we inched toward the head of the line.

I tried to wipe the scowl from my face, though I'm not sure I succeeded. "You are going to owe me for this big-time," I muttered, and out of the corner of my eye, I saw his lips curve into a faint smile.

"Maybe you'll enjoy yourself," he suggested, handing his invitation to the Knight with the clipboard.

Knights are Fae warriors, and there was something just *wrong* about seeing one standing there with a clipboard. Of course, he probably had about a hundred weapons concealed on him, and I could feel the prickly sensation of magic surrounding him. Supposedly only true Fae could sense magic, but I was apparently the exception. Because being a garden-variety Faeriewalker didn't make me freakish enough. I'd managed to keep my affinity with magic hidden from almost everyone—even my father—so far, and I planned to keep it that way.

The Knight waved us through, and we climbed a set of red-carpeted stairs into a cavernous marble entryway. There were more Knights inside, directing the crowd down a long hallway and making sure no one strayed from the path. They were dressed in tuxes, just like all the other men in the crowd, but they stuck out like sore thumbs anyway, with their muscular builds, their severe expressions, and their not-so-covert surveillance.

"Yeah, this is going to be tons of fun," I mumbled, keeping my voice low so it wouldn't echo off the marble. I didn't need any prior experience with state dinners to guess it was going to include a lot of long, boring speeches. And that Dad was going to introduce me to a lot of people with whom I was supposed to make polite small talk and smile. Just how any sixteen-year-old likes to spend the evening, right?

I could, of course, be a total brat and play the part of the sullen, bored teenager, making my dad regret dragging me along. But he and I were still sort of learning our way around each other, and if I was going to be difficult about something, it would be something more important than whether or not I had to sit through a bunch of speeches.

At the end of the hallway, we had to stand in line again, but this was worse, because I could see—and hear—what was in store for us when we got to the head of the line. There was a tall, thin Fae man standing there, and everyone stopped when they stepped up beside him, then waited for him to announce their names in a loud, deep voice, after which they could finally enter the room and go through an endless-looking receiving line.

Groan! If it took this much time and effort to even get in, I didn't want to know how long the dinner was going to take. I wondered if I could convince Dad I'd suddenly developed a migraine, or the flu. Maybe Ebola.

"You're scowling again," Dad whispered, and I gave him a dirty look.

"This counts as cruel and unusual punishment," I told him. "And I haven't even done anything wrong." The bratty, sullen teenager idea was beginning to hold a certain appeal. Maybe I could embarrass my dad enough to make him send me home.

Dad sighed, but we'd reached the head of the line so he made no comeback. We stood on the landing right outside an honest-to-goodness ballroom, and I was painfully aware that even though we hadn't been announced yet, and even though there was a lovely Fae woman currently making her way through the receiving line, practically all eyes in the room were on *us*. My palms felt clammy, and I hoped my face wasn't flushed with embarrassment.

"Seamus Stuart," the gatekeeper, or whatever you call him, intoned, and anyone who hadn't already been looking at us turned their heads in our direction. "And Dana Stuart," the gatekeeper finished, and I had to clench my teeth to resist the urge to correct him.

I could count the weeks I'd known my dad on one hand, and I'd always gone by my mother's name, Hathaway. Guess my dad had "forgotten" that when he had me added to the guest list. If it weren't for our audience, I'd have ripped into him on the spot. Instead, I plastered on the world's fakest smile and promised myself a good temper tantrum later.

The next forty-five minutes were about as much fun as sitting in the dentist's chair. Each time my dad ran into someone he knew—and I swear he knew every person in the room—it was the same thing.

They'd exchange some stupid small talk, Dad would introduce me, and then they'd start talking politics.

The high heels were pinching my toes, and I was losing sensation in the balls of my feet as we continued our circuit of the room. My face hurt from the fake-smiling, and I was so bored I had to swallow a yawn every three seconds. And we weren't even to the speeches yet!

Throughout the torturous meet-and-greet, more people kept arriving at the party, each one announced in a voice that cut through all the chatter. At first, I couldn't help looking every time someone new came in, but since it was never anyone interesting, I stopped paying attention. Until a wave of silence swept over the room, and even my dad turned to look.

The party had been under way for over an hour, and the Important Dignitaries in the receiving line had abandoned their posts to come mingle with us little people, so there was no line waiting to come in. As a result, everyone in the room had a crystal-clear view of the figure who stood regally in the doorway. I immediately suspected he'd planned things that way.

In some ways, he was a typical Fae man. Tall, lean, with angular features that were painfully beautiful. And yet, he was like no Fae I'd seen before. He was dressed in an outfit that looked like it came straight out of some artsy historical movie, complete with a crimson velvet coat with enormous cuffs and elaborately embroidered lapels, knee breeches, and a frothy white neckcloth. Crimson wasn't a good color for him, not with his typical Fae pallor and the long red hair that framed his face under a thin gold circlet, but his lack of fashion sense didn't make him any less breathtaking.

"His Royal Highness, Henry, Prince of the Seelie Court," the announcer said into the silence that had overtaken the room.

Many of the Fae bowed or curtsied. I glanced at my dad out of the corner of my eye and saw that he didn't, even though he was a card-carrying member of the Seelie Court. Avalon had seceded from Faerie about a hundred years ago, and in theory, its Fae citizens weren't supposed to belong to either the Seelie or the Unseelie Court. In reality, there were very few Fae in Avalon who didn't align themselves with one Court or the other.

Prince Henry soaked in the attention for a moment, standing nearly motionless in the entryway as his gaze swept the room. My stomach did a flip-flop when the prince's eyes stopped on my father's face, then slid to me. A smile curled his lips, and there was something oily and unpleasant about it. I took an instant dislike to him and didn't care that it probably wasn't fair of me.

The prince finally stepped into the room, breaking the spell of silence he had cast. People started talking again, and the folks who'd been in the receiving line swarmed to greet their royal guest. I rubbed my sweaty palms together and looked at my dad. It didn't matter that as his daughter, I was generally considered to be Seelie even though I hadn't sworn allegiance. The Queens of *both* Courts felt threatened by my abilities and wanted me dead. That made Prince Henry the enemy in my book.

"Who is Prince Henry?" I asked Dad in an urgent undertone. "And shouldn't we be heading for the nearest exit?"

Dad patted my shoulder in one of his reserved Fae gestures of affection. "You're perfectly safe here," he assured me. "Henry is one of Titania's sons, but she'd never use him in an assassination attempt. And she certainly wouldn't do it *here* of all places."

I'm sure Dad meant that to be comforting, but my mouth had gone dry and my heart was speeding. I couldn't see it as anything but a bad sign that a member of the royal family was in town. Not when the royal family wanted me dead.

"Did you know he was going to be here?" I asked.

Dad shook his head slightly. "I had no idea. I don't know what

Titania's playing at, but I have a feeling we'll find out before the evening is out."

I watched the knot of people surrounding the prince move closer and closer to us, and my throat tightened. "Is it my imagination, or is he moving in our direction?"

"It's not your imagination."

"Great," I muttered. Not that I thought I was in any real danger. I had a feeling that if a member of one of the royal families showed up at a state dinner and killed one of the guests, that might start an international incident. Maybe even a war. So I was pretty sure Dad was right and Prince Henry wasn't making his way toward us with murder on his mind. I just didn't think whatever *was* on his mind was something I'd like any better.

"Isn't it time to go in to dinner yet?" I asked, looking around longingly for some sign that the crowd was moving toward the dining room. No such luck.

"Nice try," Dad said with one of his wry smiles. "Royalty isn't avoided so easily."

The prince was getting closer, and though many people were gathered around him, there were four Knights, dressed in clothing just as archaic as the prince's, keeping the crowd at a respectable distance. I could feel the magic coming off the group when they were still, like, twenty yards away. Seemed a little rude to me to be so blatantly guarding the prince's safety in the midst of the Consul's mansion—as if the mansion weren't a secure location—but what did I know?

Although the prince bore zero resemblance to my dad, I knew my dad had been Titania's consort once, a long, long time ago, so I couldn't help asking, "He's not another half brother you've forgotten to tell me about, is he?"

My dad isn't the most expressive person in the world, but I was getting to know him well enough to see the slight tightening at the corners of his eyes that said I'd hit a nerve. "Connor is my only son," he said softly, "and you are my only daughter."

I wished I hadn't asked. Connor had been captured and basically enslaved by the Erlking, the leader of the Wild Hunt, a group of Fae huntsman who in the olden days preyed on human and Fae quarry. Now, because of an agreement the Erlking had with the government of Avalon, humans were off their menu. And because the Erlking had also made an agreement with both Queens of Faerie, the only Fae they hunted were ones the Queens condemned. None of which helped Connor, who'd been captured before any of these agreements had been made, centuries ago. My father still grieved for Connor as if he were dead, and I wished I could do something to help.

I didn't have much time to brood about my insensitive question, because Prince Henry had made it through the throng and was now standing face-to-face with my dad. The annoying tingle of the Knights' magic made the hairs on the back of my neck stand up.

"Seamus," the prince said with a big smile, "you're looking well."

My father returned the smile, but there was no warmth in it. Come to mention it, there wasn't a whole lot of warmth in the prince's smile, either. Maybe it was just Fae reserve, but I had the instant impression the two of them didn't like each other. I didn't think Titania's desire to have me killed was going to improve their relationship.

"As are you, Henry," my father said, and though no one's expression overtly changed, I could feel the mingled outrage and surprise of the people around us. My guess was that calling the prince by his first name was "not done." The Knights in Henry's entourage stopped pretending they were oblivious to all but their duty and stared at my father. It didn't seem to bother him. "Such splendor as yours is rarely seen in our fair city," he said with a respectful half-bow, and Henry's smile froze for just an instant.

Wow. Dad really knew how to take something that sounded like a compliment and make it obviously an insult. All the while smiling as if he were being perfectly pleasant.

I had to admit, as . . . resplendent as Prince Henry looked in his fancy velvet, he also looked like an escapee from a costume party. The Fae—especially those who live in Faerie—take being old-fashioned to the extreme, and I had no doubt that they had yet to embrace modern fashion. But I doubted the prince was so behind the times that he didn't know how out of place he'd look in Avalon in that getup.

Prince Henry continued to smile. "And *you* have been absent from our fair Court for too long and have been sorely missed."

They shook hands heartily, but I was pretty sure *that* had been a veiled insult as well. It occurred to me that I'd never asked my dad why he'd left Faerie to live in Avalon. I wondered if he'd come to Avalon because he'd lost status when Titania had put him aside as her consort. Or if it had something to do with their son being captured by the Wild Hunt.

"Avalon is my home," my father said simply, "and I find myself reluctant to leave it even for the joys of Titania's Court."

"I hope you can be persuaded to change your mind," Henry said, then turned his gaze to me.

Maybe it was because my father so obviously didn't like this guy, or maybe it was just because he belonged to one of the Courts that wanted me dead, but his gaze felt almost slimy, and it made me want to squirm. But I'd stood up to the Erlking a couple of times—mostly to my detriment, I must admit—and I wasn't about to let Henry intimidate me. At least, I wasn't going to let him *see* that he intimidated me. So I met his gaze and fought my urge to squirm, despite the malice I could have sworn I saw in his eyes.

"This must be your daughter, the Faeriewalker," Prince Henry said.

Dad put his arm around my shoulders, which was a positively effusive gesture for him. "Yes, this is Dana," he said, a hint of warning in his tone.

"What a great pleasure it is to make your acquaintance," Prince Henry said, reaching out his hand as if to shake.

I didn't want to touch him—he was giving me that bad a vibe—but there were about a million people watching us, and I didn't want to be openly rude. Unfortunately, instead of shaking my hand like I'd thought, he raised my hand to his lips and planted a kiss on my knuckles. His lips were uncomfortably wet, and I had to resist an urge to yank my hand from his grip and wipe it on my dress.

He held on to my hand longer than necessary, looking at me expectantly. I suppose he was waiting for a polite response of some sort, but he'd creeped me out so badly that my throat had closed up and I couldn't say a word.

There was a flare of satisfaction in the prince's eyes when he finally let go of my hand, and I cursed myself for being such a wimp. There'd been a battle of wills going on, and I'd lost. I turned my hand slightly as I brought it back to my side, letting the back of it where he'd kissed me rub against my dress. I was trying to be subtle about it, but I can't say I was overly upset when the slight narrowing of the prince's eyes told me he'd seen it.

"There are many people more important than us eager to greet you," my father said, his arm tightening around my shoulders. "Please, don't let us monopolize your attention."

What I heard—and, judging by his expression, what Henry heard—was "get out of my face." For a moment, I thought the prince was going to lose his cool and say something openly rude, but he recovered.

"I have one more item of business to discuss with you," he said through what I suspected were gritted teeth. He held his hand out to one of the Knights, who gave him something that looked very much like a scroll. "My mother, the Queen, is very anxious to meet this long-lost daughter of yours." He handed the scroll to my father. "She invites you to bring your daughter to the Sunne Palace to be formally presented at Court."

I felt my father's jerk of surprise through his arm, and it was all I could do not to gape in shock myself.

"Is this a joke?" I found myself asking. "She wants to—" My dad's hand tightened painfully on my shoulder, and I swallowed the rest of my sentence. I'd already said enough to win me some sharp looks of disapproval from our audience. But really, how else was I supposed to react to an invitation like that? The Seelie Queen wants to kill me, so I should leave the relative safety of Avalon and travel to her palace in Faerie to meet her in person? Either Titania was nuts, or she thought *I* was.

Prince Henry was staring at me again, his shoulders stiff and an expression almost like a snarl on his lips. "Rarely is an individual with mortal blood so graced by Her Majesty. She does you an unprecedented honor." One Henry didn't think I deserved, if the look on his face was any indicator. "You would do well to remember that and be appropriately grateful."

Wow, my outburst must have seriously rubbed him the wrong way. I felt like I'd just been called to the front of the class and yelled at by the teacher while everyone watched. My face was hot, and I tried to keep my gaze focused on the prince so I didn't have to see how many people were watching. I bet my dad was wishing he'd let me stay home after all.

Prince Henry turned to my dad. "It is past time you bring your daughter to receive the Queen's blessing. One would not want to foster the impression that there is bad blood between your family and the Queen after your sister's unfortunate actions."

He was referring to my Aunt Grace, who'd concocted some crazy plan to use my powers to help her usurp the Seelie throne, but I didn't see what that had to do with anything. Grace was dead, and it wasn't like my dad and I had conspired with her.

My dad bowed his head respectfully. If he was pissed off by my outburst or Henry's public reprimand, he hid it well. "We are, of course, greatly honored by the invitation. However, Queen Mab has shown rather less hospitality, and I fear it would not be safe for my daughter to travel into Faerie."

I bit my tongue, hoping I didn't look as indignant as I felt. I knew Mab wanted me dead, but I thought Titania's murderous intent was more relevant at this point.

Prince Henry made a face that I think was supposed to express polite concern. "Of course, Her Majesty would never dream of endangering the dear child." He smiled, raising his voice a little so that all the observers could hear his every word. "You will travel to the Sunne Palace with me as my honored guests. Rest assured that none of Mab's people would dare to trouble my entourage. You will be quite safe. We leave in three days. Now, if you will excuse me . . ."

He didn't wait for an answer, simply turned his back to us and approached one of the high-society types who'd been listening in. The prince's Knights then stepped between us and the prince, just in case we didn't get the hint that we were dismissed.

chapter two

It would have been nice if Dad and I could have slipped away from the dinner party now that Prince Henry had completely ruined it for both of us. Unfortunately, my dad wasn't going to let a little thing like a summons from the Seelie Queen interfere with his political campaign, and he carried on as if nothing had happened. Me, I just fumed. Making polite conversation with self-important assholes was even harder now, and I didn't exactly make a whole lot of friends. I kept expecting Dad to give me hell about it, but he seemed to understand.

The worst part was we couldn't talk about what we were going to do until we were out of the public eye. I was under no illusion that saying no to the Queen's invitation was going to be easy, and I wouldn't have been particularly surprised if Prince Henry planned to kidnap me if I didn't go voluntarily. He wouldn't be the first who'd tried.

The state dinner itself was torture, as expected. I'm sure the food was fantastic, but I was too anxious to have much of an appetite. And the speeches! Honestly, I don't know how anyone managed to stay awake.

It was after midnight when we finally got away. Even then, we didn't talk much. At first, it was because there were too many people around. Avalon didn't have much of a night life, but some parts of the city were more lively than others, and the Consul's mansion was in one of the hot spots.

Because I had such powerful enemies, I didn't live in the city proper with my dad. Instead, I lived in a safe house, hidden deep inside the mountain on which Avalon is built. There's an extensive tunnel system under the city, some of it populated and some of it not. My safe house was in a very definitely unpopulated section, although my dad had somehow arranged for me to have all the modern conveniences like electricity and water and Internet.

I had a kind of love/hate relationship with that safe house. On the one hand, I did feel pretty safe there, which was nice when people were constantly trying to kill me. On the other hand, I felt horribly isolated and longed for a normal house, one with windows I could look out of, or with a convenient little grocery store right around the corner.

It didn't matter where in Avalon we were—getting to my safe house was always a hike. Tiresome at the best of times, but much worse when my high heels were killing my feet and my dad was ignoring the conversational elephant in the room.

I waited a while to see if he was going to say anything, but as far as I could tell, he was lost in his own thoughts. When we made our way into the unpopulated section of the tunnel system, and my dad switched on the flashlight he carried, I slipped off my shoes with a sigh of relief. The floor of the tunnel was cold and dusty, but I didn't care as long as I didn't have to wear the heels anymore.

"Okay, Dad," I said, "it's time you clue me in on what we're going to do about this invitation."

Dad shook his head, the corners of his mouth tight with displeasure. "There isn't much we *can* do about it. As I'm sure you figured out, it wasn't so much an invitation as a summons."

"So? I'm not a member of the Seelie Court." Despite everyone's assumption that because my dad was Seelie, *I* was Seelie. "And *you're* a citizen of Avalon," I reminded him, though I didn't expect it to do much good. My dad was Seelie to the bone, and no amount of time living in Avalon was going to change that.

"You wouldn't be in danger," Dad said, ignoring my argument completely. "If you're appearing in Court in answer to the Queen's summons, you'd be protected by the laws of courtesy. It wouldn't matter if you were her worst enemy—she'd make sure you were safe until you returned to Avalon."

"Hold on," I said, stopping in my tracks, because I really didn't like the sound of that. "You're not seriously considering *going,* are you?"

Dad looked at me grimly. "We're going," he told me, making no attempt to sugarcoat the truth that I had no say in the matter. "If Titania has chosen to honor you with a presentation at Court, you have to go."

"But she wants to kill me!" She'd let me know that when she'd sent a couple of her Knights into Avalon to jump me, only it hadn't been *me* who ended up getting hurt. To get her message across, the Knights had beaten my bodyguard, Finn, to within an inch of his life, and he hadn't defended himself because they'd threatened to kill me if he did. They'd then pinned him to the floor by driving a knife through his shoulder and warned that I would be next if I didn't get out of Avalon and stay out. The knife had had a white rose—the symbol of the Seelie Court—inlaid on its handle.

"I'm no longer so sure about that," Dad said.

I shook my head. "Those Knights left that dagger behind for a reason," I argued. "I think the message was loud and clear."

"Yes, but there's no guarantee they were sent by Titania. Certainly they meant to imply it, but that doesn't mean that it's true."

None of this was making a whole lot of sense to me. "Let me get this straight: just a few hours ago, you were completely convinced Titania wanted me dead, and now a few words from Prince Henry has you convinced it was all a big misunderstanding?"

"Convinced? No. But I'm willing to entertain the possibility. And even if she *was* behind it, this summons suggests she's changed her mind."

"And you're willing to risk my life based on what could be wishful thinking." My dad was so overprotective I lived underground and had a bodyguard. It made no sense that he'd suddenly be okay with the idea of me waltzing into Faerie.

Dad put his hands on my shoulders, focusing his intense blue gaze on me. "I'm afraid you don't understand, Dana. We don't have a choice. Henry insinuated that we might have been involved in Grace's plot and that he has orders to arrest us if we decline the invitation."

I blinked in surprise. "Where was I when this happened?" I asked, although I'd been at Dad's side all night.

" 'One would not want to foster the impression that there is bad blood between your family and the Queen after your sister's unfortunate actions,' " Dad quoted in a fair imitation of Henry's pompous tone.

I shook my head. "And that meant he was threatening to arrest us?"

"He went out of his way to bring it up, and he made sure to remind us she was a member of our family. It might not have been an overt threat, but he knew I'd understand exactly what he meant."

Something told me that the Fae had no problem with "cruel and unusual" punishment, and that I didn't want to find myself a prisoner in Faerie. "But he couldn't *really* arrest us, could he? He doesn't have any authority in Avalon."

"Authority, no. But he has influence aplenty. If he requested extradition, I doubt the Council would find grounds to deny him."

He smiled gently at me. "It is not only the Fae who feel threatened by you."

That was a reminder I could have done without.

"You see now why we have to accept," my dad said. "Our choices are to go as honored guests or reviled prisoners. I prefer the former, don't you?"

"I still think going is a bad idea," I said, though with considerably less conviction than before.

"I'll take that under advisement," he said, then urged me to start walking again.

I barely slept that night, my mind spinning as I tried to figure out how to convince my dad to see things my way—without having us both dragged off to Faerie in chains. There was a part of me that *wanted* to go to Faerie, to see the world that no other human being could ever see. That part of me said that maybe my dad was right, and maybe a trip to the heart of the Seelie Court would be perfectly safe and lead to getting my enemies off my back. But living with my mom and her alcoholism had given me a heavy streak of realism—or pessimism, depending on your point of view—and I felt little hope that things would go that well.

I finally fell asleep at some ungodly hour and was awakened the next morning by the ringing of my phone. Barely conscious, I reached for the phone and hit a few buttons until I got the right one.

"Hello?" I said in my lovely, too-early-in-the-morning croak.

"I heard the news!" Kimber said in a voice that was just short of a squeal.

Kimber is my best friend, and really the closest friend I've ever had. When I was growing up, my mom kept us constantly moving, because she didn't want my dad to find us. (Not that Dad could have come into the mortal world, but if he'd known I was out there, I don't doubt he'd have sent humans to track me down.) Moving so often made it hard enough to make friends, but when you add in my mom's alcoholism and my desperate need to keep it hidden, you have a dedicated loner on your hands. In a lot of ways, Kimber was the best thing that had happened to me since I'd come to Avalon. Ethan, her older brother and my sort-of boyfriend, might object to me saying that, but my relationship with him was a whole lot more complicated.

"Heard what news?" I yawned and wished I could get a coffee IV. A glance at the clock showed me it wasn't all that early, but I'd been deeply asleep and my body wanted to get back to it.

"You're going to be presented at Court!"

The memory woke me up in a hurry. Too bad I couldn't have at least a few minutes of sleep-addled amnesia before I had to think about going to Faerie. "Why do you sound so excited about it?" I asked. She sounded like she was going to start jumping up and down and clapping with glee at any moment.

Kimber hesitated, like she wasn't expecting my surly response. "Um, well, it's a big honor. You get to go to Faerie and meet the Queen and you'll be a guest in the palace."

I guess it did sound rather exciting, if you left out the part about potentially getting killed in the process—or the part about being arrested on some trumped-up charge if you didn't go. I didn't suppose Kimber knew about that, and I didn't see any reason to rain on her parade with the grim truth.

"But the best part," Kimber continued enthusiastically, "is you get to wear a court dress!"

I stifled a groan. Kimber is an incredible girly-girl when it comes to clothes. She loves to dress up, and the fancier and frillier the outfit, the more she likes it. Me, I'm more a jeans-and-hoodie sort of girl.

"I don't know what a court dress is," I said, "but if you're this excited about it, I bet I'm going to hate it."

She sighed happily. "You're going to be absolutely stunning! But if you're leaving in two days, we need to get you in with the dress-maker, like, *now*."

"Dressmaker?" That sounded worse than I'd imagined.

"Of course, silly. You don't wear something off the rack to be presented at Court. As if you could even *find* a court dress off the rack. Has your dad set up an appointment yet?"

"How should I know? I didn't even know I was going to need some fancy dress for this thing." I instantly regretted being so snap-pish about it. "Sorry. I'm not exactly down with this whole plan, but I shouldn't take it out on you."

"It'll be all right," Kimber assured me. "No one would dare at-tack you when you're a guest of the Queen. They take matters of etiquette very seriously in Faerie. You'll be perfectly safe."

"Yeah, that's what my dad said. I just have a bad feeling about the whole thing."

"You always have a bad feeling about *something,* so you should be used to it by now."

"Ha-ha. Very funny."

"Well, someone got up on the wrong side of the bed this morn-ing!"

I snorted. "No, someone hasn't gotten out of bed at all yet. And some other people should know better than to call at oh-dark-thirty in the morning."

Kimber laughed. "I don't think ten o'clock counts as oh-dark thirty. Besides, you have to get your butt in gear. You've got a lot to do before you leave. Now get out of bed and go see if your dad's set up an appointment for you."

"Let me guess, you want to come with me."

"Well, you need someone with at least *some* fashion sense to help you out."

"I think I've just been insulted," I said, though her teasing had put a reluctant smile on my face. "I need some coffee in my system first."

"Call me back when you know the when and where. This is going to be so much fun!"

I suspected that in this instance, Kimber's idea of fun and mine weren't going to be quite the same.

It wasn't until I met Kimber outside the dressmaker's shop—with Finn trailing in my wake, because I wasn't allowed to go *anywhere* without a bodyguard hanging over my shoulder—that I realized the potential problem. You see, there was this mark on the back of my shoulder . . . A stylized blue stag that looked like a tattoo, but wasn't. It was the Erlking's mark, and he tricked me into triggering a spell that put it on me. The mark allowed the Erlking to find me wherever I was—kind of like one of those microchips you put in your pet dog.

I hadn't told anyone—not even Ethan—about the mark, and the last thing I wanted was for Kimber to see the mark while I was trying on clothes. I gnawed my lip with worry as Kimber and I stepped into the shop together with Finn bringing up the rear. There were a lot of things about my encounters with the Erlking that I'd failed to tell Kimber. In fact, I'd out-and-out lied about some of them. I was the worst best friend ever. But guilty as I felt about the deception, I just wasn't ready to tell her the truth yet.

The dressmaker's shop was unlike anything I'd ever seen. The front of the shop was a cozy-looking sitting room with overstuffed blue velvet chairs and a side table with cups, an electric kettle, and about twelve million different varieties of tea. There were a handful of magazines on another side table, but otherwise the room was empty and not like a shop at all.

"In the old days," Kimber told me, "this is where the gentlemen would sit while waiting for their ladies." She gave Finn a saucy look. "Are *you* a gentleman?"

Finn is actually a really nice guy, even if he isn't a big talker. But he's a completely different person when he's in bodyguard mode. He wears suits that would look just right on James Bond and wears *Men in Black* sunglasses even when it's raining. And he rarely, if ever, cracks a smile.

"I'll wait here while you girls meet with the dressmaker," he said, dead serious though he had to know Kimber was teasing him, "but I'm going to check out the back before I let you out of my sight."

Just then, the dressmaker herself emerged from the curtained doorway at the back of the shop. She was a drop-dead gorgeous Fae woman wearing a powder blue silk suit and killer heels. Both the suit and the shoes screamed haute couture, even to someone like me who generally wouldn't know haute couture if it bit me on the nose.

"Good afternoon," she said, in what sounded suspiciously like a fake French accent. "I am Madame Françoise."

I blinked at her stupidly for a moment. There was no such thing as a French Fae. Not to mention that *I* could probably do a better fake French accent than "Madame Françoise" was doing.

"Bonjour, Madame," Kimber answered for me, then rattled off something quick and much more genuinely French-sounding. My foreign language was Spanish, so I had no idea what she was saying.

Madame Françoise laughed lightly and said something in response, her accent still sounding phony as hell.

"Show off," I muttered to Kimber, who winked at me.

"If you don't mind," Finn broke in before we were subjected to any more French, "I need to take a look around back before I allow the young ladies to proceed."

"Why, of course," Madame Françoise said cheerfully, holding

the curtain open and inviting him back with a sweep of her arm. "I will show you."

As soon as the curtain closed behind them, I turned to Kimber. "If her name is really Madame Françoise, then my name is Jack the Ripper. What gives?"

"This shop has been here for at least three hundred years. There was a time when high society thought having a French dressmaker was a status symbol. Madame Françoise is hardly the only person to have faked being French to lure in clientele."

Sometimes, the Fae are just freaking weird. "Yeah, but no one would actually believe she's French. And hello, it's the twenty-first century. Who even *goes* to dressmakers anymore, much less cares if the dressmaker is French?"

Kimber shrugged. "From what I've heard, some of the English women who took on French names were just as blatantly fake. And I suppose once she'd been talking like that for a century or so, it became habit."

Finn and Madame Françoise emerged from the back before I could come up with a witty response. Finn declared the shop safe, and then I was swept into the back with Kimber and Madame, and if it weren't for Madame's modern outfit and the electric lights, I might have thought I'd been swept back in time.

It turned out Madame Françoise specialized in making clothes for Avalon Fae who were traveling to Faerie. Apparently, Prince Henry's ridiculous outfit at the dinner was the height of "modern" fashion in Faerie, and there was nowhere else in the city you could buy appropriate attire.

Madame sat me down at a table with Kimber and plonked a couple of heavy books down in front of us.

"Zeez are pattern books," Madame said, opening the first one to a line drawing of a woman wearing something that looked vaguely

Victorian, with a long train running behind it and a hat that was about half again as tall as she was. Madame turned the page, displaying two more drawings, both of similarly ornate dresses. "Look through. Tell Madame what you like."

Kimber drew the book to her and began flipping through, not at all fazed at the idea of me wearing one of those ridiculous dresses. Madame smiled approvingly, then moved away, giving us time to look without hovering over our shoulders.

"You have got to be kidding me," I said, keeping my voice down so Madame wouldn't hear. "I'm not wearing a freaking bridal gown!"

"I like this one," Kimber said, pointing at a frilly monstrosity, "and it won't be white like a bridal gown. One does not wear all white to Court unless one is royalty."

"I don't care about the color," I said through gritted teeth.

Kimber shrugged. "This is what a court dress looks like." She flipped a couple more pages. "What about this one?" she asked, pointing at a dress that was mercifully free of feathers or ruffles, but just as ornate, with short puffed sleeves, tons of lace, and yet another incredibly long train.

"I'll look like I'm trying out for a part in *The Tudors*," I grumped. "And do *not* tell me I have to wear a corset, because all those dresses sure look like the kind that have corsets under them."

Kimber let out a huff of irritation. "You'd never get a part in *The Tudors* wearing one of these—they're more Regency and Victorian style. That's later than the Tudors, in case you don't know."

I glared at her. Kimber's an intellectual prodigy—she's only seventeen, but she was going to be a sophomore in college in the fall. Her specialty is math and science, but I guess she actually paid attention in history class, too.

"I think this would be perfect for you, as long as we choose the right colors," she continued, ignoring my death glare.

I looked more closely at the drawing. "It has a freaking *bow* at the back." I could see Kimber wearing something like that and being totally stunning. Me, I'd just look silly.

"We can ask Madame to skip the bow," Kimber said. "And I'm sure she can alter the design enough so it fits without a corset."

I sighed, knowing I was fighting a losing battle. "What about the train? Can we lose the train?"

Kimber shook her head. "Nope. That's a requirement." There was a sudden glint in her eyes. "In fact, you'll need someone to *help* you with that train. I'm sure the Queen would be happy to lend you one of her ladies, but maybe you'd be better off bringing your own. Like, say, me."

There was a suspicious tightening in my chest as I looked at my best friend's excited face. The idea of having a friend with me for the trip to Faerie made the prospect a lot less daunting. I wanted Kimber to come so badly I could taste it. And yet . . .

"I don't care what anybody says," I said. "I think this trip is going to be dangerous, and I don't want anyone else to be dragged down with me." Of course, I knew better than to expect Kimber to give in.

"If it's going to be dangerous, then all the more reason to have friends at your side. Not that the prince's entourage isn't plenty of protection, but their main focus will be on protecting *him*." She slung a companionable arm around my shoulders. "You need someone whose main focus is protecting *you*."

"My dad'll be with me," I reminded her. I hoped I was keeping a good poker face, because Kimber wasn't exactly bodyguard material. She pretty much sucks at magic, which is usually a Fae's primary weapon. I'd seen her kill a Spriggan with a knife, so she wasn't completely incapable of defending herself, but I surely wouldn't drag her into Faerie as some kind of protection for myself.

Kimber nodded. "Your dad, and probably Finn, too. But having a couple of extras couldn't hurt."

I narrowed my eyes at her. "*A couple* of extras?"

"Well, if I go, you know Ethan's going to want to go, too. And Ethan generally gets what he wants."

There was a touch of jealousy in Kimber's voice. She loved her brother, but there was some serious sibling rivalry between them. Ethan is a magical whiz-kid, and magic trumps brains in the Fae hierarchy, so Kimber always felt like second best.

I didn't know how I felt about Ethan coming with us. Yeah, he was sort of my boyfriend, but our relationship was so complicated . . . You see, Ethan had been captured by the Wild Hunt, and I'd been determined to save him. I made a devil's bargain with the Erlking, and now I had to live with it. The Erlking had offered to release Ethan if I promised to give him my virginity.

I'd known from the moment the Erlking made the offer that there was something more to it than just a desire to get me into bed. However, making the promise—enforced by magic—was the only way I could save Ethan, and the Erlking would let me pick the time to fulfill my promise. As a bonus, he would release Connor, my brother, if and when I ever did the deed. Later, I'd found out that the Erlking wanted my virginity because he had the secret ability to steal power from virgins. If I ever slept with him, he'd steal my powers as a Faeriewalker, and ride out into the mortal world on a killing spree. Obviously, I couldn't let that happen, which meant I couldn't give him my virginity. But if I slept with anyone else, Ethan would be drawn back into the Wild Hunt.

So I'm doomed to die a virgin, and no matter how much Ethan tells me he doesn't care that I can never put out, I have trouble believing him. I couldn't find it in myself to say no when he asked me out, and I wanted to be with him so badly it hurt, but always in the back of my mind, I was searching for signs that he was getting restless. Which doesn't make for a very comfortable relationship at all.

I frowned as I thought about Ethan and Kimber coming with

me to Faerie. "Would you two even be *allowed* to come with me to the Seelie Court?" Ethan and Kimber were Unseelie, and usually the two didn't mix well.

"I don't see why not," she answered. "Our Courts are not at war. We might not be received with the same enthusiasm you are, but it's not like we're not allowed to travel in Seelie territory."

So much for that objection. "What about your dad? Would he let you put yourself in that kind of danger?"

Kimber put on a wan smile. "For the chance to help *you*? In a heartbeat."

I looked away, hating the reminder that both my dad and Kimber and Ethan's dad, Alistair, considered me a pawn in their political chess game. Alistair would do anything possible to encourage my relationships with his children, and if they could win my gratitude by helping me, that was even better in his book. I guess he hoped that if I was grateful enough to his kids, I'd be willing to support him if he became Consul.

Kimber sighed. "Sorry. That came out wrong. He wouldn't send us with you if we didn't want to go. And remember, theoretically at least, there's no reason you or anyone with you should be in danger during this trip."

I wished I could believe that. "All right. If you guys can convince my dad and yours to let you come along, you can come."

"Gee, thanks," Kimber said with a droll look. "Your enthusiasm's overwhelming."

I opened my mouth to protest that it wasn't lack of enthusiasm, it was fear for their safety, but Kimber didn't give me a chance.

"Now, let's show Madame the dress you've chosen and we can start picking fabrics."

I would have argued that I hadn't actually chosen anything, but Kimber was already waving Madame over.

. . .

In the end, we spent almost three hours at the dressmaker's shop. If I never see a bolt of cloth again it'll be too soon. Kimber, of course, loved every minute of it. I tried my best to keep the dress as simple as possible, but Kimber would have none of it and Madame always agreed with her. Two against one just wasn't fair!

The bodice was going to be white silk with gold embroidery, with a red taffeta train about a mile long. The train, too, would be decorated with gold embroidery. I absolutely put my foot down about the big gold bow they wanted to put at the back. The dress was outrageously girly and froufrou enough already. Kimber and Madame finally backed down, but I put the odds at about fifty/fifty that when the dress was ready, there'd be a honkin' shiny bow on it after all.

There was an uncomfortable moment when Madame wanted me to undress so she could take precise measurements. To keep from having to reveal the Erlking's mark, I pretended to be painfully modest, stammering and looking pathetic. Madame took pity on me and agreed the fit would be close enough if I kept my clothes on while she measured.

I couldn't imagine how Madame could create a dress that ornate in time, but she didn't seem concerned, and I suspected there'd be copious amounts of magic involved. I didn't even want to think about how much the dress was going to cost. When I'd lived with my mom, we'd always had to pinch pennies, because alcoholics aren't the best at getting and holding high-paying jobs. But my dad was loaded, and he'd arranged for Madame to put everything on his tab with no spending limit. Too bad the dress wasn't for Kimber—she'd have appreciated it a lot more than I did.

Kimber wanted to do some more shopping afterward, telling me

I needed a fancier wardrobe to travel in Faerie. Only for the presentation at Court—the ceremony during which I would be formally introduced to the Queen—would I need to dress like a native, but Kimber was certain I wanted a whole new wardrobe, just because hey, what girl wouldn't?

I was saved from the ordeal of being bullied by my personal fashion consultant when my cell phone rang. Unfortunately, an even bigger ordeal was in store for me: my mother had just found out I was going to Faerie.

chapter three

When my mom had come to Avalon looking for me, my dad had tricked her into handing over custody of me. (Tricked her because she'd been too drunk at the time to pay attention to the papers she was signing. Yep, she was a paragon of parental responsibility all right.)

Aside from losing legal custody of me, she'd also been declared legally incompetent, which involved my dad using either his influence or his money to manipulate the courts of Avalon into giving him what he wanted. That meant she was also in my dad's custody. To make me happy, Dad had promised that as long as she was in his custody—living in something resembling house arrest—he would make sure she had no access to alcohol. The weeks I'd been in Avalon were by far the longest stretch of time my mom had been sober in my memory.

The phone call I'd gotten was from my dad. He'd broken the news to my mom that we were leaving for Faerie the day after tomorrow, and she'd gone ballistic. There was a hint of what sounded like desperation in his voice when he asked me to come over and talk to her. Unlike me, he didn't have sixteen years of experience dealing with her fits of hysteria, and I could tell he was in completely over his head.

Strange how I could move all the way to Avalon, find out I was a Faeriewalker, have people trying to kill me, and yet some parts of my life remained exactly the same. I'd hoped that once my mom stopped drinking, she'd also stop being a drama queen, but that was obviously asking too much. It also occurred to me, as Finn and I hurried through the streets of Avalon to my dad's house, that with both me and my dad going off to Avalon, my mom's house arrest was about to come to an end.

The thought made my stomach tie itself in knots. No house arrest meant no way to stop her from drinking. No way to stop her from drinking meant that when I came back from Faerie (assuming, of course, that I made it out alive), Mom the Drunk would be here waiting for me.

Once upon a time, I'd let myself believe that if she would just sober up for a little while, my mom would come to her senses and decide she was staying off the booze forever. Dad tried to explain to me that we couldn't cure her alcoholism by force, but I hadn't wanted to believe him. The fact that she *still* wouldn't admit she had a drinking problem made my dad's point of view more convincing.

My head wasn't in a good place when I arrived at my dad's house, and I wanted to talk to my mom about as much as I wanted to stick my head in the toilet. I'd halfway decided to tell my dad to just deal with it, but when he opened the door and I saw the glassy look in his eyes, I swallowed my words. I didn't like it, but I was far better equipped to handle my mom than he was.

"She's in her room," my dad said as he led the way up the spiral staircase from the garage to the first floor, which was where his living room, kitchen, and dining room were located.

As soon as I set foot in the living room, I smelled the distinctive scent of tea in the air, although I saw no sign of any mugs. Then I saw the dark, wet stain against the wall beside the plasma TV.

"Let me guess," I said with a sigh, "she threw her tea at you?"

Dad crossed his arms and nodded. "I've never seen her like this before." He looked completely mystified, and if I weren't caught in the middle of the mess, I might have found it amusing.

"I have," I grumbled. I looked back and forth between Dad and Finn. "You guys stay down here no matter what, okay? She's not going to throw deadly weapons at me, but you're a different story."

Finn was giving me a look of pity I could have done without, but I think Dad was just glad he didn't have to face Mom again in the near future. With a sigh of resignation, I trudged to the door to the stairway and climbed to the third floor.

Mom's door was closed, and I braced myself for battle before I knocked on it.

"Mom?" I asked. "Can I come in?"

The door opened almost before I got the last word out, and before I knew what was happening, I was wrapped in a smothering hug, Mom's arms so tight around me I could hardly breathe.

"Dana," she said, then started to sob, holding me and rocking me like she'd just found out I had a terminal disease.

I let her hug me for as long as I could stand it, then wriggled out of her grasp. She looked terrible, her eyes all swollen and puffy, her nose red, her hair disheveled. *But at least she's sober,* I reminded myself. *For now.*

I invited myself into my mom's room and sat on her bed. Sniffling, she reached for a tissue and scrubbed at her eyes.

"I'm not going to let him take you," she said. Her voice was hoarse, either from all that crying or from an earlier shouting match with Dad.

She didn't have the power to stop him, and we both knew it.

"I'm sure Dad told you what will happen if I don't go."

She dismissed that with a wave. "Some nonsense about your aunt Grace. I don't believe it for a moment. He's just using that excuse to scare you into doing what he wants."

My dad can be majorly manipulative, but he wasn't sneaky about it, at least not with me. I wasn't sure Henry really would have me arrested and carted off to Faerie if we refused the "honor" of the Queen's invitation, but I was sure my dad believed he would.

"I *want* to go," I told my mom. It was a total lie, but I wasn't above lying if it was the only way to get my mom to calm down. She'd obviously run through her repertoire of hysterics with my dad, and if I could get her to skip the repeat performance with me, I was all for it.

She shook her head. "It's too dangerous."

"Not if I'm the Queen's guest. I'll be fine."

I'd been angry with my mom for almost as long as I could remember. Angry at her drinking, angry at her neglect, angry at the way I had to function as the adult of the family from the time I was about four. Until I'd run away from home, I'd been real, real good at hiding that anger, stuffing it down inside me so I could do what I had to do to take care of her and run the household.

I was out of practice keeping my anger under control, and I ground my teeth to keep myself from saying anything about how absurd it was for *me* to be comforting *her* under the circumstances.

"Dana, honey," Mom started, but she couldn't seem to figure out where to go from there. At least she wasn't throwing things.

She came to sit on the bed beside me, her head bowed, her shoulders slumped. "I can't stand the thought of you going off somewhere where I can't protect you."

A little more tooth-grinding was in order. Since when had she ever protected me? It wasn't that she wouldn't protect me with all the ferocity of a mama bear if I were in danger and she were sober enough to realize it. The *will* was there, and I knew that she loved me. But being willing to protect me and being *able* to protect me were two very different things.

"You can't even protect me *here*," I said, trying to keep my voice gentle. "Not with the kind of enemies I have."

Ever since she'd stopped drinking, she'd been fidgety, constantly moving like a hummingbird on caffeine. The more upset she got, the more she fidgeted, and she had a major case of the fidgets this time. I took a deep breath and reminded myself that this couldn't be easy for her. She'd tried very hard to keep me away from my dad and from Avalon precisely because she wanted to keep me safe from the political intrigue. She might not be a candidate for mother of the year when she was drinking, but I knew she loved me.

Once upon a time, I'd thought that if she would only stop drinking, she'd become more like a normal mom, that she'd take care of me and protect me, et cetera, et cetera. But all the evidence suggested that she was pretty damn needy even without the booze.

"I want you to make me a promise," I said.

"Of course, sweetheart," she said after a momentary hesitation. "Anything."

I refrained from snorting. My mom wasn't big on making promises, and she was even worse at keeping them.

Why was I asking her to keep one, then? Because it was the only thing I could think of to do, the only faint hope I had that when I returned from Faerie, she wouldn't have morphed back into her drunken alter ego.

"I want you to promise me you won't drink while I'm gone," I said, then braced myself for her inevitable reaction.

She stood, too agitated to hold still, and I could see the emotional barriers going up. "Dana, really!"

How she could act offended when she had to know why I was asking this of her is anyone's guess. I don't care how deeply in denial she was. There was no way I believed she didn't know she had a problem.

My fists clenched in my lap, and I forced myself to relax them. "It won't be for that long," I said, hoping it was true. "You keep telling me you're not an alcoholic, so it really shouldn't be that hard for you, should it?"

"I am not an alcoholic! But you don't get to decide whether I can have a drink or not. I'll be a nervous wreck while you're gone, and if I can't even have a calming drink now and then . . ."

A calming drink now and then. That's what she called starting her day with whiskey in her coffee and ending it passed out with an empty bottle or three at her side?

"What happened to 'I'll promise anything'?" I asked bitterly. "You only meant anything that didn't really matter to me."

I could see from the look in her eyes that she was hurt as well as angered by my accusation. At that point, I didn't care. I was pretty hurt and angry, too.

"That isn't fair," she said, and I wanted to scream.

"I'm going to be out there risking my life, and it's too much of me to ask that you stay sober for a little while? That's just great, Mom. Thanks a lot. Glad to know I matter to you so much."

I was so mad I felt like hitting something, and tears burned my eyes. Why didn't she care how much her drinking hurt me? I might not be perfect or anything, but I thought I was a pretty good daughter. I never got into any trouble—at least, not until I came to Avalon—and I'd always taken care of her. Above and beyond the call of duty, no less. I got good grades, and I usually managed to keep my anger securely hidden.

She'd been the one constant in my life, when my life revolved around moving from place to place every year or so. I couldn't make any long-term friends, had never had any other family. My mom had been my everything for as long as I could remember.

My lower lip quivered, and a tear trickled down my cheek. Usually, I fight tears with everything I have, especially when I'm not alone. Today, I let them come. I let my mom see just how hurt I was.

The look in her eyes softened into one of dismay, and she came back to sit beside me and take my clenched fists into her hands.

"Dana, honey, of course you matter to me."

She pulled me to my feet and wrapped her arms around me. I was far too angry to return her embrace, but she didn't let go.

"I love you more than anything," my mother said as I stood stiffly in her arms and cried. "You have to know that."

"But not enough to stop drinking," I said, my voice muffled by her shoulder. "Never enough for that."

Mom's hands slid to my shoulders, and she pushed me away a little bit so she could look into my eyes. I wanted to look away, but she took hold of my chin.

"My drinking has nothing, *nothing* to do with how much I love you." She smiled wanly and brushed a lock of my hair away from my face, like I was a little girl who'd skinned her knee. "Just because I don't always do what you want me to do doesn't mean I don't love you."

I swallowed the lump in my throat. "But you don't care that it hurts me to see you destroying yourself."

"I'm not going to destroy myself," she said, sounding like she meant it. "There are lots of people in the world who drink, honey. It's just . . . something adults do. I am truly sorry it bothers you, but please don't worry about me. I'm going to be just fine."

What was the use in fighting it? Even if I somehow managed to get her to promise, there was nothing I could do to make her keep the promise. Nothing sent her diving for the booze faster than stress, and she was going to be stressed to the max for the entire time I was gone.

I jerked away from her, no longer able to stomach the excuses or the hollow reassurances. "Fine," I said. "Drink as much as you want. Pickle your liver and pass out on the floor in a puddle of your own puke. See if I care!"

"Dana!" Her cheeks went white with shock, although this wasn't the first time since we'd been in Avalon that I'd given in to the temptation to let her know what I really thought of her. I was being a mean-spirited, ungrateful little bitch, and I didn't give a damn. I was tired of pretending all was well when it wasn't, tired of humoring her, tired of forcing my feelings into a little mental box so I could be the polite, dutiful daughter.

"Go home, Mom," I said, pulling away from her when she tried to reach for me. "I'm sure Dad will give you your passport back before we leave for Faerie. Go back to the States and *stay* there. There was a reason I ran away in the first place, and obviously nothing has changed."

I slammed out of the room before she could respond. I half expected her to chase after me, but she didn't. Maybe my words had cut too deep, maybe she needed time to recover. Or maybe she knew I'd say something even uglier if she came after me. Whatever the reason, the fact that she stayed up in her room and made no attempt to get me to come back just made me that much angrier.

Both my dad and Finn looked at me in dismay as I slammed the door to the stairway and stomped into the living room where they were waiting for me. There was no way either of them could miss how upset I was. I might have wiped the tears away, but I'm sure my eyes and nose were all red. I suspected this was not what my dad had in mind when he asked me to come over.

"I don't want to talk about it," I declared before either of them could say a word.

If either one of them had been human, they might have tried to talk to me anyway. However, the typical Fae reserve worked to my advantage. Finn was never big on talking, and my dad looked lost and uncomfortable.

"I want to go home now," I said, staring at the floor so I wouldn't have to see their faces.

There was a moment of silence.

"Call me if you decide later that you want to talk after all," my dad said. "Anytime."

His gentle tone almost made me start crying again. A few weeks ago, he hadn't even known I existed. Now he was the only parent who acted like he loved me.

As it was, I managed to croak out a thanks, then made a beeline for the door so fast Finn had to run to catch up.

The rest of my afternoon sucked—I brooded about my mom and what she would do when Dad let her go. I racked my brain for something I could do or say that would make her decide to stay off the booze, but I'd already proven that nothing I said or did mattered.

There were probably a million things I should have been doing to prepare myself for the trip to Faerie, but the drama with my mom had robbed me of my will. Instead of being productive, I spent hours playing stupid Internet games on my laptop, lulling myself into a zombielike trance.

I was playing a really convoluted game involving dice, cards, and—ha-ha—zombies, when I was startled out of my stupor by a knock on the door to my suite. I blinked and glanced at the clock on my screen, seeing it was already eight o'clock at night. Finn is really good at being unobtrusive, and he usually confines himself strictly to the guard room, giving me some semblance of privacy in my suite. I don't get too many knocks on my door, especially not at night.

My pulse jumped, and I feared more bad news was on its way.

"Come in," I called, crossing my fingers.

The door opened to reveal not Finn, but my father. I was surprised to see him, because he usually called before coming.

"Is something wrong?" I asked before he had a chance to say a word.

"No, no," he said as he came in and took a seat on the sofa in the homey little sitting area. "I just wanted to see if you were okay."

"I still don't want to talk about it," I warned, gearing up for an argument.

Instead, Dad nodded. "Understood. I don't know what happened between you and your mother, but I know it's my fault for asking you to come over when she was so overwrought. I'm afraid I was a little out of my element, and I leaned on you when I shouldn't have. I'm sorry."

My throat tightened with gratitude. There was no denying that sometimes, my dad could be a pretty cool guy. " 'S okay," I said, not completely sure how to respond to a sincere parental apology.

There was a long silence as both my dad and I tried to think of what to say next. This whole father/daughter relationship thing was equally new to both of us.

Eventually, my dad cleared his throat and said, "I thought you might have some questions to ask me about Faerie and the logistics of our trip to the Sunne Palace."

Wow. My dad, volunteering information! I wanted to accuse him of being a pod person, but I didn't think he'd get the joke. Humor is not his thing, though considering what little I knew about his life, that wasn't a surprise. My father was something like a thousand years old, and you can pack a hell of a lot of trauma and heartache into a thousand years.

"If I start asking questions, you're going to be here all night," I warned.

He smiled at me. "A fact of which I'm fully aware. Make me a spot of fortifying tea and I'll be fully prepared to face the Inquisition."

All right, maybe he had a sense of humor after all. It was just on the subdued side. "One tea with thumbscrews, coming up."

I made coffee for myself while the water boiled for Dad's tea. I could drink tea in a pinch, and I could drink it to be polite, since everyone in Avalon apparently worshipped at the Holy Church of Tea, but I would never learn to love it.

I set my coffee and Dad's tea down on the coffee table, then curled up comfortably on the couch beside my dad. With typical Fae formality, he was sitting up straight with both feet flat on the floor. I wondered if it made him uncomfortable to have my bare feet up on the couch so close to him. If it did, he made no sign of it, merely stirring some honey and lemon into his tea as he waited patiently for my first question.

It was hard to decide what to ask first. I had so little idea what to expect from this trip, or from Faerie. But instead of asking a sensible, practical question, the first question that came to my mind was far more personal.

"What's up with you and Prince Henry?" I asked. "You obviously don't like each other."

Dad hesitated a moment, probably as surprised as I was that that was the first thing I wanted to know. Then he grimaced and took a sip of tea.

"No, we don't like each other. In fact, we'd each be happy to see the other dead."

I couldn't help a little gasp. My dad always seemed so cool and rational, even in the face of danger. It took a lot to crack his facade, but what I saw in his eyes now was nothing less than pure hatred.

He smoothed the expression away and then took another sip of tea. "I have enemies at Court, Dana. Everyone who's ever spent any significant time at Court does, and I was Titania's consort for well over a century."

"Enemies who want to kill you."

"No, enemies who'd like to see me dead. There's a difference." He gave me one of his wry smiles. "If one is a courtier, one does not kill one's enemies. That would be far too vulgar. I told you once that at Court, lying and deceit is an art form. I was speaking rather more literally than you probably imagined. The Court awards figurative style points for the subtlety and ingenuity with which one destroys one's enemies."

Geez, and I was going there to meet a whole bunch of courtiers and the Queen herself. Fabulous.

"So why are you and Henry enemies?" I asked.

"Titania is never without a consort. Prince Henry's father was her consort before me. There was a noticeable reduction in both their statuses at Court when Titania put Henry's father aside. Henry, quite naturally, blamed me for it. He was only twenty when it happened, and I was a far more experienced and polished courtier. He tried to start various unsavory rumors about me, but I always managed to turn them back on him. And he never could control his temper, which is a fatal flaw in the Court. To lose one's temper is to admit defeat, and I had little trouble making Henry do it, even in public." Dad smiled like he was reminiscing about the good old days. "Every attack he made saw his status within the Court slip just a little more. He was forced to leave Court or eventually he'd have faced total social ruin despite being the Queen's son."

I gaped as Dad took another sip of tea. This was a side of him I'd never seen before. Sure, he was manipulative, and had a politician's way with words, but I'd never thought he'd take such obvious satisfaction in basically ruining someone's life. Henry seemed like a total jerk, but still . . .

Dad saw my expression, and he put down his teacup and turned to face me on the sofa.

"The primary reason I left Faerie and came to live in Avalon was to escape Court social politics. I am still capable of playing the game, but that isn't who I am. Not anymore."

That didn't make me feel a whole lot better, and nothing he'd said so far made me any more pleased with the idea of going to Court. "So are you and Henry going to be taking potshots at each other for the whole trip, like you were at the dinner?"

"Undoubtedly. And he's gotten a lot better at it since he was that sullen, untried boy. Luckily, my standing at Court is no longer of great concern to me." Dad's smile held a touch of malice. "And his temper is clearly still a liability. He must be beside himself at the thought that Titania would invite my daughter to Court. And he must have done something to annoy her for her to send *him,* of all people, to escort us."

Glad to know Henry saw having Dad and me traveling with him as some kind of punishment. "But she didn't really *invite* me," I pointed out. "Not if she's really planning to have us arrested if we don't go. Or is that part Henry's idea?"

"Hardly," Dad scoffed. "I'm sure he'd have been happy to drag us off to Faerie in chains, but it certainly wasn't his idea to blackmail us into going. He'd rather eat iron nails than see my daughter honored. No, he'd have loved nothing better than if we'd been free to refuse the invitation and mortally offend his mother."

I grunted in exasperation. "How much of an honor can it possibly be when she's blackmailing me into going?"

"Trust me. It's an honor, no matter what inducements she felt it necessary to offer in order to be certain we come. The end result is that you will be presented at Court, and that is a very public show of favor."

"Okay. I'll take your word for it." And try to remember that the Fae don't think like normal people.

"Good. Now, what's your next question?"

"How long will we be gone?"

"I can't say with any great certainty, but count on it being at least three weeks."

"Three weeks!" I'd been assuming—why, I don't know—that it would take a couple of days.

Dad smiled at me. "Remember, this is Faerie we're talking about. There are no cars or planes. The trip from Avalon to the Sunne Palace should take roughly four days on horseback, and you can be certain Titania will keep us waiting for at least a week before she finds it convenient to hold the ceremony. And afterward, we'll be expected to stay awhile to fulfill our social obligations."

Horseback? This just got better and better. I'd never ridden a horse in my life, and I'd have been just as happy to keep it that way. Though I supposed if the alternative was walking, horseback would have to do.

"It won't be until after the presentation ceremony that we'll be able to speak with Titania. However, I have had a chance to question several members of Henry's entourage today, and I feel reasonably certain Titania did not send those Knights after you."

I shook my head, not believing it for a moment. "Just because they say so?"

"No, because I know Titania. Getting her to change her mind at all takes something just short of a miracle. If she wanted you gone so recently, she would not have invited you to Court unless something catastrophic occurred, and it hasn't.

"Of course, *someone* was behind the attack," my dad continued. "Someone with enough clout to command a pair of Knights to carry out a personal errand."

I shivered. "You mean someone like Prince Henry?"

Dad grimaced. "The thought has crossed my mind. Although hiring Knights to make threats and do bodily harm is not his style. Remember what I told you about the Fae love of subtlety. An overt attack like that would be considered gauche in the extreme."

"Gee, I feel so much better knowing that him murdering me would be a social faux pas."

"Princes can't afford faux pas like that, so it's more of a deterrent than you think." He leaned forward a little and gave my shoulder a squeeze. "Don't worry. I'll be keeping a careful eye on him, just in case."

"Do you think whoever *was* behind that attack would be happy to see me being presented at Court?"

His face wasn't what I'd call expressive, but even the studied lack of expression was an expression in itself. "You will be well guarded. I'll be with you, and so will Finn and Keane."

Keane was Finn's son and my self-defense instructor. I had what I think of as a like/hate relationship with him. When he's beating the crap out of me on the practice mats, I really hate him. When we're not sparring, he can be a pretty decent guy, though things were currently a little uncomfortable between us because I suspected he liked me a whole lot more than I liked him. Still, I would definitely feel safer with him by my side.

"What about Ethan and Kimber?" I asked, because I was sure Kimber would have already started bugging her dad and mine to let them come with me.

My dad managed to look disapproving without changing his facial expression, which was a neat trick. He didn't insist I stay away from my Unseelie friends, but I knew he'd be a lot happier if I stuck to my "own kind." If I ever start choosing my friends based on which Court they belong to, just shoot me.

"Alistair has suggested they come along," he answered. "I hesitate to take the risk when they are both so young and untried."

"Kimber's a couple months older than me, and Ethan is the same age as Keane."

"I know how you feel about Ethan," he said with a little smile, "but . . . He and Keane may be physically the same age, but Keane is an adult while Ethan is still a boy."

I knew what my dad meant, and when I'd first come to Avalon, I might even have agreed with him. But Ethan wasn't quite the same since I'd rescued him from the Erlking's clutches. He was still bound to the Erlking in ways I didn't fully understand, and the ordeal had aged him. He was not the same carefree boy I'd first met.

"However," my dad continued, "if Alistair is determined that they come along, I shall have to take them. I fear that if I refuse, he might send them after us anyway, and that would be far more dangerous for them."

I was glad to know I'd have plenty of company, but I hated the thought that Alistair would put his political ambitions above his children's safety. As ambitious as my own dad was, he was practically fanatical about keeping me safe.

"I don't believe you will be in danger," Dad said, "especially not when you are so thoroughly guarded. However . . ."

I felt the faint prickle of magic, and suddenly there was a pink faux-leather case, about six inches long, in his hand. He extended the case toward me, and I took it. I hadn't a clue what was in it, and Dad ignored my inquiring look.

With a shrug, I lifted the lid, then almost dropped the case when I saw what was inside, nestled in a bed of red velvet: a gun. The logo on the underside of the lid said "Lady Derringer."

"It's only for emergencies," Dad said. "I'll teach you how to use it, but I certainly don't expect you to need it. I just think we'll both feel better if you have a mortal weapon available."

Swallowing hard, I touched the ivory-colored grip, which had a picture of a white rose on it. Despite my dad's reassurances, I didn't think taking a gun with me into Faerie was going to make me feel safe at all.

The next morning was one of my regularly scheduled lessons with Keane, which meant I had to get up indecently early and couldn't have any breakfast until afterward. Not unless I wanted to risk it coming back up while we sparred. If my teacher were anyone but Keane, I'd have expected him to give me the day off on the day before I left for Faerie, but I knew better.

I stood in front of the bathroom mirror, examining the new high-backed tank top I'd ordered from an athletic catalog. In the catalog, it had looked like the top might give me enough coverage to hide the Erlking's mark on the back of my shoulder. It covered part of the mark, but not all of it. I sighed regretfully, then headed to the bedroom to pull a T-shirt on over the tank. It was easier to fight without the loose, comfortable T-shirt giving Keane something to grab on to, but I didn't have a choice.

I opened my bedroom door to find that Keane had already arrived. He'd pushed the furniture in my sitting room to the walls and was rolling out the practice mats. I admired the view for a moment, because even if I didn't like him *that* way, there was no denying he was a treat to look at. He had a typically beautiful Fae face, but his hair—dyed jet black, with a lock perpetually hanging in his eyes— along with the earrings in his left ear, the Celtic armband tattoo, and a wardrobe that seemed to consist entirely of black, gave him a bad-boy edge. What could be sexier than a Fae bad boy?

"You're late," he said to me without looking up.

"Good morning to you, too," I responded, approaching him warily. Keane didn't believe in giving me a warning before he attacked—he said my enemies wouldn't do it, so *he* wouldn't do it—and that meant my lesson could start at any moment, even when it looked like he was thoroughly engaged in something else. I watched his body language carefully, searching for any sign that he was about to leap into motion.

"We've had this discussion before," he said as he finished arranging the mats. "I expect you to show up on time *every* time."

I rolled my eyes at the rebuke. And, of course, that was when he attacked.

Despite his high-handed, annoying, and often painful training techniques, Keane was a great teacher. Not that I'd ever admit it to his face. Even though I'd let my guard down, I reacted fast enough not to take his punch in the face. My arm jerked upward like it had a will of its own, blocking the punch.

In a real fight, that block might have saved my life, because a blow that hard to my head might knock me out and would certainly at least knock me down. And in a real fight, I'd be thanking my lucky stars right now as I ran like hell to get away from whoever had attacked me.

But this wasn't a real fight, so my reaction—very mature, I know—was to yell "Ow!" loud enough to burst a few eardrums. I knew in theory that Keane pulled his punches when we sparred, but it still hurt like hell when he made contact, even when I managed to block.

"Don't be such a baby," Keane said, even as he kicked out in an attempt to knock my legs out from under me.

This was the reason I hated him so much when we were sparring.

I jumped backward, avoiding Keane's kick, and after that there was no time for complaining. Even if I'd had enough air in my lungs to make a complaint.

I knew I was getting better, knew that if I was fighting someone who wasn't any good, I'd probably be able to get away, but I would never, ever come close to Keane's skill level. Being the son of a

Knight, he'd been taught how to fight from an early age. He'd even started to go through training to be a Knight himself, but he wasn't Knight material. Not because he couldn't fight well enough—I'm sure if he'd had the whole training, he'd be ridiculously good—but because he was too much of a rebel to accept the lifestyle.

The upshot of all this is that I almost never succeed in landing a blow, and despite knowing all the right moves, I could rarely escape one of his holds unless he let me. Frustration and I have become good friends. And like any friend who's a bad influence, frustration sometimes made me do things that were, in retrospect, stupid.

Like trying to tackle my self-defense instructor.

There isn't a single instance I can think of in which tackling your attacker is a good self-defense move. If you have enough distance to try to tackle your attacker, you have enough distance to run like hell and maybe get away. But since doing the "correct" moves never seemed to work, every once in a while I couldn't stop myself from trying to catch Keane by surprise.

The problem is, even if I catch him by surprise, he's bigger, quicker, stronger, and far more experienced than I am.

My tackle surprised him enough to take him down. Unfortunately, he twisted like a cat in midair, and somehow I ended up on the bottom when we landed. The landing knocked all the wind out of me, and while I was lying there trying to breathe, he landed a light blow to my face, demonstrating just how bad a position I'd gotten myself into. Not that I didn't already know.

Escaping one of Keane's holds when we were both on our feet was hard enough, but escaping him when we were on the floor with him on top was impossible unless he purposely gave me an opening. As soon as I managed to drag in a full breath, he gave me one of those openings, and I went for it.

Just because he left me an opening didn't mean he was making things easy for me, so I had to work like crazy to get free. At the last moment, just as I was trying to triumphantly jump to my feet after slipping his hold, his hand closed on the back of my T-shirt.

I mentioned that the loose T-shirts gave Keane convenient handholds. He'd certainly taken advantage of it before. But I don't know if the T-shirt was just getting threadbare from having been worn and washed too often, or if one of us was pulling harder than usual, or if it was just the angle of the pull. Whatever it was, there was an ominous ripping sound, and I lurched forward, caught off balance and by surprise.

Keane, with his Fae reflexes, managed to grab me before I hit the floor with my face, but I could feel the cool sweep of air over the skin of my back and shoulder where my T-shirt had torn. Right where the Erlking's mark lay.

"What the fuck?" Keane asked in a horrified whisper.

chapter four

This was officially Not Good.

I tried to twist away from Keane, to pull the torn T-shirt back over the mark, but he turned me with rough hands, pulling aside the strap of the tank top so he could get a better look.

"Let go of me!" I snapped while trying to introduce his face to my elbow. I missed, of course, but Keane let go and took a couple of hasty steps away from me, like I had a contagious disease or something.

"What the fuck?" he said again, his face ashen. "Dana, what did you do?"

I considered my options. I was a pretty good liar—years of trying to cover up for my mom had given me plenty of practice—but I wasn't sure I was creative enough to come up with a plausible explanation for the Erlking's mark. Other than the truth, that is, and there was no way Keane was getting *that* out of me. Which left stonewalling as my only option.

"It's none of your business," I told Keane, rearranging the strap of my tank top so the mark was mostly covered despite the rip in my shirt. It came out harsher than I meant it to, and Keane actually flinched at my tone.

I let out a heavy sigh, trying to let the tension ease out of my body while I did. It didn't work too well.

"Look," I said, "if I wanted to talk about it, I wouldn't be keeping it hidden like this. It's between me and the Erlking, it's complicated, and it doesn't affect anyone but me. That's all you need to know."

Keane shook his head, the horror in his eyes slowly mixing with anger. "You'll have to do better than that."

I jutted my chin out stubbornly. "You're not the boss of me, and that's all you're going to get."

"Fine," he said, eyes boring into me. "I guess I'll just have to ask your father."

Like I said, I'm a pretty good liar, but my poker face failed me just then. My dad was the absolute last person I wanted to know about the Erlking's mark. If he found out about the mark, he wouldn't rest until he'd wrested every single detail out of me about how I'd gotten it. And if he learned I'd snuck out of my safe house, I'd be grounded for the rest of my life. Maybe even longer.

Not that I felt bad about keeping secrets from him, mind you. He was still keeping what he thought was a whopping secret from me. He was bound by his ties to the Seelie Court not to tell me what would happen if I gave the Erlking my virginity. Thanks to the agreement the Erlking had made with Titania, there was a geis—a magical restriction—that prevented my dad from even talking about the Erlking's secret.

But when my aunt Grace had tried to kill me, she'd been so determined to hurt me before I died that she'd severed her ties with the Seelie Court just so she could tell me the horrifying truth of what I'd agreed to. That was when I realized that as much as my dad loved me—and he did love me, I knew that—he was a Seelie Fae, too deeply devoted to his Court to consider leaving it, even to protect me.

He *had* to know what I'd promised the Erlking in order to free Ethan. And yet he hadn't been willing to renounce the Seelie Court so he could warn me. If he was going to keep a secret like that from me, then I didn't feel bad about hiding the Erlking's mark.

"Shall I go talk to your father right now?" Keane prompted. "Or are you going to explain why you have something that looks suspiciously like the Erlking's mark on your shoulder?"

I considered calling his bluff. He wasn't generally what I'd think of as a tattletale kind of guy. But like just about everyone else in my life, he'd do any crappy thing you could name if he thought it was for my own good.

"You're blackmailing me?" I asked, stalling as I tried to make up a half-truth that would get him off my back.

Keane shrugged, but the gesture was tight and tense. "Call it what you want. But if you're the Erlking's creature, then I think I have a right to know it before I travel into Faerie with you."

"I am *not* the Erlking's creature!"

"No? Then why do you have his mark, like a brand, on your skin?"

"You mind if I go change before we have this conversation? I don't like standing around in a torn shirt." I plucked at the shredded shoulder for emphasis.

Keane took a step closer to me, his jaw set. "Yes, I mind if you take a little extra time to work out the details of whatever lie you're about to tell me." There was a hint of a growl in his voice, and I wondered if he was mad enough to hit me in anger. I didn't think so, despite the clenched fists and the smoke coming out of his ears, but I couldn't help my primal instinct to take a step back.

Keane blinked, like he was surprised. Then he seemed to realize just how aggressive his body language was, and he visibly relaxed. His fists uncurled, and his shoulders lowered, but I could still see the metaphorical smoke. He wasn't any less pissed. And he wasn't going to give me time to think things through before I spoke.

"Start talking!" he commanded.

I wished I could squirm my way out of talking, but I couldn't, so I tried to keep my explanation as simple as possible. "The Erlking put a spell on me when I was trying to get him to free Ethan." I left out just *how* he'd put the spell on me, because there was no way I was telling anyone about the Erlking's brooch. I'd used it three times to make myself invisible, and the third use had activated the mark. I hadn't used the brooch since—despite the Erlking's promise that it contained no other secondary spells—but I didn't want to risk having it taken away.

I resisted the urge to reach up and touch the mark. It didn't hurt or anything, but somehow I was always very conscious of it on my skin, knowing exactly where it was even when I couldn't see it.

"It's like a tracking device. He claims it's for my own good," I said, "because he wants me alive so I can take him into the mortal world."

I hadn't thought it was possible for Keane to look any more horrified, but I was wrong. Most of the people around me had accepted that the Erlking, despite being one scary dude, wanted me alive. They didn't know that he wanted me alive so much he'd saved my life, but it was pretty obvious a dead Faeriewalker wasn't going to do him much good. From the way Keane was looking at me, I felt sure he wasn't as convinced as the rest.

"He knows where you are right now?" Keane asked. "He knows the location of your safe house?"

"Yeah, he knows. He's known for a long time and he hasn't come down here after me, so you can stop looking like the world just came to an end."

"You're unbelievable! You didn't think it was important to tell anyone this shit?"

"What good would it do? No one can do anything about it." A geis prevented the Erlking from attacking anyone in Avalon, but the geis was deactivated if someone attacked *him*. "The bottom line is he can't attack me, and I don't want anyone getting all protective about this and maybe giving him an excuse to hurt them." That was, after all, how Ethan had been captured by the Wild Hunt.

Keane didn't look convinced.

"You're not going to tell my dad, are you?" I asked, then chewed my lip when he didn't answer immediately.

Keane let out a heavy sigh and shook his head. "How many other secrets are you keeping?"

I didn't want to think about that. The Erlking had once suggested that all my secrets were going to come back and bite me in the butt someday. I had a feeling he was right, but I was determined to put off dealing with it until absolutely necessary.

"Are you going to tell on me or not?" I asked, ignoring Keane's question.

"I won't. At least for now. But you really should tell him yourself. Have you ever considered that when you go into Faerie, the geis that keeps the Erlking from hunting anyone in Avalon won't be in effect anymore? And that you're not officially a member of the Seelie Court and therefore aren't protected by the Erlking's agreement with the Queens?"

I'm sure my face went pale. No, I hadn't thought of that.

"There will be nothing to prevent him from hunting you, and if you've got the equivalent of a radio collar on you, he won't have to look very hard to find you."

It was true that the Erlking didn't want to kill me. However, if he was free to hunt me, then if he captured me, he could force me to join his Wild Hunt. And then the Hunt would have its very own pet Faeriewalker to take them out into the mortal world and wreak havoc.

I swallowed hard. "I hadn't thought of that," I said, "but I'm sure my dad has. He wouldn't take me into Faerie unless he's sure the Erlking can't get me."

"How can he be sure when he doesn't have all the facts?"

Geez, Keane was full of uncomfortable questions today. And I was sorely lacking in satisfying answers. Dad had assured me I'd be protected by the rules of Court etiquette. The Erlking didn't belong to either Court, but maybe he followed their rules of etiquette anyway. I trusted my dad and his judgment.

"I'm going to go change," I announced, because continuing this conversation wasn't going to do anyone any good. I could feel Keane's angry gaze on my back even after I escaped to my bedroom and closed the door behind me.

My day didn't get any better after that. I had a lot of packing to do, and my mom called about a zillion times. I refused to answer, despite the weepy messages she left. I couldn't face talking to her. I was too freaked out by the reality that I was leaving for Faerie the very next day, in the company of a prince who would be happy to see my dad—and me, by extension—dead, to deal with any more drama.

As if all this wasn't enough to make me a nervous wreck, my dad came by in the afternoon and took me to a gun range to teach me how to fire the derringer. Shooting the little gun was a stark reminder that this supposedly safe trip of ours might be far more dangerous than we knew. I also discovered that I was not destined to be an expert marksman. I had to fight my instinct to close my eyes every time I pulled the trigger, and I jumped at the noise, despite the earplugs.

Dad was pretty patient with me, but I think he was regretting the impulse to give me a lethal weapon by the time we left the range.

There was one bright spot to my day, though it wasn't the kind of bright spot that soothed my nerves: that night, Ethan and I were going on our first honest-to-goodness date. We'd planned it before the summons, and there was no way I was going to cancel. Although this being our first real date, I couldn't help being nervous. (As if the knowledge that I would be leaving everything familiar behind and traveling to Faerie in less than twenty-four hours didn't make me nervous enough.)

It didn't help that this morning's session with Keane had made me so painfully aware of all the secrets I was keeping, even from my family and my closest friends. For example, I'd never told Ethan about the Erlking's mark. His head would probably explode if he ever found out I'd told Keane and not him. I could give Ethan some watered-down version of the story I'd given Keane, but Ethan was more likely to push for details—and I was more likely to cave to his pushing.

The last time Ethan and I had gone out together was before the Erlking had sunk his claws into Ethan. I'd insisted we were just friends, and it *wasn't* a date. We'd gone to a movie, and I'd discovered just how creative Ethan was capable of being in a darkened movie theater. Even with Finn sitting there just a few rows back, Ethan had gotten away with things I'd never meant to let him get away with.

Figuring I'd learned the hard way that going to a movie with Ethan was dangerous, this time we were going out to dinner instead.

I have to admit, I felt pretty sophisticated and grown up as I headed out to meet Ethan at a tiny little Italian restaurant he swore was fantastic. Most kids my age did school dances or trips to the mall for their dates, but Ethan had outgrown high school dating practices. He could act majorly childish and immature at times— especially when he was bickering with Kimber—but at the ripe old age of eighteen, he considered himself an adult, and for this date, he'd chosen to act like one.

He was waiting for me just outside the restaurant, and I felt the familiar flutter of excitement in my belly when I first caught sight of him. The Fae are all ridiculously good-looking, but from the moment I'd met Ethan, he'd pushed my buttons in a way no one else did.

His hair was a very pale blond, and it reached to his shoulders when he didn't have it tied back. His eyes were a shade of teal blue humans can only achieve with contacts. And the slight imperfection of his nose—which looked like it had once been broken—gave him just enough character to save him from being pretty.

Of course, these days, the first thing that drew my eyes when I caught sight of him was the Erlking's mark, which looked like a tattoo of a stylized blue stag curling around the side of his face. It was the mark that said that even though he was no longer a member of the Wild Hunt, he was still bound to the Erlking. It always gave me a little chill when I saw it, although if I didn't know what it meant, I might have thought it kinda sexy.

Ethan broke into a smile when he caught sight of me. That smile still had the power to make my insides quiver, but there was a haunted look in his eyes that made my heart ache for him. He was not the same boy I'd first met. Once upon a time, Ethan had been cheerful and carefree. You couldn't apply either of those words to him now. Everything he had gone through had been because of me, and sometimes I felt like I was drowning in the guilt.

Glancing over my shoulder at Finn—who, of course, had to come with me even on a date, because that's what bodyguards do—Ethan put his hands on my shoulders, then leaned forward to give me a chaste kiss. Even that slight brushing of lips made me tingle all over. I wanted to pull his head back down to mine, wanted him to give me a deeper, longer kiss. But although Finn wasn't officially my chaperone, I knew he'd interrupt if things got too hot and heavy. Besides, I couldn't help being self-conscious with him watching.

"You look beautiful tonight," Ethan told me, still smiling as he held the restaurant door open.

I was glad he thought so, because I'd spent the better part of an hour deciding what to wear. I felt like a total loser for doing it, but I couldn't seem to help myself. I'd gone for jeans, paired with a cozy sweater that would not only keep me warm on this typical chilly Avalon summer night, but would also feel nice if Ethan should happen to touch me.

The restaurant was even tinier than I'd imagined, with only ten tables and a bar about the size of your average walk-in closet. Nine of those tables were occupied, and there were a number of twenty-somethings hanging around the bar. I was acutely aware of how much Finn stood out as he positioned himself against the wall near the door.

Most people were dressed pretty casually—one couple, who were probably tourists and didn't know the average temperature for summer here was in the sixties, were even wearing shorts. Finn, on the other hand, was wearing his usual dark suit and tie, as well as the dark sunglasses, and he was on the receiving end of more than one curious look.

The hostess guided Ethan and me to our table, and I tried not to feel self-conscious. The people who'd stared at Finn were one by one transferring their curious stares to Ethan and me.

I should have been used to it by now. I had to have Finn with me whenever I left my safe house—unless I had my dad instead. Which meant I was always at least a little conspicuous. But maybe because of the whole date thing, I felt more conspicuous than usual. My nerves were buzzing as I picked up my menu and stared at it with-out seeing it.

I was on a date. A real, honest-to-goodness date. With a guy so gorgeous he'd usually have a handful of cheerleaders hanging on him wherever he went. I know that compared to all the crazy stuff that had happened to me so far in Avalon, this was nothing. But it made my heart beat a little quicker. And it made me feel about as mature as your average twelve-year-old.

Ethan leaned over the table, dropping his voice. "Is something wrong?"

Great. Bad enough that I felt so awkward and uncomfortable. Did I really have to be so obvious about it that Ethan could tell?

Way to look sophisticated, Dana.

I forced a smile and told myself to get over it. Not only had Ethan and I had more, um, intimate encounters before, but I had absolutely no reason to be nervous around him. At least, so I told myself.

"Nope. Not a thing."

Ethan rolled his eyes. "Yeah, right. That's why you look like you want to jump out of your chair and run."

That shook me out of my little bout of self-pity. "I do not!"

"Do too."

I narrowed my eyes at him. For the moment, his smile looked normal, like the friendly smile he'd used to devastating effect before the Erlking had come into his life. But then he seemed to remember himself, and the smile wilted.

"Sorry," I said. "I guess I'm obsessing a bit about this trip to Faerie." It made as good an excuse as any.

Ethan nodded and picked up his menu. This time, he was the one deliberately avoiding my eyes. "It's going to be a fun time all right. You, me, Kimber, and Keane all hanging out together twenty-four/seven."

I snorted. "*That's* what you think is most disturbing about this whole thing? That the four of us are going to be spending so much time together? I'm more worried about stuff like, oh, you know, dying a slow and horrible death."

The look in Ethan's eyes hardened. "You're not going to die," he said, reaching across the table to take my hand in his. The touch made my belly flutter again. "I'm not going to let anything happen to you." He grimaced. "And neither is anyone else."

I squeezed Ethan's hand and smiled. "Thanks. I know you'll all do your best. And maybe I'm getting myself all worked up over nothing. Maybe it'll end up being as safe as a school trip."

The look on Ethan's face told me he didn't believe that any more than I did. The waiter chose that moment to come over and take our orders. Neither one of us had done more than glance at the menu, but Ethan knew what he wanted, and I made a snap decision, more interested in Ethan's comment about our traveling companions.

"Do you think it's a bad idea for all four of us to go?" I asked when the waiter was out of earshot. "Are you and Keane going to try to kill each other before the first day's travel is through?"

To say Ethan and Keane disliked each other was an understatement. Ethan, for whatever reason, was jealous of the time I spent with Keane. Time I spent getting my butt kicked, not making out or anything, but Ethan didn't seem to make the distinction. And apparently, Ethan had stolen Keane's girlfriend when they were in high school, so Keane hated him. I didn't know whether anyone but me realized Kimber was into Keane, but I'd bet if the boys found out, it wouldn't help the situation. So far, I'd never been around Ethan and Keane together, but I'd be shocked if sparks didn't fly.

Ethan scowled at me. "Having the two of us so close together is a recipe for disaster. But I won't start anything if he doesn't."

And didn't that just fill me with confidence?

"This trip is going to be miserable enough without you two going all MMA on us."

Ethan cocked his head to the side. "MMA?"

"Mixed Martial Arts. I guess that's a U.S. thing, huh?" Or maybe just a *human* thing. I suspected the Fae might find MMA . . . undignified.

"I guess. What is it?"

I shrugged. "Some fighting thing. Lots of blood and testosterone. Not my cup of tea."

Ethan grinned, but the expression didn't reach his eyes. "I'm not a complete idiot, you know. Keane teaches self-defense for a living. I'm not about to 'go all MMA' on him. Not unless I want to have my ass handed to me."

Ah. That was what was chafing Ethan. He might be a magical prodigy and everyone's golden boy, but he knew Keane could take him in a physical fight. Boys and their egos.

"We'll find a way to get along," Ethan assured me. "You should have all the protection you can get, and I'm sure Keane is a good man to have in a fight." There was an edge in his voice, like it was practically killing him to admit that. I must have made some kind of face, because Ethan reached out and gave my shoulder a squeeze.

"It won't be so bad," Ethan said. "Even if tensions run a little high, you should be looking forward to your first look at Faerie. It's a pretty cool place."

"What could be more fun than traveling in a place where creatures like Water Witches and Spriggans live?" I grumbled.

"Water Witches and Spriggans are both Unseelie," Ethan reminded me. "We'll be traveling through Seelie territory."

"Oh, yeah, and all the creatures of the Seelie Court are sweetness and light."

He smiled sheepishly. "Well, no. But they're unlikely to bother Prince Henry."

I was far from convinced, though I resisted the urge to say so. This was supposed to be a romantic night out, and so far I'd spent most of it whining and complaining. Real attractive.

Ethan's hand found mine under the table. Our fingers twined. It was a simple touch, but it sent a pleasant shiver through me anyway. Our eyes met and locked, and the rest of the world seemed to fade away. His thumb stroked gently over my knuckles, and I wished that after we were done with dinner, we could have some quiet time together, just the two of us.

But, of course, that wasn't going to happen. If I was lucky, I *might* get a goodnight kiss, but with Finn watching our every move, it would be a chaste, G-rated kiss that wouldn't even begin to satisfy our hunger.

Ethan leaned toward me, dropping his voice to a conspiratorial whisper. "We're going to be traveling together for weeks. I bet if we're clever enough, we can carve out some time for ourselves."

My heart fluttered at the thought, though I suspected getting time alone on this trip was going to take more than a little cleverness. And even if we did . . .

Ethan and I could never do much more than make out. I knew I should be satisfied with that, at least for now. It wasn't like I was ready to go all the way with him even if I didn't have the Erlking's bargain hanging over me. But I've never been good at living in the moment. Taking care of my mom had taught me from a very young age that I always had to look three steps ahead, had to be ready for the curveballs life was going to throw at me. My forethought had helped keep food on the table and kept us from getting evicted, but sometimes—like now—I really wished I could just switch it off.

Ethan leaned even farther over the table. "I can read you like a book," he said. "Forget about the Erlking for a while. We can have plenty of fun together without crossing the line." There was a wicked twinkle in his eyes that made my heart flutter. "I can be very creative, you know."

I swallowed hard, both excited and intimidated by his words. Just kissing Ethan was almost enough to make me completely lose my head. If we were alone together without a bodyguard/chaperone, I suspected he could completely overwhelm me. There was something very tempting about the idea of being overwhelmed like that, of letting him kiss me until my rational mind went on sabbatical and I just allowed myself to *feel* without thought.

It was a dangerous temptation. Especially with a guy like Ethan, who was no doubt used to girls who could and would put out. Could I trust him to stop on his own if I let down my guard? Or did we need me to remain in my role as the voice of reason?

I wished I knew.

chapter five

The day of the big trip was a typical Avalon summer day, meaning it was gray and gloomy with a hint of chill in the air. Dad had arranged for my bags, except for my backpack, which I refused to part with, to be delivered to the baggage wagon in advance. In the backpack, I put everything that couldn't exist in Faerie outside a Faeriewalker's aura, like the little gun. At the last minute, I threw in a digital camera. I would be the only mortal ever to have photographed Faerie. I might have thought that was cool, if I weren't so nervous.

Prince Henry's caravan was leaving from the Northern Gate, and when Dad and I arrived, it was to see that the bridge leading to the gate had been cordoned off, only official members of Prince Henry's party allowed through until after he was gone. I would have thought that was a show of royal arrogance, but blocking off the gate was the only practical solution. The entire parking lot was packed, only a few cars visible in a corner that I suspected was employee parking. The rest of the lot was teeming with people, and horses, and wagons. Some of the Fae were wearing modern clothing, but most were wearing long dresses or breeches. The whole scene looked like something out of a Renaissance Faire.

"Geez, are we traveling with a freaking army?" I muttered to Dad. I'd known it wouldn't be just my friends and Prince Henry, but I hadn't realized his entourage would be this substantial.

Dad's lips curled into a wry smile. "Henry goes nowhere without an army to serve and protect him. It would be beneath his dignity as a prince."

Of course, not everyone down there was part of the prince's entourage. I'd dragged my feet a bit about leaving my safe house, so we were among the last to arrive. At the near side of the bridge, waiting for us, were Ethan, Keane, Kimber . . . and my mom.

Keane and Ethan were standing about twenty yards apart and pointedly ignoring each other. Kimber and my mom stood between them, looking uncomfortable. I wondered if the boys had started fighting already.

I never returned any of Mom's calls yesterday. I'd known I'd have to face her again before I left, so I wasn't surprised to see her. But I was still too angry at her to force an apology I didn't mean. Maybe if I rode off into Faerie without caving to her oh-poor-me eyes, she'd finally understand just how much this drinking thing meant to me.

I held up my head when I caught her eye, knowing the look on my face was pure stubbornness. She took a step toward me, her arms opening as if to give me a hug. I gave her a cold glare instead of the welcoming embrace I'm sure she was expecting, or at least hoping for.

Mom's smile wilted, and hurt flashed in her eyes. A hint of guilt stabbed through me, but I ruthlessly shoved it away. If my mom couldn't even stay off the booze for a few weeks, then I didn't feel like protecting her delicate feelings.

She opened her mouth as if to say something, but I guess the look on my face was forbidding, because she didn't get anything out. In my peripheral vision, I saw Ethan, Kimber, and Keane looking away, trying to give us an illusion of privacy. My dad wasn't in-clined to do us the same courtesy.

"Give your mother a hug, Dana," he said, giving my shoulder a little push. "You don't know how long it's going to be before you see her again."

I gave him a dirty look over my shoulder. "Thanks for the pep talk. I wasn't freaked out enough by the whole idea of going into Faerie, so I'm glad you put it in perspective for me."

"It's all right, Seamus," my mother said before my dad could tell me what he thought of my smart mouth. She smiled sadly at me. "Dana and I have to work this out between ourselves."

I crossed my arms over my chest, just in case she wasn't getting the hint that I wasn't open to an affectionate, teary farewell. "Do you have any promises you'd like to make me before I go off into Faerie, potentially never to be seen again?"

She blanched, and I knew I was being unnecessarily cruel. But, dammit, *I* was the one who was plunging headfirst into danger. It wasn't my responsibility to try to make her feel better about it.

My mom stood up a little straighter and tried to look stern. "My life is my business," she told me firmly. "You don't get to make the rules, and I'm not going to make promises I can't keep."

I ground my teeth. Couldn't she hear herself? If she couldn't keep a promise not to drink, didn't that obviously make her the alcoholic she claimed she wasn't?

"Well, I'm not going to pretend it doesn't bother me," I told her. "I'm through with that act."

I'm sure this wasn't the sentimental send-off she'd been hoping for. But if she thought we could fix this thing between us in the few minutes we had standing out here surrounded by all these people, she was nuts.

Mom reached out and touched my shoulder briefly. "I love you,

Dana," she said, her voice low enough I could barely hear it, her eyes now swimming with tears. "I hope you know that."

There was a time in my life when the minute my mom turned on the waterworks, I gave up whatever fight we'd been having and tried to get her to stop crying. My mom had aced Emotional Manipulation 101 and was now on to graduate studies. But whatever else had happened to me since I'd come to Avalon, I seemed to have become immune to the magical effects of her tears.

I didn't reassure her that I knew she loved me, nor did I reassure her that I loved her. Even though I did. No matter how angry I was, no matter how scared I was of what she would do to herself, she was still my mom, and her drinking wouldn't have bothered me so much if I didn't love her. But I didn't tell her, despite the little voice in my head that said I should, just in case this was the last time we ever saw each other. I told that little voice that it was being morbid and should shut up.

Mom bowed her head, then nodded. Accepting reality, I guess. Now there's a shock!

"Be safe, baby," she said, and she let loose the tears she'd been trying—not very hard, I suspect—to suppress.

Moving faster than I could dodge, she threw her arms around me and hugged me tight. I could feel her body shaking as she cried, and I knew I'd have a damp patch on my shoulder before she let go.

With a sigh of resignation, I put my arms around her and gave her a brief squeeze before squirming out of her grasp. "I'll see you soon," I said, which was about as close as I was going to come to giving her the reassurance she'd wanted.

"I won't let anything happen to her," my dad said.

"I know," she responded, then gave him a hug, too. He was taken by surprise, but he hugged her back with more enthusiasm than I had. They fought almost all the time, as far as I could tell—mostly about me—but I guess they had loved each other once upon a time, and they didn't hate each other now.

"I'll bring her back safe and sound," my dad said, though I doubted phrasing his reassurance a different way was going to make my mom any more convinced.

She nodded, still clinging to him.

Mom held on to Dad for a moment, then let him go and took a couple of steps back. Her eyes were still shimmery, her cheeks wet with tears. I had a nasty suspicion that the first thing she would do when we were gone was find a liquor store. But there would have been nothing I could have done to stop her even if I weren't running off to Faerie, into what was, as far as I was concerned, enemy territory.

Dad put an arm around my shoulder and steered me toward the bridge. My friends fell in behind us. I looked over my shoulder once and saw my mom waving forlornly. I thought about waving back, but didn't.

When we reached the parking lot, one of the prince's men was waiting for us with an expression of impatience on his face. He looked like he was about to say something about us being late, but my dad gave him an icy look, and he thought better of it. Instead, he motioned to some guy dressed like Robin Hood, who led a bunch of horses our way.

By "led," I don't mean he held on to their halters and guided them toward us; I mean he beckoned to them with a wave, and they perked up their ears and followed. I tried to tell myself that meant the horses were easygoing and well-behaved, and I would have no trouble trying to ride one.

"These are the mounts your Knight chose for the children," Robin said, and my dad was the only one who didn't stiffen up at the word *children*. Yes, I know, to thousand-year-old Fae, we were infants, but still . . .

Robin Hood introduced each of us to our horses by name as if they were people. I half-expected them to offer to shake hands. My horse was an enormous white mare named Phaedra. Being a Fae horse, she was a thing of beauty, with sleek lines, intelligent brown eyes, and a mane and tail so white they practically sparkled. She was also about half-again as tall as I was. My palms began to sweat.

"Is this a good time to mention that I don't know how to ride?" I asked my dad as Robin Hood, or whatever his name was, left us to our own devices. Was it my imagination, or was Phaedra giving me the stink eye?

Dad smiled at me and stroked Phaedra's nose. She seemed to like that. "You'll do fine," he said. "She knows where we're going better than you do. All you have to do is sit in the saddle, and she'll take care of the rest."

I eyed one of the wagons that was currently being loaded with crates and boxes. "Couldn't I ride in one of the wagons?"

Phaedra snorted and tossed her head, like she'd understood me and was insulted. Maybe she had, but more likely it was just my imagination running away with me.

"Riding in wagons is for the lower classes, or for the injured and infirm," Dad informed me. "I'm sure Henry would be happy to have you ride in a wagon so he and his courtiers could snicker at you behind your back. They'd see it as a sign of weakness. As I'm sure you understand, we can't afford signs of weakness."

Guess I was going to have to learn to ride after all. *How hard can it be?* I asked myself, then wished I hadn't as good as jinxed myself. Dad guided me to Phaedra's side.

"Put your left foot in the stirrup and hop up," he instructed me.

"Here goes nothing," I said. The stupid stirrup was about eighty feet from the ground, and I had to pull on the saddle to haul myself up. When I got settled, the ground was disturbingly far away. I most definitely did *not* want to fall off. "You sure I don't need an oxygen tank up here?" I asked, and Dad laughed while handing me the reins.

"Take good care of my daughter, Phaedra," he said, patting the horse's shoulder, and then he turned away from us.

Finn emerged from the crowd riding a dappled gray horse, a riderless black horse following on his heels. Dad headed toward them. The black horse's ears flicked forward, and it made a happy-sounding noise, like it was glad to see my dad. From the way my dad smiled and rubbed its nose, I guessed he was glad to see it, too. He looked completely at ease as he climbed gracefully into the saddle. I, on the other hand, found myself squirming to find a comfortable position. Phaedra snorted and stomped her foot, which I interpreted to mean "stop fidgeting." I put one hand on the saddle to steady myself and did my best to hold still.

We must have been among the last to arrive. No sooner had we all mounted up than the caravan started forward, a pair of Knights leading the way to an oversized doorway in the gatehouse. A handful of uniformed border patrolmen guarded the doorway, but they were more concerned with not letting any unauthorized creatures of Faerie come into Avalon than with paying attention to who went out. (Which was how the Knights who'd attacked Finn a few weeks ago had managed to escape without the slightest repercussions or even an investigation.)

I took a deep breath as Phaedra danced impatiently beneath me, waiting for her turn to join the procession.

It took a while. The prince apparently had to be in the absolute center of everything, so there were a handful of Knights telling everyone when they could and couldn't move. I couldn't help noticing that even though we were supposed to be under the prince's protection, we were directed almost to the very back of the procession, with only one Knight and a baggage wagon behind us.

I saw from the tightening around my dad's mouth that it was

exactly the insult I thought it was, though he didn't protest. I remembered him saying that the prince's men were going to be more focused on defending Henry than on defending me, and I was glad that I had both Keane and Ethan with me.

Finally, it was our turn to move. Ethan rode up beside me, giving me a jaunty salute, while Keane and Kimber slipped in front and my dad and Finn took up the rear. I was well protected. But that didn't stop my hands from sweating as Phaedra bore me ever closer to the door that gaped open.

"Be sure you focus on Faerie when we get to the end of the passageway," my father called to me from behind.

My power as a Faeriewalker meant that when I looked out over the border of Avalon, I could see what was known as the Glimmerglass, a blurry double image of the mortal world and Faerie, superimposed upon each other. If I focused my gaze on the mortal world, then when we reached the end of the passageway through the gatehouse, I would see nothing but a brick wall, which I wouldn't be able to pass through. I'd have to make sure not to let my fear blind me to Faerie.

When we entered the passageway, my hands were not only sweating, they were shaking. I was about to leave everything that was normal and familiar behind, and enter a world where magic reigned supreme. A world where at least one Faerie Queen wanted me dead, and where creatures who haunted mortals' nightmares lived. I wanted to turn around and gallop the other way.

Okay, so maybe if I went through with this and made friendly with Titania, I would no longer be in any danger from the Seelie Court. That would be great, but it was only a maybe. And I still had to get there, which didn't seem like any sure thing to me.

Staring ahead, I saw the wall that marked the border between Avalon and the mortal world. It was slightly indistinct, but I couldn't make out the image of Faerie that I knew was there, too.

With another deep breath, I tried to relax and let my eyes lose focus, searching for the second image in the Glimmerglass.

For a moment, I feared my nerves were going to get the best of me and my subconscious was going to refuse to let me see anything past the mortal world. But then my stomach gave a familiar sickening lurch as my vision blurred and things seemed to move within the bricks. I swallowed hard, hoping I wasn't going to puke, and tried to focus my gaze on the movement behind the bricks as Phaedra carried me ever closer. I wondered what would happen if I couldn't get my gaze focused on Faerie in time. Would Phaedra go through the wall? And would I then find myself dumped to the floor, trapped on this side?

The added worries about humiliating myself didn't help. Blood clamored in my ears, and I had to remind myself to breathe every once in a while. I kept my gaze as unfocused as possible, letting the images blur until I could make out vague shapes behind the bricks, rather than just movement. The shapes resolved themselves into figures, the members of the caravan who had already passed over the border and into Faerie. I picked out one figure, a Knight on an imposing black horse, and stared at him until I could see him clearly, the brick wall now nothing but a faint afterimage making him look almost like he had scales.

I managed it in the nick of time. The moment I was finally able to focus on something that was purely Faerie, Phaedra stepped through where the wall in the mortal world had been.

chapter six

There was a part of me that expected the transition from Avalon to Faerie to be dramatic and flashy, that thought it should be like going through the looking glass into a world that was completely foreign and unfamiliar. This despite the fact that with my Faeriewalker's vision, I'd had numerous glimpses into Faerie already and knew it wasn't a world of giant toadstools and beanstalks. When I'd dared the disorientation of looking through the Glimmerglass, I'd seen what looked like untold miles of forest. Trees, trees, and more trees. Which, if you think about it, really isn't that unusual a sight, unless you'd never been outside a city before.

I held my breath as Phaedra crossed the border into Faerie, waiting for the thunderclap, or whatever, and I was almost disappointed when nothing particularly out of the ordinary happened. There was a broad dirt road leading away from the gate, but it curved out of sight within a hundred yards or so. The prince and his entourage were already making their way down that road.

I forced myself to start breathing again, looking all around me in search of something to give me the immediate evidence that we weren't in Kansas anymore, but there was no yellow brick road, no lollipop trees, no monsters from out of my nightmares. The trees were a little odd in that I could identify almost none of them. Not that I'm a naturalist or anything, but I could usually recognize your basic pines, maples, and oaks. I spied a couple of oak trees, but aside from that, they were all mystery trees, which made the forest suddenly look a lot more foreign. Still, if I didn't look too closely, I could almost fool myself into believing we were riding down a nature trail somewhere back in the U.S.

"You were expecting more fanfare?" Ethan asked, grinning at me. He looked like he was having fun, although there was still that hint of sadness in his eyes that reminded me how much he had changed. As if the Erlking's mark on his face wasn't reminder enough.

I shrugged a bit sheepishly. "I don't know what I was expecting," I admitted.

"Something more exotic, I presume. I know that's what I was expecting the first time I came to Faerie. But it's really a fairly normal place—except where it's not."

I rolled my eyes at him. "Yeah, normal. I'm sure." Never mind that I hadn't seen anything outlandish yet. I was sure that would come.

"*Fairly* normal," he said. "And the exceptions can be a bit unsettling."

"Fantastic." Phaedra snorted and tossed her head, the movement startling me enough that I almost fell off. I patted the side of her neck uneasily. "Take it easy," I said. "I didn't mean to insult your homeland."

She snorted again, as if to say, *Yeah, right.* Ethan smothered a smile, and I felt the heat rising in my face. We'd been in Faerie two whole minutes, and I was having a conversation with my horse. Not cool.

"Phaedra hates me," I told Ethan in what I hoped was a haughty voice. "I figured it wouldn't hurt to kiss ass a little in hopes that she won't dump me on my head."

Ethan laughed again. I noticed he seemed to have no trouble with his own horse. He rode with a kind of easy confidence I would have envied, if I'd had any desire to become a better horsewoman. He looked fantastic astride that white horse, with his blond hair loose around his shoulders, his comfortably worn jeans clinging to the muscles of his thighs. For the thousandth time, I wondered how I'd managed to catch the eye of someone like him, who could have any girl he wanted.

Ethan caught my admiring stare and winked at me, totally aware of how sexy he was. I'd once found that arrogance annoying, but now it just made me smile and shake my head. Yes, I had it bad for him. And at that moment, I didn't mind a bit.

The nerves and anticipation that had kept me so hopped up I could barely sleep last night quickly gave way to boredom and discomfort. Because of the baggage wagons, our caravan moved at a plodding walk, and all I could see on both sides of the road was trees, trees, trees.

At first, I kept staring at the trees, strangely weirded out by their unfamiliarity. The occasional familiar oak only made the rest of the trees seem more foreign. The air was filled with what sounded like bird song—though again, nothing I could recognize—and sometimes, I caught flashes of color out of the corner of my eye. Whenever I turned to look, there was nothing there. Eventually, I learned to stop looking, but that didn't make me any less aware of the phantom flashes that constantly reminded me of the thinly veiled strangeness of the forest.

Luckily, the torture that was horseback riding provided plenty of distraction from my unsettling surroundings. My butt began protesting the hardness of the saddle within about fifteen minutes, and Phaedra's impressive girth gave my inner thighs a serious stretch.

I was sure that when I dismounted I'd be walking like a cowboy—assuming I could walk at all. It was only force of will that kept me from asking how much longer we were going to go without a rest, but I didn't want to be like the little kid in the backseat going, "Are we there yet?" Even if that was what I was thinking.

We'd been on the go for about four hours when the road took a sharp curve, and a huge, breathtaking lake came into view. I could catch only occasional glimpses of it through the trees, but the water was a sparkling shade of blue I associated with Caribbean beaches. I'd never seen a lake that wasn't muddy brown in color before, but maybe Faerie didn't do muddy water.

The caravan came to a halt, a runner traveling down the line and telling us we were stopping for a rest. It seemed a bit of an odd stopping place to me, the road being narrow, with no room for anyone to spread out and no easy access to the lake. Still, as long as I got to get off my horse, I wasn't about to complain.

When I slid off of Phaedra's back, I practically fell on my butt, my legs so rubbery they could barely hold me. Phaedra gave me a disdainful look as Ethan hurried to my side to give me a little support in case I took a nosedive.

Oh. My. God. I don't think I'd ever been so sore before in my life! And this was just a rest stop, a chance to water our horses and stretch our legs. In less than an hour—according to the runner—we'd be mounting up and heading out again. I honestly wasn't sure I was capable of getting back up on the horse, much less riding several more hours.

"You guys seriously need to invent some kind of alternative to the car," I muttered at Ethan, who gave me a crooked smile.

"Believe me, people have tried. There are some aspects of technology that magic can mimic, but I'm afraid cars aren't one of them."

At that moment, all the trees on the lake side of the road started to move. At first, I thought I was hallucinating or dreaming, but then I felt the faint tingle of magic in the air. No one else seemed particularly alarmed when the trees pulled up their roots and trundled aside, those roots working like giant crab legs. I shivered in a phantom chill as the underbrush, too, pulled up roots and cleared a large swath of land between the road and the lake. People began leading their horses to the water's edge to drink as if nothing unusual had happened. I just stood there and gaped like an idiot.

"Fairly normal," Ethan reminded me. "Except when it isn't."

"Yeah," I said, unable to think of anything clever to say.

Phaedra hadn't bothered waiting for me to lead her to the water; she headed toward the lake, swishing her tail in my face as she passed. I could have done without the tail-in-the-face bit, but I was just as happy to take a break from her—and no one seemed to think the horses needed constant supervision. Phaedra wasn't the only one going to the water without a rider. Ethan put his arm around my shoulders and guided me toward the water.

Out of the corner of my eye, I saw Keane, his eyes narrowed and flashing. He looked like he was about to hit something, which meant he was watching Ethan, not me.

I stifled a sigh. I had no doubt Ethan had put his arm around me specifically to provoke Keane, but I didn't feel inclined to shrug him off. We'd had very little alone-time, and though we were hardly alone here, the anonymity of the crowd gave us some semblance of privacy.

I slipped my arm around Ethan's waist and laid my head against his shoulder, enjoying the feel of him against me as we walked to the shore of the lake and then stood there together, taking in the view. Up close, the lake looked just as blue as it had from a distance. Near the shore, the water was crystal clear, showing a bottom of pebbles, but even that water had a blue tinge to it. The color shaded to aquamarine as the water got deeper, and then was an almost sapphire blue in the center. I wondered if maybe there was some kind of algae in the water that made it blue like that, but I didn't ask, because "Why is water blue?" seemed like a dumb question.

"You doing okay?" Ethan asked, squeezing my shoulders.

"Nothing's attacked us yet, so I'm doing great," I said, crossing my fingers in case I just jinxed us.

Ethan laughed. "Nothing's going to attack *this* party. There are a dozen Knights with us, along with some serious magic users. We're not exactly an appealing target."

I glanced over my shoulder at the prince's entourage. Everyone was scurrying around busily, and I wondered if anyone other than me, my friends, and the prince was actually getting a chance to rest at this rest stop.

Ethan pulled me a little closer, his chin nuzzling the top of my head. I tore my gaze away from the lake and looked up at him, meeting his eyes. I had come so close to losing him forever, and I'd promised myself that I was going to savor every moment we had together from now on. His head bent toward mine and his lips parted. I closed my eyes and held my breath in anticipation of his kiss.

Someone cleared his throat behind us. I jumped like a startled cat, although Ethan didn't seem surprised at all. I tried to pull away, feeling guilty and embarrassed about our near public display of affection. Until I turned my head and saw who had just interrupted us.

"You should get something to eat," Keane said, holding up a shiny red apple and then taking a bite. "This is as close to a lunch break as we're going to get."

I saw that he had a second apple in his other hand. He tossed it to me, and I impressed myself by catching it one-handed. (I had to catch it one-handed because Ethan was squeezing me so tightly against him my other arm was trapped.)

"Thanks," I said warily. I was pretty sure Keane hadn't come over here just to give me an apple. I didn't think it would take much for this to turn ugly.

"You didn't bring one for me?" Ethan asked with exaggerated outrage.

Keane took another bite of his apple, the fruit making a crisp crunching sound that would have made my mouth water if I weren't so aware of the rising testosterone level. I'd known from the start that having both of them traveling with me was a recipe for disaster, but which one of them would I have told to stay home? Not that it would have mattered, because neither one would have listened to me.

"Sorry," Keane said around his mouthful of apple. "Only have two hands."

Yeah, he sounded really sorry. Looked it, too.

I think Ethan was about to say something scathing, but I gave him a poke in the ribs with my elbow. "Can we skip the posturing and chest-pounding, guys?" I asked, trying to put some distance between myself and Ethan. I liked having his arm around me, but not when he was doing it just to piss Keane off. I couldn't help wondering if he'd tried to kiss me only because he knew Keane was watching. I wouldn't put it past him. I knew Ethan was really into me—I was over suspecting his motives every two seconds. Well, *mostly* over it. But I'd seen his darker side, and I knew he was capable of some world-class scheming.

Keane grinned at me. "I promise not to pound my chest, though I'd get a kick out of it if Ethan tried a Tarzan yodel." He took another bite of his apple, his eyes alight with hard-edged amusement.

My skin prickled with a hint of magic, and I figured things were going from bad to worse. Ethan had lost his easygoing manner and was staring daggers at Keane. I didn't think Keane had said anything all that bad—at least, not for him—but apparently Ethan was touchier.

"Maybe you should demonstrate the yodel," he said, the magic around us growing thicker.

Keane had to feel the gathering magic, too, and had to know what it meant. Keane was a great fighter, but I seriously doubted he had the chops to go up against Ethan in a battle of magic.

"Ethan," I said in a warning tone, "you'd better not be thinking about casting any nasty magic." Of course, I already knew he was more than thinking about it.

Keane raised an eyebrow. "What makes you think he's about to cast something?"

Dammit! Keane didn't know I could sense magic, and I couldn't afford for that to change. I'd been so annoyed at the boys and their machofest that I'd forgotten to be cautious.

I shrugged, hoping my chagrin didn't show on my face. "I know Ethan," I said, giving Ethan my sternest look. "Don't do it."

He blinked and tried to look innocent. Considering the air still prickled with magic, it wasn't a very convincing act.

"I'm not a bully," he said. "I'd never pick on someone who couldn't defend himself."

Keane made a growling sound and stepped closer to us. The sensation of magic built even more, and I suspected Keane was responsible for at least some of it.

"Who the fuck says I can't defend myself?" Keane asked, green eyes flashing.

Geez, could he take the bait any easier? I wondered if I'd get myself hurt if I stepped between the two of them. Neither one of them would hurt me on purpose, but I had a feeling if they started fighting, there'd be collateral damage.

Ethan's grin widened. He was really getting a kick out of pushing Keane's buttons. Not that Keane was making it hard for him.

"Far be it from me to insult your manhood," Ethan said. "I'm sure you'd have no trouble whatsoever defending against my magic."

Keane sneered. "Just like you'd have no trouble whatsoever defending yourself in a fair fight. Right?"

They both seemed to have practically forgotten I was there. They met each other's eyes in furious alpha-male stares, and the magic was so thick in the air it was hard to breathe. I wanted to say something to them, to get them to back off, but so far nothing I'd said had made a dent in their animosity. In fact, my very presence was probably making things worse.

"Whoever throws the first punch, magical or otherwise, gets to deal with me," Finn said, and we all jumped.

We'd all been so focused on the looming fight we hadn't heard him coming. I checked over my shoulder and saw that my father and Kimber were only a few steps behind him.

Ethan and Keane both turned to Finn, the belligerence far from gone. And now there was a third person's magic stealing the oxygen from the air. I hoped they'd all cut it out soon, or they'd start to wonder what was wrong with me as I did my gasping fish impression.

Keane opened his mouth as if to say something smart—or stupid, as the case may be—but he wasn't a complete idiot. I'd seen him fight his father once before, when Finn was teaching him a lesson about the difference between a skilled teenaged self-defense instructor and a trained Knight of Faerie. It hadn't been pretty.

Ethan didn't back down quite as fast, though I'd seen signs before that he respected Finn's power. Maybe he was too hopped up on testosterone to remember that at the moment. Finn grabbed hold of Keane's arm and gave it a yank.

"Go tend to your horse," he snapped, giving Keane a shove. Keane was practically trembling with rage now, but he knew when he was beat. He turned and stomped back into the crowd of Fae who bustled around our makeshift camp. Probably just as well that the rest of the caravan was ignoring us.

With Keane out of the picture, Ethan finally relaxed, shaking out his hands and letting the magic slip away. I didn't think Finn had done Keane any favors by intervening. I could only imagine what kind of crap Ethan would give Keane for it whenever he had a chance.

"The last thing we need is the two of you acting like children," Finn said to Ethan in his sternest voice. "You don't like each other. Fine. I don't give a damn. But you're both supposedly here to help guard Dana, and getting into pissing matches with each other isn't helpful."

To my surprise, color rose to Ethan's cheeks, Finn's rebuke taking root. He wasn't usually one to take criticism gracefully.

"Sorry," he mumbled. "You're right. It won't happen again. But you might want to give Keane the same reminder."

Finn made a sound somewhere between a snort and a laugh. "Don't worry, I will. Now why don't you get yourself something to eat before we hit the road again?"

Ethan gave me a quick sidelong glance that said he'd rather stay here with me and pick up where we'd left off. But I was pretty annoyed at him and Keane both, so instead of speaking to him, I polished the apple Keane had given me and took a bite. Ethan took the hint and went off in search of food.

chapter seven

Getting back on Phaedra was even worse than I'd anticipated. I felt like an arthritic little old lady as I hauled myself into the saddle, my legs and butt screaming in protest. No one else seemed to be having as much trouble, not even Kimber, who I doubted had much more experience riding horses than I did. But then, she was a full-blooded Fae, and they had lots of physical advantages. I suppose being half Fae myself, I was better off than if I'd been a mere mortal, but that didn't make the misery of the saddle any more fun.

As soon as we were all mounted up and on our way, magic prickled the air again, and the trees and bushes started moving back to their original positions. I bet by the time we'd been gone ten minutes, there would be no sign of the "clearing" we'd just spent the last hour in. Creepy!

We rode for the rest of the day, a steady, boring procession along the road. There was still nothing but forest, though when I asked, my dad assured me that there was more to Faerie than this. Occasionally, we'd run across some other Fae traveling the same road, but we saw only Sidhe—the most humanlike of the Fae.

We traveled for what felt like about twenty days, though my watch insisted it was about six more hours, before the caravan sud-

denly veered off the main road, following an even narrower dirt
road that was so artfully camouflaged I probably wouldn't have
spotted it if the caravan hadn't turned off. We followed the narrower road for maybe a mile or two until we came to a wall of
greenery that was obviously man-made. Squinting at the wall, I
could discern the trunks of individual trees, planted so closely together that their branches intertwined from ground level all the
way to their flattened tops.

The road continued on through an arched opening in the wall.
When Phaedra and I passed through the opening, I felt the distinctive prickle of magic against my skin. I suspected it was some kind
of barrier spell that the prince had overridden. I hoped that meant
we were nearing our stopping point for the night, and my hopes
were confirmed when the forest widened into a massive clearing.
In the middle of the clearing towered a building that at first glance
looked like a humongous dirt hill, until I noticed the evenly spaced
rectangular windows. I blinked, and then I made out a number of
outbuildings dotting the edges of the clearing. Artfully placed
greenery made the buildings practically disappear into the surrounding forest.

A handful of plainly dressed Fae hurried out of one of those
outbuildings, one of them sprinting for the main house while the
others converged on the pair of Knights at the front of our procession. I couldn't hear what anyone was saying, but I could tell
from the body language that (a) we weren't expected, (b) Prince
Henry didn't care, and (c) saying no to royalty came under the
heading of Things Not Done in Faerie.

People began dismounting, and Henry started barking orders as
servants bustled around, hauling crates out of some of the baggage
wagons and unharnessing horses.

The servant who'd run for the main house soon emerged, a
harried-looking couple hard on his heels. They were both much

better dressed than the servants, and they carried themselves with the self-important dignity of the wealthy and powerful despite their obvious dismay at finding the prince with several dozen of his closest friends parked in their front yard.

I hadn't noticed my father dismounting, but he came up beside me and patted Phaedra's neck.

"I know you'd rather spend the night on Phaedra's back," he said to me with a hint of a smile, "but you might as well get down. It appears Henry has other plans for us."

I was more than happy to get down, though every movement of my body caused shooting pains in my legs and butt. I held on tightly to the saddle as I slid off and had to suppress a groan of mingled misery and relief.

"The people who live here don't seem happy to see us," I murmured as I swayed on my feet, tempted to just curl up on the ground and go to sleep because that would save me the trouble of having to walk. The couple who'd come out of the house to greet Henry were both smiling, but there was a hint of a manic gleam in their eyes that made the smiles false.

Dad made a sound that was half snort, half laugh. "They'll be expected to feed and house everyone in our party, whether they're prepared for us or not. It's considered an honor to host the prince and his entourage, but it's a damned expensive nuisance, too."

"And they're not allowed to say no, right?"

"Right," Dad confirmed as servants came to commandeer our horses and lead them toward one of the outbuildings, which was apparently a stable.

The prince's servants were all frantically busy, and the Knights were still visibly on duty, keeping a careful eye on their liege. A couple of the servants were directing the more aristocratic of Henry's entourage toward the main house, where I gathered they would be given lodgings. By the time one of those servants reached us, Ethan,

Keane, and Kimber had joined us. In the distance, I saw Finn leading his horse toward the barn, and it burned me that he was considered to be of lower class than people like my father. I know humans
have a class system, too, but the Fae take it to a whole different level.

The servant bowed slightly before addressing my father. "You
and your daughter will be in the main house," he said. He turned
to Keane. "You and your companions"—his gaze flicked briefly to
Ethan and Kimber—"will be in the servants' quarters."

I felt an instant surge of indignation on my friends' behalf, and
despite my best intentions to abide by the local customs in Faerie,
there was no way I was letting that one go. I opened my mouth to
protest, but to my surprise, my dad beat me to it.

"That is not acceptable," he said, sounding every bit as snooty as the
prince at that moment. "These young people are my daughter's companions, and they are under my care. They will be lodging with us."

I never would have expected my dad to stand up for the son of a
Knight and a pair of Unseelie kids who were de facto second-class
citizens in Seelie territory, but there was no hint of give in his voice.

The servant looked alarmed and distinctly uncomfortable. "I beg
your pardon, sir, but our hosts—"

"We will need three rooms," my dad said over him. "One for me,
one for the boys, and one for the girls."

I felt bad for the servant, who was obviously getting stuck in the
middle of this mess, and sorry for our beleaguered host and hostess,
whoever they were. I considered suggesting we all stay in the servants' quarters, but knew there was no way that would fly with my
dad. Maybe being relegated to the servants' quarters was one of
those "signs of weakness" my dad had told me we couldn't afford. I
bit my tongue on a number of comments that would probably have
been unwise under the circumstances.

Another servant, this time a smiling woman I was pretty sure
worked for our hosts rather than for Henry, hurried over to us. "Of

course, sir," she said, shooting Henry's servant a disparaging look, "we will be happy to accommodate you and the children. There has obviously been a misunderstanding. Please, follow me."

Gee, it felt so good to be called "the children" again. Made me feel real grown up and respected. I suspected it bothered the boys, who were both eighteen, even more than it did me. I glanced at their faces, and realized they were too busy giving each other dirty looks to notice. Putting the two of them in a room together might be dangerous. I hoped the house would still be standing by the time we hit the road again tomorrow.

My first day in Faerie ended with me sharing a large feather bed with Kimber in a room made almost entirely of dirt. Not that you could tell it was dirt unless you looked at it real closely. The floor and ceiling were of packed red clay so smooth it looked like tile, and the walls were an intricate pattern of earth tones from ivory to nearly black, giving the impression of a series of mosaics. I tried touching a finger to the designs in the wall, and though the texture felt rough and grainy—you know, like dirt—it was packed in so solidly that even when I scratched it with my fingernail, nothing came loose.

"What happens when it rains?" I wondered aloud, trying not to imagine all that dirt turning to mud and collapsing on my head while I slept.

"Remember, we're in Faerie," Kimber reminded me, yawning behind her hand. "This house is held together by magic. I'm sure it could weather a storm."

Her yawn was contagious, and I eyed the bed longingly. I'd never shared a bed before, and if I were any less tired, I might have worried I wouldn't be able to sleep. As it was, that wasn't an issue. The only issue was forcing myself to clean up before collapsing into bed, but I was tired of smelling like horse. With a minimum of exploring, Kimber and I found a bathroom, which had a soaking tub and a steaming waterfall that served as a shower. Claiming excess modesty once more, I insisted Kimber and I take turns, even though we probably could have fit a half dozen people under that waterfall. It delayed getting to bed even longer, but it once again allowed me to keep the Erlking's mark hidden.

I fell asleep the moment my head hit the pillow. About sixty seconds later, there was someone sitting on the side of my bed, shaking my shoulder. I made an incoherent sound of protest and tried to swat the hand away, my eyes firmly closed. The hand just shook me harder, and Keane's voice hissed in my ear.

"Wake up, lazy," he said. "It's Thursday morning."

This time, the sound I made was more like a snarl, and I sat up in bed, jerking away from the touch of his hand. Pink-tinged light streamed in from the windows. I rubbed my eyes, but the light was still there. Guess I'd gotten more than sixty seconds of sleep after all. I glanced at my watch and saw that it was six AM. I'd slept for eight hours, and I was more than willing to collapse back into bed and sleep eight more.

"What are you doing here?" I growled at Keane, who was already fully dressed and showered, looking wide awake and completely impatient.

"Thursday morning," he reminded me. "I know we don't usually practice this early, but I'm not sure what time we're going to hit the road this morning."

Thursday morning. Practice. I groaned. "You have *got* to be kidding me. We are *not* having a lesson today!"

He crossed his arms over his chest and raised his eyebrows. "Says who?"

Beside me, Kimber stirred and mumbled, "Turn the radio off."

"I see no reason to skip practice just because we're on the road," Keane replied, ignoring Kimber's sleepy protest. "Now get your ass out of bed, get dressed, and meet me in front of the stables in thirty minutes or less."

Kimber seemed to realize now that the noises disturbing her didn't come from a radio after all. She raised her head and squinted at Keane. Her hair was a frizzy, tangled mess, and there were pillow lines on her face, but I saw Keane's eyes stray to her and widen. Even with bedhead, she was disgustingly gorgeous, especially in the royal blue silk nightgown she was wearing. Me, I'd gone with a ratty T-shirt and flannel boxer shorts, and I suspected I looked about as appetizing as roadkill.

I reminded myself that Keane was an annoying jerk who woke me up at an ungodly hour because he wanted to spar after one of the longest days of my entire life. I didn't *care* if he thought I'd give Medusa a run for her money in the Ugly Olympics.

"Sorry to wake you," Keane said to Kimber. "Just give your bedmate a nice kick in the ass to get her moving and we'll let you get back to sleep."

Kimber pushed her hair back from her face. "Thirty minutes, in front of the stable, is that what you said?"

"Yup."

"I'll get her there."

"Traitor," I grumbled, belatedly remembering that Kimber was much more of a morning person than me. She was already starting to look almost perky, while I was still wishing for toothpicks to hold my eyes open.

"I hate you," I told Keane, inspiring a self-satisfied grin.

"Not as much as you will in thirty minutes if you're not down by the stables like I told you."

I gave his shoulder a shove. I knew he'd have no compunction about throwing me over his shoulder and carrying me down if I didn't show up. "Get out of here so I can get dressed. I am going to be *so* motivated you're going to wish you let me sleep in."

It was an empty threat, of course. I was sure that as usual, I'd have trouble landing a single blow unless he let me. But it sure wasn't going to stop me from trying.

The last thing I wanted was an audience for my sparring session with Keane. I was self-conscious about my lack of skill, and I was pretty sure some of the positions we ended up in were . . . less than dignified. But once Kimber got the idea in her head of seeing Keane in action, there was no stopping her from tagging along. There was a definite sparkle in her eyes and a spring in her step as we both hurried to get dressed and get to the stables.

"It's really not going to be that interesting," I told her, hoping I was just imagining the hint of desperation in my voice. Kimber was always so graceful and elegant, and I was anything but. I suspected I'd be even more of a klutz today, considering how stiff and sore every muscle below my waist felt. I was *not* looking forward to another day on horseback.

Kimber gave a huff of exasperation. "I'm not going to be watching *you*, dummy." She grinned at me and waggled her brows. "Do you think you can get him sweaty enough to take off his shirt?"

I rolled my eyes. "I'll be lucky if he works hard enough for a hair on his head to move. Like I said, not that entertaining."

"I'll be the judge of that," she replied as she led the way out of our room.

As reluctant as I was to have Kimber watch me make a fool of myself, it was probably a good thing she came along, or I'd have made at least three wrong turns before I found my way out of the massive house. My sense of direction sucks, and I'd been so tired the night before I'd barely paid attention to where I was going.

It seemed the people of this house were not exactly early risers. The halls were deserted and silent as Kimber and I made our way toward the front door. Which made it even more shocking when we turned one corner and came upon a brown-skinned creature about three feet in height. Its back was to us, but when I made a little squeak of surprise, it whirled around, displaying a mouth full of teeth that would have looked at home in a shark.

The creature was naked except for a loin cloth, its skin a wrinkled, leathery brown like it had spent a lifetime baking in the sun. Saggy boobs that hung to its waist like partially deflated balloons declared the creature was female.

Sure it was going to pounce on me and sink those wicked-sharp teeth into my throat, I let out a choked cry of alarm and leapt backward, practically knocking Kimber down. The creature made a very similar sound, leapt backward . . . and disappeared.

Hyperventilating, I grabbed hold of Kimber's arm as I looked wildly around.

"Where is it? Where'd it go?" I was still waiting for the attack, adrenaline pumping through my system. In fact, I was so primed for attack that it took me a moment to realize Kimber was laughing. Laughing so hard tears were leaking out of the corners of her eyes.

Her laughter calmed my panic, and I let go of her arm. The heat in my cheeks told me I was blushing, though I wasn't yet sure exactly what I was supposed to be embarrassed about. I was sure she'd enlighten me as soon as she stopped laughing uncontrollably.

I glared at Kimber. "What the hell was that? And where did it go?"

Kimber cleared her throat, and I could see she was still struggling against laughter. "That was a Brownie. I'm sure there are at least a dozen of them on staff here, but they don't like to be seen."

If the one I'd just laid eyes on was typical, I could see why. "*That's* a Brownie? As in the helpful little fairies who clean house and cook?" I'd never put much thought into what a Brownie might look like, but it sure as hell wasn't like *that*. I was going to have freaking nightmares.

"Brownies as in the lowest ranking of all the sentient Seelie Fae, who are employed for menial labor by the Sidhe. Not only do they not like to be seen, but the Sidhe don't like to see them. Don't tell anyone you caught sight of one, or they might track her down and dismiss her."

Geez, it sounded like being treated like a second-class citizen would be an upgrade for the poor creatures. The Fae and their stupid class system! "I'm surprised Henry doesn't have an army of them traveling with us to take care of his every need," I grumbled as I started forward again. The adrenaline rush had been as effective as any cup of coffee, and I was finally feeling awake and alert.

"I'm sure he does," Kimber said as she fell into step beside me. "They're just better at their jobs than this one."

I came to a stop. "Wait. You mean there are a whole bunch of those creatures traveling with us? And we've never caught sight of them?"

She nodded. "Yes, of course. Now hurry up or we're going to be late."

We hurried up, but we were still late. Keane had his arms crossed over his chest and was tapping his foot impatiently when we arrived. He frowned when he caught sight of Kimber, though that didn't stop him from giving her a quick, head-to-toe examination. She looked fabulous as always, with her stylish khaki pants and her blue silk tank top. Not exactly rugged, horseback-riding wear, but Kimber was a big believer in form over function. I felt like an ugly stepsister standing beside her in my loose, faded T-shirt and my black yoga pants. (Pants I had to carry in my backpack, because they were made with Lycra and would disintegrate if they got outside my Faeriewalker aura.)

"Dana would probably be in Outer Mongolia right now if she didn't have someone to guide her here," Kimber said to explain her presence, and she and Keane shared a good laugh at my expense. I decided to take a page out of Keane's book and go on the offensive before our lesson had officially started.

While he and Kimber were yucking it up, I aimed a sweeping kick at his calves. If he'd have been as unprepared as he looked, I might have had the satisfaction of seeing him land on his butt in a patch of what I suspected was horse poop. But, of course, I never get that lucky.

Keane jumped nimbly over my kick and was on me almost before he came down. His fist connected with my right shoulder, and my entire arm went temporarily numb. I tried to backpedal to avoid the next blow, but he was too fast for me. I partially blocked his next punch with my left arm, but it's my weak side, and I found myself sprawled on the ground anyway. I hoped I hadn't landed in the patch of manure, but I didn't have time to worry about it as I rolled to avoid Keane's pounce. He kindly allowed me to get to my feet before launching himself at me again. He locked his arms around me, pinning my own arms against my sides. I head-butted his chin—I'd have liked to aim for his nose, but I was too short to reach from this position. My forehead slammed into his shield spell, and I know for a fact it hurt me more than it hurt him.

"Good," he said, still holding me there, arms pinned, "but you need to follow up in case the first blow wasn't enough."

No matter how much training Keane had given me, I was still squeamish about going for his groin. I knew I wouldn't hit anything except his shield spell, but still, aiming a kick or a knee there just felt wrong.

"Let's just pretend I followed up with a knee and leave it at that," I panted.

"Sure," Keane agreed, too easily. "Then we'll also just pretend I let go."

He dropped to the ground, and with my arms pinned, there was nothing I could do to soften the fall. My breath whooshed out of me, and then Keane's weight came crashing down on top of me, and I thought I was about to die as my lungs fought for oxygen.

Dammit, would I never learn?

Keane lay still on top of me as I struggled to get air into my lungs. His eyes widened as they locked on something behind me I couldn't see, and then his lips split into a grin. I figured Kimber was probably giving him an adoring "oh, my hero" look, appreciating his manly prowess. I tried to lurch into action before I was truly ready, which was never smart. I tried a sharp roll to my right, but it was hard to put much oomph in it while I was still struggling for breath, and we moved all of about two centimeters. Keane punished me for it with a tap on the chin—not a real punch, just a reminder that I hadn't improved my situation by being impatient.

I sucked in a couple more breaths, regaining my strength as Keane continued to grin down at me. We were on the ground now instead of standing up, but we were essentially in the same position as we'd been before: my best shot at escape was brisk head butt, followed by a well-placed knee. I got Keane's message loud and clear: he was not letting me go until I did what he wanted.

"Fine," I gritted out from between clenched teeth, then jerked my head upward until I slammed into his shield again. He pretended to be in horrible pain, dropping his guard so he wasn't primed to protect himself. I jerked my knee up between his legs, wincing in anticipation despite knowing I wouldn't hurt him.

From behind me, I heard someone yell, "Down!"

Magic tingled across my skin, and my knee made solid contact with something that most definitely was not Keane's shield spell.

Keane made a strangled noise and rolled off me, curling up practically in half as he clutched himself.

I hastily pushed myself into a sitting position and looked over my shoulder. And discovered that Kimber was no longer our only audience. Standing beside her, grinning smugly, was Ethan, and I belatedly realized it was his voice I'd heard yelling. I glanced over at Keane, who was still writhing.

"You took his shield spell down!"

Ethan looked completely unrepentant. "Serves him right for hitting a girl."

"He's my self-defense instructor, you asshole! He's *supposed* to hit me."

Does it make me a bad person that I couldn't help feeling just a little pleased by what Ethan had done? Considering how many times Keane had hurt or humiliated me during our sparring, it was kind of poetic justice. Not that I liked seeing him in pain or anything. Well, maybe just a little.

Ethan shrugged, not at all bothered by my rebuke. "*You* don't have a shield spell. Why should *he*?"

"Because," Keane gasped out, sitting up although the look on his face said he was still in dire pain, "if I don't have a shield spell up, Dana will hesitate to practice full out because she's afraid she'll hurt me. Good job reinforcing that fear so she might hesitate when someone attacks her for real."

For the first time, the humor in Ethan's eyes dimmed. Kimber, who'd been standing to the side as if trying to stay out of the middle, came over and knelt by Keane's side.

"Are you all right?" she asked Keane, giving her brother a scathing look. She laid her hand on Keane's shoulder, and I could see in her eyes that she really cared.

Keane nodded. "Will be, in a minute or two." He fixed me with a stern look. "Don't you dare let this make you hesitate."

I didn't like his commanding tone, and I honestly didn't think this little episode had done any permanent damage to my psyche or anything. I might hesitate to hit Keane if I knew Ethan was watching, but if it was just our normal sparring session, or if I was being attacked by a bad guy, I was pretty sure I'd act normally. Still, I didn't want to let Ethan off the hook—not when doing so might encourage the stupid feud between him and Keane—so I put a hint of uncertainty in my voice when I answered.

"I'll try not to," I said. Out of the corner of my eye, I saw Ethan grimace. Then, he made a beeline back to the house without another word.

chapter eight

By the time my friends and I returned to the house, people were stirring. In fact, from the looks of the servants rushing around carrying luggage, our caravan was going to be heading out pretty soon. Not before I hit the shower, though. I was covered with mud and filth from my sparring session. Still trying to keep the Erlking's mark hidden, I waited until the bathroom was completely empty before I took my turn, hurrying as best I could, though I had to wash out my clothes as well. The pants, being black, were salvageable despite my roll in the muck, but the mud stains on the T-shirt were *never* going to come out. I threw the sopping shirt into what I hoped was a wastebasket, then rushed back to the room to pack the few items I'd taken out.

Servants were already leaving the room when I arrived, one of them carrying my suitcase. I figured whatever I'd left out I could just stuff in my backpack, but when I entered the room, Kimber informed me that our bags had been packed when she'd arrived.

I made a face. "I don't like the idea of someone pawing through my things," I said, uncomfortable at the invasion of my privacy.

Kimber shrugged. "It was probably Brownies, and I'm sure they left your suitcase more neatly packed than ever. Now come on.

We've apparently missed breakfast and we're leaving in about fifteen minutes."

Being reunited with Phaedra was not the highlight of my day. My butt started aching the moment I set eyes on the saddle, and when I patted her shoulder like I'd seen my dad do, hoping to make friends, she stomped her hoof, barely missing my toes. I narrowed my eyes at her.

"It's not my fault I'm a city girl and don't know how to ride," I told her, like I thought she'd understand. She tossed her head in what looked suspiciously like disdain.

Ethan showed up at my side to help me into the saddle. I blushed when his help involved him giving my butt a boost. I guess he was over his chagrin about having potentially sabotaged my self-defense instincts. When I gave him a dirty look, he winked at me, showing me a glimpse of the playful side I thought he'd completely lost since his time with the Wild Hunt.

Once again, my friends, my father, and I were directed to travel near the very end of the caravan. My dad didn't look any happier about it today than he had the day before, but I suppose he had to pick his battles. I was glad he'd chosen to put his foot down about my friends being housed in the servants' quarters instead of about our place in the procession.

As we made our slow progress, the land around us changed. The road began to rise and fall over gentle hills, and the trees thinned out. I caught occasional glimpses of woodland creatures, some very like those I'd seen in the mortal world, some very much not.

By early afternoon, the trees had thinned out so much that there were only patches of them, the rest of the terrain brush-covered hills and rock outcroppings.

"Troll country," my dad told me.

I knew a troll, though I sometimes had trouble thinking of him as one because he wore a human glamour. His name was Lachlan, and he was a really nice guy, even if his size made him seriously intimidating. Sometimes, he served as an extra bodyguard when my dad thought I needed more protection, so I felt safe around him. Still, I'd never seen Lachlan without his glamour, and if trolls were anywhere near as ugly as Brownies, I'd rather not know about it.

I must have looked alarmed. My dad smiled at me. "Don't worry. I highly doubt we'll meet any. They're very clannish and tend to keep to themselves."

There was just a hint of disdain in his voice, as there always was when he talked about trolls, making it clear that they were considered low-class. Dad trusted Lachlan and was polite to him to his face, but when Lachlan wasn't around, Dad didn't hesitate to let his snobbishness shine through. He claimed that he was too old and set in his ways to change, but that generally didn't stop me from trying to bring his attitude into the twenty-first century.

"Gee, I can't imagine why they'd rather keep to themselves when the Sidhe are so kind and gracious to them."

Dad's smile disappeared and he regarded me with annoyance. "We aren't in Avalon, Dana. You may not like or approve of how the Fae interact with one another, but you'd best learn to respect it, at least until we get home. I sincerely doubt Henry or his people would appreciate being lectured or judged."

"I'm not lecturing or judging *them*," I said, the already long day in the saddle making me grumpy. "I'm lecturing and judging *you*. You're supposed to be a citizen of Avalon, not of Faerie."

This was becoming an old argument. Dad seemed perfectly happy to rehash it with me, even though neither of us was likely to convince the other. He didn't get a chance, however, because his retort was cut off by a shout of alarm from somewhere up the line.

Dad went on instant alert, his magic flaring up faster than I could turn my head to see what was going on. Phaedra sidestepped and made a nervous little sound not quite like a whinny. The caravan came to a screeching halt, the Knights in Henry's entourage drawing their weapons and converging on their prince. They formed a circle around him as he rose in his stirrups, looking for the cause of the disturbance.

We were still near the back of the caravan, with only one Knight and a baggage wagon behind us. That Knight spurred his horse forward, heading toward the prince—and leaving us behind.

"Go," my dad said to me, pointing for me to follow the Knight. "Get as close to Henry as possible. It'll be the best-defended area."

"What's happening?" I asked, my heart hammering as I kept glancing around, looking for the threat.

"I don't know," Dad said. "But move!" He turned to point at Kimber. "You, too."

Ethan jumped off his horse, a silver knife appearing in his hand. Keane followed suit, but he had *two* knives. I supposed it was hard to fight with knives on horseback, but I didn't like the idea of them being on foot when everyone else was on horses. I wouldn't put it past Henry to run like hell and take his people with him.

Kimber was quicker to follow my dad's order than I was. She slipped past me, beckoning me to follow.

"Better go with her," I said to Phaedra, giving her a light kick in the sides for extra emphasis. She snorted and shook her head, showing no sign of wanting to follow Kimber to the relative safety of the center. Stupid horse!

There was another shout from someone ahead of me. And then something sprang out from behind one of the outcroppings of rock. Something that looked suspiciously like a monster, though I had no idea what it was. It was squat and vaguely humanoid, but it was covered in black scales and had a long, barbed tail. And, of course, impressive claws and fangs. It reminded me of a reptilian chimpanzee, though it was wearing leather armor and a helmet that suggested it wasn't just an animal. It also wasn't a troll, because trolls are supposed to be huge, and this thing was the size of a small human.

Whatever it was, it roared, the sound much louder than such a small body should have been able to produce. Up ahead, a woman screamed, and there was another roar. Horses everywhere began making sounds of alarm as the shouting increased.

Things went to hell in less than five seconds. The creature I'd spotted leapt through the air, landing on the seat beside the driver of the baggage wagon behind me. He was not a Knight, but he wasn't completely defenseless. The creature swiped at him with a clawed hand, but the claws grazed off of an invisible shield as the driver dove off the wagon's seat.

"Get to the center!" Dad shouted at me as he unleashed some kind of spell at the creature.

The spell knocked the creature down mid-leap, but it didn't seem to hurt it. Finn charged forward while it was still stunned, putting his sword through its torso.

"Move, Phaedra!" I urged, giving her another kick as two more of the creatures popped out from behind the rocks.

Phaedra whinnied and tossed her head, dancing nervously sideways, her eyes ringed with white. All around us, people were screaming and shouting. The monsters roared, and I heard sounds of battle as the Knights protected their prince.

Kimber turned back, calling to Phaedra in an encouraging voice, although even I could hear the fear in it. She knew Phaedra and I weren't the best of friends. Maybe Phaedra objected to the way I shouted at her, but I couldn't worry about her delicate feelings while we were under attack.

Phaedra didn't seem any more moved by Kimber's coaxing than

she was by my attempted bullying. She whinnied again, then reared, her front hooves slashing the air in front of her. I squeezed my legs tight around her and clung to the saddle with everything I had.

One of the creatures went flying, its head split open where Phaedra had apparently kicked it in mid-leap. I'd have thanked her for taking out one of our attackers, except at that moment, she finally leapt into motion—running *away* from the center of the battle and the safety of the Knights.

"Dana!" my dad cried, reaching out to me.

"Phaedra, stop!" I yelled, still clinging to the saddle, but she ignored me, dodging past the baggage wagon until there was nothing but open road in front of her. I tried pulling back on the reins, but she just jerked them out of my hands.

I looked over my shoulder and saw my dad trying to follow, but one of the creatures jumped in front of him, and he had to stop and fight. Behind him, Ethan and Keane stood back to back, fighting three of the creatures as Finn took on four all by himself. The caravan was completely overrun, and there were enough creatures that some of them could chase after Phaedra and me while still leaving my dad and my friends overwhelmed with enemies.

"Go back!" I pleaded with Phaedra, tears streaking my cheeks as I tried not to imagine those creatures tearing the people I loved apart.

Phaedra paid no attention to me, galloping down the road as fast as she could, her hooves pounding the packed dirt and throwing up a cloud of dust that made it hard to see how many of the creatures were chasing us.

The dust also hid the battle from view, so I had no idea if we were winning or not. What I *did* know was that I was in deep shit if Phaedra couldn't keep up her breakneck pace, because even though I couldn't see them clearly, I was painfully aware of the horde of dark shadows that was still pursuing.

Phaedra kept running, and I kept clinging, as we left the rest of the caravan behind, putting more and more distance between us and them. Unfortunately, the distance between us and the monsters wasn't getting any bigger. They didn't look like they should be able to run so fast, but they were keeping up.

More than keeping up. They were gaining!

"Faster, Phaedra!" I urged, and for once she actually did what I asked and put on another burst of speed.

But horses, even Fae ones, aren't made for long-term galloping at top speed. She was tiring, and even her fear of the pursuing creatures wasn't enough to fuel her into outrunning them.

Glancing over my shoulder, I saw at least half a dozen shadows moving in our dust cloud. They were much closer than they had been the last time I'd looked.

I doubted any of the self-defense tactics Keane had taught me was going to help against these creatures. I had the gun in my backpack, but with Phaedra's jarring gait, I figured there was no way I could dig it out without dropping it or falling on my head. Besides, the gun only held two bullets. That left me with only one weapon.

Closing my eyes and trying not to hyperventilate in my fear, I started humming. I was too panicked to think of an actual song, so I hummed a scale. A bit off-key, and very wobbly due to the constant bouncing of Phaedra's gait, but the magic didn't seem to care anymore how well I sang. It came immediately to my call, making its presence known by prickling at my skin in what felt like a series of small static shocks.

I kept humming, kept summoning the magic, drawing it to me desperately. I didn't know exactly what I'd done when I'd used the magic against Aunt Grace. I hadn't been thinking very rationally, and had been reacting on pure instinct. I had no idea if I'd be able to re-create whatever I'd done now. And no idea if doing so would help me. My spell hadn't exactly dropped Aunt Grace in her tracks, and if it hadn't been for Ethan and the Erlking, it wouldn't have done any good at all. But I had to try *something*.

Phaedra screamed and stumbled.

My eyes flew open as I almost toppled from the saddle. Terror gave me the strength to hold on, but the situation had gone from bad to worse.

The creatures were gaining on us, just barely out of leaping range. Or, judging by the bleeding red furrows on one of Phaedra's hind legs, maybe not out of range after all.

Shaking with terror, I kept humming until I was sure I had as much magic as I could possibly hold. Then I let out a shrieking high note, the kind that would probably shatter glasses if there were any around. I imagined that note carrying my magic out to the creatures and turning them into stone. Not that I really expected that to happen, but visualizing the effect I hoped for seemed like the thing to do.

The magic wasn't visible—I wouldn't have even known it was there if it weren't for that Fae magic sense I wasn't supposed to have—but I could almost see it as it bowled into the pursuing creatures, flinging them back so far they disappeared into the dust cloud, so I couldn't tell if they were hurt or not. The spell hadn't had so violent or obvious an effect when I'd used it on Aunt Grace, so I wondered if something drastically different had just happened.

The good news was that even if my spell hadn't hurt them, it had flung a handful of my pursuers back so they were no longer in pouncing range. The bad news was there were more than a handful after me. The remaining creatures howled in rage and put on another burst of speed.

I started humming again, meaning to call more magic, but we were out of time. Phaedra's hide was flecked with foam, and I could hear her labored breathing as she struggled to keep running despite her exhaustion. Our pursuers had more stamina, and if they were tired from the long run, they showed no sign of it. One of them swiped at Phaedra's legs with its claws.

Phaedra couldn't quite manage a scream—I didn't think she had enough air for it—but her cry of distress still made me wince in sympathy. She stumbled again, and this time, the stumble was her undoing, allowing the creatures to cross the last little bit of distance between us.

Another swipe of claws to Phaedra's legs, and instead of just stumbling, she fell. I tried to jump off before she hit the ground. Almost managed it, too, although it no doubt looked more like a fall than a jump.

Phaedra landed so hard I felt the vibration through the hard-packed earth, even as I slammed into it myself. My foot was tangled in the stirrup, though at least I'd gotten clear enough that Phaedra hadn't landed on me.

She thrashed frantically, trying to get back up as the creatures swarmed her, sinking fangs and claws into her haunches. One hoof flailed dangerously close to my head as I struggled to free myself from the stirrup.

I was too out of breath from the fall to manage a hum, and I doubted I'd be able to gather enough magic to save us anyway. We were doomed!

One of the creatures jumped over Phaedra's flailing legs and landed directly in front of me. It bared bloody fangs, then swiped at me with razor-sharp claws, and there was nothing I could do to defend myself, not when the stirrup had me trapped.

Something thwipped through the air over my head, and the creature jerked away from me, falling over backward. I blinked in momentary confusion until I saw the black-feathered arrow sticking through its throat.

Another arrow sailed over my head, taking another creature in the throat. Then, there seemed to be a veritable storm of them, zipping through the air, each one finding its target.

"Stay down, Faeriewalker," shouted a familiar voice.

I froze in my struggles to free myself from the stirrup and glanced over my shoulder to see if I'd really heard what I thought I'd heard.

On the road in front of me were a band of horsemen, all masked and armored, each one armed with a bow. Most of them were firing away, taking out the last of my attackers. But one sat silently on his massive black horse, and though I couldn't see his eyes behind the camouflage of his terrifying horned mask, I knew he was watching me with predatory fascination.

How long had the Erlking and his Wild Hunt been following me? And should I be happy they had just saved my life, or terrified of whatever was going to happen next?

chapter nine

I managed to get my foot out of the stirrup while the Huntsmen finished off the rest of the creatures. I lost my shoe in the process, but I didn't much feel like crawling closer to Phaedra to get it. Her body was streaked with bloody gashes. There was so much blood I could hardly believe she was still alive. However, her sides were heaving, so she was obviously breathing.

The Huntsmen stopped firing, and I both felt and heard the thud as the Erlking slid off his horse and hit the ground. He was not a small man, and his mask and armor made him even larger and more intimidating.

As usual, he was dressed entirely in black, except for the silver studs and spikes on his armor. He looked like a porcupine on steroids, and I wondered how he managed to ride his horse without gutting it. And let's not even talk about the mask, with its huge silver antlers and grotesque fangs.

The Erlking grasped the edges of his mask and lifted it carefully off. Long, thick, blue-black hair slipped out from underneath. He was the only naturally dark-haired Fae I'd ever encountered. He hung his mask from a hook on his horse's saddle, then turned to face me.

Every time I laid eyes on him, it was like a punch to the gut. He was probably the most frightening and dangerous person I had ever met, and he was also the most breathtakingly gorgeous. Even for a Fae, which is saying a lot. He was a bad boy to the nth degree, only there was nothing remotely boyish about him.

The Erlking smiled at me. It was a knowing smile that said he guessed why I was still sitting there on my butt gaping at him instead of climbing to my feet in a dignified and mature fashion. I willed myself not to blush as I forced myself to look away, pretending to search for my shoe even though I already knew where it was.

Climbing to my feet, I hopped over to Phaedra's side, trying to avoid looking at her wounds as I gingerly picked up my sneaker and shoved my foot into it. I heard the clanking of his armor as the Erlking approached me, and I turned to face him, trying to look unintimidated. I doubt I succeeded.

"So, is it a lucky coincidence that you happened to be nearby?" I asked. Maybe I should have thanked him for saving my life, but as always with him, I thought it better to wait and see what he was up to first.

The smile turned into a grin. "What do you think, Faeriewalker?"

"I think you were following me," I said. "And stop calling me Faeriewalker." It shouldn't matter to me whether he used my name or not, but somehow when he called me "Faeriewalker," I felt more like he thought of me as a valuable piece of property than as a person.

His eyes twinkled with amusement as he made a little half-bow. "My apologies, Dana."

Somehow, I didn't think that was much better after all.

Beside me, Phaedra made a low, pained sound. The Erlking—his name was Arawn, but I had trouble thinking of him that way—turned to look at her. If I didn't know better, I could have sworn his expression was one of sympathy. I couldn't exactly say I was fond of Phaedra, but when I looked over and saw that she was con-scious and suffering, there was a pang in my chest and tears burned my eyes.

"Why couldn't you just have stayed with the others?" I asked her, wishing I'd thought to take some horseback riding lessons (in all that excess of time I'd had to prepare for this trip—ha!). Maybe then I'd have been able to guide her to safety.

"That's a very good question," the Erlking said grimly.

I turned to look at him again and saw that he'd drawn his sword. He met my eyes, his deep blue gaze making me feel weak and un-steady.

"Look away," he told me.

The burning in my eyes intensified, and I blinked frantically, trying to keep the tears from falling. "You're going to kill her," I whispered.

He had no trouble hearing me. "She's too badly hurt to save."

I could see that with my own eyes. Some of the Fae specialized in healing magic, but I was certain the Erlking and his Wild Hunt weren't among them. And maybe even the best of them couldn't have saved Phaedra. When I looked at her more closely, I saw that her throat was torn almost completely open. I don't know how she was even conscious, but the pain in her eyes was unbearable.

Swallowing hard, I shut my eyes and held my breath. I heard the Erlking's sword slicing through the air, then heard the wet thunk of it plunging into flesh. My stomach heaved, and it was all I could do not to hurl. The air stank of blood, and of something rank and rotten. The latter I suspected came from the dead creatures.

"You can open your eyes now," the Erlking said.

I didn't want to, afraid of what I would see. But despite the fact that he was an ancient, cold-blooded killer, the Erlking was capa-ble of imitating a decent human being every once in a while: when

I cracked my eyes open, I saw that he'd covered as much of Phaedra's body as he could with his black cape.

Sniffling like a baby, I dabbed surreptitiously at the corner of my eye, pretending I had some grit in it. Not that I think anyone was fooled for a moment.

It's a sign of how badly overdosed on adrenaline I was that it wasn't until then that I remembered the rest of the creatures, attacking my dad and my friends. I gasped, my heart jump-starting back into a full sprint.

"My dad!" I said. "And Ethan!" I turned away from the Erlking, meaning to start sprinting down the road back toward the battle.

Yeah, I know. Stupid. It wasn't like I could do anything to help even if I got there in time, and thanks to our long gallop, the battle was probably over already anyway. But I acted on blind instinct, almost tripping over one of the dead monsters.

Of course, Arawn wasn't about to let me go dashing off. His hand came down on my shoulder, his fingers closing on me like a vise.

"They survived," he said as I tried to struggle out from his grip. "Your father is injured, but not seriously. Ethan and the rest are fine."

I'd forgotten that the Erlking could communicate with Ethan over long distances, thanks to Ethan wearing his mark. Usually, I considered that a bad thing, but right now I was so grateful for it that I was almost dizzy with relief.

"You're sure?" I asked.

"Positive. Bogles are no match for such an impressive collection of Knights and magic users."

I glanced at one of the dead creatures. Bogles. Yet another Fae creature I'd never heard of. There were a lot of them. "What's a Bogle? I mean—"

"They are Unseelie," the Erlking interrupted, having correctly guessed my question. "They have a sort of primitive intelligence, but nowhere near that of the Sidhe. Or of humans, for that matter. And they are at least fifty miles outside their territory. Bogles don't stray from their territory. Ever. Someone went to a great deal of trouble to get them here. And because they are closer to animals than to people, Titania cannot take offense over their trespassing."

I swallowed hard. I knew it couldn't be a coincidence that our party had been attacked. I'd thought for a moment that Prince Henry might have led us into enemy territory, but I immediately dismissed the notion. For one thing, it wasn't *supposed* to be enemy territory. For another, I hoped he wasn't so callous that he would risk so many of his own people on the off chance I or my dad might get killed in the battle.

"Why were you on your own?" the Erlking asked. "How did the Bogles manage to cut you from the herd? As it were."

I gestured at Phaedra's body. "She panicked and ran." My throat tightened again as my mind forced an image of Phaedra's pain-filled eyes on me. I hadn't liked her, and she hadn't liked me, and here I was practically bawling because she was dead.

The Erlking frowned and cocked his head. "Panicked? Really?"

I nodded, remembering the nervous sounds she'd started making the moment the first shout went up. "I wasn't a good enough rider to control her."

He shook his head. "It wasn't your fault. A Fae horse shouldn't have bolted. If she felt panicked, she should have run for safety, which in this case would have been anywhere but away from the herd."

I gaped at him. "So what are you saying?"

"Someone tampered with her. Maybe cast a compulsion spell. One that prompted her to carry you off so you'd be more vulnerable."

Dammit. That was so not what I wanted to hear. So much for my dad's assurances that Titania wouldn't have invited me to Court if she still wanted to kill me. I sure hoped this meant we were going to turn around and go home now. Maybe I could get back before my mom slid fully back into her old ways.

"I should be used to people trying to kill me by now," I muttered under my breath.

Arawn smiled. "Indeed. You have made an impressive array of enemies."

"My dad was so sure Titania wouldn't break her word."

"She wouldn't. Not when you're here under safe passage. That would be an unforgivable breach of etiquette. Even *I* honor the rules of Court etiquette."

"I'm glad people would think she was rude if she killed me, but someone just tried, and she's the logical suspect."

"But she isn't. Your father is right: she would not make an attempt on your life, nor would she condone someone else's attempt, when you are traveling under her guarantee of safe passage."

"I suppose it could be Mab," I said, reluctant to give up my beef with Titania. If I could blame the attack on Titania, then surely my dad would agree that we had to go home. Of course, if we tried to go home, Henry might decide to arrest us after all.

"Also unlikely," Arawn said. "Sending members of her Court into Seelie territory and then attacking someone under Titania's protection would be an act of war."

I gave him my most skeptical frown. "Right, and the Seelie and Unseelie Courts have never gone to war before. They're just bestest buds."

One corner of his lip twitched, but he didn't quite break into a smile. "They have warred more times than I can count, and they will war again. But this is not how it would start. There would be a pattern of escalating tension before someone declared war. And there would be a formal declaration before battle began."

"The Fae don't do surprise attacks?"

He shook his head. "Not like this. In Faerie, war is much more formalized than it is in the mortal world. At least from what I know of the mortal world."

"So if it isn't Titania, and it isn't Mab . . ."

"Then you have another enemy. One who is willing to risk the Queen's wrath by defying protocol."

My suspicions fell immediately on Henry. He obviously didn't like me, if only because I was my father's daughter. But I got stuck again on the fact that his own people were attacked. Yes, he might have arranged for Phaedra to panic and run, separating me from my defenders, but still . . .

"Let's get you back to your father, shall we?" the Erlking suggested. "Ethan has assured him that you're all right, but your father is strangely reluctant to trust you to my care."

I rolled my eyes. "Gee, I wonder why."

The Erlking laughed and beckoned to his horse, which came to him with evident eagerness. Of course, he was an immortal hunter, and I imagined horsemanship came with the territory. He climbed easily into the saddle, then held out a hand for me.

I felt the blood drain from my face. It hadn't occurred to me that he meant for me to get up on that horse with him. For one thing, the beast was monstrously huge, way more intimidating than Phaedra could ever have been. Not to mention that he was heavily armored, to make him even more huge. And then, there were all those spikes on the Erlking's armor.

"I think I'd rather walk," I said, although I doubted Arawn would give me a choice. It wasn't like I could do anything about it if he tried to carry me off.

"I won't hurt you," he assured me, and in the blink of an eye, his armor disappeared, replaced by the black leather biker gear he'd worn in Avalon.

Wow. The ultimate quick change. Kimber would just die of jealousy if she knew he could do that.

I glanced around at the other Huntsmen. None of them had dismounted while Arawn and I talked. They just waited there, silent and watchful.

Of *course* they were silent. The members of the Wild Hunt never spoke. I'd once worried that meant he'd cut their tongues out, but Ethan told me it was the result of a spell.

I couldn't tell the Huntsmen apart, not behind all that armor and those masks. The Erlking made it very difficult for anyone to see his Huntsmen as individuals.

"Is Connor here?" I asked quietly. "I'd rather ride with him." Not that I knew Connor even vaguely. But he was my brother, and though it was probably illogical of me, I knew I'd feel safer with him.

The Erlking gestured at one of the Huntsmen, who nudged his horse forward and slid his mask up so I could see his face. It was like looking up into my dad's eyes, though it took only a moment to take in the rest of his features and realize that he was not my dad. He was stockier, his face less narrow and his nose less pointed, but the resemblance was obvious.

"He is here," the Erlking said unnecessarily, "but you will ride with me."

Why had I known he'd say that? I knew the battle was already lost, but I tried to stand my ground anyway.

"I'd like to get to know my brother," I said.

The Erlking laughed. "He is not a very entertaining conversationalist."

I flinched. Usually, the Erlking at least pretended to have some human feelings, so I hadn't expected cruelty from him. I glanced over at Connor, but if he was offended by the Erlking's joke, there was no sign of it. He was watching me, a hint of a smile on his face.

Connor waved a hand between me and the Erlking. Telling me to go with the Erlking, I supposed. He could just have been following the Erlking's silent orders, but something told me he wasn't. I still didn't want to get on the giant black horse, nor did I want to get so close to the Erlking. The last thing I wanted was him touching me.

Unbidden, an image came to my mind of when we'd sealed the deal for Ethan's freedom—with a kiss. Because of the wild surge of magic that had accompanied the spells that bound us both to our word, that kiss had been embarrassingly passionate. I knew that it had only felt that way because of the influence of magic, that I hadn't been in my right mind, and that even Arawn had been affected. But sometimes, I couldn't help thinking about it. Logically, I knew that touching him wouldn't set off any fireworks, that the kiss had been a one-time deal, but still . . .

The Erlking's horse snorted and stomped its hoof, apparently as impatient with me as Phaedra had been.

"Come along," the Erlking said. "Your father is nearly beside himself. If you don't make an appearance soon, he's likely to say something Prince Henry might make him regret."

As far as I could tell, Arawn had never lied to me. Deceived me, yes, but never outright lied. I couldn't imagine my staid and usually unemotional father being "beside himself" over my absence, but if Arawn said it was so, then it probably was.

With a sigh of resignation, I took the Erlking's offered hand and allowed him to pull me up onto the saddle in front of him. I'd expected him to put me behind him, but he and his horse dwarfed me so much that he could easily reach around me to hold the reins. This meant I was smushed up against him uncomfortably close, and I was painfully aware of the warmth of his body behind me. I was also painfully aware that he, uh, enjoyed having me there. My cheeks burned, and I prayed that he wasn't going to comment.

It was worse when the horse started moving. Arawn's body

rubbed against mine, and his arms seemed like they were practically trapping me against his chest. And then there was that other thing, rubbing against me with every jolt of the horse's stride. My hands gripped the edges of the saddle, not because I needed to hold on but to keep me from doing something drastically stupid like poking my elbow into his gut to make him back off.

"Relax," the Erlking said, his voice soft as he spoke right into my ear, bringing his face uncomfortably close to mine. "You are in no danger from me. I promise."

I managed to swallow the hysterical laugh that wanted to bubble out of me. He might not be liable to hurt me, but that wasn't the same as not being in danger. And there was our bargain, hanging there menacingly. If I ever wanted to have sex in my life, I would have to do it with Arawn first. I doubted I'd ever have been able to do that even if I didn't know he could steal my powers and ride out into the mortal world on an unchecked killing spree.

It took only a minute or two for us to reach the area where I'd unleashed my magic against the Bogles, and for the first time, I saw the results of what I'd done. Arawn reined his horse to a stop, staring at the collection of armor, helmets, and shoes that lay strewn across the road. Of the Bogles themselves, there was no sign.

"What happened here?" Arawn asked.

Usually, I was very secretive about my magic, but Arawn had already seen me in action once, and I was too wrung out to make something up.

"They got too close," I said as his horse picked its way gingerly through the stinky leather. "I hit them with some kind of spell, and it threw them backward. I couldn't see what happened after that." I didn't know exactly what I'd done to them, but they were definitely dead. To my shock, I felt a shudder run through Arawn's body behind me.

"You did the same thing to them you did to your aunt Grace," he said softly, and if I didn't know better, I would have sworn his voice held a combination of awe and fear. But that was ridiculous. No way was the Erlking afraid of *me*! "You made them mortal."

I shook my head in denial. "But it *wasn't* the same spell. Whatever this was, it threw the Bogles backward. It didn't do that to Aunt Grace."

Arawn was quiet for a moment before he spoke again. "Magic is an almost sentient force. It understood the intent of your command. It had to get them outside of your Faeriewalker aura so that making them mortal would kill them."

I didn't tell Arawn I'd been thinking about turning the Bogles to stone, not making them mortal. Somehow, I didn't think that would have been any kinder or gentler a spell to have cast. There was no denying I'd intended to kill the Bogles.

"It was self-defense," I said, telling myself that it was silly to feel guilty about killing things that had been trying to kill me.

I felt Arawn nod, but he didn't say anything more. And, ridiculous as it seemed, I now felt certain he was . . . well, maybe not *afraid* of me, exactly. But unsettled by me, for sure. We had already established that I was unlikely ever to use my magic against him. Now we knew I could reproduce the spell I'd used against Aunt Grace, but I still didn't know if I could do it when I wasn't under attack. I *was* sure I couldn't use it to cold-bloodedly kill someone.

"It bothers you, knowing I can do this," I said, though I probably should have just kept my mouth shut and hoped Arawn let it go. So far, he'd saved my life twice—not because he was so all-fired fond of me, but because if I was dead, I couldn't give him my virginity. But what if he decided I was too dangerous? After all, I might be the only person in either of our worlds who was capable of killing him. I had a feeling that if he sided with those who wanted me dead, my life expectancy would be less than sixty seconds.

Behind me, I felt Arawn's shoulders lift in a shrug. "I won't pretend it isn't disturbing. But I know you would only use it against your enemies, and as a last resort. And I am not your enemy."

I supposed it depended on how you defined *enemy*, but Arawn had declared himself my ally, and I believed he meant it. At least, he'd meant it *before* he'd seen what my magic could do. There was something . . . off in his tone of voice. And he had put a little bit of space between us on the saddle. Not so much that I didn't keep bumping into him, but enough so that he wasn't rubbing up against me anymore. I appreciated the personal space, but I really hoped it didn't mean Arawn was starting to reconsider my value to him. I had more than enough enemies already.

chapter ten

It seemed to take forever to catch up with the caravan. Phaedra had covered a lot of ground in her headlong rush.

The wind was blowing into our faces, and I smelled the carnage before it came into view. Bogles stink to high heaven, and there was an overlay of blood and fear that made it almost overpowering. Or maybe I was just imagining it.

When we finally rode around a bend to the site of the attack, my stomach heaved, and I had to close my eyes and hold my breath in hopes that I wasn't going to barf all over myself.

There were bodies everywhere, though in my first brief glimpse, I saw only Bogles and a handful of horses. No humans. Er, Fae. Of course, maybe the prince's people had already carried the dead away from the battlefield.

I opened my eyes again, bracing myself for what I was going to see.

Still lots of bodies, and lots of blood. Some of the prince's men—servants, not Knights—were piling the dead Bogles together. The pile was already alarmingly high, and there were plenty more bodies littered all around the outskirts of the road. Not all of them were whole, and I did my best not to look at them.

A couple of the wagons had been knocked over, and there were at least three dead horses, but considering the staggering number of Bogles that lay slaughtered on the ground, the battle had gone fairly well. It told me a little something about the power of the Fae I traveled with that they could fight off an attack of this magnitude with so few obvious casualties.

People were hard at work fixing wagons, bandaging wounds, and cleaning weapons. Too busy to see us approach at first. But then someone spotted us, and a cry of alarm went up among the assembled Fae. Behind me, I felt the Erlking sit up straighter, like he was trying to make himself even bigger and more intimidating than he already was.

The prince's Knights moved quickly to stand between the Wild Hunt and their liege, although it wasn't like the Erlking could attack anyone from the Seelie Court, not with the geis he'd allowed the Queens to put on him. But that didn't stop him and his Hunt from being a source of terror. Several of the Fae looked like they were about to pass out from fear, although the Knights just looked grim.

I heard my father's voice call my name. I strained my eyes trying to see around the Knights. I caught sight of movement, then saw my father, pushing his way through the gawking Fae, Finn and Ethan following close behind him. Keane and Kimber were coming from the other side of the gathering, moving more slowly because they weren't as aggressive about shoving people out of the way.

The Erlking reined his horse to a halt while still about fifty feet away from the Knights. My dad finally made it to the front, but the Knights blocked his way. I saw the spark of fury in my dad's eyes, and realized that Ethan hadn't been exaggerating when he said my dad was "beside himself." He looked like he was about to explode. I wasn't close enough to tell, but from the way the Knights whirled toward him, I guessed my dad was pulling magic, maybe about to do something stupid.

"Dad! Don't!" I yelled. I tried to slide off the horse, but Arawn put an arm around my waist and held me.

"Not yet," he said. "Someone might get twitchy if you make any sudden moves."

"Let go of me," I growled, but he just held me tighter.

I prayed Dad wouldn't cast anything on the Knights who were blocking his way. I suspected that would be the kind of breach of etiquette that could get him in a whole lot of trouble, especially when the prince had it in for him anyway.

Finn reached out and laid a hand on my dad's arm, leaning forward and saying something I couldn't hear. Dad winced, then closed his eyes, visibly taking a deep breath to steady himself. When he opened them again, he looked outwardly calm, his bland Court mask back in place. But the Knights still regarded him warily.

"*Now* you can get down," Arawn said. "But move slowly. They're on edge, still in battle mode. It wouldn't take much to trigger them."

I didn't much want his advice, but I listened to it anyway. I kept a close eye on the Knights as Arawn helped me slide to the ground. I was glad for his steadying hand, because it was a long way down. The Knights looked every bit as on edge as he'd said, so I walked slowly and held my hands away from my sides, trying to look as harmless as possible. Not that that was hard. As my aunt Grace and the Bogles could have told you, I'm not actually harmless, but I definitely *look* it.

My dad said something to the Knight closest to him. The Knight frowned, then stepped aside with apparent reluctance. My dad slipped past him, although Finn and Ethan stayed behind. Dad walked slowly toward me. After everything I'd seen and been through in the last half hour or so, I wanted to run to him and fling my arms around him—a gesture of affection I'm sure he'd have had no idea what to do with.

We met about halfway between the two groups. I wished the

Erlking would take his Hunt and leave, because as long as he loomed there, the tension was going to stay dialed up to maximum.

"Are you all right?" my dad asked, his voice controlled and tight.

"I'm fine," I assured him, though I wasn't sure it was quite true. I'd seen more death since I'd come to Avalon than I'd ever imagined, but I'd never seen anything like today. Breaking down and having a fit of hysteria seemed like a reasonable thing to do, although at that moment, I was pretty numb. "What about you?" There was blood on his shirt, and I gasped when I saw the five parallel tears in his sleeve. Blood soaked his shirt around the tears, although there was no sign of a wound.

"I'm fine, too," he said, then followed my eyes to the tear on his shirt. "It was just a scratch, and Finn healed it for me." He reached for me, startling me by pulling me into a hug. "I thought I'd lost you," he said into my hair, his voice choked with emotion.

I hugged him back, my throat tightening up so much I couldn't talk. Sometimes, I felt like my dad saw me as nothing more than a tool to help further his political ambitions. Then there were times like these, when he let me see what lay beneath his polished exterior, and I realized he really did love me. And I loved him right back.

Dad broke the hug before I had a chance to say something sappy and started guiding me back to the caravan. The Knights were still blocking the road, and I saw that Kimber and Keane had joined Ethan and Finn, waiting for me just beyond the barricade. Maybe it was my imagination, but I could have sworn I felt the Erlking's eyes on me the entire time.

I looked back over my shoulder as the line of Knights parted to let us through. Arawn gave me a jaunty wave, then turned his horse and led his Hunt back down the road away from us. I had no doubt he'd be staying close on our tail, even if he was pretending to go away.

The Knights finally relaxed, and the rest of the prince's people lost interest as the Wild Hunt rode away. Except for the prince, that is. Surrounded by his Knights—not a mark on him and not a hair out of place—he stormed in our direction with murder in his eyes. This didn't look good.

Dad put his arm around my shoulder and made a little shooing motion at my friends. "I suggest you retreat," he said. "This may get unpleasant."

Ethan drew himself up, all offended dignity. "I'm not the type to run away from trouble."

Keane and Kimber both took up similarly stubborn stances. Maybe they all thought they could help protect me, but if the prince had his panties in a twist, I didn't think it fair for my friends to be caught in the middle.

"Just give us a little space, guys," I begged them. "I'll be fine."

I think they were planning to argue some more, but Finn put one hand on each guy's shoulder and started pulling them out of the way. Keane tried to break his father's hold, to no avail, and Ethan didn't even bother to try. With an apologetic shrug, Kimber hurried after them.

Just in time, too, because Henry was practically on top of us. Everyone else had scattered at the sight of Henry's fury. I didn't know what he was so pissed off about, seeing as he was the one who'd led us into an ambush. An ambush I couldn't help suspecting he had something to do with.

"What is the meaning of bringing the Wild Hunt here?" he spat, and I didn't know if he was talking to me or my dad.

My dad decided Henry was talking to him and answered. "I didn't bring them here. I'm sure they were just following, and Dana happened into them when *her horse carried her away.*" There was a sharp edge to those words, and I wondered if Dad suspected that someone had cast a compulsion spell on Phaedra, as the Erlking believed.

Henry chose to ignore the implications, instead curling his lip as he looked at me. "Interesting company you keep. Unseelie friends and the Wild Hunt at your beck and call. Perhaps my mother made a mistake by inviting you into our lands."

Probably the smart thing to do would have been to keep my mouth shut and let my dad handle the obnoxious jerk of a prince. But keeping my mouth shut isn't my way.

"At least *I* didn't lead us into an ambush," I countered. "And it was nice of you to make sure all your Knights were gathered around you while the rest of us were under attack."

Beside me, Dad made a little choking sound. I couldn't tell if it was smothered laughter or alarm. I did know that the prince was not amused. He glared at me as if he hated me more than anyone in the world.

"Perhaps we would not have been ambushed if you hadn't insisted on bringing your Unseelie companions!" he snapped.

It was my turn to sputter with outrage. "You seriously mean to tell me you think Ethan and Kimber arranged for us to be attacked?"

The outrage lost a little of its steam when I remembered Ethan arranging for me to be attacked by a Spriggan, back when I'd first come to Avalon. Well, actually, it was Ethan's dad who arranged the attack, but Ethan was in on it. He was supposed to save me from the Spriggan so he could be my hero and I would fall madly in love with him. Things had gone horribly wrong, because of course things always do when I'm around, but I'd long ago forgiven Ethan. And I was sure he had nothing to do with the Bogles.

Henry made a sour face. "They are no friends of the Seelie Court, and—"

"Really, Henry," my father interrupted. "They live in Avalon, and their father preaches that citizens of Avalon should not align themselves with a Court. Look first to your own people before you accuse mine."

"You dare!" Henry spat, as if he'd never heard anything so outrageous in his life. His cheeks were growing red with anger. My dad hadn't been exaggerating when he said he was good at rousing Henry's temper.

I noticed a couple of Henry's Knights edging closer, watching my father and me with suspicious eyes, like they thought we were about to attack their prince. But my dad's voice remained calm and level as Henry's grew more shrill. If anyone was going to attack, it would be Henry.

"My daughter is supposed to be under your protection," my dad said. "And yet an attempt was made on her life right under your nose. The Bogles did not venture so far into Seelie territory without some interference, nor would my daughter's horse have run off with her like that. The obvious conclusion is that someone in your party arranged it."

Henry clearly didn't know how to quit when he was behind. "Perhaps it is you yourself who arranged the attack," he said. His face was now almost purple with rage, and his voice had gone up about an octave. "As a way to discredit me!"

My dad gave that suggestion exactly the respect it deserved: he laughed.

The argument had drawn a fair amount of attention, and more than one of the observers snickered. I doubted even Henry believed what he was saying, but he clearly didn't like being laughed at. There was a young, redheaded servant girl—I'd guess her age at somewhere around fourteen—standing respectfully to the side awaiting his attention. To my horror, Henry turned to her and slapped her so hard one of the Knights had to catch her to keep her from falling.

"How dare you laugh?" he shouted, though she hadn't been one of the ones who'd snickered. Those people got the message, though, ducking their heads and slinking away.

"Tell me, Henry," my dad said, "do you make a habit of bullying children, or do you only do it when your temper is piqued?" If he was particularly upset that Henry had just clobbered an innocent bystander because of his needling, you couldn't tell it by looking at him. I, on the other hand, wanted to demonstrate some of the most deadly kicks and punches Keane had taught me, and I had no doubt that thought was clear on my face. I wouldn't actually have *done* it—I swear, I'm not a moron—but my dad put a restraining hand on my shoulder just the same.

Belatedly, Henry seemed to realize he was making a total fool of himself. I could see him visibly battling his temper, trying to resist the urge to respond to my dad's latest taunt. He managed it, but not by much.

"Your daughter may ride in one of the servants' wagons," he said, still spitting mad. "I have no spare horse to give her now that she's lost her mount."

I had no doubt being relegated to the servants' wagon was meant to be an insult, but if it got me out of any more horseback riding, I was all for it. I didn't much appreciate Henry's implication that I was to blame for losing Phaedra, but I kept my mouth shut. I wondered if my dad was going to argue about me riding in a wagon, but he seemed satisfied that he'd come out on top and didn't object.

Henry turned sharply away, stomping off. "Elizabeth!" he bellowed over his shoulder, and the poor redheaded girl went scurrying after him, her head held low.

"Shouldn't we be turning around and heading back to Avalon?" I asked my dad as we both watched Henry's indignant retreat. "I'm obviously not as safe here as you thought."

He looked grim and unhappy. "Apparently not. But we can't turn back. It would be an unpardonable insult to imply that Henry can't protect you."

"You're kidding me, right? Because I'm pretty sure I'd be dead right now if it weren't for the Erlking. Even if Henry's people weren't behind it, they didn't lift a finger to help me. I think it's fair to say he can't—or *won't*—protect me."

"Maybe so, but if we offer him an insult of that magnitude—no matter how well-deserved—he could use it as an excuse to revoke our safe passage." Dad swept his gaze pointedly around the caravan, with its Knights and magic users. "We are not among friends, and without the protection of safe passage . . ."

I suppressed a groan of frustration, but I got the point. I had a good idea what Henry and his people would do if they were no longer under any obligation to play nice, and I did not want to find out firsthand I was right.

chapter eleven

When we were finally ready to depart again, one of Henry's servants directed me to my assigned wagon. It was more comfortable than riding horseback, but not by much. The only seats were hard wooden benches. As if that weren't uncomfortable enough, two of the baggage wagons had been beyond repair, and their cargo was stuffed under the benches so there was only one seat where you could actually put your feet on the floor. The servants put me in that seat, but I couldn't help feeling guilty when I saw the rest of them contorting themselves to find a place to put their feet. The women, who had to deal with the ridiculous bustles right over their butts, had an especially hard time of it. I wondered if all the crap in those crates was strictly necessary, but I knew better than to think Henry might leave something behind for the comfort of mere servants.

I don't know if it was a result of post-traumatic shock, or if Henry's servants were so beaten down they'd lost all desire to be sociable, but try as I might, I couldn't get anyone in that wagon to speak to me in more than monosyllables for the entire afternoon. They all rode with their heads bowed, not looking right or left, not talking to each other any more than they talked to me. I thought surely I could strike up a conversation with the redheaded girl,

Elizabeth, since I guessed she was near my own age, but she was even quieter than the rest. Her eyes went wide with what looked like fear every time I tried to strike up a conversation. I felt so sorry for her I wanted to go over and give her a hug, but of course, I didn't. I was sure she wouldn't have appreciated it.

I expected Henry to commandeer someone's house for the night as he had yesterday, but apparently he had other plans. Maybe we were too far out in the boonies to find a convenient host.

Whatever the reason, our caravan came to a halt in the middle of what seemed to me a nondescript patch of road. The servants in my wagon practically stampeded in their hurry to get to work as soon as we came to a halt. Magic pulsed in the air, and the surrounding forest began shifting in a way that I didn't think I'd ever get used to.

I assumed everything was going to move out of the way and make a big clearing like the trees had at yesterday's rest stop, but that didn't seem to be what was happening. As far as I could tell, the trees were scurrying about as haphazardly as the servants. I jumped down from the wagon and tried to stay out of the way so I wouldn't be trampled.

After a couple of minutes, I realized with a start that the trees and bushes were forming themselves into a multitude of enclosures, like they were the giant, living walls of a cubicle farm. The tallest of the trees bent over each of the enclosures, forming roofs.

"Cool," I murmured, forgetting for a moment to be weirded out.

I wandered through the crowd until I found my dad and my friends. Servants were unloading wagons, carrying luggage and crates into the enclosures. Others were tending to the horses, while still others were setting up what looked like an open-air kitchen.

"If Henry can manage all this," I said to my dad, "why did he have to invite himself and the rest of us to stay over at someone's house last night?"

"I'm sure you can guess the answer to that," he responded drily, and he was right. Commandeering someone's house like that had been a power play, something Henry did just to show that he could. What a jerk! And because the Fae were completely fixated on their archaic class structure, they just had to take it.

Eventually, a servant came for us and led us to a cluster of tree-lined enclosures, informing us that once again, Kimber and I, and Ethan and Keane would be sharing "rooms." I doubt Henry's people planned it that way, but Finn decided to join Ethan and Keane, which seemed positively forward of him. I immediately suspected he was worried about what kind of trouble the two of them might get into if left unsupervised.

When Kimber and I entered our "room," it was to find our luggage already delivered, suitcases stacked neatly in the corner. There were two feather mattresses on simple wooden frames, and there was a wooden folding table, complete with a basket of fruit, a pitcher of some dark liquid I suspected was wine, and a couple of silver goblets. Considering we were basically camping in the forest, this looked suspiciously like the Ritz. Not that I was complaining, mind you. My body was just as sore after hours in the wagon as it was after hours on horseback, and, to tell the truth, I was still seriously shaken up by the Bogle attack. I collapsed onto the bed, heedless of the fact that I stank of horse with a hint of dead Bogle. Kimber stood in the doorway for a moment, then said, "Be back in a few," before slipping out.

"Where are you—" I started to ask, but she was already gone. I was too tired to get up and see what she was up to. Instead, I closed my eyes and tried hard not to think.

I had almost fallen asleep when I heard the sound of footsteps approaching. I cracked my eyes open and saw that Kimber had returned, carrying two ceramic mugs and an earthenware pitcher from which wisps of steam rose. I sniffed the air as I propped myself up on my elbows and caught a whiff of a familiar scent.

"Hot posset?" I asked, my mouth automatically watering. I'd never even heard of hot posset before I came to Avalon, and now it was nearing chocolate at the top of my list of best comfort foods ever.

Kimber looked very proud of herself as she filled both mugs to the brim. "I figured we could use it after everything that happened today."

I forgot my exhaustion as I wrapped my hands around the mug Kimber handed me. "Where did you get hot posset?"

"From the kitchen," she answered simply.

Ask a stupid question . . .

I sniffed at my mug before taking a sip, and the smell of whiskey practically made my eyes water. "Geez, Kimber, how much booze is in this?" She knew I wasn't a big fan of alcohol, so she usually used only a touch of whiskey for flavor when making hot posset for me. Except when she took it upon herself to prescribe "extra-strength," that is.

Kimber took a sip of her posset, then gave a satisfied sigh before answering. "Just enough."

I rolled my eyes but didn't have the energy to protest. I blew lightly on the surface of my posset, then took an incautiously large sip. Not only did I burn my tongue, but that sip kept burning all the way down my throat and into my belly. No doubt about it, this was the extra-strength version. I drank it anyway.

The second sip burned less than the first, and the third less than that. The flavor was rich and heady—no skim milk here—and I started to relax almost in spite of myself. Until I thought about my mom, sitting at home enjoying similar beverages in much higher quantities. My heart squeezed in my chest, and the sudden sense of loss made me feel hollow inside. I'd had Sober Mom for a grand total of about four weeks, and thanks to Titania and her "invitation," that was all gone now.

"What's wrong?" Kimber asked, sitting on the bed across from me.

I forced a little laugh. "After everything that happened today, you have to ask?"

But Kimber was coming to know me uncomfortably well. "It's not that," she said, not a trace of doubt in her voice.

Kimber knew about my mom's drinking problem—she was the only person I'd ever told—but that didn't mean I liked to talk about it. I'd considered my mom my shameful secret for so long and was so used to covering up for her that it was always my first instinct to avoid the subject. I took another couple swallows of posset without answering, hoping Kimber would decide to change the subject. But she doesn't give up that easy.

"I noticed some tension between you and your mom when we left yesterday," she said.

I froze with my mug halfway to my mouth. Damn. She was much too observant—and much too understanding—for my own good. I might have thought she wouldn't have caught the connection between the alcoholic beverage I was drinking and the alcoholic mother I'd publicly given the cold shoulder to yesterday, but no, not Kimber.

Figuring this conversation would end a lot quicker if I just gave in to the inevitable and talked, I told Kimber about my doomed-from-the-start attempt to get my mom to promise she'd stay sober. I stopped frequently for sips of posset, so my muscles felt all loose and comfortable, and my head was spinning just a bit. All signs that I'd had too much posset already. And all signs I ignored as I drained my mug.

Kimber gave me a look of sympathy, although she wasn't giving me that pitying look some people give me when they see me with my drunken idiot of a mother. It was a look of compassion, and it was one I could accept without shame.

"Parents stink sometimes," she said, finishing her own posset and setting the mug on the floor at her feet. "At least your mom is around, however screwed up she may be."

I winced in sympathy. Kimber's mom had left to live in Faerie when Kimber was twelve. I knew how much that had to hurt. "When did you see your mom last?" I asked.

She scrunched up her face. "It's been about two years, I think. We went to see her in Faerie over a Christmas break. I guess that means it's about two and a half years."

"And she never comes to Avalon to visit?"

Kimber shook her head. "Not once since she left. She always seems glad to see us, and when we visit, it sometimes feels almost like the old days. Only it isn't." She reached for her mug, then grimaced when she saw it was empty. "It can never be like the old days again. I can never unlearn that she didn't love me enough to stay in Avalon."

I am not a touchy-feely person. But the bitterness and hurt in Kimber's words inspired me to heave myself off my bed—and wow, that was harder to manage than it should have been—and sit beside her. I gave her the hug I thought she needed. She patted my back and pulled away, smiling sadly at me.

"You don't need to comfort me," she said. "We're supposed to be talking about *you*, not me. I'm just trying to make you feel better by letting you know I understand."

"Thanks," I said, my veins practically buzzing with the after-effects of my posset. That she would try to make me feel better by opening her own wounds and sharing them . . . humbled me. And made me feel even guiltier about all the secrets I was keeping from her. She deserved more from me than I was giving her.

Maybe it was the alcohol. Or maybe it was just that the guilt had reached critical mass and forced my hand. But at that moment, my mouth seemed to take on a life of its own, moving without any conscious thought.

"I lied to you," I blurted. The part of me that had never truly trusted another person started screaming at me to shut up before it was too late.

Kimber blinked in surprise. I guess my confession did sort of come out of the blue. "Oh? About what?"

She's never going to forgive you, my inner voice told me. I feared it was right. I knew *I* wouldn't forgive me in her shoes. But I'd already said too much, and it was too late to back down. I opened my mouth to blurt out my secret—at least one of them, the biggest one—but I couldn't get any sound out. Tears swam in my eyes. I was terrified I was about to lose my best friend—just like I was losing my mom to the alcohol again.

Kimber put her hand on my back. "About the 'geis' the Erlking put on you so you can't talk about your agreement?" she prompted gently. I could hear the mental quotes around the word *geis*.

Come to think of it, when I'd first told her that a geis prevented me from telling her what I'd done, she'd been openly skeptical. But I'd been too humiliated by the agreement to tell her the truth. I was such a pathetic coward.

A tear dribbled down my cheek, and I swiped it away angrily. I'd made the decision to lie, and it was too late to cry about it now. "You never really believed me, did you?" I asked in a tear-raspy voice.

"Not for a moment," she confirmed. Strangely, she didn't sound angry. Maybe just because this wasn't coming as a surprise, which I probably should have known from the beginning. Kimber was pretty sharp.

"You're not mad?" I asked, risking a glance at her face.

"I was at first," she admitted. "But I figured you were keeping it secret for a reason and that you'd tell me when you were ready. And you don't have to tell me now if you're still not ready. I'm not going anywhere." She made a face. "Well, not anywhere *you're* not going, anyway."

I managed a hint of a smile. Then I took a deep, steadying breath and told her just what I'd had to promise the Erlking to get him to release Ethan.

Kimber didn't interrupt my halting explanation. I sneaked glances at her face every now and then, but I couldn't read her expression. She was certainly surprised, and horrified, but I couldn't tell if she was pissed or not.

I told her about the day I'd gone to see the Erlking and bargain for Ethan's freedom, and about the magic that had sealed our deal. I even told her about the kiss the Erlking had given me and how the magic had made that kiss feel good despite the fact that I knew he was a cold-blooded killer.

There was a lot I left out, some things—like the Erlking's mark—because I didn't want to talk about them, some things—like my magical abilities—because I *shouldn't* talk about them, and one thing—the real reason the Erlking wanted me to give him my virginity—that I *couldn't* talk about. I wasn't covered by the geis that kept the members of the Seelie Court from talking about it, but the Erlking had promised me that Connor would suffer for the rest of his immortal life if I told anyone. Maybe if I told Kimber, the Erlking would never know, but I didn't dare risk it.

"There are things I still can't tell you," I said to assuage my guilt. "I'm sorry." I clasped my hands together in my lap and stared at them, wondering if all the years I'd been a loner had made me incapable of being a good friend. "And I'm sorry I lied to you about the geis. I just . . ." I shuddered. "The truth was too embarrassing, and I'm used to keeping embarrassing things to myself." I swallowed hard. "Do you think you can ever forgive me?" I asked in a pathetically tentative voice.

Kimber sighed and ran a hand through her hair. "I'm not in any position to throw stones," she said, not looking at me. "Practically every word out of my mouth when we first met was a lie, and *you* managed to forgive *me*."

She had a point, but I couldn't help noticing that she hadn't actually answered my question. *She'd* lied to me when we'd barely known each other, when there weren't any bonds of friendship to betray. What I'd done was entirely different, and we both knew it.

"What are you going to do?" she asked.

"There's nothing I *can* do. I'm not having sex with the Erlking, and I'm not letting him take Ethan back. So . . ." I shrugged. "I guess I've taken a lifelong vow of chastity. Maybe I should join a convent or something."

Kimber made a little snorting sound that might have been a reluctant laugh. "Don't. You'd look lousy in black."

I smiled and whapped her shoulder. She smiled back, though the expression didn't reach her eyes. She was either pissed at me or hurt—or maybe both—but if she was going to pretend she wasn't, that was fine with me. I'd had all the turmoil I could take for one day.

"Do you think the prince's people have managed to magic up a shower somewhere?" I asked. "I feel all gross and stinky."

"That's because you are," Kimber said, jumping to her feet before I could whap her upside the head. "I believe I did spot an impromptu bathhouse on my way to the kitchen. Follow me."

I wasn't quite as steady on my feet as I would have liked, but I managed to get upright and totter off after Kimber.

I began day three of my trip through Faerie with a headache I suspected might be a hangover. Maybe I shouldn't have drunk the second dose of hot posset Kimber had nagged me into downing before bed. Then again, I *had* actually slept, which after the day's nightmarish events was a minor miracle. I would have loved a nice, strong cup of coffee for breakfast, but the Fae don't do coffee, so I was stuck with strong, weird-tasting tea that probably didn't have anything resembling caffeine in it.

I was not looking forward to a full day in the servants' wagon. So when Ethan suggested I ride double with him on his horse, I jumped at the offer.

"It's going to be pretty uncomfortable," Ethan warned. "These saddles aren't meant for two."

I waved off his concern. "It won't be much more uncomfortable than the stupid wagon."

As soon as I climbed on behind Ethan, I realized I was dead wrong about the comfort level. The edge of the saddle dug into my butt so hard I would probably have bruises, and since there was only one set of stirrups, my legs were dangling. Still, I *was* with Ethan, my body pressed up against his back, my arms around his waist. I rested my cheek against his shoulder, closing my eyes and breathing in the scent of the minty Fae soap he favored even when we were in Avalon. I hadn't realized how much I'd begun to associate that scent with Ethan until I'd used a bar of the same stuff to wash with last night.

"Are you miserably uncomfortable?" Ethan asked as we started forward. "I can take you to the wagon if it's too—"

"I'm fine," I told him, despite the way the saddle dug into me in unfortunate places. I was happy to put up with the discomfort, as long as I got to spend some time with Ethan, even surrounded by an audience as we were.

We passed a few minutes in companionable silence before Ethan said, "Seeing that horse run off with you yesterday was one of the worst moments in my life."

I tightened my arms around him, hearing the genuine pain in his voice. "I didn't enjoy it a whole lot myself," I said. I remembered the sick feeling in my stomach as I'd watched Ethan and Keane fighting off Bogles as Phaedra carried me helplessly away. "I felt like I was abandoning you."

He turned to look at me over his shoulder, his face a mask of amazement. "You've got to be kidding! It's not like you *chose* to run off. And it's not like you could have done anything to help the rest of us. Besides, we were more than a match for a bunch of Bogles."

It was true that no one had died, and it was also true that I hadn't left them behind voluntarily. That didn't make the memory any easier to bear.

"Actually, I could have helped in the fight," I said, then told Ethan about what I'd done to the Bogles that had attacked me.

"But you would never try to cast a spell in front of witnesses, right?" he asked, and I could feel the tension in his body and hear it in his voice. He was convinced that if anyone learned about my affinity with magic, I'd be viewed as even more of a threat than I already was.

I sighed, not sure what I would have done if I'd been in the middle of the battle and found myself or one of my friends in life-threatening danger. I had a sneaking suspicion I'd have cast the spell even with witnesses around, but Ethan didn't need to hear that.

"Of course not," I told him. "Besides, like you said, you didn't need my help."

I think Ethan heard the falseness of my tone, but he didn't challenge me on it, which was a good thing. I didn't want to waste this precious time we had together with arguing.

I shifted in the saddle, trying to find a more comfortable position. My arms were still locked around Ethan's waist, and I could feel him holding his breath.

"Is something wrong?" I asked.

"Nope. Not a thing," he replied, his voice a little breathy. "But if you don't hold still, things could get a little embarrassing."

I froze, thinking about how my fidgeting caused me to rub against him. The moment I thought of it, I forgot all about the discomfort of the saddle, my mind focusing on the fact that my breasts were smooshed up against his back and his butt was cradled between my legs. My cheeks heated with embarrassment, even as the tingle of awareness spread throughout my body and made me want to rub up against him harder. I wondered if he was even now thinking about our venture to second base the night I'd snuck out of my safe house to see him. I knew *I* was, my mind conveniently editing out the strain we'd both been under at the time and the anger and desperation that had tainted the encounter.

Maybe accepting Ethan's offer to ride double with him had been a bad idea.

"Sorry," I said, willing myself to be still.

"No worries," he said, his voice still strained and breathy. "This is kind of fun." He turned to wink at me, as if he were perfectly satisfied with a little playful flirtation. As if he weren't used to getting girls into bed, and my enforced chastity were no big deal.

Not that any of that mattered right now. Even if I were a total slut, we wouldn't be doing anything more than flirting, in full view of dozens of people. But the tingly feeling of excitement from being close to him never failed to rouse my worries and concerns. I was desperately addicted to Ethan, and the fear of losing him could be debilitating at times, no matter how logically my rational mind explained that we had no future together.

"Maybe I should ride in the wagon after all?" I suggested tentatively.

"No way," Ethan said with gratifying speed. "I'm not missing out on my chance to have you so close to me." He sighed, and some of the tension eased out of him. "Besides, we won't be riding all that long today."

"We won't?" From what my dad had told me, the Sunne Palace

was at least a couple hundred miles from the Avalon border. I didn't know how much ground we were covering at our plodding speed, but I was pretty sure it wasn't a couple hundred miles yet.

"No. Finn showed Keane and me a map of our route last night. We're going to take a shortcut through some standing stones."

"Huh?" I said intelligently.

"Standing stones. Like Stonehenge, only with real magic. There are tons of them in Faerie. They can be tricky to use, but if you've got the skill, you can travel from one set to another in the blink of an eye."

"Tricky to use? What exactly does that mean?"

"Each set of standing stones is naturally connected to another, and they're active in the moonlight. So if you don't mind traveling at night, and if you want to go where the stones will naturally take you, using them is a piece of cake. But if you want to travel in the daytime, or if you want to control which set of stones you travel to, it takes some serious magic. And screwing up the spell could be the last mistake you ever make, if you know what I mean."

I liked the idea of taking a shortcut—the sooner we got to the Sunne Palace, the sooner I'd be able to go home—but the way Ethan was describing it made it sound like a really bad idea to play with standing stones.

"Don't worry," he said, no doubt sensing my tension. "Prince Henry wouldn't risk using standing stones if he thought there was any chance a hair on his head might be ruffled. And once we go through them, we'll have only a few more hours to ride. We should be sleeping in luxury at the Sunne Palace tonight."

Sleeping in luxury sure sounded nice, but an uneasy voice in the back of my head told me the standing stones would not turn out to be such a great idea after all.

. . .

I was right, only not for the reasons I thought.

We'd been traveling for about two hours, and I was pretty sure riding double on Ethan's horse had already crippled me for life, when the caravan came to a sudden and unexpected halt. It was too soon for a lunch break, so I hoped that meant we'd reached the standing stones, even though the idea of passing through them made me decidedly nervous. I leaned to the side for a better view, but there were too many riders between me and the front to see why we'd stopped. At least there weren't any shouts of alarm.

"Are we there yet?" I murmured, and Ethan laughed.

"Don't know," he said. "Let's go see."

We were still in hilly terrain, and Ethan guided his horse off the road and up the side of the hill that bounded it. We were pretty far toward the back, but the extra height allowed us to see why we had stopped. In the distance, at the crest of a flat-topped hill, were the standing stones: about ten big slabs of gray rock arranged in a circle, making it look like the hill was wearing a crown. But that wasn't why we'd stopped. The road we were on forked, one branch leading right up to the standing stones, the other leading around the hill and off into the distance. The road that led to the standing stones was blocked by what looked like a big hedge. The hedge was about six feet high, and wide enough to span the entire road.

"This looks like a setup for an ambush," I said, looking nervously around, wondering if there were more Bogles about to descend on us. "Except no one seems the least bit worried."

"I don't think it's an ambush, exactly," Ethan said cryptically as he nudged his horse forward. Either he was taking us closer to the prince's position, where it was supposedly safer, or he was taking us closer to the front line, which didn't seem like such a good idea to me.

From our vantage point, we could see Henry slide from his horse, then talk to one of his Knights—having a conniption fit, if the way he was waving his arms around was any indication. Ethan continued to urge his horse closer, but by the time we got within earshot, the discussion/argument was over. The Knight got back on his horse and started weaving his way through the stopped caravan toward the rear, and Henry stomped up to the hedge. When he started talking to it, I wondered if he'd lost his mind.

"What is the meaning of this?" he demanded, his fists on his hips and his jaw jutting out. "Do you know who I am?"

The hedge . . . moved. Not like the trees and underbrush did when they got out of the way, more like some multi-limbed amoeba changing shape. The vines rustled and quivered, drawing in from the edges, and I could see now that although the leaves looked kind of like ivy, there were wicked-sharp thorns all along the branches. Whatever the hedge was, it definitely wasn't ivy.

"Shite," Ethan muttered under his breath. "It's a Green Lady."

"Do I even want to know what a Green Lady is?" I asked.

"Probably not."

"That's what I thought."

The vines reshaped themselves until they formed the figure of a woman in a flowing green gown, looking very much like an animated topiary. The Green Lady bowed her head.

"I know who you are, my prince," she said, although her head was just a featureless oval with no mouth that I could see. "It goes without saying that you may pass freely. These others, however, must pay the toll."

"This is outrageous!" Henry shouted. "You dare to impede my progress?"

"Not at all, my prince," the Green Lady said, and there was unconcealed amusement in her voice. "As I said, you may pass unhindered."

"You will remove yourself from this road immediately," Henry said, not a bit appeased. "My chattel are exempt from your toll."

Even some of Henry's most loyal Knights looked offended at being referred to as chattel. Even if being his chattel meant they didn't have to pay whatever toll the Green Lady was demanding.

"Can't they just hack their way through the hedge?" I asked Ethan, keeping my voice down, because the last thing I wanted to do was draw Henry's or the Green Lady's attention. There was enough firepower in our caravan to fight off what had seemed like an army of Bogles. It seemed like this one Green Lady should be no match for them.

"Yeah," Ethan agreed, keeping his voice just as soft, "but that's one of those things that's 'not done' in Faerie. To kill a Green Lady is to poison the land, and they can demand their tolls whenever it suits them."

"And what, exactly, is this toll she's demanding?"

"Blood, of course," said my dad, and I practically fell off the horse in surprise. I felt Ethan's body jerk, too, so I guess I wasn't the only one who hadn't noticed my dad riding up beside us. "Virgin blood, more specifically," Dad said, and I felt the prickle of his magic.

A chill passed down my spine. "You think Henry's going to throw me under the bus."

Dad gave me a quizzical look, but even if he wasn't familiar with the saying, he took my meaning. "He can try," my dad said grimly, and I realized we might be in more trouble now than we had been yesterday when the Bogles attacked. There was no way my dad would allow Henry to hand me over without violence, and Henry might be enough of an ass to try find a way around the safe passage agreement to do it.

It wasn't a fight my dad could win, and we both knew it.

"These people are not all your chattel, my prince," the Green Lady said. "I'm afraid I must insist they pay the toll. Or, of course, you can take the long way." She gestured with one leafy arm at the road that led around the hill.

Henry sputtered a little more.

"Come, come," the Green Lady said. "What is a little blood between friends? You do wish the land to prosper, do you not?"

At that moment, I noticed the Knight who'd been talking to Henry coming back. And I noticed, to my horror, that Elizabeth was sitting behind him on his horse, her face once more wet with tears.

"Oh, no," I said. "He's not going to . . ."

My dad's shoulders slumped in relief. "Better her than you," he said; then he turned to me and made a calming gesture before I could bite his head off about his callousness. "The blood toll isn't fatal," he assured me. "But it is unpleasant."

I didn't doubt that. What did Henry have against this poor girl? She was only a kid! Then again, the rest of the women in his caravan were all adults and could be thousands of years old for all I knew. Maybe Elizabeth and I were the only virgins in the bunch. Well, except for Kimber, but I doubted Henry would be allowed to offer up an Unseelie girl.

I got the impression that the Green Lady was eyeing Elizabeth hungrily, even though she didn't technically have eyes.

Henry had obviously decided to give Elizabeth to the Green Lady from the very beginning—otherwise why would he have sent his Knight to fetch her?—but he still pretended to be completely indignant about the sacrifice. He scowled fiercely at the Green Lady, making thinly veiled threats and reminding me of a three-year-old having a tantrum.

Elizabeth was clearly terrified, and my heart squeezed with pity for her as the Knight dismounted, dragging her down with him. Her face was so white I was surprised she didn't faint dead away, and even from a distance, I could see how badly she was trembling. She was just a kid. And Henry was going to hand her over to the Green Lady like she was exactly what he'd called her and all the rest of his people: chattel. When she balked, Henry turned on her impatiently.

"Stop blubbering," he said with a truly overwhelming level of compassion. "Just hold still and it will be over in a moment."

His words weren't exactly comforting, and Elizabeth flinched from the sharpness of his tone. An angry red flush was creeping up his neck, and I had no doubt he was on the verge of beating her into submission.

Without having consciously made a decision to act, I found myself slipping off the back of Ethan's horse. My thighs and butt groaned in protest, and when my feet hit the ground I found my legs were all wobbly, but I managed not to fall on my face.

"What are you doing?" Ethan asked me, and my dad turned to me in obvious alarm.

I remembered the Erlking telling me once that I was very protective of the people who mattered to me, and that it took very little to make someone matter. I guess he had me pegged. Elizabeth had never spoken a single word to me, but I couldn't just stand by and let Henry hand her over to the Green Lady.

I ignored Ethan's question and avoided my dad's eyes as I walked around their horses toward the road. Elizabeth was trying to pull away from the Knight's grip, and Henry was yelling at her, ordering her to march straight into the Green Lady's clutches.

"Leave her alone!" I shouted, and everyone in hearing range went silent. Except for my dad.

"Dana, no!" he barked, and I heard the sound of his horse as he came after me.

Henry turned to me, and there was an ugly gleam in his eye that gave me a chill. "We cannot pass without a sacrifice," he said as his gaze bored into me. "Unless you're volunteering to take her place, my servant *will* give her blood to the Green Lady."

Dad's horse came up beside me, and Dad reached down for me. I dodged out of his reach but kept most of my attention on Henry.

"I'll take her place," I said, wondering if I was completely crazy.

I didn't know exactly what would happen during this blood sacrifice, and here I was volunteering for it in the place of a girl I didn't even know.

"Dana, no!" my dad said again, this time with even more heat. "I forbid it!"

I turned to look up at him as he glowered down at me from his horse. "You said the blood sacrifice is non-fatal, right?"

"That doesn't matter," he said through gritted teeth. "You are not doing it!"

"Dad, *look* at her," I argued, indicating Elizabeth with a sweep of my arm. The poor girl was still crying, though she held one hand over her mouth as if trying to stifle the sobs. If she were a human girl, I'd be afraid she might die of terror if she was forced to act as a sacrifice. As it was, I doubted she would actually die, but she would no doubt be emotionally scarred. Maybe I was overestimating my own toughness, but I was pretty damn sure the sacrifice would damage me a lot less than it would her.

I don't think my dad felt nearly as sorry for Elizabeth as I did, and I was sure he was about to put his foot down, but the Green Lady spoke before he got a chance.

"A willing sacrifice is of far more value than one that is forced," she said, turning her featureless head toward me. "I will take the willing sacrifice." She held out a thorny arm, beckoning to me.

"No!" my dad said, a hint of desperation in his voice.

"She has already offered herself," Henry snapped. I didn't think he was a bit unhappy at how things were turning out. "It is too late to renege."

"I am her father, and I forbid it!"

"Then none of you shall pass," the Green Lady said. She pointed at Elizabeth, who cowered at the gesture. "I do not want that one."

I could practically see the calculation in Henry's eyes as he looked back and forth between my father and me. Our guarantee of safe passage probably meant Henry couldn't give me to the Green Lady by force, but I doubted it would be any kind of violation if I volunteered. Which meant Henry was currently within his rights, and my dad was within a heartbeat of getting himself in serious trouble.

I didn't think letting my dad and Henry keep up a dialogue was a good thing, so instead of waiting to see who said what next, I broke into a run, surprising everyone around me.

"Dana!" my dad cried, and I was sure the next thing I'd hear was the thundering of his horse's hooves.

I was wrong. The Green Lady was apparently eager to accept my sacrifice, and she quickly lost her humanoid shape and tendrils of thorny vines shot out toward me.

I was a willing sacrifice, but I *am* human (at least mostly), and I couldn't help pulling up short at the sight of those vines reaching for me. The thorns were as long as my fingers, and a hell of a lot sharper.

My dad yelled out something else that I couldn't hear over the thundering of my heart. In seconds, the vines had surrounded me, trapping me in a circle of greenery. A circle that grew darker and darker as the vines packed themselves together around me until I was completely buried within them. If I so much as twitched, I was going to get firsthand knowledge of just how sharp those thorns were.

I'd been feeling really brave a couple of seconds ago, but right now I was so scared I could barely suck in a breath. I closed my eyes, hoping that would make me feel less claustrophobic, and forced myself to think of poor Elizabeth and her terror. Sure, I was scared. But I knew without a doubt that I wasn't as scared as *she* would have been.

"Do not struggle," the Green Lady's voice said. Maybe I was crazy, but I could have sworn there was a touch of gentleness in that voice.

The vines pressed closer, until I could feel the prick of thorns against my skin. I couldn't help the little half-gasp, half-whimper that escaped me.

"Shh," came the Green Lady's voice, coming from all around me. "Be still, and this will not hurt so badly."

And suddenly, the vines contracted around me, driving the thorns into my flesh.

The thorns were everywhere, piercing me from head to toe, and it was all I could do not to scream. My most primitive instincts urged me to struggle, to pull away even though there was no escape, but I fought those instincts. I understood now why the Green Lady told me to be still. I felt like a human pincushion with all of those thorns sticking into me, but although they hurt plenty, the pain was . . . manageable. If I struggled, those thorns would tear me to shreds.

"Well done," the Green Lady said, and just like that, the thorns withdrew from my body and the vines retracted, giving me room to breathe.

My knees were wobbly, and I would have fallen on my butt if several of the vines hadn't wrapped themselves around me—without piercing me with their thorns—and held me up. Greenery still surrounded me, but it was less dense now, allowing light and air into the Green Lady's center. I glanced down at my hands and saw lots of tiny pinpricks of blood. I suspected my whole body looked the same.

"You honor the land with your willing sacrifice," the Green Lady said. "Such courage and generosity of spirit I have not seen for a long, long time."

I almost said a reflexive thank you, then remembered at the last moment that there were certain creatures of Faerie you weren't supposed to say that to. For all I knew, that was nothing but a legend—certainly the Sidhe seemed to have no problem with the words—but instinct told me that if the restriction applied to *any* creatures of Faerie, it would apply to the Green Lady.

My knees steadied, and the vines that held me snaked away.

Then the circle around me receded, and the Green Lady reformed into her humanoid shape. People rushed in to help me, so I didn't see the Green Lady disappear back into the forest.

Ethan was the first to reach me, wrapping me in his arms, practically smothering me. His magic tingled over me, and I knew he was healing the myriad pinprick wounds the Green Lady's thorns had left. I put my arms around him and clung to him, burying my face against his chest, reveling in his warmth and comfort.

"That was one of the bravest, stupidest things you've ever done," he said into my hair. "You just scared ten years off my life."

I let out a little laugh, adrenaline still pumping through my system. "You're immortal, dummy."

"I was before I met *you*," he quipped.

I would have loved to have stayed right where I was, oblivious to the outside world as I reveled in the glory of Ethan's arms. Unfortunately, the outside world had other plans. Henry was barking out orders, trying to get us all mounted up and on the move again. I reluctantly let go of Ethan and found my dad practically on top of us, glowering.

"You'll ride with me the rest of the way," he informed me. The look on his face promised I would *not* have a fun ride.

"Um, maybe I should go back to the wagon," I suggested. "I'm kind of sore . . ."

"Nice try," he said with a strained smile as he gestured his horse over.

I sent Ethan a pleading look, but he held up his hands and backed away. "Not getting in the middle of this one."

"Wise," my dad agreed, giving Ethan a significant look that sent him scurrying.

I expected my dad's lecture to start the moment I groaningly got on the horse behind him. The fact that it didn't just heightened the anticipation—which I'm sure was exactly what my dad wanted.

With the Green Lady no longer blocking the way, our caravan mobilized once more, climbing the hill to the circle of standing stones. It was a tight fit to get all the horses and wagons within the circle, but we managed it, packing into the center, leaving about a foot or two between those of us on the outside of the circle—like my dad and me—and the stones.

Apparently, we were leaving that space so that Henry would have easy access to the stones. On foot, he walked from stone to stone, touching each one and whispering something under his breath. I felt the magic gathering, stronger with each stone Henry touched.

By the time Henry was halfway around the circle, there was enough magic in the air that I had trouble drawing in a full breath. I closed my eyes and concentrated on breathing, knowing it was only going to get worse.

"Dana?" my dad asked, concern in his voice. "Are you all right?"

"Yeah," I said, hoping I sounded convincing. "Just a bit of delayed reaction. And a little freak-out about whatever's about to happen." I sucked in a breath of air, wishing Henry would just get on with it and let go of the magic before I passed out. I *had* to act as normal as possible, unless I wanted everyone in the entire caravan to know I could sense the magic.

"There's no need to 'freak out,'" Dad assured me, the words sounding kind of awkward coming from him. "Using the standing stones requires a lot of magic, but you won't feel anything except for a moment of disorientation."

Yeah, right, I thought as I fought for air.

"Hold on," my dad said. "He's going to activate the stones in a second, and the vertigo can be a bit uncomfortable."

I figured the magic overload was so uncomfortable already I wouldn't even notice a little vertigo on top of it. I was wrong.

You know that feeling you get in the pit of your stomach when a roller coaster is whooshing down a really steep hill? Well imagine that, only ten times worse, and combine it with the feeling of that roller coaster going upside down and sideways at the same time. That would be about how I felt when Henry's magic activated the standing stones.

Even sitting down and holding on to my dad wasn't enough to quell the falling feeling, and if he hadn't held my arms against his body, I might have tumbled off the horse.

The only good news was that the effect didn't last very long. Oh, and that I didn't hurl, though my stomach gave the possibility serious consideration.

When I opened my eyes, we were still in the middle of a circle of standing stones, but these were situated in a broad clearing rather than on the top of a hill. I had to admit, that was rather cool—if also terrifying. The caravan started forward again, following a road that was far broader and more busily trafficked than any we'd yet been on. (Not surprisingly, considering we were now only a couple hours' travel from the Sunne Palace.)

It was once we'd taken our habitual place near the back of the caravan that Dad's not unexpected lecture began.

I bit my tongue and didn't argue with him, because I knew it would do me no good. I hoped I'd never again have to step up to the plate like I had today, but I wasn't about to promise not to. Elizabeth, in her terror, would have been shredded by the Green Lady's embrace, and I would have drowned in guilt if I'd let that happen. I had done the right thing, and nothing my dad said was going to change my mind.

chapter twelve

It was about one hour after we'd passed through the standing stones when we came upon the first real town we'd seen since we'd left Avalon. Of course, this being Faerie, the town was like nothing I'd ever seen before. The Fae—according to my dad—were much more connected to the land than humans. They didn't do row houses or apartment buildings or stuff like that. Even small homes came with at least a couple acres of land.

The homes were designed to blend with the surrounding forest, and some of them did it so well they were almost invisible, walls thickly covered in ivy, rooftop gardens making the whole house look like nothing more than an unusually steep hill. If I didn't look closely at my surroundings I might have thought we were still traveling through uninhabited forest.

The illusion of traveling through empty forest was somewhat lessened when doors and windows opened, and people popped their heads out to watch our procession. I half-expected people to come running out of their houses throwing garlands of flowers—isn't that how pompous princes are supposed to be received when returning home?—but no one did more than stand there and stare.

I know the Fae are way more reserved than humans, so I wasn't *really* expecting such an enthusiastic greeting; however, I couldn't shake the feeling that there was a tinge of disapproval in our reception, like Henry wasn't everyone's favorite person. It didn't help that we were traveling down the only major road, and Henry's people were forcing other travelers off to the side, like they didn't have as much right to be on the road as he did.

No one protested the unfair treatment—stupid Fae class values!—but I caught more than one person shooting irritated and impatient glances our way. Once the prince was far enough past not to see, of course.

I thought after passing those first few houses we might eventually come to some kind of business district, a place with stores or inns or other, more town-like buildings, but the landscape remained the same, small, unobtrusive houses, spaced widely apart. There were no farms, no pastures, no orchards—nothing other than residences.

"Where's the downtown?" I asked my dad.

"You're looking at it," he responded, and I wondered at first if there was more to the houses than met the eye. My father soon clarified. "The Sidhe do not engage in commerce as humans do."

"But they have to get food and supplies from *somewhere*, right?"

"Yes, but those transactions are considered unattractive and are kept out of sight."

"Like Brownies," I grumbled under my breath. "Heaven forbid the Sidhe be seen doing something so vulgar as buying food," I said aloud. My dad just sighed and let the subject drop.

Shortly after we crossed the border into the town, the road stopped all its gentle meandering and straightened out, giving me my first glimpse of the Sunne Palace in the distance.

Fae houses might blend into the background of the surrounding forest, but the palace was very much meant to be seen.

When I'd pictured the Faerie Queen's palace, I'd imagined something beautiful and dainty and feminine. You know, like Cinderella's castle at Disney. The imposing structure that rose out of the trees was about as far from my expectations as it could get.

What met my eyes was a solid, towering wall of stone with a crenellated top, punctuated by tall, skinny windows—arrow slits? Hexagonal towers, made of the same gray stone, rose from each of the corners, with tall, skinny turrets sticking up from the top, making it look like the towers were giving the rest of the world the finger. There was nothing remotely pretty or dainty about the place, and it looked more like a fortress—or a prison—than a palace.

This was a palace meant to remind everyone who caught sight of it that the Queen who resided there was untouchable and steeped in power, meant to intimidate the outside world and defend its Queen from attack. I suppose that considering the history of war between the Seelie and the Unseelie Courts, having a cozy little fortress to hole up in was only practical. No matter how ugly it was.

"I guess subtlety isn't one of Titania's strong suits," I said, keeping my voice down so no one but my dad could hear me.

My dad chuckled softly. "No, it is not. In the eighteenth century, someone brought Titania a sketch of the Caernarfon Castle in Wales, and she fell in love with it. Titania had her palace rebuilt in its likeness, though it's not an exact replica. To the Fae, mortal architecture is considered exotic, and this palace is stunningly beautiful." He laughed again. "In a few hundred years or so, she will probably remodel it to resemble what you Americans would call a McMansion, because that will have become the new pinnacle of the exotic."

"Uh-huh," I said, feeling an uncomfortable flutter of nerves as we approached the forbidding walls. I wouldn't be surprised if instead of a welcome mat, the front door had a sign over it that said ABANDON HOPE ALL YE WHO ENTER HERE. I wanted quite desperately to go home.

The road led right up to a set of massive wooden gates, beyond which was a bustling cobblestone courtyard. The gates were open, but I didn't know if that was the norm, or if someone had seen Prince Henry coming and opened them. I hoped like hell the gates weren't going to close after us. I already had more than enough of a sensation of entering a prison, thank you very much.

The bustle of activity in the courtyard became a downright frenzy as our caravan trickled in. Henry, of course, made sure he was the center of attention, snapping out orders and generally being a self-important spoiled brat. Dad reined his horse to a stop and slid gracefully from the saddle. My own dismount was far less graceful, and I was glad for my dad's steadying hand. I thought I'd been sore after riding solo, but that was nothing compared to my misery after hours of riding double. I kept a nervous eye on the gates, but no one closed them behind us. We weren't trapped, no matter what the hairs on the back of my neck were trying to tell me.

Together, Dad and I rounded up Kimber, Ethan, and Keane, and Dad started leading us to one of the enormous arching entrances.

"What about Finn?" I asked, dragging my feet.

"He'll stay in the Knights' barracks," Dad answered over his shoulder.

"Yeah," Keane said with a sneer, "he's a *Knight,* not a freaking *guest.*"

Dad gave him the same kind of exasperated look he usually gave me when I commented on the Fae class system, but didn't otherwise respond.

At the entrance, my dad was greeted familiarly by several people, one of whom seemed to be something like a butler. The butler gave the rest of us a bit of a snooty look, then led us deeper into the palace, to a suite of rooms where we would stay until the Queen summoned me for the official presentation ceremony.

I expected the inside of the palace to be as gloomy and forbidding as the outside, but it was much more pleasant. The floors were stone, but they were covered by luxuriously thick rugs, all featuring white roses on various jewel-tone backgrounds. The walls, too, were stone, but I could barely see them past the potted plants and climbing white roses that lined them. If I didn't know better, I would have sworn I was walking through a greenhouse. I wondered how the high, narrow window slits provided enough light to keep the plants alive and flourishing. Maybe they didn't need so much light because they were sustained with Fae magic.

The high stone ceilings were all painted with wall-to-wall murals, sometimes depicting the sky, sometimes sunlit nature scenes. I guess that even while living in this stone monstrosity, Titania wanted to keep the illusion that she was one with nature.

The butler directed each of us to our assigned rooms, but as soon as he had hurried off, leaving us to our own devices, Dad shuffled us around. Originally, we had each been given our own room. Dad didn't want me staying alone, so he ordered me and Kimber to share, and he traded rooms with me, making sure that my room was the one farthest down the hall, and thereby putting himself, Ethan, and Keane between me and the main staircase. At least he let Ethan and Keane have their own rooms so the rest of us wouldn't have to worry about them getting into a fight and bringing the palace down around our ears.

"I don't suppose anyone will give you any trouble," my dad said, "but after the incident with the Bogles, I think it's better to be safe."

The room Dad put me and Kimber in was inviting, if a little . . . excessive in its floral theme. Floral carpet, floral bedspread, potted flowers on shelves against one wall, a mural of wildflowers on another. But I couldn't have cared less about the decor once I spotted the bed. I very much looked forward to making its acquaintance, the sooner, the better, but Dad insisted on inspecting the room first. I didn't know what he was looking for. Until he found the doorway against one wall, hidden by an illusion spell. I felt Dad's magic gather, and he cast some kind of spell.

"I can't prevent the door from opening," he told me. "But I've set an alarm spell on it. If it should open, everyone nearby will know it."

For someone who kept insisting Titania's promise of safe passage meant I wasn't in danger, he seemed awfully paranoid. When he left Kimber and me alone in the room, we looked at each other nervously, then started laughing.

"Bogle attacks, Green Ladies, standing stones, secret doorways . . . Was this what you expected when you volunteered to come with me?" I asked Kimber when we got our laughter under control.

She shrugged. "Well, I wasn't expecting a walk in the park. And hey, your first trip to Faerie *should* be memorable, right?"

Oh, I was going to remember this trip all right. And as far as I was concerned, this was both my first and my last trip to Faerie. Nice place to visit, wouldn't want to live there, and all that.

I let out a groan of pleasure as I sank into the feather bed that was even softer than it looked. I could do with a long soak in a hot tub and then a massage, but I figured a late-afternoon nap was the best I could hope for at this point.

"If I never see a horse again, it'll be too soon," I declared as I stretched out on the bed. It occurred to me that I really should have gone in search of a bathroom before even sitting on the bed if I didn't want the covers to smell like horse, but it was too late now. "Try not to wake me up for at least three days."

Kimber snickered. "If you think we're going to have that much time to ourselves, you don't know jack about Faerie hospitality."

Unfortunately, Kimber was right. I hadn't been lying down more than ten or fifteen minutes before my dad came knocking on the door to let us know that Titania was bestowing another "great honor" on us. We'd been invited to dine with Princess Elaine, who was one of the Queen's granddaughters. According to my dad, I couldn't be in the Queen's presence until I'd been officially presented, but the princess would serve as a proxy because Court etiquette required someone play hostess.

The last thing I wanted to do after the exhausting, too-eventful journey was socialize with *anyone,* much less a princess of Faerie who might be cut from the same cloth as Henry. I stifled a groan.

"I suppose it would be a horrendous insult if we declined?" I asked.

Dad laughed like that was really funny. "We have ninety minutes to clean up and get dressed. The servants should deliver your bags shortly, and there are bathrooms at the end of the hall. The dress code is casual, which means wear the dressiest clothes you brought."

Better and better, I thought sourly as I reluctantly abandoned hope of a nap.

We met in the hallway at what my watch said was six thirty. The sun hadn't gone down yet, but there were torches lit anyway. They must have been fueled by magic, because there was no smoke, and when I got close to one, I realized I could feel no heat coming off of it. Then I caught sight of the ceiling, and my jaw dropped.

When we'd been shown to our rooms, the ceiling mural had been of an azure blue sky, artfully dotted with fluffy white clouds. Now the mural depicted a stunning sunset in tones of peach and pink and purple, and the clouds were thin and wispy.

Kimber followed my gaze and smiled. "Cool," she said.

"Yeah," I agreed, but I was more inclined to call it creepy.

My dad had dressed in a charcoal gray suit that looked fantastic on him, especially with the splash of red from his power tie—not that I thought people in Faerie would recognize a power tie when they saw one. Kimber had chosen a light blue sundress paired with cute wedge heels, and I was wearing khakis with a button-down shirt, which was about as dressed up as I ever willingly got. Keane wore his usual all-black, and Ethan had chosen a polo shirt with dress pants. All in all, we were a bit of a motley crew, and we probably looked as silly to the Fae as Prince Henry had looked to me at that state dinner.

I frowned when I realized Finn was nowhere to be seen. I glanced up at my dad, and he read the question on my face before I had a chance to ask it.

"We're in Faerie," he reminded me. "Knights do not dine with royalty. And he would not have felt comfortable sitting at table with us anyway."

I narrowed my eyes at him, though I suppose I should have guessed Finn would be left out. "Then why can Keane come?" I asked.

Out of the corner of my eye, I saw Keane stiffen, and I realized I'd made it sound like I didn't want him coming to dinner with us. "You know that's not what I meant," I said to him.

Keane's face said he was less than mollified. "I can come as your guest because I'm not a Knight. And because I was born and raised in Avalon, I don't give a rat's ass if someone of my 'class' isn't supposed to eat with royalty." His lip curled in his trademarked superior sneer.

"Charming," Ethan muttered. "I'm sure you'll win us all kinds of new friends with that mouth of yours."

I groaned. "Don't you two start!" I warned. "This dinner is going to be long enough already without the rest of us having to play referee."

They both subsided, but the hard feelings between them hadn't exactly been softened by the time they'd spent together on this trip.

Dad led the way down to a smallish dining room on the first floor of the palace. Apparently, there were quite a few dining rooms in the palace, some designed for grand dinners, some for more intimate affairs like this one. Of course, "small" in a palace meant big enough for my entire safe house to fit into.

Like every other room I'd seen in the palace so far, the ceiling, walls, and floor were all stone. And like in every other room, the decor was designed to hide that stone. More rugs, more murals, more plants. The walls were lined with liveried servants, and the entire room was lit by the multitude of candles on the dining table. Everything was both ornate and delicate, from the furniture, to the china, to the silverware. And the male servants' livery included breeches and fluffy white neckcloths, while the women wore ankle-length gowns with bustles.

The princess wasn't there yet, but one of the servants directed us to our assigned seating, and another hurried around the table filling wine glasses. With a start, I recognized Elizabeth. I hoped that didn't mean Henry would be dining with us. I smiled at her as she poured my wine, but she wouldn't meet my eyes. She seemed to be in a perpetual state of fear, and it made me hate Henry just that much more. When I thanked her for the wine, she practically flinched.

"I'm sorry," she said in the faintest of whispers.

I didn't know if she was apologizing for being so jumpy, or for me having to take her place in the Green Lady's embrace. Either way, the apology struck me as a little strange, but she hurried away before I had a chance to respond or ask her what she meant. I guess she was so scared of Henry that she was edgy even when he wasn't around.

I had been seated next to Keane near the head of the table, and I turned to share an inquiring glance with him. He'd noticed Elizabeth's skittishness, too, but he shrugged to indicate he was as clueless as me.

Everyone else picked up their glasses and sipped the wine, but I wasn't much of a drinker, thanks to my mom. And I didn't like the smell of wine, so I suspected I wouldn't like the taste much better. No one talked, the room seeming somehow oppressive in its formality.

There was a very definite sense of waiting, like we weren't allowed to move or even breathe until the princess graced us with her presence. I tried to shake the feeling off, to no avail, and I wished more than ever that I could have a nap, followed by a quiet meal in my room.

The princess kept us waiting for half an hour before sweeping into the room. My dad pushed back his chair and stood when she entered, gesturing for the rest of us to do the same. I was grumpy enough to want to stage a sit-down strike, but I decided that would make this ordeal last even longer.

Stifling a yawn, I appraised our hostess. She looked remarkably like Henry, although the features that looked harsh on him somehow looked lovely on her. Her neck seemed impossibly long, almost swanlike. Her gown of lush green silk glittered with jewels, and despite the bustle—a fashion accessory that looked just plain silly to me—her fashion sense was considerably better than Henry's. The green of the gown was a perfect complement to her green eyes and strawberry blond hair.

She began making the rounds of the table, greeting each one of us by name without need of an introduction, and though the gesture came off just as formal as the room, she seemed a lot less stuck-up than Henry. She had an easy smile, and there was genuine warmth in her eyes.

When she got to me, she took both my hands in hers. "My uncle has told me so much about you," she said, and I realized she meant Henry.

"Umm . . ." I had no idea what to say to that. I seriously doubted Henry had said anything even remotely good.

She patted my hand, laughing lightly. "Never fear, child," she said. "I have always chosen to form my own opinions rather than rely on others'."

I hoped that meant she wasn't a charter member of the Prince Henry fan club. I tried to smile, but the expression felt forced. "Thanks." I felt once again like there were undercurrents I didn't understand here, and I figured my best bet was to say as little as possible. What I didn't say couldn't hurt me. At least, that was my theory. I wished she would let go of my hands, but I didn't want to pull away and be rude.

"I have never been to Avalon," she said, releasing my right hand, but keeping my left and bringing it closer to her face. I realized she was looking at my watch. "This is beautiful," she said, touching the face of the watch gently, as though it might break. I almost laughed, because the watch was a cheap digital with a fake leather band. I'd bought it at a drugstore, and it was about as far from beautiful as could be.

"Is this technology?" The word sounded strangely alien and un-comfortable, like she was trying out a foreign language.

"Um, yeah. I guess."

The princess's gaze slid to my backpack, which I of course had to carry with me even to dinner to preserve my mortal goods. "Have you any other technology you can show me?"

The excitement and eagerness in her voice made me wonder why she'd never gone to Avalon herself. She could have seen a lot more "amazing" things there than what I had in my backpack. But there was no reason for me to say no, so I rooted through the backpack and pulled out my digital camera.

I hadn't taken as many pictures in Faerie as I probably should have, seeing as I was the only person capable of doing it and this was the only time I ever planned to come here. Still, I had a few, and I showed them to the princess one by one. She seemed amazed, if a little unnerved by it, especially when I took a picture of her. The flash made all the servants in the room jump, and I felt an instant surge of magic in the air. Someone in here was more than just an ordinary servant.

"It's just a flash," I hurried to explain. "It's too dark in here to get a good picture without it. See?" I held the camera up, showing everyone the princess's picture. Dad gave me a reproachful look. Maybe I should have known better and should have warned her about the flash in advance, but I hadn't thought of it.

The princess looked at the picture a bit warily, but the magic in the room died down, and I let out an internal sigh of relief.

"Would you like to try taking a picture yourself?" I asked, holding out the camera to her.

There was a hint of wistfulness in her gaze, but she didn't take the camera. "I think I'd best not." She smiled and took a step back from me. I wasn't sure if the flash had made her suddenly afraid of me, or if she had just decided that playtime was over.

"I have been remiss as a hostess," she said, smiling at everyone. It was the kind of practiced smile you see on the face of celebrities who were posing to have their pictures taken, looking ever so slightly false. "Please, take your seats and let us have some dinner."

Princess Elaine moved toward the thronelike chair at the head of the table. The rest of us, taking our cue from my father, remained on our feet. I presumed we were waiting for her to sit first.

The princess touched her chair, and one of the servants hurried forward to pull it out for her. He didn't get the chance.

A deafening boom shattered the stillness of the room, and a wall of heated air punched me in the chest, throwing me to the floor. Flames leapt from the princess's chair, catching on the tablecloth and linens as splinters of wood rocketed through the room like arrows. Smoke and dust filled the air, making it hard to breathe.

I'd fallen hard on my back, and for a moment I lay there in shock, having no idea what had just happened. But the fire was advancing along the tablecloth, the wood beneath it beginning to burn, and I knew I couldn't lie there until I got reoriented. I pushed myself up unsteadily to my elbows and peered through the smoke toward the head of the table.

The princess's chair had been almost completely obliterated, and flames now consumed it. And the princess lay facedown, bloody, and unmoving on the floor beside it.

chapter thirteen

My head ached, and my ears were ringing, and my brain still wasn't quite working at peak capacity. For a moment, I just sat there, staring, coughing as each breath brought more smoke and dust into my lungs.

Everywhere around me, people were screaming. The servant who had been pulling on the princess's chair lay crumpled in a bloody heap against the wall, and it looked like a couple of the other servants who'd been nearby had been hurt as well.

I glanced frantically around, looking for my dad and my friends. Ethan was just staggering to his feet across the table from me, helping Kimber up as he did. Neither of them seemed badly hurt, thank God. Beside me, looking almost as dazed as I felt, Keane pulled a wooden splinter the size of a steak knife out of his shoulder.

"Are you all right?" I yelled at him, probably talking too loud because my ears were ringing.

He coughed and nodded. And then my dad jumped over the flaming table—no doubt assisted by magic. There was blood on his face, and it looked like his suit had been singed, but otherwise he looked okay. He bent and put his arm around me, hauling me to my feet.

"Come on," he said.

Instinctively, I grabbed my backpack, just barely getting a grip on it before my dad shoved me toward the nearest door and beckoned for Keane to follow. A couple of the Fae servants were trying to put out the fire by beating it with their jackets, but that didn't seem likely to work. They needed fire extinguishers, but there weren't any available in Faerie.

"Ethan! Kimber!" my dad shouted over the noise of the flames and the frantic servants. "Come on. Hurry!"

They had to take the long way around the table—I guess Ethan's magic wasn't up to carrying him and Kimber over without them being French fried—and by the time they reached my side, Dad was practically sprinting out the door, still holding my arm.

I stumbled to keep up as my friends followed close behind.

"Where are we going?" I asked. My throat was raw, and I had to cough before I could find my voice again. "People need help in there!"

I tried to slow down, but Dad was having none of it. And Keane pushed on my back, just in case I didn't get the hint.

"A bomb just went off in that room," my dad said to me as we continued to run. "There are no bombs in Faerie."

I coughed again, then checked over my shoulder to make sure Ethan and Kimber were still there. They were. Ethan's face was a study of determination, and Kimber looked pale and shaky, leaning on him a bit as they ran. I hoped she wasn't hurt.

There are no bombs in Faerie. Of course there weren't, not naturally. But with a Faeriewalker in the vicinity . . .

Oh, shit.

I started shaking my head as we ran. We were beginning to pass others who were running the other way, investigating the blast. A couple of them tried to stop us to ask what was going on, but Dad kept forcing us to run.

"They won't think . . ." I started, but I didn't finish the sentence, because oh, yes, they *would* think! I was the only Faeriewalker in the world, and a bomb could only work if it was in a Faeriewalker's presence—and had been for the entire time since that Faeriewalker had crossed the border from Avalon to Faerie. Anyone would assume I was the one who'd brought the bomb.

"Oh my God," I breathed as we pounded down the hallway then burst out of a door into the courtyard. The imposing stone walls and turrets loomed over us menacingly, making me feel even smaller and more scared than I already was. Torches lit the courtyard brightly, but their light didn't reach the tops of the walls, which disappeared into the darkness.

There weren't a whole lot of people around at this time of night, but those who *were* there didn't seem particularly alarmed. I wondered if they'd been able to hear the blast out here with all those layers of stone to muffle it. Maybe even if they had, they wouldn't know what it was, might think it was just thunder.

Dad looked at me with wild, frightened eyes. "You have to keep running," he said to me, pointing toward the gate that we'd passed through earlier today. "Get back to Avalon." He turned to Ethan. "If you have any concealment magic, I suggest you use it. They're confused by the blast right now, but they'll quickly regroup and come after you. I know you're good at magic, but don't risk the standing stones. Take the long way around." Then he turned to Keane. "Keep her safe!" he ordered.

"Wait a minute!" I cried, but Dad wasn't listening to me. I felt magic building around us, and I didn't know whose it was.

"Run," my dad said, giving me a shove.

I was too confused to do more than stumble forward. Okay, I knew things probably looked kind of bad right now, but surely once things settled down, people would realize that I couldn't be the one responsible for the bomb. Right? After all, I wasn't guilty.

Only, it sort of *had* to be me. During the Bogle attack, I'd been carried miles away from the rest of our caravan, so if someone there had brought a bomb with them, meaning to stick close to me until they had a chance to set it off, then their plan would have been foiled. But I'd had nothing with me but my backpack when Phaedra had run away, and I was damn sure there hadn't been a bomb in it.

"Come on," Keane said urgently, grabbing my arm.

"Dad?" I asked, realizing that he was telling us to run but wasn't running himself.

"I'll hold them off as long as I can," he said grimly, then looked back and forth between Keane and Ethan. "Get her out of here before it's too late."

"Wait! No!" I cried, but Ethan grabbed hold of my other arm, and he and Keane started dragging me toward the gate, Kimber limping along behind us.

"We can't leave my dad here alone," I protested, turning a pleading gaze on Keane. "Or yours!"

I had a strong suspicion that if I wasn't around to take the blame, my dad and Finn—wherever he was—would pay the price for me. And if I wasn't around, it would be pretty damn hard to prove my innocence.

"We have to," Keane said, still pulling me. His eyes were glassy, as if he were on the verge of crying, although he was too much of a manly man to allow that to happen.

I still didn't want to go, didn't want to leave my dad and Finn to face the wrath of the Seelie Court. But Ethan, Keane, and Kimber weren't going anywhere without me, and even if I wanted to stay and defend myself, I couldn't in good conscience drag them down with me. Maybe Titania would hold them blameless, maybe she would figure the blame belonged entirely on me and my dad, but I didn't dare take the chance. Dad was telling me to run for a reason, and it wasn't because he expected things to go well when the members of the Court figured out what had happened and decided I had to be responsible.

With a sound somewhere between a sob and another hacking cough, I allowed my friends to drag me away. I looked over my shoulder as we passed through the gate. The last thing I saw before I turned and ran was my father, standing there alone, with those prison-like walls all around him as he prepared for a battle he knew he couldn't win.

We managed to make it through the gate without anyone chasing us, though we weren't exactly inconspicuous, running at top speed as we were. At least we would have the cover of darkness once we got away from the torches that lit the gate area.

"We have to get off the road ASAP," Keane panted, then coughed. It worried me that he was out of breath, seeing as he could usually spar for like an hour without being even slightly winded. How much smoke had we all inhaled?

"No shit, Einstein," Ethan responded, and I couldn't believe he was wasting breath on his feud with Keane at a time like this.

Keane gave him a dirty look, but otherwise didn't respond, which I thought showed admirable restraint. Magic prickled in the air around me, and Ethan pulled me close enough to put his arm around me. "Stay close," he told me. "I've been working on my invisibility spell, and I can cover us with it, at least for a while."

Of course, I had the ability to make myself invisible without Ethan's help. I almost opened my big mouth to tell everyone about the Erlking's brooch, but decided at the last minute not to. Not because I wasn't willing to face their anger at my long deceit—well, yeah, maybe a little because of that—but because I was afraid that if they knew about the brooch, they'd make me use it to run off without them.

There was only so long Ethan's little spell was going to last, and once he ran out of juice, we were probably going to be sitting ducks.

I could already see the strain on his face, and I could only imagine how much power it was taking for him to extend his invisibility shield over all of us while running at top speed. And still coughing from the smoke inhalation, to boot. If I knew my friends at all, if they knew about my brooch, then once Ethan's spell gave out, they'd want me to use the brooch and go on without them. I supposed I'd be safer without them if I could be invisible and they couldn't, but there was no way in hell I was going to abandon them, no matter how practical it might be. I wouldn't have run in the first place if my father and the boys hadn't bullied me into it, and I still felt terrible for leaving my dad and Finn to face the music.

We ran down the road until we rounded a bend that hid us from the view of anyone hanging around the gate, and then Keane directed us off the road and into the trees. Personally, I didn't have high hopes that we were going to evade anyone. It might take a little while for the folks at the palace to figure out what had happened, pin the blame on me, and organize a pursuit, but we were on foot, and we didn't know our way around. Surely we'd have to stick close to the road so we wouldn't get completely lost, and that would make us pretty damn easy to find. At least the heavily forested town gave us some cover.

Ethan slowed down as we crashed through the underbrush, and because he had his arm around me, I was forced to slow down, too. Keane and Kimber both kept going full speed for a moment, then stopped and looked back at us with wide eyes.

"What are you doing?" Keane cried. "We've got to haul ass."

Ethan shook his head. "You can bet they have a tracker who can follow the trail we're leaving." He pointed at a couple of bushes we'd just plowed through. It was dark out here under the trees, although the moon was bright and close to full. I had to be practically on top of the bush to see what Ethan was pointing at, but then I saw a couple of broken branches. If *I* could see our trail, then someone with superior tracking skills would have no trouble picking it up.

"Shite," Keane muttered, and I couldn't have agreed more.

"Well, we can't just stand here!" Kimber said, and she was right, too.

Ethan's brow furrowed. "I can create an illusion to hide our trail if we move slowly enough."

"And by the time we've gotten a hundred yards, they'll be on top of us," Keane argued. "Trail or no trail, we've got to move."

"No point in moving if they're just going to catch up with us immediately," Ethan countered. "We need to hide. They're going to assume we're running like hell for the Avalon border, just like Seamus told us to. If we can hide ourselves, we can let the pursuit go straight past us. Once they're gone, *then* we can get moving again."

"So you want us to just sit here and cower," Keane growled, and there was that curl of his lip again.

I knew the boys were going to keep arguing if I didn't intervene, and we didn't have time for it.

"If you can hide us, do," I said to Ethan, then turned to Keane. "We're not cowering. We're trying to be smart about this, and Ethan's right. Leaving a trail anyone and their brother can follow is going to get us caught real fast."

Keane didn't like it one bit, and I thought he was going to waste more time arguing with me. But I guess it was easier for him to concede the argument to me than to Ethan, because he nodded tightly.

"This had better work," he warned Ethan, giving him a narrow-eyed stare that would have been more intimidating if we weren't running for our lives. If this didn't work, Keane was going to be the least of Ethan's worries.

"It will," Ethan said, though I wondered if that was confidence, or arrogance. "I'll run back to the road and do what I can to hide the evidence of where we veered off." He looked back and forth between the three of us. "If I get caught, I'll holler." His eyes landed on Keane. "If that happens, it'll be up to you to protect the girls."

Kimber punched Ethan in the shoulder. "We're not helpless damsels in distress. We don't need protecting."

Even in the darkness, I could see Ethan rolling his eyes. "Fine, you two protect Keane. Just don't try to play hero if I get caught."

"Don't worry," Keane muttered, "we won't."

Ethan pretended not to hear him, slipping away from us and heading back toward the road. Leaving the three of us alone and strung out on adrenaline in the darkness of the forest.

At first, I could hear the rustle of Ethan's footsteps as he moved away. Then there was nothing but the sound of crickets and the occasional hoot of an owl.

My heart was still thudding in my throat, and I still felt like my lungs were coated with soot. I didn't dare cough, not when the road was so close by, but the very fact that I didn't dare cough made the urge even stronger.

Keane had taken a couple steps toward the bushes through which Ethan had disappeared, putting himself between Kimber and me and the road. He probably thought he was being subtle, but you could bet that if Ethan shouted an alarm, Keane would stand there to cover our retreat while ordering Kimber and me to run. What he could do to protect us when he was apparently unarmed, I didn't know.

And that was when I remembered the gun my father had given me before we'd set out. Like every other mortal artifact I'd brought with me, it was in my backpack. I wasn't sure I could shoot anyone, even in self-defense, and I doubted killing our pursuers would make my situation any better, but at least I didn't have to feel completely helpless.

Moving as quietly as possible, I slid the backpack off my shoulders and lowered it to the ground. Keane jerked at even the small noise I made, turning to me and putting his finger to his lips. I ignored his furious look, digging through the backpack until I found the case at the very bottom.

When I pulled out the small silver gun, Keane gaped at me. I hadn't told anyone I had it. Kimber looked at me with a raised eyebrow, but she seemed less shocked and more amused by my possession of a firearm. I stood up slowly, keeping the gun pointed at the ground and the safety on.

"Do you know how to use that thing?" Keane asked in a whisper so quiet you could almost mistake it for the wind.

I put my finger to my lips, happy to be able to return his gesture, then nodded. Hey, he only asked me if I knew how to use it, not if I was any *good* at using it. I think he read between the lines, based on the look of pure skepticism he gave me.

"Just don't shoot me in the back," he said, and this time both Kimber and I put our fingers to our lips. He shook his head and turned back to face the remnants of our trail.

We were quickly back to the oppressive silence, although soon an unfamiliar, high-pitched whine added to the cricket-and-owl chorus. I hoped it was just some harmless kind of Fae insect or frog rather than some terrifying night-stalking monster. I comforted myself that neither Kimber nor Keane seemed alarmed by it.

The quiet of the night made it easier to hear the pounding sound of horses' hooves on the road, nowhere near far enough away for my tastes. Kimber reached over and took my hand, squeezing my fingers and biting her lip. I squeezed right back, my heart racing once more as the sound of hooves got closer.

Had Ethan had enough time to cast his illusion spell? It seemed like he'd been gone forever, but time tends to get sort of wonky when you're in danger, so I wasn't sure. I flicked the safety off my gun, though I was careful to keep it pointed at the ground and to keep my finger off the trigger. It would be ready for use if worse came to worst, but it would be my absolute last resort.

I couldn't tell from the sound how many horses there were in the pursuit, but it sure sounded like a lot. I heard at least four distinct voices as the Fae search party called to each other. They were moving pretty fast by the sound of it. I hoped that meant they were moving *too* fast and wouldn't notice any telltale signs of our passage even if Ethan hadn't had enough time to cover us.

I held my breath and squeezed Kimber's hand more tightly as the sounds moved ever closer . . . And then moved past, without stopping. The relief made me practically dizzy, and I could see Keane's shoulders relax as some of the tension drained out of him.

We all listened intently as the search party continued down the road, but there were no shouts of alarm, and no indications that they were turning back. As the sound of the horses faded into the distance, I heard the rustle of undergrowth, and then Ethan appeared before us seemingly out of nowhere.

Keane jumped, and it was probably a good thing he didn't have the gun, or Ethan would have gotten shot for the second time since I'd met him. Ethan smirked at his nemesis, and though it was too dark to see, I'd have bet anything Keane's face was turning a uniquely angry shade of red.

"It's just me," Ethan said unnecessarily.

"You're lucky I'm not armed," Keane said, echoing my sentiments.

"I guess it worked?" I asked, hoping to head the two of them off at the pass.

Ethan made a face, but nodded. "It will keep them off our tail for the time being. I made sure the illusion covered any tracks we might have made near the road, but it only reaches about ten yards into the forest. It'll hold during the night, but when daylight hits, it's likely someone will start combing the woods and see around the illusion."

Ethan's face looked pale in the moonlight, and he swayed ever so slightly on his feet. He'd probably expended more energy than was wise creating his illusion, especially after inhaling a ton of smoke and then running like hell. Not that he was going to admit it.

"So we need to put as much distance as possible between us and the palace before the sun rises," Keane said, stating the obvious.

"Without getting ourselves hopelessly lost," Kimber muttered.

"Or getting eaten by Bogles," I added, because hey, if we were going to be so cheerful and optimistic, we might as well go all out. "Who has the best sense of direction? I know it isn't me."

All three of my friends stifled laughs at that. I'd have been offended if I'd been the least bit sensitive about my ability to get lost in a closet.

"Um, that would probably be me," Kimber said, surprising me—and Keane, by the look on his face.

Ethan nodded. "No doubt about it," he agreed, then grinned at Keane. "Unless you've got bloodhound in your family tree we don't know about."

"The only hound here is you," Keane retorted.

Kimber and I gave stereo groans, and both the boys shut up, though not without giving each other macho glares.

"Lead the way," I prompted Kimber, then flicked the safety back on my gun and stuck it in my pocket. Ethan noticed it for the first time, but though he gave me an inquiring look, I didn't comment, and he didn't ask any questions.

Trusting Kimber to keep us from straying too far from the road, we all fell into step behind her and started making our way through the darkened forest toward the impossibly distant Avalon border.

chapter fourteen

This may come as a shock, but traveling on foot through unfamiliar woods in the dark of night is not easy. The moon was high in the sky, and when there was any break in the tree cover, a fair amount of its light would reach the forest floor. We trudged onward, making painfully slow progress as we tried not to leave too obvious a trail and tried to avoid the houses that were so skillfully hidden in the trees.

My full-blooded Fae companions seemed to have better night vision than I did, although even they struggled as the night wore on and the moon sank lower in the sky, hiding its light little by little. We were all stumbling over tree roots and getting whacked in the face by unseen branches, probably leaving a trail that could be spotted from orbit, and there wasn't a thing we could do about it. Obviously, we'd be able to move more easily in the morning; but then, so would our pursuit.

I tried really hard not to think about what might have happened to my dad and Finn once the rest of us had fled. I felt like a total coward for leaving them behind, and I kept halfway deciding that I had to turn back immediately. Then I'd wake up and realize that if I decided to go back, either my friends were going to stop me, or they were going to come with me. There were already enough people I cared about in trouble because of me. If I had a chance of getting my friends to safety, then I had to take it.

Who had really planted that bomb? I kept stumbling against the fact that for a bomb to work, it would have had to be in my presence continually since we'd left Avalon. The more I tried to figure out how I could have unknowingly carried a bomb—and how, if I'd been carrying it, it ended up under the princess's chair—the more frustrated and stumped I became.

Stress had done a hatchet job on my brainpower. When the answer to the riddle came to me, it was so obvious I stopped in my tracks and slapped myself on the forehead. The bomb had to have been planted by a Faeriewalker. I hadn't planted the bomb. Therefore . . .

"Duh!" I said as the others stopped around me. "I'm not the only Faeriewalker in the world after all!"

The boys both gaped at me, but Kimber just looked grim. "So it would seem," she said, and I realized she'd figured it out on her own.

"The redhead," Keane said, then said something Gaelic-sounding that I was pretty sure was a curse.

"What redhead?" Ethan asked.

"Elizabeth," I said, remembering how jumpy she'd acted at the dinner, the apology that had come out of nowhere, and the way she'd refused to meet my eyes. And realizing that she—like most of the women in Henry's entourage—always wore a bustle in her skirts. You could probably hide a whole suitcase full of mortal items in one of those things. Maybe she hadn't been apologizing for what happened with the Green Lady after all. Maybe she'd been apologizing in advance for framing me.

"Who's Elizabeth?" Kimber asked with a frown.

"The redheaded girl who served us wine at dinner," Keane answered. "She was one of Henry's servants, wasn't she?" he asked me.

I nodded. "Yeah. She's been with us all the way from Avalon." Hers had been the only familiar face I'd spotted in the dining room, though I had to admit I hadn't been looking all that closely. "But she can't be more than, like, fourteen years old," I said, appalled.

"She's completely terrified of Henry," Keane said. "I'm sure she'd do anything he ordered her to, even if she didn't like it. And it would explain why she was serving at the dinner. I doubt Henry's usually terribly anxious to share his servants."

I remembered the terror in her eyes, and I remembered the abuse Henry had heaped upon her. The poor thing was thoroughly downtrodden. The evidence suggested she was the one who'd planted the bomb, that she was the one who'd tried to kill the princess—and maybe succeeded—while framing me for it. But there was no doubt in my mind that it was Prince Henry who was really behind it.

Kimber was nodding. "You said Titania claimed not to have been behind the threats against you. Can you imagine being a power-hungry asshole like Henry and having a secret Faeriewalker under your thumb? I bet you someone like him would do *anything* to make sure his was the only Faeriewalker in the world. So he sent those Knights to threaten you, figuring everyone would assume it was Titania who sent them. And as long as they didn't kill you, there'd be no reason for your father to confront Titania and find out the Knights weren't hers."

"Guess he must have been thrilled when she sent him to invite me to Court," I said. But I couldn't be terribly satisfied by the thought of his annoyance. "We're letting him get away with it," I said bitterly. "By running away, I'm making myself look guilty. Guiltier than I already looked, I mean."

"You have no choice," Keane said. "I haven't spent a whole lot of time in Faerie, but I do know that it's not famous for its fair and impartial justice."

"He's right," Ethan said, making a face to show how little he enjoyed agreeing with Keane. "You wouldn't even be entitled to a trial if the Queen was pissed off enough not to give you one. If we hadn't gotten you out of there, you might have been summarily executed. You could be dead already." His voice went low and raspy, and he pulled me into an unexpected hug.

His words sent a chill racing down my spine. It was one thing to imagine myself locked up and subjected to the Fae version of a trial, but another to think about being judged guilty without being given a chance to defend myself. Not that I thought speaking out in my own defense would do much good—if we were right, it was the Queen's own son who was behind the bombing, and she most likely wouldn't *want* to find him guilty. I made a really easy scapegoat.

Ethan squeezed me tighter, and I burrowed my face into his chest, wishing I could hide there in his arms forever. His shirt stank of smoke, and the temperature was somewhere in the eighties, making it way too hot for cuddling, but for the moment, I didn't care.

"We have to keep moving," Keane said.

With a sigh of regret, I eased myself out of Ethan's arms. Maybe if we managed to evade capture and get all the way back to Avalon, I'd be able to find someone who could help my dad and Finn. Dad was a citizen of Avalon, after all, and considering his political influence, the Council might want to negotiate for his release. Titania might even give in to keep the peace between Avalon and Faerie.

The hope felt fragile, and I wasn't sure that even if things happened exactly the way I hoped, Finn would be released with my dad. I wasn't even sure whether Finn was an Avalon citizen or not, and he certainly didn't have my dad's influence.

Of course, all of this would be a moot point if the Queen had already had them both killed.

"Should we try for the standing stones?" Kimber asked as we started picking our way through the darkness. "I know Seamus said not to, but it'll take us ten times as long to get to Avalon if we have to walk the whole way."

"I think I can work them, even if it's daylight when we get there," Ethan said, though his tone didn't exactly fill me with confidence.

Keane shook his head. "It's too risky. Even supposing you've got enough juice left to activate the stones and enough power to control them, you can be sure Titania will have already dispatched Knights to guard it."

We absorbed that unpalatable reality in silence for a moment.

"The long way it is," I finally said, and tried not to think about how slim our chances were.

I don't know how long we traveled that night, though it felt like it was about twelve hours. We all held our breaths every time we had to sneak past one of the Fae houses, but no one spotted us, and eventually the houses petered out and the woods thickened. When the moon disappeared over the horizon, the only hint of light came from the stars. And as if that wasn't enough to slow us to a crawl, clouds started coming in and the wind started to pick up. In the distance, there was a flash of lightning and a roll of thunder.

"Oh great," I said as I tripped over yet another tree root. "I've always wanted to walk through the woods in a thunderstorm."

The way my luck was going, I'd be crisped by a bolt of lightning.

The first drop of rain plopped on my nose just a few seconds later, quickly followed by another. When the lightning flashed, the thunder followed more closely on its heels.

"We'd better find a ditch or something to hole up in," Keane said. "If we stay close enough together, I can stretch my shield spell to cover all of us. I don't know if it will hold against lightning, but it's better than nothing."

"I don't need your protection," Ethan protested, all offended dignity.

"Fine," Keane snapped. "Use your own shield spell. Or go climb a tree and play lightning rod. I don't care."

Even in the oppressive darkness, I could see the way Ethan's eyes glittered, and I hoped he wasn't going to start something with Keane. Judging by how the wind was kicking up, we didn't have time for it. The temperature had dropped at least ten degrees in the last few minutes, and the rain that had at first felt almost refreshing now just felt cold.

"Let's just find that low ground, shall we?" Kimber said, stepping between the boys. She gave her brother a quelling look. "Have you suddenly developed a shield spell I didn't know about? Because if you haven't, then you're going to use Keane's just like the rest of us."

"I'm sure I can learn to cast one myself," Ethan countered, and magical whiz-kid that he was, he probably could.

Kimber nodded. "Yeah, play around with learning a new spell when you're in a life-threatening situation. That's real smart. We'll all be sooo impressed. Right up until you get yourself killed or maimed because you don't have all the kinks worked out yet."

Ethan scowled fiercely, but he had to know Kimber was right. He wasn't happy about it, but at least he stopped arguing.

The rain came more heavily as we scanned the area for somewhere safe we could hole up. The prospects weren't promising. The terrain was generally flat, and most of the places that looked vaguely shelter-like were actually the insides of trees. The harder the rain fell, the more tempting those hollows looked, but the escalating thunder and lightning reminded us that trees are nature's lightning rods.

We were getting close to desperate when we found a huge tree that had fallen, pulling up a massive clod of dirt in its roots when it did. It must have fallen recently, since you could still see the hole in the ground where it must have stood.

It wasn't much, more like a divot when we wanted a ditch, but we all agreed it was the best we could do. The sharp crack and crash of another tree falling somewhere in the darkness had us hurrying into the hollow's questionable shelter. The wind was now howling, the tone almost musical. I hoped that wasn't the sound of some bloodthirsty Fae storm-critter out for a hunt.

"Everyone stay close to me," Keane said, and I felt the spark of his magic starting up.

I sat down beside Keane in the mud and tried not to notice the spark of jealousy that lit Ethan's eyes. Kimber sat on Keane's other side, and Ethan plopped down beside me and put a possessive arm around my shoulders.

"Closer," Keane said, shifting until his hip and leg were pressed up against mine. I didn't know if he was doing it because his shield spell didn't stretch far enough, or if he was just trying to annoy Ethan. The tension in Ethan's body told me how *he* interpreted the gesture.

Ethan got even more tense—which I hadn't thought was possible—when Keane put his arm around Kimber and drew her onto his lap. Kimber couldn't hide her surprise or her pleasure as she cuddled up against him, and I really hoped he wasn't doing it just to get at Ethan. Kimber deserved better.

"Are you covered?" I asked Ethan, because he was the farthest away from Keane. To emphasize the danger, a heavy branch crashed to the ground just a few feet away from our hiding place. Every time the wind gusted, the raindrops flew parallel to the ground, and the trees were bent practically double. I hoped they didn't have tornados in Faerie.

"I'm covered," Ethan assured me through gritted teeth.

"Don't be an asshole," Keane said. "My shield isn't reaching that far and you know it. Sit next to me and put Dana on your lap."

At first, I thought Ethan's macho pride was going to get the best of him and he was going to refuse—at which point I'd have had to resort to drastic measures to make him act like a sensible adult. (Don't ask me what those measures would have been, because I'm nowhere near as good at bullying as the guys are.) Luckily, Ethan didn't make that necessary, though he grumbled darkly under his breath as he pulled me onto his lap and shifted reluctantly closer to Keane.

The hail started coming down just then, nuggets the size of marbles pounding onto the ground—and onto Ethan's right leg and shoulder, which apparently were still outside the shield.

"For God's sake!" Keane snapped. "I don't have cooties and I'm not going to bite."

Ethan probably was going to snap right back, but Kimber shifted on Keane's lap until she could reach out and put her arm around Ethan's shoulders, pulling him flush up against Keane's side. Figuring she had the right idea, I shifted my own weight and grabbed Ethan's leg, dragging it under the shield. If it offended his manly sensibilities to sit so close to another guy, tough! Even the few hailstones that had hit me while I reached past the shield spell to grab him had stung like hell, and they seemed to be getting bigger.

Ethan was totally fuming, hating every second of being forced to accept Keane's protection. Keane wasn't exactly making things easier, but at least he hadn't hesitated to offer that protection, no matter how he felt about Ethan. I rested my head against Ethan's shoulder, and when that didn't lessen the tension in his body, turned my head and brushed a kiss across his neck.

His skin felt warm and smooth beneath my lips, and I heard the way his breath hitched even over the howl of the wind and the pounding of the hail. I kissed him again, a little higher, and the angry tension he'd radiated moments ago dissolved into a different kind of tension altogether.

Yes, I was a little self-conscious with Keane and Kimber right there beside us, but Ethan needed the distraction, and I needed the comfort. I let my kisses travel up the side of Ethan's neck while he conveniently lowered his head and turned his face toward me.

I was wet, I was cold, sitting outside in a ditch during a dangerous thunderstorm, but when Ethan's lips came down on mine, it was like I'd been momentarily transported to heaven. I didn't have a whole lot of experience with kissing, but I was sure Ethan was one of the best kissers in the universe. My traitorous mind conjured the image of the Erlking and the wild, ravenous kiss we'd shared under the influence of magic, but I shoved the thought away. That hadn't been a real kiss, nor had my reaction been real pleasure, not like it was when I kissed Ethan.

Ethan's tongue was teasingly licking my lips as his arms crushed me against him. I had no complaints, melting into his arms and kissing him back eagerly. His hand slipped under the hem of my shirt. It was a relatively innocent caress, his fingers touching the skin of my lower back, but I felt a little pang, knowing these innocent caresses were all we would ever have. I told myself to live in the moment and not think about it. But I'm not good at not thinking about things, and though the kiss still felt good, the thrill was suddenly dampened—no pun intended. No, Ethan and I weren't going to get it on here in front of Keane and Kimber even if the Erlking's bargain weren't coming between us, but I couldn't enjoy even this simple kiss without worrying about everything I *couldn't* do.

I think Ethan sensed me cooling off, because he sighed against my lips then pulled away, tucking my head under his chin. My throat tightened and my eyes burned, but I refused to cry. Somehow, I was going to find a way to be happy with what I had rather than pining for what I couldn't have, but I hadn't managed it yet.

Ethan went tense under me again, and it was as if our whole little make-out distraction session hadn't happened. From the feel of his chin on my head, I could tell he was looking at Keane, so I turned to look myself, ready to jump in and stop them from fighting again if necessary.

Kimber was cuddled in Keane's arms in a pose very similar to my own, her head against his chest. One of his arms was around her shoulder, and the other rested lightly on her thigh. There was a little smile on her face that said she was happy to be there, and I knew she was probably thrilled that Keane was touching her like that. But Keane was barely paying any attention to her and was instead locked in a staring match with Ethan. I wanted to slap them both, but I kept my feelings to myself, because if I opened my big mouth I'd only make things worse. The storm might have been getting a little less savage, but the lightning was still too close for comfort, and I couldn't risk that testosterone would make the boys do something stupid that might get us all killed. So instead, I took one for the team, grabbing hold of Ethan's head and planting another kiss on him.

My valiant sacrifice did the trick, and Ethan and Keane didn't try to kill each other. Considering the absolutely rotten day we'd just had, I chose to take that as a good sign.

By the time the storm died out completely and the clouds cleared, the first hints of sunrise were coloring the horizon.

Keane's shield spell had more than likely saved our lives. The forest floor was littered with broken branches, some of them slim and harmless, some of them as big as small trees all by themselves. One of those big branches lay across the ditch beside us, where it had come to rest after bouncing off of Keane's shield spell.

The shield spell had died before the storm had. Keane practically passed out straining to keep it up, but eventually he ran out of strength and we all huddled miserably together in the soaking rain and blustering wind. Luckily, the thunder and lightning had moved on, and the wind wasn't ripping trees apart anymore.

It was tempting to just lie there in the mud and take a nap. It had been an exhausting night, and none of us had been able to sleep under the circumstances. But we were all too wet and miserable to sleep, and we had to take advantage of the daylight to get farther away from the Sunne Palace and the Queen's forces. The storm had actually done us a huge favor, wiping out any trail we might have left, but it wasn't like any of us felt even remotely secure. I didn't know how far we had traveled in the night before the storm stopped us, but I *did* know it wasn't far enough.

We dragged ourselves to our feet and started moving again, trusting that Kimber was leading us in the right direction. In some ways, the going was easier because of the light, but we were all a hell of a lot more exhausted than we'd been the night before, and that made even the Fae clumsy. It didn't help that the ground was muddy from the storm, sucking at our feet and making everything slippery.

Keane in particular was struggling, having used so much of his energy shielding us last night. Being a typical male, he was unwilling to admit it—especially in front of Ethan—but we could all see the dark circles forming under his eyes, and he was even more unsteady on his feet than I was. By the time we'd walked for a couple of hours, his eyes had glazed over and he moved with all the speed and grace of a zombie.

"We need to rest," Kimber said suddenly, startling us all because we'd barely spoken two words since we'd gotten started this morning.

"We're still too close to the palace," Ethan immediately protested.

"We can't afford a rest, not when we sat there not moving for hours last night."

Kimber was about to retort, but she fell silent, her face going pale.

"What?" I asked, looking frantically around. "What is it?"

But then the rest of us heard it too: the baying of hounds in the distance. Not anywhere near distant enough, either.

"Shite," Ethan and Keane said together, and I didn't have anything better to add. I doubted a mortal bloodhound would have much trouble catching our trail, and I knew that Fae hounds would be even better at tracking than mortal ones.

"Is it my imagination, or are they getting closer?" Kimber asked in a small voice.

"They're getting closer," Keane said. "Come on, we've got to run!"

It wasn't hard to catch his sense of urgency, and we all took off running through the trees, painfully aware of the baying of the hounds growing louder. There was no way we were outrunning dogs, but we weren't going to just sit there and wait for them to catch us.

"Would your shield spell keep the dogs from smelling us?" I panted at Keane as we ran. Not that I thought he had enough strength to cast it after last night.

He shook his head. "I wish."

I turned to Ethan. "You got anything?"

"Nothing!" he said, grabbing my arm and urging me to run faster.

I was already stumbling from exhaustion, and I was never as graceful as the full-blooded Fae anyway. When I tried to eke a little more speed out, the tip of my shoe caught on something, and I went sprawling. Ethan was there hauling me to my feet practically before I hit the ground. I managed one more hunched-over stumble-step, and then went down again, realizing I was still tangled up in whatever I'd tripped on.

And that was when I noticed the tendril of ivy wrapped around my ankle.

"Come on!" Keane urged, he and Kimber coming back to me as Ethan tried again to yank me to my feet.

The ivy didn't let go, and soon a sea of it flowed toward us, creeping out from behind bushes and crawling down the trunks of the trees.

I swallowed a scream as the ivy leapt into the air, tendrils raining down around us, forming a dense green wall, trapping us. Familiar, needle-sharp thorns sprung from the vines, though the Green Lady made no attempt to prick us with them.

"Be still and be silent," a disembodied voice ordered us, and I don't think any of us was inclined to argue. Not with all those thorns pointing our way. I slipped my hand into Ethan's as we crouched within the shelter of the ivy. Beside us, Kimber was clutching Keane's arm, and he was looking a little wild-eyed.

The baying of the hounds drew nearer and nearer, and I felt the vibration of hoofbeats, though I couldn't hear the horses over the racket the dogs were making. It sounded like the dogs were right on top of us.

Suddenly there was a rustling sound and a dog gave a high-pitched yip. The baying stopped, replaced by anxious-sounding whimpers. Moments later, I finally heard the sound of hooves. The horses came to a stop, and a man's voice shouted, "Let us pass."

"You will pass when you have paid the toll," the Green Lady said.

I'd assumed this was the same Green Lady who'd accepted my blood sacrifice, but her voice sounded subtly different.

The man made an impatient sound. "We have no suitable sacrifice to offer, and we are in pursuit of a fugitive from the Queen's justice. Let us pass!"

"Come back when you have a suitable sacrifice," the Green Lady said. "Until then, you will go no farther."

The man said something I figured was probably a curse, though I didn't recognize the language.

"You are impeding the Queen's justice!" he said, all offended-sounding.

"I am within my rights," the Green Lady replied. "There is no requirement that my tolls be extracted only upon roads, and I choose to extract one here. Surely you do not begrudge the land its nourishment."

There was some grumbling. Our pursuers most definitely did begrudge the land, but none of them was stupid enough to say so. Depending on how thoroughly tied the Green Lady was to the land, she probably could make the lives of anyone who annoyed her pretty damn difficult.

"The fugitives you are aiding plotted the assassination of the Queen's granddaughter," the lead pursuer tried again. "Every moment we spend arguing increases the chances that they will escape the punishment they deserve."

It was only then that I realized the Green Lady was hiding us so thoroughly that our pursuers didn't even know we were there.

"Then you'd best hurry back with your sacrifice, don't you think?" the Green Lady said, and there was no missing the hint of annoyance in her voice. Her leaves rustled, and I imagined she was making an impressive display of her thorns.

The man cursed again, but soon afterward, we heard him stomp away. Then we heard the hoofbeats as the riders retreated, taking their chastened and whimpering hounds with them.

When we could no longer hear the echo of the horses' hooves, the Green Lady's vines receded, forming themselves into a tall woman in a flowing green gown.

"I will delay them until the sun goes down," she said. "I would merely have waited until they brought me a sacrifice, but their arrogance and rudeness requires they be taught a lesson. Their hounds will be unable to scent you until I allow it."

I swallowed my urge to say thank you. "Would it be rude for me to ask why you're helping me?"

"You gifted my sister with the treasure of a willing sacrifice. As you have seen, the Sidhe are no longer as gracious about providing sacrifice as they were of old. It is time to remind them of the importance of good manners."

"Is there any chance you could help us get to the standing stones without being caught?" Ethan blurted.

Kimber's eyes widened, and she punched Ethan in the arm. "Shut up, Ethan!" she hissed.

The Green Lady didn't have any features on her face, and yet even so I could feel the glare she turned on Ethan, who held his hands up and tried to look innocent.

"Sorry. I was just asking. I'm not a native of Faerie. I don't know the rules, and I apologize if I just broke one."

The Green Lady kept her disapproving gaze on Ethan. "If you don't know the rules, then perhaps it's best not to speak." She swept her gaze over all of us, and we obediently kept our mouths shut. "The standing stones you used to travel here will be heavily guarded. I'd advise you to avoid them. However, there is another set you can try for, one they will not expect you to know about and will be less likely to guard. Depending on how fast you travel, you should find a small stream sometime tomorrow. It runs parallel to the road for several miles, and then turns west. Follow it when it turns, and it will lead you to the standing stones. They will take you to another set that is close to Avalon's southern border."

The Green Lady's words kindled a spark of hope in my chest. Instead of traveling through these woods for days, or even weeks, dodging pursuit and hoping the elements didn't finish us off, we could reach Avalon as soon as tomorrow. Our flight might not be as impossible as we'd thought. I refused to let myself think about how many problems I would still have once I reached the safety of home.

"Go now," she said, her voice cold. "I will delay your pursuers as promised."

She started to lose shape, apparently finished with our conversation. Her head melted into her body, and then the vines became just a tangle of greenery, creeping away into the forest, blending with the underbrush until all traces of the Green Lady vanished.

chapter fifteen

We walked until we were ready to drop, keeping ourselves relentlessly moving despite our exhaustion, determined to put as much distance behind us as possible before we lost the Green Lady's protection. A couple of times, we heard hounds baying in the distance, but it was always far away.

Around midday, we found a little ground-fed spring and each drank about five gallons of water to ease our parched throats. A little later, we found a patch of what looked like blackberries, and we were hungry enough to eat them even though they didn't *taste* like blackberries, and we all knew eating mysterious berries wasn't the brightest idea. Lucky for us, there was no sign of them being poisonous—i.e., no one got sick or died—and I wondered if the Green Lady was giving us a little extra help, helping us find just enough food and water to keep going.

It wasn't till the sun went down that we finally admitted we had to stop and get some rest. After last night's rainstorm, the temperature never quite got back up to what it had been, and as the sun disappeared, the temperature took a nosedive. I'd never once been cold on the journey in, but tonight the breeze gave me goose bumps. And that was *before* the misty drizzle started.

We groaned in chorus. The drizzle was just enough to dampen our clothes and make us all clammy without being enough to provide us with any water. We ate the last of the blackberries—or whatever they were—as we searched for another place to hide for the night. The trees here didn't have any convenient hollows, and the ground continued to be flat, not even providing any rocks we could use as shelter from the wind.

Eventually, too tired to move another step, we made our halfhearted camp among the roots of an enormous tree. It blocked a bit of the wind, and the drizzle had subsided, but we were all shivering in our damp clothes. Well, *I* was shivering. The Fae weren't much affected by the cold, but that didn't mean they were comfortable. We huddled together, me with Ethan and Kimber with Keane, but there was no kissing or teasing or secret smiles. Even the shot of hope the Green Lady had given us, the hope that tomorrow night we might sleep in our own beds, wasn't enough to lift us out of our misery.

After about a half hour, Ethan rose to his feet. "I'm going to collect some firewood," he announced.

Keane snorted. "Oh, yeah, that's a good way to hide. Light a fire that anyone can see. With wet wood, I might add."

Ethan scowled at him. "I can create a localized illusion that will hide us and the fire. And I don't care how wet the wood is, I can make it burn."

Usually, Keane would have argued more, but I think he was too tired to bother. "Fine, do what you want," he said, then laid the back of his head against the tree and closed his eyes.

"Stay close," Kimber warned as Ethan moved away. He spared time for a "well, duh" look before he disappeared into the darkness.

· · ·

Ethan was as good as his word, returning to our makeshift camp with an impressive pile of branches. It took a while to get them burning, since he didn't have a handy "light wet wood on fire" spell ready. From what I understand of magic, most of the Fae would take hours or even days of practice before they could train the magic to do a new spell, but Ethan managed it in about fifteen minutes. I could tell even Keane was impressed, though he would never dream of admitting it. At least Ethan refrained from acting all smug.

I can't say we were exactly comfortable after that, but the fire was a welcome relief, and our silence as we huddled around it was almost companionable.

It didn't take long for us to start yawning, the warmth of the fire making us even sleepier than we already were. We set up a watch schedule, because even though we'd neither seen nor heard signs of pursuit in the last several hours, it was still out there. Ethan took the first watch, and the rest of us curled up on the damp ground.

Exhaustion pulled me into sleep with alarming speed. My dreams were filled with images of blood and death and a man in a hideous horned mask chasing me down darkened roads. The man in the mask chased me into a dead-end alley, and I came to a stop in front of a high brick wall I could never climb. Heart pounding in my throat, I turned to watch helplessly as the man in the mask—the Erlking, I remembered with a sudden start—stalked down the alley toward me.

"My magic can destroy you," I reminded him, then started to hum under my breath.

"I don't think so," the Erlking responded, and though I couldn't see his face behind the mask, I heard amusement in it.

I kept humming as he continued to approach, but the magic was coming only sluggishly to my call. Unlike the flood I was now used to, there was only a trickle, and terror almost stole my voice.

The Erlking was too close. I couldn't wait any longer or he would have me, so even though I hadn't gathered enough magic to do much of anything, I let loose my screaming high note.

He was on me before the sound rose from my throat, his hand clamped over my mouth, trapping my scream. I flailed.

And woke up to find a hand over my mouth and my wrists held together in a bruising grip. But it wasn't the Erlking's eyes burning into mine, it was Ethan's.

My first thought was that I'd been thrashing around, having a nightmare, and Ethan was trying to keep me quiet so I wouldn't draw any search parties. Still sweating from the terror of my dream, I forced myself to relax in his grip and signal to him that I was awake. But he didn't let go of me.

Ethan dragged me to my feet, one hand still clamped over my mouth, his other arm wrapped around my waist, trapping my own arms at my sides. His grip was bruisingly tight, and he didn't ease up when the pained whimper of protest rose from my throat. Then, he started to drag me off into the forest.

I didn't know what the hell was going on, but I *did* know something was horribly wrong with this scenario. Ethan was hurting me, dragging me away from the campfire and my sleeping friends. But I hadn't suffered through all my self-defense lessons with Keane for nothing.

I stopped struggling against Ethan's hold, then stomped down hard on his instep. He cried out in pain, the sound jerking both Keane and Kimber out of sleep. They jumped to their feet while, wincing, I took advantage of Ethan's distraction to give him an elbow to the gut.

I didn't have the courage to do it very hard—this was *Ethan!*—but it was enough to make him let go. I whirled around to face him, opening my mouth to ask him what the hell he thought he was doing. But Ethan had already recovered from my admittedly wimpy blow, and before I could get a word out, his fist was swinging toward my face.

A few weeks ago, I'd have been helpless in this situation, and even now shock made me a little slow. But Keane's training kicked in again, and I managed to block the punch with my arm. It hurt like hell, but better to take a punch on the arm than in the face. Ethan took another swing while I was still reeling, but that blow never landed because Keane jumped in between us.

The air filled with the prickle of magic, and the boys swung at each other furiously.

"What is going on?" Kimber wailed, coming to my side and reaching out helplessly toward her brother and Keane.

I'd have answered her if I had a clue, but I could only stare in horror as my friends tried to pound the crap out of each other.

Ethan never had a chance. Not with Keane's skill at hand-to-hand fighting. I was certain that some of the magic in the air was Ethan's, but even *he* couldn't get a spell off when someone was kneeling on his chest and pounding on his face.

"Keane! Stop it!" I cried, because Ethan was clearly already down and beaten.

Keane, of course, ignored me. I stepped forward, meaning to try to drag him off of Ethan, but Kimber grabbed my arm.

"Don't," she said, and I turned to her in shock. This was her brother who was being beaten senseless!

Kimber's eyes were wide and frightened-looking, and she winced with every thud of fist hitting flesh. She spoke to me without looking away from the fight.

"I don't know what's going on, but as long as Ethan is conscious, he's dangerous." A tear leaked down her cheek, and her hand tightened on my arm, like it was taking everything she had not to interfere.

I knew she was right, no matter how much I hated it. Ethan was ridiculously good at magic, and I had no idea what the limitations of his power were. If he had suddenly gone crazy during the night, then he could probably kill us all with a single spell.

Eventually, Ethan went limp, and Keane stopped hitting him, though he remained sitting on his body, poised for action and panting with exertion. After the incident when Ethan had taken Keane's shield spell down during our sparring session, I might have thought Keane would enjoy beating him unconscious, but he didn't look like he was having fun.

"Get something to tie him up with," Keane ordered, not taking his eyes off of Ethan. "I don't know how long he'll stay out."

I didn't know if he was talking to me or to Kimber, but since I was the only one who had anything other than the clothes I was wearing, I ran to my backpack and yanked the zipper open. My hands were shaking, and I was having a hard time catching my breath as I pawed blindly through my belongings.

I'd been locked in a nightmare about the Erlking when Ethan had attacked me. I didn't think that was a coincidence. I had freed Ethan from the Wild Hunt, but because he wore the Erlking's mark on his face, Ethan was still subject to his will. I'd been off-limits to the Erlking on this journey because of Titania's guarantee of safe passage. I suspected that guarantee had been revoked and the Seelie Queen had just sicced the Wild Hunt on me.

I didn't exactly have rope stuffed in my backpack, and my frantic searching didn't find anything even vaguely ropelike. I flinched when I heard the sound of fist hitting flesh again.

"Hurry up!" Keane barked.

Kimber yanked a T-shirt I was pulling out of the backpack from my hands, and I turned to see her easily tear a shred off of it. Well, that solved that problem.

Still shaking and almost sick to my stomach, I watched as Kimber and Keane ripped apart my shirt, then bound Ethan hand and foot. Ethan's face was badly bruised, and bloody from a split lip. I couldn't help suspecting Keane had beat on him more than necessary to subdue him, but I bit my lip to keep myself from saying so. Starting another fight was not going to improve the situation.

When Ethan was thoroughly trussed, Kimber turned to me while Keane hovered over her brother with a watchful eye.

"What happened?" she asked, but from the look on her face I thought she'd already guessed.

"I was dreaming about the Erlking," I said, "and when I woke up, Ethan was trying to drag me away into the woods."

Keane cursed, and Kimber looked like she was on the verge of tears. I don't even want to know what *I* looked like. The pain in my heart was almost too much to bear, even though I knew Ethan hadn't been responsible for what he'd done. Gingerly, I rubbed the spot on my arm where I'd taken the punch. It throbbed steadily, and I was going to have a humongous bruise in the morning.

Ethan moaned softly, and we all went on red alert. Keane knelt beside him, ready to grab him if he went berserk despite being tied up like a Thanksgiving turkey. Kimber hugged herself and looked worried while I knelt at Ethan's other side.

"Ethan?" I said. "Ethan, can you hear me?"

He dragged in a shaky-sounding breath, and his eyes fluttered open. He hissed and quickly closed his eyes again, his skin going a sickly shade of green.

"You puke on me and we'll be going another round," Keane growled, all heart as usual.

Ethan's Adam's apple bobbed as he swallowed hard. "I'll keep that in mind," he said, his eyes still firmly closed, his voice tight with pain.

"Are you all right?" I asked, then wanted to slap myself for the question. No, he *wasn't* all right. In more ways than one.

He shrugged as best he could with his hands tied. "Been better." He cracked his eyes open again. His wince said it hurt.

"Are you *you* again?" Keane asked.

Ethan sucked in a deep breath. "Yeah. For the moment, at least. Whatever you do, don't untie me."

"Wasn't planning to," Keane said.

Ethan looked up at me, his expression stricken. "I'm so sorry, Dana. He ordered me to bring you to him, and I *couldn't* disobey him. I tried to be noisy about it so Keane and Kimber would stop me, but that was the best I could do."

"I know," I assured him, laying my hand on his shoulder. I wished I could think of something to say that would make him feel better, but he'd been bitter about the hold the Erlking had on him *before* this.

"You're still connected to the Erlking," Keane said. "That means he can find you through the bond, right?"

I heard Kimber's gasp of dismay, but I already knew just how much deep shit we were in. It wasn't just Ethan that the Erlking could track anywhere in Faerie.

"You're going to have to leave me behind," Ethan said.

"No!" Kimber said. "Absolutely not!" She looked back and forth between Keane and me, waiting for our chorus of agreement, but we didn't join in. For entirely different reasons, I suspect. I couldn't help thinking that Keane would get some amount of satisfaction from abandoning Ethan, but maybe I wasn't giving him enough credit.

"We have bigger problems than just Ethan if Titania's set the Wild Hunt on me," I said. "I bear the Erlking's mark, too."

Kimber gasped in surprise. Keane, of course, already knew about the mark, so it made sense that he didn't look shocked. I expected more of a reaction from Ethan, but there was no sign he was surprised by my announcement.

"You knew!" I said to him with a hint of accusation in my voice.

"He told me," Ethan responded, and I didn't need to ask who "he" was.

"Seems like you have some explaining to do," Keane prompted me. "What were you saying about the Erlking's mark?"

I said a silent thank-you to Keane for not telling anyone he'd already known about the mark. I doubt either Kimber or Ethan would have taken it well if they'd found out.

Wishing I'd found the courage to fess up earlier, I gave Kimber the same abbreviated version of the story I'd given Keane.

chapter sixteen

Keane was still all for leaving Ethan behind, though I think he was saying that just to be irritating. Much as he disliked Ethan, he wasn't truly spiteful at heart. We would have to keep Ethan tied up and under close watch, otherwise he might try to drag me off into the night again, but there was no way we were going to abandon him. Even if he *did* side with Keane for the first time in known history.

"The Erlking's orders were vague enough that I could at least try to work around them this time," Ethan argued. "But he's not stupid. He'll find a way to make me do what he wants."

"You won't be able to do much of anything all tied up like you are," Kimber said, and Ethan gave her a condescending look.

"If he forces me to use magic, it won't matter that I'm tied up."

"So we'll gag you, too," she said, never one to give up easily. "You're good, but even *you* can't work magic without words or gestures." She sounded really certain of herself, but she ruined the effect by tacking on "Right?" at the end.

I had already made up my mind that we weren't leaving Ethan behind, so I wasn't paying a whole lot of attention to the argument. I'd already been forced to leave my dad and Finn, and I was damned if I was going to do something like that again. Besides, as long as I had what amounted to a homing beacon set into my flesh, leaving Ethan behind wouldn't do any good. The Erlking was a supernatural hunter, and he was no doubt even now hot on our trail. He had horses and was familiar with the terrain, and we were on foot and the next best thing to lost. Not to mention we had no food or water. He could be on us in a matter of hours.

"We need to destroy the mark," I blurted, interrupting yet another argument I hadn't been listening to.

My friends all turned to me with varying expressions of confusion and wariness.

"What do you mean, destroy the mark?" Kimber asked, staring at me intently.

"As long as I have this mark on my shoulder, the Erlking can find me. Let's not kid ourselves: we're not going to be able to outrun him or hide from him. So the only way we can stop him from catching me is to destroy the mark."

"Destroy how?" Keane asked grimly.

My palms were sweaty, but I shivered as I tried not to think too much about what I was proposing. The Erlking's mark was like a tattoo, and I was hoping that like a tattoo, it was only skin-deep. Trying not to look as scared as I felt, I turned to look at the remains of our fire, which had burned down to embers over the course of the night.

"No!" Ethan shouted, struggling against his bonds. "We are *not* doing that!"

Kimber's face was almost green, her eyes wide with horror as she clapped her hand to her mouth. Only Keane looked like he was actually thinking about what I said, so I focused on him.

"If we don't find a way to destroy the mark, then the Erlking will catch me and he'll force me to join the Wild Hunt. As if that isn't bad enough, he'll make me take him out into the mortal world so he can hunt defenseless human beings. If it's a choice between that and dealing with a few minutes of pain, I'll take the pain." My throat tightened with panic even as the words left my mouth, and I forced myself to take a deep breath.

"No!" Ethan insisted again. He was struggling against the bonds so much I was afraid he was going to hurt himself.

Keane sneered at him. "Are you worried about *her*, or about your own pretty face?"

I thought sure my heart was going to stop. I'd been so focused on my own mark that I'd allowed myself to forget about Ethan's. There was no point in destroying mine if his was going to lead the Erlking right to us anyway.

"Think what you want, asshole," Ethan growled at Keane. "I'm not just going to sit around and let you burn a hole in my girlfriend."

"No? How are you going to stop me?"

Ethan opened his mouth for a response, and Kimber jumped on him, clapping her hand over his mouth as magic suddenly filled the air. Ethan glared at her, but she ignored him as she gave Keane a pointed look.

"Taunting Ethan probably isn't the best idea," she said, trying for a tone of grim humor and failing miserably. She was visibly shaking, and I wished I'd never dragged her into any of this, never allowed her to come to Faerie with me.

"My bad," Keane said, holding up his hands and looking embarrassed.

Kimber waited until the last hint of magic faded before she took her hand away from Ethan's mouth, and she was poised to slap it right back into place if necessary.

"I wasn't going to hurt him," Ethan said, but I wasn't so sure he was telling the truth.

"Don't try that again," I said. "If you'd rather we leave you behind, we'll do it." The words came out low and raspy, but *he* wasn't the one who was in danger from the Erlking. I wasn't sure I'd be able to get Kimber to go along with it, but it turned out I didn't have to worry about it.

"I'm not worried about myself," Ethan said. "If I'd thought about burning it off before, I'd have tried it already. But it's not really a tattoo. I don't know if burning it will destroy the magic."

His brows drew together as if he were concentrating hard, and then he shook his head and looked me in the eye. "The Erlking says to tell you to spare yourself the pain. It won't work."

My stomach did a nervous flip-flop. I knew Ethan could really communicate with the Erlking—thanks to the damned mark. But I also knew that if burning the mark would destroy it, Arawn would hardly say so. And that Ethan could have made this message up as a way to stop me from hurting myself.

"We'll just have to find out for ourselves," I said firmly, "because there's only one way to know for sure."

Ethan started to protest again, but Kimber grabbed a leftover strip of my T-shirt and stuffed it in his mouth. The glare he aimed at her was positively terrifying, but she was unaffected.

"We don't have a choice," she said hoarsely. "This could be our only chance."

Ethan still didn't agree, I could see it in his face. But by now he had to know that the rest of us had decided and he couldn't change our minds, so when he managed to force the impromptu gag out of his mouth, he didn't argue.

"Do me first," he said instead. "I'll be able to tell if it works, and I'm not sure Dana will."

He was right about that. The Erlking had told me that if I fed magic into the mark, I could call him to me—though why I'd ever want to do that was anyone's guess—but it produced no sensation right now, no tingle of magic that told me it was active. If I couldn't feel it working, then I wouldn't be able to feel it *not* working, either.

"Problem with that," Keane said as he moved over to the remains of our fire and started poking at it, coaxing out some reluctant flames, "is that if you tell us it isn't working, we won't be able to believe you. The Erlking could force you to tell us that even if it isn't true."

Ethan grimaced, but Keane was clearly right. If the Erlking could force Ethan to try to drag me out of camp, then he could force him to lie. The only way we'd know if burning the mark worked was if we managed to evade the Erlking against all odds.

Keane found a piece of green wood that poked out of the fire, its end a glowing ember despite its obvious reluctance to burn. I swallowed hard and tried to slow my racing heart. I felt deep down in my gut that this was what I had to do, but that didn't make it any less terrifying.

"You get to decide who goes first," Keane said, "not him." He jerked his thumb at Ethan.

I was scared to death of what was about to happen to me, but I suspected watching it happen to Ethan first was just going to make me feel worse. Besides, I had to make sure I wasn't going to chicken out at the last minute. No reason to put Ethan through hell if I wasn't going to be able to go through with it myself. I dragged in a deep, unsteady breath.

"I go first," I said, then pushed my hair to one side of my neck. I unbuttoned the first couple buttons of my shirt and pushed it down, exposing the mark.

Kimber knelt beside me and adjusted the shirt and my bra strap. Her eyes were glistening with tears, and her hands were shaking.

"I'll be all right," I told her, hoping it was true.

She sniffled. "I know you will be. But this is still going to suck."

"Tell me about it," I mumbled.

"Maybe you should lie down," Keane suggested. "Your instinct is going to be to pull away, and you have to hold still."

I nodded, then positioned myself as comfortably as possible on the ground, my head pillowed on my hands. I felt Keane's weight as he straddled my back and pressed one hand down on the opposite shoulder blade. I heard Ethan's growl of protest at the intimacy of the position. Then, before I had time to think about it anymore, the ember touched my skin, and it was all I could do not to scream.

I'd burned myself on the hot stove a couple of times when I was cooking for my mother—she was often too drunk to be trusted near an open flame—so I thought I'd be prepared for this. I was wrong. The pain that radiated from my shoulder was like nothing I'd ever felt before, and though I managed to hold back the scream, I couldn't help a moan of protest.

Keane was right about the instinct to pull away, and if he hadn't been holding me down we would never have been able to finish. As it was, I felt woozy and sick from the pain, but I couldn't escape it.

It felt like it went on for five minutes, but I know it was only a few seconds. My stomach heaved as I caught a whiff of burning flesh, and I thought for sure I was going to pass out. When it was over, I was shaking and sweating at the same time. I'd have liked to escape into unconsciousness, but I stayed wide awake and clear-headed.

With Keane's help, I sat up, trying to keep my shirt and bra away from the wound. I knew it was only a small spot on my shoulder, but the pain seemed to be radiating throughout my body. I wondered if that was normal, or if it had something to do with the magic of the mark. It seemed to me having a burned shoulder shouldn't be making my feet hurt, for example. I told myself that it was some kind of positive sign, that we'd done real damage to the mark, but I couldn't be sure.

"Are you all right?" Kimber asked, still looking like she was on the verge of tears.

"Yeah," I lied hoarsely. I hoped that out here alone in the wilderness the wound wouldn't get infected or something.

"I'm sorry," Keane said, and I knew he meant it. He'd been acting all tough about this, but I noticed there was a slight tremor in his hand as he stuck the end of the branch back in the fire. I couldn't help being sort of glad it bothered him.

Ethan didn't look too good either, his face unnaturally pale in the firelight. I didn't know if he was dreading his own ordeal, or whether he was freaking out about mine. Maybe it was some of both.

None of us could find anything to say as we watched the end of the branch, waiting for it to reheat. Keane poked around a bit, looking for another one that would do the trick, but he had no luck. I had a feeling that despite his dislike of Ethan, and despite his tough-guy facade, Keane was going to have a hard time with this. At least with me, he hadn't had to look me in the face while he was hurting me.

"I should do it," I whispered, because this was all my bright idea in the first place. And because I was the one the Erlking was after.

"No," Ethan and Keane answered in unison. They shared a glance that had none of their usual animosity.

"You've been through enough," Ethan said. "Let someone else do the hard thing just this once."

It felt like cowardice, letting Keane take all of this on his shoulders. I could tell by the haunted look in his eyes that this was bothering him way more than he was willing to say. But the boys were nothing if not stubborn, and they had both made up their minds.

I think watching Keane burn Ethan's face was worse even than having my own mark destroyed. Ethan barely made a sound, but I almost screamed for him. And then to see that horrible burn on his face where the stag tattoo had once been . . .

"I'd rather have the burn than the mark," Ethan said, noticing my stare. "And if it makes you feel any better, I think it worked. I can't feel my connection to the Erlking anymore."

"We can't untie you," Keane said, and I thought he was aiming his words more at me than at Ethan. "If this didn't work, the Erlking would make you tell us it did so we'll let down our guard."

Ethan nodded grimly. "That's true. You shouldn't untie me, and you should always have someone on guard, if for no other reason than that we aren't sure the marks will stay inactive. The Erlking's magic is like nothing else I've ever seen, and it's possible they'll start working again when we heal."

Oh, fabulous!

Logic told us that even if we had successfully destroyed the Erlking's marks, he would still be making his way toward our last known location. Which meant we had to move. The pain in my burned shoulder made me want to curl up in a little ball and moan in misery, but we didn't have time for that.

We did the best we could to rub out all traces of our camp, but I didn't think it would fool anyone. Certainly not an immortal hunter like the Erlking.

After a long argument that we couldn't afford, we decided to head for the road. It was unlikely people would be searching for us on the road in the dead of night, and we'd be able to move a lot faster—and leave a much less obvious trail—on the road than in the woods. Plus dragging around a guy whose hands were tied in the deepest dark of the woods was slowing us down way too much, and every time Ethan stumbled or fell, he left another link in the trail the Erlking would follow. Keane glared every time, no doubt suspecting that Ethan was doing it on purpose. Maybe he was, but if so, it meant the Erlking was still controlling him through the mark, in which case the Erlking knew where we were anyway.

Kimber's sense of direction didn't fail us, and we found the road within about fifteen minutes of breaking camp. We watched from the bushes for a while, but there was no sign of activity in either direction, so we left cover.

The road wasn't exactly smooth, its surface pitted by hoof marks and the ruts left by wagon wheels, but it was a whole lot smoother than the woods. Smooth enough that we were able to travel at a slow jog, at least for a while. My workout sessions with Keane had given me pretty decent stamina, but there was only so long I could keep up with full-blooded Fae. Even Kimber in her cute wedge heels ran better than I did, and we eventually had to slow to a fast walk.

We stayed on the road for several hours, tense and jumpy and sure we would hear the thunder of hooves chasing us down at any moment, but no one except us was out and about at this time of night. Well before dawn, we ducked back into the woods. There was no way of knowing how far off those standing stones were, but the Green Lady said we'd probably find them sometime today, so we didn't dare take a chance that we'd run right past the stream that would lead us to them.

Fighting our way through the underbrush was grueling work, and more than once, a stray branch poked at my burn and made me whimper in pain.

The sun was just beginning to rise when we heard the distinctive burble of water in the distance. We were lucky the day was quiet and still, or we might have missed it, because it was farther from the road than we'd imagined. Our hearts all rose at having successfully found the landmark, and our footsteps quickened as we began to follow the stream's meandering course.

With my sense of direction, I had no idea when the stream's course veered away from the road, but by the time the sun was high in the sky, Kimber informed us we were now traveling west, instead of continuing south like the road. Unfortunately, we had no clue how far we still had to go before we found the standing stones, and we were all terrified that we would somehow miss them. The Green Lady had told us the stream would lead us to them, but she hadn't told us what to look for.

It turned out we needn't have worried about missing them. After we'd been following the stream a few hours, it widened out until it was almost broad enough to call a river. A very rocky river, interrupted by frequent outcroppings and sandbars. It was on one of those sandbars that we found the standing stones.

This circle was much smaller than the one we'd traveled through with the prince's caravan. There were six stones, each only about six feet high, and we would have to wade through the water to get to them. Luckily, the water didn't look too deep, though the current was dangerously swift.

We stood on the banks of the stream and stared at those stones, our impossible escape route that now seemed possible. Home was so close . . .

And yet, we were still hours from nightfall, when the stones would be naturally active, and we didn't dare let our most powerful magic user call magic.

"I can work them," Ethan said quietly, and I'm sure I wasn't the only one who was sorely tempted to take him up on it.

"Are you *sure* you can work them?" Kimber asked. "Or do you just *think* you can?"

Ethan didn't answer, and we all knew what that meant.

"We can't risk it," Keane said. "Even if we were willing to risk letting you call magic—which I, for one, am not—you'd get us all killed if the spell failed."

"I know that," Ethan said irritably. "It just sucks to be this close to getting home and not be able to take that final step."

"Yeah, it sucks, but that's the way it is," I said, though I felt as frustrated and anxious as Ethan did. "Let's find somewhere to hole up for a few hours. Preferably somewhere out of sight of the stones.

They aren't exactly conveniently located, but that doesn't mean we're the only people who'd ever use them."

No one found any flaws in my suggestion, so we wandered down the banks of the stream until we found a sheltered embankment where we could wait out the rest of the day. We were all exhausted, and determined to spend as many of the remaining hours of daylight sleeping as possible.

"I'll take the first watch," I told the others, though I had to stifle a yawn as I forced the words out. Tired as I was, I wasn't sure I'd be able to sleep if I tried. Now that I was sitting down and not fighting my way through the brush, I was much more aware of the searing burn, and it might well be enough to keep me up. The thought that I might fall asleep and accidentally roll over onto that shoulder was enough to make me break out in a cold sweat.

Kimber and Keane shared a look I couldn't interpret.

"I'll stay up with you," Kimber said.

I shook my head. "Get some rest. I promise I'm not going to fall asleep on duty or anything."

There was another of those looks between Kimber and Keane, like they were communicating silently.

"That's not what we're worried about," Kimber finally said.

I heaved a sigh of exasperation, because this evasion was so not what I was in the mood for. "Then what *are* you worried about?" I asked, and I didn't even try to hide my irritation.

"They're worried about me," Ethan answered for them. "If one of them is on watch and I start to call magic, they'll feel it and be able to stop me. You won't."

It was time for Ethan and me to share the knowing look, because Ethan knew perfectly well I could sense magic. He even knew what I could do with it, having seen me turn Aunt Grace mortal. But obviously he still thought I should keep my ability secret, even from my best friends.

Maybe he was right. Maybe it was a case of the fewer people who knew, the better. Maybe I was being irrational because I was scared and in pain. But I was sick and tired of lying and keeping secrets.

"I can sense magic," I told them all bluntly. "I know Faeriewalkers aren't supposed to be able to, but I can. I can call it, too."

Kimber and Keane gaped at me, and Ethan shook his head in disapproval. I figured since I'd gone that far, I might as well go the rest of the way.

"I don't seem to be able to cast regular magic spells," I continued, "but when I'm in danger I can do this spell that turns Fae into mortals. I'd never have survived the Bogle attack otherwise. A bunch of them almost caught me, and . . . and I turned them mortal." The Bogles were monsters, and they'd been trying to kill me at the time, but I still shuddered with horror at the memory of what I had done. Monsters they might have been, but they were living beings.

"You turned them mortal," Keane repeated flatly. I wasn't sure he quite believed me, but whether he believed me or not, he was plenty mad that this was the first he was hearing about it. He shifted his gaze from me to Ethan. "And you knew about this. Don't lie—you obviously weren't surprised by what she said." And yeah, Ethan knowing something he didn't was not going to put Keane in his happy place.

"I knew," Ethan admitted. "I'm the one who told her not to tell anyone, and if you care about her at all, you'll keep your mouth shut and try to forget she said anything. People feel threatened enough by her powers as it is."

Keane said something snarly in response, but I couldn't hear it over the pounding of my heart when I risked a glance at Kimber's face. Keane was mad at me for keeping such a big secret, but Kimber . . .

She'd handled learning the secret of my bargain with the Erlking pretty well, and she hadn't punched me out when she learned about the mark, either. But this was apparently the camel's last straw.

"I shouldn't be surprised," she said in a furious undertone. "You've lied about so many things, why not one more?"

I flinched from the anger and hurt in her eyes. "Ethan is the only person who knew. I didn't even tell my father." I realized I was telling yet another lie, but this time it was by accident. I'd allowed myself to forget that the Erlking knew about my power, too. I was going to clarify, but Kimber didn't give me a chance.

"You know what, Dana?" she cried, pushing to her feet so fast she almost fell over. "You can take your secrets and your lies and you can shove them! You and my brother are like peas in a pod, and you deserve each other."

Kimber turned her back and scrambled up the bank of the stream, disappearing into the underbrush in an adrenaline-and-anger-fueled sprint. I wanted to follow her, but I doubted I could catch up to her, not with her Fae speed, and even if I did, there wasn't anything I could say that she'd want to hear right now.

Keane looked back and forth between Ethan and me, and I could see he was torn between going after Kimber and staying to make sure Ethan didn't try anything.

"Go after her," I begged him. "She's upset enough she could get into trouble." Even with her good sense of direction, I was afraid she'd get herself lost in the woods if the energy from her rage kept her running long enough. Not to mention that there were people hunting us.

Keane glared at Ethan. "If anything happens to Dana while I'm gone, I will kill you. Understand?" He looked like he meant it, too.

"Got it," Ethan said. "Now bring Kimber back so *I* don't have to kill *you*."

Keane gave him one more bone-chilling glare before clearing the bank in a ridiculously graceful leap and tearing off in the direction Kimber had gone.

chapter seventeen

I felt like crying, but that was a cop-out. I'd chosen to keep my secrets, even from the people who were supposed to be my best friends; it was time to face the consequences of my decisions.

Thanks to my mom, her drinking, and our constant moving from town to town, I'd learned that the only person I could ever fully trust was myself. I knew this wasn't a good way to go about life, but time and time again, when I'd put my faith in my mom, the only constant in my life, she'd let me down. I'd let that turn me into a suspicious, secretive little bitch, and that wasn't the kind of person I wanted to be. I should have trusted Kimber with the truth, and I didn't know if I could ever make it up to her.

"I suck," I said beneath my breath.

Ethan laughed, but it was a bitter, haunted laugh. "Maybe Kimber's right and we deserve each other. Two natural-born liars." He closed his eyes and thunked the back of his head against the wall of dirt and roots behind him.

"You were supposed to comfort me and tell me I don't suck." God, how pathetically needy I sounded.

Ethan opened his eyes and met my gaze. "I'm the one who told you to lie about it in the first place. And in case you didn't get the mental telepathy message I was trying to send you, I wanted you to lie about it again just now. In other words, *I* suck, not you."

I tried to run my hand through my hair in frustration, but it was a dirty, snarly mess. I had a mirror somewhere in my backpack, but I had no desire to see how hideous I looked right now.

"Maybe I should have lied again," I said. I wouldn't even have had to say anything. All I had to do was keep quiet and let the lie stand, and Kimber wouldn't now be running blindly into the woods, hating my guts.

"And maybe you were right to tell the truth. It's not like I have all the answers."

I wrapped my arms around my legs and laid my chin on my knees, hurting, heartsick, and exhausted both mentally and physically. I had screwed up so many times, and it was mostly the people I cared about who suffered for it instead of me. That was just . . . wrong.

"Come here," Ethan said, beckoning with a jerk of his chin. "I can't give you a proper hug with my hands tied, but we can sort of pretend."

Was he hoping to lure me into untying his hands?

I wanted to slap myself as soon as that thought crossed my nasty, suspicious mind. Two seconds ago, I was thinking about how I needed to trust people more.

Ethan nudged me with the tip of his shoe, which was all he could reach me with.

"Hey, it's okay. I'm not offended that you don't trust me right now. You know I may not be myself."

"But you're not feeling any insane urges to grab me and carry me off to the Erlking right now, right?"

One side of his mouth quirked up in a grin, though I didn't think his expression would ever be quite as boyish as it had once been. "Nope. You're mine, and I'm not sharing."

Those words made me squirm, though they also brought a pleased blush to my cheeks. I would never really be his, not as long as my bargain with the Erlking lasted. I didn't see any reason why the Erlking's decision to hunt me would free me from our bargain.

I shouldn't even have been *thinking* about that under the circumstances, but I couldn't help it. Ethan was looking at me with a familiar hunger in his eyes, though I had to look about as appealing as moldy cheese and didn't smell much better. Of course, Ethan was looking kind of rough himself, his hair all tangled, his clothes filthy, and that livid burn on his face constantly reminding me of the pain he must be in. My shoulder hurt like hell, but his mark had been bigger, so his burn was, too. I couldn't imagine what it must feel like, and yet it didn't stop him from looking at me like he wanted to get me into bed.

Knowing that Kimber and Keane would tell me I was being stupid if they were here, I scooted over until I was sitting right beside Ethan, then laid my head on his shoulder. The warmth of his body was comforting, but I desperately longed for the feel of his arms around me. I was severely tempted to untie his hands, but it was a temptation I managed to resist.

"Reach into my right front pocket," he whispered.

I glanced up at his face and saw that he was serious, and that it wasn't an attempt at flirtation. I frowned at him, having no idea why he wanted me to put my hand in his pocket. I hated having to be so suspicious of him, but it would be stupid of me not to think things through when I couldn't be sure if the Erlking was influencing him.

"Hurry, before the others come back," he urged.

Still, I hesitated, and even though Ethan understood my caution, there was a flash of annoyance in his eyes.

"I'm trying to give you back your brooch," he said.

I gasped and reached for my own pocket, where I'd been keeping the Erlking's brooch carefully hidden. The pocket was empty.

"The Erlking told me about it and made me take it from you before I tried to kidnap you," Ethan explained. "I didn't want to give it back to you while Kimber and Keane were around, because I knew you must be keeping it secret for a reason."

There was no hint of accusation in his voice, and his casual acceptance of one more lie on my part almost brought me to tears. I couldn't think of what to say—my reasons for keeping the brooch secret didn't seem as good today as they had before—so I did as he asked and reached into his pocket. I tried not to think too much about just where I was putting my hand, but I couldn't help but be aware of it as I felt around for the brooch, which of course was buried at the very bottom of the pocket.

Maybe if we'd been back in Avalon, alone and out of danger, I'd have found the courage to take advantage of our positions. Ethan was my boyfriend, after all, and though we could never go for the home run, we could certainly give the bases a try. It would be a dangerous game, because it was possible Ethan would let his hormones get the best of his common sense. I might not be the most experienced sixteen-year-old in the world, but I knew that boys' brains sometimes resided in their pants. The only reason I was willing to risk even kissing him was that I trusted my own brain to stop us from going too far.

I was blushing again, but then my fingers found the brooch and I carefully pulled it out of Ethan's pocket. I held it in the palm of my hand. It was a beautiful piece of jewelry, the metal gleaming silver that neither tarnished nor scratched, the stylized stag looking ready to leap off my hand at any moment.

"You don't think the Erlking can track us through this, do you?" I asked. I had been so focused on the marks that I hadn't even thought of that before, but the brooch was a rendering of the Erlking's symbol.

"I don't think so," Ethan said. "Why would he need to track you through the brooch when he'd already put the mark on your shoulder?"

"Still," I said, the words coming reluctantly, "maybe it would be best if I left it behind."

"Don't. If the Queen's forces catch up with us, you need to be able to use the brooch to escape."

I narrowed my eyes at him. "I am *not* running away and leaving you guys to face the music." Maybe I'd been right all along about keeping the brooch secret.

"You'd damn well better!" he responded with some heat. "*You're* the person they hold responsible for the bomb. *You're* the one they'll execute. The rest of us might be seen as accessories, but the Queen won't kill us. Especially not Kimber and me, considering we're Unseelie and killing us might cause an incident."

I knew enough about Fae politics to be doubtful. No, Titania might not execute Ethan and Kimber, but she'd be happy to hand them over to Mab, the Unseelie Queen, who might well execute them as a gesture of goodwill or something stupid like that.

But Ethan was right about one thing: if Titantia's forces caught me, I was dead. And if Henry had anything to do with it, I'd be dead even before I was brought back to the palace for the Queen's pleasure. Maybe no one would believe me if I started pointing fingers, but why would he risk it? How hard would it be for Henry to bribe or bully the search party into taking me dead or alive, with the emphasis on dead? I suspected not hard at all.

With a sigh of resignation, I slipped the brooch back into my own pocket. I hoped I wouldn't need to use it.

. . .

Kimber and Keane were gone long enough that I began to worry about them. If they'd been gone even five minutes longer, I probably would have gone out in search of them, no matter how dangerous it was for someone with my sense of direction to go wandering around in the woods alone.

I sighed with relief when I heard their voices approaching, but when they jumped down into the hollow with Ethan and me, I sensed trouble was about to start. Again.

There was a distinctive red mark on Kimber's neck, and the tiny buttons on the bodice of her sundress were mis-buttoned. As if that weren't bad enough, Keane was looking unbearably smug, and it didn't take a rocket scientist to guess what he and Kimber had been up to for all the time they were gone. Maybe he'd thought he was "comforting" her.

Once upon a time, Keane had made it obvious—without ever saying it out loud—that he was interested in me. I had made it just as obvious that I didn't share his interest, though I'd been flattered by it, and I'd felt little tugs of irrational jealousy when he'd started paying attention to Kimber. I wanted to be happy for Kimber, I really did. It was just that I couldn't help suspecting Keane's motives. Ethan had stolen his girlfriend when they were in high school, and Keane made no secret that he held a major grudge. Was it a coincidence that Keane had shown interest in me and then shifted his attention to Ethan's sister when I didn't respond?

If he wanted to get a rise out of Ethan, Keane succeeded beyond his wildest dreams. The moment Ethan caught sight of them and saw the hickey on Kimber's neck, magic flooded our little hollow. I whirled on Ethan, rushing to cover his mouth before he could get a spell out.

I was too slow.

"Back!" Ethan yelled in the instant before my hand landed on his mouth.

Kimber then did something either very brave or very stupid. Maybe a little of both. She stepped between Ethan and Keane.

Ethan's spell slammed into her, and Kimber screamed as she was lifted off her feet and propelled backward. She bounced off Keane, who tried to grab her but managed to catch an elbow in the face for his efforts, then crashed into the trunk of a large tree. Her back hit first, the impact hard enough to rattle the tree's branches, and then the back of her head smacked the trunk and she fell limply to the ground.

I tried to keep my hand over Ethan's mouth, afraid of what else he might do, but he broke my hold easily, despite his bonds, and surged to his feet.

"Kimber!" he cried as he stumbled and ran to her side.

Keane was there before him, his hand at Kimber's throat, feeling for her pulse. Logically, I'm sure we all knew she wasn't dead. The Sidhe are very hard to kill, and though the impact had been hard, it hadn't been *that* hard. Ethan had meant to hurt Keane, not kill him. That didn't make it any less terrifying to see Kimber lying there, not moving.

We all relaxed marginally when Keane said, "She's alive."

She proved he was right by groaning softly, although her eyes didn't open.

"Untie my hands!" Ethan ordered. "I can heal her."

I'd seen Ethan heal wounds before, and I knew that whatever damage he'd done to Kimber, he could most likely fix it. But either Keane didn't know that, or he was too furious to care.

"Put a fucking gag on him!" he barked at me. "We apparently can't move fast enough to block his magic after all."

"Don't be an ass," Ethan snapped back. "Untie my hands so I can heal my sister. I'm not about to waste magic on you now."

Despite Ethan's considerable talent, using magic did drain him, and he had limits to what he could do. I doubted the spell he'd hit Kimber with had done much to drain his magical reserves, but he'd already had plenty of time to lob another spell at Keane if he wanted, and he hadn't done it.

Keane, however, didn't see it that way. "I can heal her myself," he said, talking to me instead of Ethan. Practicality demanded that Fae fighters learn some healing magic, but my impression was that it was just rudimentary stuff. Maybe it was enough to heal Kimber, or maybe not. "For all we know, this whole thing has been a plot to get us to untie his hands. Now put a gag on him before I break his pretty face. Again."

"Try it," Ethan growled. "See how easy it is when I'm ready for you."

Magic filled the air once again, coming to Ethan's silent call at incredible speed.

I already knew I wasn't getting a gag on Ethan, not unless he felt like letting me. He'd torn out of my grip a minute ago with ease, after all. But if he decided his anger with Keane was greater than his concern for Kimber, this could get even uglier than it already was.

I swallowed hard, knowing there was only one way I could keep Ethan from casting anything, but fearing he would never forgive me if I did it. He was ignoring me, all his attention focused on Keane. I wasn't sure I could knock him out with one blow—my lessons with Keane had been focused on defense, not offense—but I had to try.

My moment of indecision was more than enough to let Ethan unleash whatever spell he planned, but he didn't do it. Which made me hesitate even more.

Keane shook his head in disgust. "Go ahead. Hit me with your goddamn spell while your sister is lying here unconscious from your last one."

"All right, I will," Ethan said, and suddenly the strip of T-shirt that bound his hands together behind his back disappeared.

I ordered myself to hit him before he did something disastrous, but I just couldn't do it. This was *Ethan,* and for better or for worse, I had to admit to myself that I was probably in love with him. I might have been able to hit him in self-defense, but not like this, not in cold blood.

The magic in the air grew thicker, no doubt the result of Keane raising his shield spells, but Ethan didn't attack him. In fact, he seemed almost to forget that Keane was there, instead leaning over and putting his hands on Kimber's shoulders.

"Kimber?" he asked. "Can you hear me?"

She groaned and her eyes fluttered open. "Unfortunately," she said, her face twisted with pain. "I think you broke my ribs."

Ethan winced, and his cheeks reddened with shame. "I'm so sorry. I'll fix it, but it's going to hurt."

Tears of pain leaked from Kimber's eyes, but she still managed a first-class glare at her brother. "You are so off my Christmas list this year." She reached a hand out toward Keane, who still looked like he wanted to ignore everything and beat the crap out of Ethan.

"For God's sake, hold her hand!" Ethan snapped. "I'm not a real healer, and I can't do anything for the pain."

Keane grumbled something under his breath, but he moved closer to Kimber and wrapped his fingers around hers. Their eyes met and locked, and for the first time, it looked to me like he genuinely cared about her, that he wasn't showing off for Ethan's benefit. I wanted to hold her other hand, but I was surely still in her doghouse so I didn't think she'd appreciate it.

Ethan's magic swelled, and he whispered something so softly I couldn't hear it. Kimber's back arched, and she gasped in pain, her knuckles going white as she clasped Keane's hand with desperate strength. And then it was over.

We all breathed a sigh of relief. Kimber was sweaty and shaking, but the expression on her face no longer screamed of pain. Keane kept hold of her hand, his thumb stroking back and forth idly.

"So you could have untied yourself anytime," he said to Ethan, who shrugged. We had all badly underestimated his power, and we were lucky he hadn't made us pay for it.

"Yeah. If you hadn't damaged the mark, it would have been bad."

"And you're not under the Erlking's influence right now, but you didn't tell us that we weren't taking enough precautions."

Ethan reached up to rub his face, then remembered the burn and thought better of it. "I didn't want to be gagged, which I figured was the next logical step." His shoulders drooped. "But if the mark heals any more than it already has, I guess I'll have to live with it."

"More than it already has?" Keane asked, sounding horrified.

Ethan nodded grimly. "It doesn't hurt as much as it should, and I think that means it's healing."

We all looked closely at the burn on his face. It definitely looked less angry than it had when it was fresh. But I had no idea how fast a burn would heal naturally on one of the Sidhe, except that it was faster than it would heal on a human or a half-blood like me. Maybe this was normal. Or maybe there was magic that would keep the mark from being permanently damaged.

My heart sank at the thought, then sank even lower when I considered all the ramifications of the mark healing. If Ethan's mark healed, then mine probably would, too. And even if we could make it safely to Avalon, the Erlking would still be able to track me there. Titania had officially set him on me, which meant that the geis that prevented the Erlking from hunting indiscriminately in Avalon wouldn't be in effect. Which meant my only hope of escaping him was to leave Avalon for the mortal world and never return.

I was still trying to absorb that unpalatable reality when Keane's head suddenly popped up, his eyes going wide. I was going to ask him what was wrong, but then I heard it, too. The sound of someone moving through the underbrush, coming in our direction.

I remembered Kimber's startled scream when Ethan's spell had hit her, and realized we had been anything but quiet. Maybe whoever was approaching was some stray Fae, someone who wouldn't be inclined to detain us and report us to the authorities. Or even someone we could overpower, between Keane's fighting abilities and Ethan's magic.

But my luck had been lousy for so long I wasn't exactly hopeful that it was going to change now.

chapter eighteen

"Use the brooch," Ethan whispered to me urgently as once again magic filled the air.

Kimber and Keane both gave me quizzical looks, but now wasn't the time to explain. I shook my head.

"Don't argue!" Ethan said. "I'll sit on you and stick you with it myself if I have to."

"What are you talking about?" Keane asked.

I wanted to scream at them to run instead of sitting here and arguing, but the reality was that we would never make it. Even if Ethan cast his invisibility spell on us as he had the night we'd fled the palace, he couldn't keep it up for very long. I doubted he'd have the time or the power to work the standing stones—assuming we were willing to risk trying them—and if we just ran off into the woods, we'd leave a trail any idiot could follow, with no storm to wipe it out and no Green Lady to draw the pursuit off.

Ethan put his hands on my shoulders and leaned into me, his eyes boring into me, deadly serious.

"If it's the Queen's forces, using the brooch is your only hope," he said. He was squeezing my shoulders so tight he was probably leaving bruises. "Leave us. Get back to Avalon and be safe."

I opened my mouth to protest, but he stopped my words with a searing kiss that took my breath away. I groaned with the pleasure of his kiss, even as a part of me knew something was wrong with this picture. Now was *so* not the time for a make-out session, but my hormones were in overdrive, and I couldn't seem to make myself push Ethan away. Even when I felt his hand delving into my pocket and grabbing the brooch.

A part of me knew exactly what was happening, was aware of the magic prickling my skin. Ethan had used a milder version of this spell on me once before, but that time I'd been able to shake it off as soon as I realized my hormones were being magically manipulated. This time, I felt like my body wasn't my own, and I kept kissing him, pressing against him, my hands buried in his hair, as he pulled the brooch out of my pocket.

Something sharp pricked my thigh, right through my pants, and suddenly the flood of arousal left me as Ethan sat back on his heels and blinked at me.

"You bastard!" I said, my eyes welling with tears. But Ethan couldn't hear me, because the brooch wouldn't let him. For the next thirty minutes, I would be completely undetectable.

"What the fuck did you do to her?" Keane growled, looking like he was about to forget everything and pound Ethan into the ground.

"The Erlking gave her a magic item that makes her temporarily invisible," Ethan explained calmly. "No one can see or even hear her while the spell is active, so she'll be able to get away even if we can't."

I felt rather like punching Ethan myself at the moment. Maybe using the brooch was the smart thing to do, but I'd vowed to myself that I wouldn't abandon my friends. I already didn't know how I was going to live with abandoning my dad and Finn.

Since no one could see me, I grabbed the brooch from where it had fallen on the ground and stuffed it back into my pocket. I quickly checked my watch so I'd know when the spell would wear off, then climbed to the top of the embankment so I could see who or what was coming.

The news wasn't good. There were at least three Knights creeping up toward the hollow where my friends sat arguing pointlessly. I suspected there were more Knights I couldn't see, circling around and cutting off our escape routes. Certainly they would have sent someone to guard the standing stones, too.

Below, I heard Keane accuse Ethan of having somehow captured me for the Erlking with his magic. I suppose it did look kind of bad, and I wished I'd come out and told everyone about the brooch. I'm sure I would have, too, if my earlier bombshell hadn't gone over so badly.

My friends wouldn't hear anything I said to them, nor would they feel it if I touched them. I'd already realized that running wouldn't do them any good, but I couldn't stand to hear them arguing about me while grim-faced Knights armed with crossbows snuck up on their position.

I grabbed a stick and scrambled back down. The Erlking's spell made it so that no one noticed the stick moving from the top of the embankment and then hanging in the air in front of them. I tried poking Keane with it, but he didn't seem to feel it. Then I dropped it on his head.

Keane reached up and brushed the stick out of his hair, then glanced up, probably looking for the tree it had dropped from.

Encouraged that he'd actually felt the stick, I bent down and grabbed a few pebbles from the stream and began lobbing them at him one at a time. He looked so confused that I would have laughed in any other situation.

"It's Dana, idiot," Ethan said. "Trying to tell you she's all right."

"Um, guys?" Kimber said. "Maybe we should run now?"

Ethan shook his head. "*Dana* should run instead of hanging

around here throwing pebbles. *We* should surrender to give her more time to get away. I don't know if they have any spells that can sense her, but if they do, she needs to be well away before they start casting them."

Keane made a low growling sound. "You surrender if you want. I'm not giving up without a fight. There's more than one way to buy time."

"Come out of there and keep your hands where we can see them," one of the Knights yelled.

Kimber peeked over the lip of the embankment, then quickly dropped back down. "Knights," she said, her face pale with fright. "They've got crossbows."

"We won't last more than a minute or two in a fight," Ethan said. His gaze darted quickly to Kimber and back, fast enough that she didn't notice. But Keane did, and he got the message. Kimber might not be totally defenseless, but she was still way more vulnerable than either of them because she couldn't even cast a shield spell. If the boys tried to fight the Knights, Kimber might very well get hurt, or worse.

Keane looked grim, but resolved. "All right," he said, and he even managed not to look like the concession caused him dire pain. "If we got ourselves killed, Dana would never forgive us."

Ethan gave a halfhearted bark of laughter, but quickly sobered. "Look, I'm sorry I tried to hit you with that spell. I guess I was being kind of childish."

Keane sighed, reaching over to take Kimber's hand. "No, you were just being her big brother."

"Come out *now*!" the Knight shouted. "This is your last warning."

I let out a scream of frustration, hating the helpless feeling of standing there watching and being unable to do anything.

"We're surrendering," Ethan yelled back. "Don't shoot."

Hands up, Ethan stepped slowly out of the hollow, Keane and Kimber close behind.

Maybe I should have just run away after that. After all, it wasn't like I could do much of anything to help my friends all by myself, unless I were willing to unleash my mortality spell on a bunch of Knights who were just following orders. And who had every reason to believe we'd been behind the bombing. I didn't believe the Knights would be able to sense me behind the Erlking's magic, so all I had to do was hide until nightfall and then travel through the standing stones right under their noses.

Maybe if I ran back to Avalon, I'd be able to get help for my dad and my friends. And at least I'd be safe myself, as long as I got out of Avalon before the Erlking found me. Ethan and Kimber's dad was as powerful and influential as my own, and he'd do everything in his considerable power to get them safely home.

But who would fight for Finn and Keane? And would my dad's political rivals try to make sure he never returned to Avalon? The only person who cared about my dad and all my friends equally, who would fight for them all, was me. Which meant I couldn't run to Avalon and hope someone else could and would save them for me.

My mind churning desperately, trying to come up with an idea that didn't suck, I watched as the Knights bound my friends' hands behind their backs and bullied them through the trees. I followed, unseen and unheard.

When I broke through the trees, I saw a narrow dirt road, much smaller than the main one. The handful of Knights who had rounded up my friends was only a portion of this search party, which consisted of about a dozen people, some Knights, some not. The air around them buzzed with magic, raising all the fine hairs on my arms and the back of my neck.

A cold-faced Sidhe woman questioned Keane, trying to find out where I was. She completely ignored Ethan and Kimber, but I supposed that was a result of the rivalry between the Seelie and Unseelie Courts. She no doubt thought Keane, as a member of her own Court, was more trustworthy.

Keane told her about Ethan's attempt to capture me for the Erlking—which earned him a look of shock from Kimber, and scorn from Ethan. Ignoring their outrage, Keane went on to explain that I'd run off after Ethan's attack, terrified that he was still tied to the Erlking and would try again.

I thought it was a pretty good story. Plausible, at least to someone who didn't know me. And if the woman believed him, she'd send at least some of her men on a wild goose chase.

I couldn't tell by her face whether she was buying Keane's story, but she didn't seem inclined to do a full-out interrogation, at least not in the middle of the road. She picked out five of her men and ordered them to carry my friends back to the Sunne Palace, where I had no doubt they would be deposited in some nasty dungeon-type place. Then she directed the rest of her men to continue searching for me.

Once again, I was helpless as my friends were hoisted up onto the backs of horses and then tied to the saddles. The rest of the search party fanned out into the woods again, one man staying behind to guard the remaining horses, while my friends and their captors took off down the road at a gallop.

I thought about trying to steal a horse, but gave up on that idea immediately. How could I get the horse to do what I wanted if it could neither see, feel, nor hear me? And even if I could, being invisible wouldn't do me much good if I was riding a horse down the road. Maybe no one would be able to see me, but they would know *something* was wrong with that picture.

Instead, I checked my watch to remind myself how much longer the spell would be working, then forced my weary legs into a pathetic imitation of a jog, following the road toward the Sunne Palace. What I was going to do when and if I actually got there was anyone's guess.

chapter nineteen

I don't know how I kept putting one foot in front of the other. My entire body ached with fatigue, and if I stood still for a rest, I found myself swaying on my feet, my head swimming. Not trusting myself to think straight, I set the alarm on my watch to go off three minutes before the brooch's spell would expire and forced myself to keep going. When the alarm went off, scaring the crap out of me because I'd been in such a daze I was practically delirious, I poked myself with the brooch again and kept going down the road. I couldn't manage a jog, or even a brisk walk, so I settled for a slow and steady plod. I had a nasty moment when the narrow road I was on met with the main road, but I was pretty sure I'd chosen the right direction.

There was plenty of traffic on the road, mostly people riding horses, but a few driving wagons and some pedestrians as well. Most were heading the same way I was, reinforcing my assumption that I'd turn the right direction. No one saw me, and I silently thanked the Erlking for giving me the brooch, even though he was the enemy. I was even able to snatch some food and water from one of the passersby without anyone noticing me.

I stuffed my face as I kept walking, trying not to eat or drink too fast. A hunk of bread and an apple had never tasted so good, even though the apple had peach-colored flesh and tasted more like some kind of melon. As long as it was edible, I didn't care, and as my body began to process the food and rehydrate, my brain started working better, too.

The Erlking's brooch was one hell of a secret weapon. I'd been able to steal the food right out from under a Fae's nose, and he'd had no idea I was there, even when I accidentally brushed against him.

If I had come to the Sunne Palace for the sole purpose of assassinating Princess Elaine—God only knows what my motive was supposed to be—then I sure as hell could have done it without having to resort to using a bomb. I could have just used the Erlking's brooch to make me invisible, followed the princess around until I was sure she was alone, and then killed her with a Fae weapon. If I'd done that, there would have been no evidence pointing to me as the culprit, and no one would have had any reason to suspect me. What kind of moron would I have be to use a bomb, something that—at least in theory—only *I* could have been responsible for?

I stumbled to a stop as I tried to find flaws in my argument. But no matter how I sliced it, as long as I had the Erlking's brooch, there were about a million easier ways for me to assassinate someone than to set a freaking bomb. And that, I realized, was my defense.

The realization gave me a taste of hope, and that hope gave me a rush of energy. My pace picked up, and my body felt less achy and awful. Maybe it was possible for me to prove my innocence. Based on my dad's reaction on the night of the bombing, I didn't think I would get anything like a fair trial if I turned myself in, and without a fair trial, I might never be able to present my side of the argument. But thanks to the brooch, I could march right through the doors of the palace and grant myself an audience with the Queen. And thanks to the gun my dad had given me, I could be sure she'd listen—and see how much more easily I could have killed Elaine if I actually wanted to.

The plan felt almost surreal, like something out of a cheesy action movie. Who was I, a sixteen-year-old half-blood girl, to storm the Faerie Queen's palace and threaten her with a gun? But if I didn't prove my innocence, my father and my friends might very well die. If the Queen hadn't killed my father already, but I tried to shut that thought out.

Crazy as my plan sounded, I had to try it. Besides, it sounded better than my previous plan, which was to somehow use the brooch to help free my father and my friends, and then somehow get us the hell out of Dodge. I wasn't any closer to figuring out either of those "somehows" now than I had been when I'd first turned back toward the palace. So Plan B it was.

For a while, knowing I had a plan gave me a burst of energy, but it could only last so long. I stole food and water a second time, but even after I'd eaten my fill, my legs were quivering with exhaustion, and I realized that if I didn't stop and rest, I was going to run myself into the ground. Reluctantly, I left the road and slipped back into the woods, looking for a place where I could hide while I rested.

I was too tired to be picky, and I ended up curled up between a couple of gnarled tree roots way too close to the road for comfort. I considered letting my watch keep waking me up every twenty-seven minutes so I could stay invisible, but I decided I needed the rest too desperately. Holding the gun in my hand and using my backpack for a pillow, I closed my eyes and was instantly sucked down into sleep.

When I awoke, it was pitch-dark out. My body yearned for more sleep, and it took a massive effort of will to force my eyes open and push myself into a sitting position. I didn't seem to have moved a muscle the whole time I was asleep, and I was so stiff and sore I felt like my bones would break if I moved too fast.

A glance at my watch told me it was ten o'clock at night. I'd slept almost seven hours! And I desperately wanted to sleep for about seven more, but I didn't know how much time my friends had. The sooner I reached the palace and proved my innocence, the sooner they could be set free, and the less chance they'd get hurt.

I picked my way carefully through the darkened woods. We'd been on the run for about forty-eight hours before the search party had caught us, but we'd been fighting our way through the woods, and I was sure I'd make faster progress on the road. I guesstimated that I'd make it to the Sunne Palace sometime tomorrow afternoon, if I kept pushing myself relentlessly.

I pricked myself with the brooch as soon as I caught sight of the road, then resumed my slow, plodding pace of this afternoon. I hoped it was a pace I could keep up indefinitely. I wanted to make it to the palace before I had to stop to rest again, because my gut told me I was running out of time.

I walked in a trancelike daze until my watch reminded me it was time to prick myself again. I was beginning to feel like a pincushion, and was heartily sick of poking myself with the damn pin.

I'd been staring blindly at my feet as I walked, but when I stopped to fish the brooch out of my pocket, I raised my head. And froze with the tips of my fingers just touching the edge of the brooch.

In my daze, I hadn't even noticed when I'd left the wild forest behind and crossed into the almost-town near the palace. I must have passed by the side road leading to the standing stones without even seeing it. For all our seemingly endless wandering, and for all the help the Green Lady had given us, apparently we'd gotten less than a day's easy travel from the palace. Probably the only reason we hadn't been caught sooner was that the searchers thought we would be more competent and be farther away.

I shook off my chagrin and once more poked myself with the pin. Maybe it was a bit embarrassing to see how sucky a job we'd done at running away, but it certainly wasn't a bad thing that I'd be able to reach the palace tonight instead of tomorrow. I wanted this whole hellish ordeal over with.

A little more than an hour later, I was walking through the gates of the palace, the hairs on the back of my neck lifting as I passed between a pair of grim-looking sentries. All well and good to say I wanted this over with, but I was scared to death of what would happen when I confronted the Queen. I found my argument about why I couldn't be the mad bomber very convincing, but how could I know if *she* would find it convincing? Especially when it was her own son who was really responsible. I wondered if maybe I should leave that part out. What I had to do was prove I wasn't to blame, not point the finger at the guilty party. I sure as hell didn't want Henry to get away with it, but if that was the best way to get my friends and my father released, then that was what I'd do.

It didn't help that the palace looked like the Bastille, the Tower of London, and Alcatraz all rolled into one from the outside. I'd thought the place looked intimidating when I was coming as a guest, but it was about three times worse now.

Ready to do whatever it took, I snuck into the palace and began searching for the Queen.

There was one problem with my grand plan. Well, more than one, really, but one that slapped me upside the head within about ten minutes of beginning my search.

I had never met Titania, and I had no idea what she looked like, except that she probably bore some resemblance to both Henry and Elaine. That wasn't a whole lot to go on, and there were tons of people in the palace. Some of them were obviously Knights and servants, but there were plenty of others who could be guests or family or the Faerie Queen herself.

All of the women were ridiculously beautiful, because that came with being Fae. And all wore gowns that made them look like actresses in a costume drama. Some gowns were showier than others, and some women wore more jewels, but I didn't spot anyone wearing a crown or carrying a scepter or doing anything else particularly queenly. My stomach did a flip-flop when it occurred to me that Titania might not even be in residence. Maybe she decided to leave the palace after the bombing, fearing for her safety.

But no, if the Queen weren't around here somewhere, I doubted there would be so much activity in the palace, especially not at this time of night. Maybe that was another dose of wishful thinking, but I clung to it for all I was worth, because it was my only hope.

One bright spot in my nerve-racking search was that I found Princess Elaine, alive and relatively well. There was an angry red scar on her face, and a haunted expression in her eyes, but I let out a breath of relief to discover the bomb hadn't killed her.

My relief dampened a bit when I realized that though she was in a room with about ten other glittering gems of Sidhe society, she was sitting alone on the edge of a chaise, and no one was looking at her, much less talking to her. Almost like she was as invisible as I was. I bit my lip as I approached her and looked at the scar. There must have been some pure iron in the bomb, because that was the only thing I knew of that could permanently scar a Sidhe's skin when there was a healer available. She should have been either dead or good as new, and I suspected from her obvious misery that she'd have preferred one or the other.

Seeing the princess made me hate Henry just that much more.

He hadn't cared what happened to her or any of the other innocent bystanders in the room, just as long as he could destroy the Faeriewalker who wasn't under his thumb.

Finding the princess was a pleasant surprise, despite her condition. I had a much less pleasant surprise when I rounded a corner and almost bumped into Connor. He and another of the silent Huntsmen were walking briskly down the hall, apparently on some errand or another.

Neither my brother nor the other Huntsman saw me, and they probably wouldn't have felt me even if I really had collided with them, but dread settled in my stomach at the sight of them. If the Huntsmen were in the palace, that meant the Erlking was, too. And he'd told me when he'd given me the brooch that, while it would work on his Huntsmen, it would not work on him. Which meant if he and I crossed paths, I was toast.

I thought my nerves were driving me crazy *before* I found out the Erlking was in the palace. Now, I jumped at every sound, my heart pounding in my throat as I wondered if I'd made the biggest mistake of my life coming here.

It was too late now. I was here, and I wasn't leaving until I tracked down Titania and gave her my side of the argument. Or until the Erlking found me and I became the only female member of the Wild Hunt.

I'd been searching the palace for what felt like twelve hours, though my watch insisted it was less than one, when I found a hidden wing. I wish I could say I'd cleverly deduced that the palace wasn't the same size on the inside as the out, but really I just got lucky. (Imagine that!)

While I was walking down a corridor I was ninety-nine percent sure I'd walked down at least twice before, I saw a Knight walk through a wall at the very end of the hall. Even my long rest this afternoon hadn't been enough to cure my exhaustion, and I wondered if I was now seeing things. I figured I'd better go check it out. After all, I was invisible, so no one would see me make an idiot of myself trying to walk through a stone wall.

I approached the wall cautiously, trying to sense any magic that might linger around it and reveal an illusion spell, but I supposed an illusion spell that left a magical signature would be pretty useless in Faerie. I didn't sense any magic around the wall, but when I reached out to touch it, my fingers passed through. Cool! Titania *had* to be back here somewhere, because I could swear I'd searched every other square inch of the palace. (This assuming she hadn't been one of the hundreds of unidentified women I'd seen in my wanderings. It was always possible she wasn't as pompous as Henry and didn't parade around in clothing that set her apart.) But this wing was hidden for some reason, and security seemed as good a reason as any.

Taking a deep breath, hoping the hidden doorway wasn't booby-trapped, I closed my eyes and stepped through the wall.

Despite my fingers having gone through, I couldn't help tensing up as though I was about to walk into something solid. I held my breath, then let it out slowly when I finished my step and hadn't smacked into anything. I opened my eyes, and my heart leapt with hope.

The hallway I'd entered was lined with Knights, all armed to the teeth and standing at grim attention. Unlike the rest of the palace, this wing hadn't been built from stone. The walls were of some kind of dense, twisted live wood, like the tallest, most solid thicket ever, and the high ceiling was formed of an archway of branches. Climbing white rosebushes punctuated the hallway at regular intervals, their blooms so tightly packed together that if I looked at them through the corner of my eye, they looked like white marble pillars.

I was pretty sure the floor under my feet was dirt, but it was carpeted by a plush layer of pristine white rose petals. How they remained so pristine when they weren't on their bushes and people walked on them, I don't know. The hall was lit by glowing chunks of translucent white rock, kind of like salt lamps, only there was no electricity and no lightbulb. I could only assume they were lit by magic, because this hall did not look like a good place to light a fire.

There was a single doorway at the end of the hall, and it was guarded by a pair of gargantuan trolls. I caught my breath at the sight of them, a shiver running down my spine. I'd seen drawings and paintings of trolls before, but the only one I'd ever seen in person was Lachlan, who wore a human glamour. I liked it better when I didn't know what he really looked like beneath that glamour. Paintings couldn't do their size and malevolence justice. Paintings couldn't capture the soulless black eyes that didn't blink. Maybe it wasn't much of a shocker that the Sidhe didn't socialize with trolls after all.

I shook my head, trying to clear the fog of terror that tried to gather around me. The trolls might look terrifying, but they weren't monsters. Lachlan was one of the nicest Fae I knew, warm and friendly and loyal to a fault. Looks weren't everything. Besides, the trolls couldn't see me, so they weren't dangerous.

I started tiptoeing down the hall, trying not to disturb the rose petals as I walked. The Erlking's brooch might keep all these guards from noticing the petals moving, but I didn't want to leave a trail that they might notice after I'd passed. I had a feeling that if they sensed there might be an intruder, I would be in deep, deep trouble despite the brooch's spell.

I was sweating and practically vibrating with tension by the time I made it to the end of the hall. My lizard brain kept telling me not to get any closer to those trolls, and every step was a fight. It was probably stupid—the Knights with their magical skills were much more dangerous than the trolls—but I couldn't convince myself of that, and I wondered if what I was feeling was the effect of some kind of spell.

Not that it mattered. I had to get past the trolls, no matter how intimidating they were. I glanced quickly at my watch to see how much longer I was going to be invisible. I had eight minutes before I'd have to reactivate the spell again, and if I could just get myself moving, maybe I'd be in position to force the Queen to listen to me by the time it wore off, and I wouldn't have to prick myself for the gazillionth time.

Knowing I had to hurry, I slung my backpack forward and groped for the gun. Better to have it in my hand and ready when I walked through that doorway. I told myself I wasn't stalling, but I wasn't entirely convinced.

I checked to make sure the gun was loaded, then double-checked to make sure it was ready to fire. I shoved a couple of extra bullets in my pocket for easier access. Then I forced myself forward again.

I let my breath out slowly as I moved into reach of the trolls, but they didn't react to my presence. They might as well have been made of stone for all the life I saw in them.

My hand was shaking as I pushed the door open, but still none of the guards moved or showed any sign of noticing me. I closed it quietly behind me, then turned to face the room.

At first, I couldn't see much, because the lights were very low. They were the same kind of lights I'd seen out in the hall, but their glow was much dimmer, leaving most of the room in shadow. I blinked a couple of times as my eyes adjusted to the gloom.

Directly in front of me was a ginormous four-poster bed, mounded with pillows. And lounging amongst all those pillows was a drop-dead gorgeous woman with curly red hair that reached to her waist. She was smiling contentedly, her eyes heavy-lidded as she held a white silk sheet to her chest in a halfhearted show of modesty. She was obviously naked underneath it, and in the shadows at the foot of the bed, I could see the silhouette of a man pulling on a pair of boots.

My first thought was: *Awkward!* This was not a good time to be bursting in on the Faerie Queen. (Not that there ever really was a good time.) My second thought was: *Thank God I didn't get here earlier.*

And then dread coiled in my gut as my mind fully processed what I'd just seen.

The man at the foot of the bed stepped out of the shadows, his boots making a familiar metallic clinking sound with each step. He leaned casually against one of the bedposts, crossing his arms over his chest and grinning at me.

"We meet again, Faeriewalker," the Erlking said, his eyes twinkling with laughter at my expense.

I was totally and completely screwed.

chapter twenty

Out of the corner of my eye, I saw Titania sit up, the sheet sliding down and showing me more of her than I wanted to see.

"She's here?" the Queen gasped.

I stood by the doorway, frozen like a scared rabbit caught in the Erlking's sights. I pointed my gun at him, but I'd seen him take a bullet to the head with barely a blink. The gun wouldn't save me.

"I told you she would come," he said, not taking his eyes off of me. "She would do just about anything for Ethan."

Great. Not only was he here, he was waiting for me. I was getting way too familiar with the sensation of falling into his traps.

I swung the barrel of my gun toward Titania. "Call him off!" I ordered her, though I suspected I sounded more frightened than threatening.

The Erlking laughed. "She can't hear you, remember?"

Dammit! I still had a couple of minutes until the spell wore off, and until it did, only the Erlking could see or hear me.

Gritting my teeth, I pointed the gun at one of the bedposts and pulled the trigger. My aim was lousy, but the bullet scraped a chip of wood off the edge of the post. Titania might not be able to see or hear me, but she could see the bullet and the effect it had had.

"Even though she can't see me," I said, "I bet she's smart enough to understand the message I just sent."

"Let's find out, shall we?" he replied, taking a step toward me.

I squeezed the trigger again. My aim was better this time, and the bullet buried itself in the bedpost.

"Arawn, stop!" Titania ordered, a hint of panic in her voice. "I rescind my permission."

The Erlking *had* to be annoyed that he'd just lost his chance to capture me and bind me to the Wild Hunt, but he didn't show it. In fact, he was still grinning like he found this all very amusing. He put his hand to his chest and bowed from the waist, though I wasn't sure if he meant the gesture as one of respect for the Queen or mockery for me. My hands shook as I loaded two more bullets into the gun and prayed I wouldn't need to use them.

The air prickled with magic as Titania slid out of the bed. She'd pulled a gauzy wrapper around herself, but it left little to the imagination. Who knew she and the Erlking were so . . . close? I would have thought the fact that he'd bound Connor to the Wild Hunt for the last thousand years or so might have put a damper on any relationship. Connor was her son, and she was sleeping with the man who'd enslaved him. Nice.

I was pretty sure Titania didn't have to see me to destroy me with her magic. And because I wasn't supposed to be able to sense magic, she had no idea I was aware she was gathering her power.

"Tell her to quit it!" I said, and Titania jumped, startled.

"Tell her yourself," the Erlking said. "The spell wore off."

Yes. I could tell that by the way the Queen was staring at me in horror. So much for my deep, dark secret.

"Quit calling magic," I ordered her. I had to stifle a laugh at the thought of me, a half-blooded teenager from the mortal world, ordering around Titania, the Queen of the Seelie Court. But however powerful she might be, my gun scared the crap out of her.

The magic faded from the air, and the Queen stood up straighter, wiping the expression of horror from her face and staring at me with the coldest blue eyes I'd ever seen.

"You dare much," she said, and if her eyes were cold, her voice was positively icy. "You tried to kill my granddaughter, and now you threaten me. For that I vow to make you suffer."

I hoped I didn't look as terrified as I felt. I suspected if Titania wanted to make me suffer, she could be very, very creative about how she did it.

"I didn't try to kill Princess Elaine," I said. I sounded calmer than I felt, which was good because otherwise my voice might have shaken too badly for her to understand. "And I'm only threatening you because I don't know how else to make you listen to my side of the story."

"She was attacked with a mortal weapon," Titania argued. "Only a Faeriewalker could have wielded such a weapon."

I nodded. "That's true. But *I'm* not the Faeriewalker who wielded it."

Out of the corner of my eye, I saw the Erlking smile. Of course, he'd known all along I wasn't behind the bomb. We might not be bestest buds, but he knew me frighteningly well. Well enough to guess that I'd come to the palace once my friends were captured. And easily well enough to know I wouldn't plant a bomb even against someone I hated, much less against someone I didn't know.

"There are no other Faeriewalkers," the Queen snapped, but I thought there might be a hint of doubt in her eyes.

"There has to be at least one other," I countered, "because I didn't set that bomb. If the Erlking weren't here, I could have walked right up to you and shot you in the head without you ever knowing I was here. I could have done the same to Elaine. Or I could have used a knife, so that no one would even guess a Faeriewalker was involved."

"If there were another Faeriewalker, I would know," Titania said, but she definitely sounded less sure of herself.

"Why would I want to hurt Elaine? I'd never even met her. And I've lived all my life in the mortal world. I don't give a crap about Faerie politics."

"I understand you were only a tool," she said, her voice going all soft and gentle. I didn't believe it for a moment. "Your father must have thought that Henry would dine with you that night instead of Elaine."

My heart lurched at the mention of my dad. If Titania had believed all along that he was the mastermind behind the whole bombing scheme . . .

"Seamus is alive," the Erlking told me.

I guess my train of thought had been showing on my face. I had to blink rapidly to keep from crying in relief. Maybe I was crazy, but I couldn't help feeling grateful to Arawn for telling me. I don't know if I'd have had the courage to ask. Titania flashed him a look of annoyance, perhaps not used to having her thunder stolen.

"Even if my father thought that," I said, "and even if he wanted to kill Henry, he wouldn't have done it that way. He wouldn't have used me. And there's no way I would have *let* him use me like that."

The Queen was still looking at me with a gentle, pitying expression. "I'm sure it seems that way to you," she said soothingly. "And I understand that it is hard for you to think ill of your father."

I had to roll my eyes at that one. I was pretty good at "thinking ill" of people. "It doesn't matter what I think of my dad. I'm telling you: I had nothing to do with that bomb. There's another Faeriewalker that no one knows about. Well, almost no one."

Magic began to gather again, and I jerked my arms up, realizing the barrel of the gun had been slowly dropping as we spoke. It wasn't like the gun was heavy or anything, but my arms were getting tired.

"No magic!" I reminded her. "I'm serious."

Titania shrugged as though it hardly mattered, but the magic dissipated. "I believe you would say anything to save your father from getting his just desserts," she said. "You will not change my mind with brute force."

Too bad brute force was my only option. I knew if I lowered the gun, Titania's magic would come back in a heartbeat, and though I didn't know what that magic would do to me, I was sure it wasn't anything good.

"You would believe her if she could prove the existence of another Faeriewalker, would you not?" the Erlking asked.

I might have thought he was trying to help me out—if I didn't know him better. He just wanted to know the identity of the other Faeriewalker in hopes that she was easier to exploit than I was.

I pictured Elizabeth in my mind's eye, her head bowed and her shoulders hunched in the face of Henry's disapproval. She had brought the bomb from Avalon and had planted it under Elaine's chair, but she truly was the helpless tool Titania imagined me to be. If I gave her up, then Titania might well kill her. And if she didn't, the Erlking would start circling her like the hungry shark he was.

But if I didn't give her up, my father and I were both going to die, and who knew what Titania would do to my friends.

Titania cocked her head, looking curious. "*Can* you prove it?" she asked me.

I hesitated, hating the thought of throwing Elizabeth to the wolves. My throat tightened, and I felt like a gutless wonder. She might not be a friend of mine, but Elizabeth was a child.

"You have no choice, Dana," the Erlking said. "This can only end in disaster for you if you refuse to unmask the real culprit."

He was right, and I knew it. It wasn't like I had enough bullets to shoot my way out of here. And even if I summoned my magic and unleashed my deadly spell, there was a gauntlet of Knights and trolls I'd have to make my way through before I escaped the palace a second time.

I wanted to scream with anger and frustration, but I didn't. Too many people's lives depended on me, and I couldn't afford to take a single false step.

"It's Elizabeth," I said, the words tasting bitter on my tongue. "And I can prove it."

There was no sign of recognition on either of their faces. But then why should Titania or Arawn know the name of one insignificant servant in Henry's entourage.

"She's one of Henry's servants," I explained. "And she's just a kid," I hastened to add. "He beats on her, and she's so terrified of him she'd do anything he told her to."

I'd thought Titania's eyes looked cold before. I'd had no idea what cold was until I saw the way she looked at me now.

"You lie," she said simply, but there was so much fury in her voice that I almost pulled the trigger in preemptive self-defense. It was no surprise that she didn't like hearing her son might have been involved with the whole plot.

"You said you can prove it," Arawn said, sounding surprisingly cautious, like he was afraid Titania was about to explode or something.

I nodded, too intimidated by Titania's glare to force out any words.

"I refuse to believe it," Titania spat. "This is your father's doing. He wishes to discredit my son, and—"

"If she thinks she can prove it, then let her try," Arawn interrupted. "If your son is innocent, then there is no harm done. You can punish Seamus to your heart's content, and you can leave Dana to me, which I assure you she would find a more than adequate punishment." He winked at me, like he thought this was all some kind of joke. It made me want to shoot him, though I knew it wouldn't do any good.

Titania speared me with her ice-pick eyes. "Very well. You have my leave to try to 'prove' my son was behind this. And woe unto you and everyone you care about if you fail."

Yeah, no pressure or anything.

"Give your weapon to Arawn," she ordered. "I will not be threatened in my own home."

Arawn took a couple of cautious steps toward me and held out his hand.

I did *not* want to give him my gun. True, I knew it wasn't enough of a threat to get me out of here with my skin, but it made a nice security blanket. Even though my arms were quivering with the strain of holding it up.

Arawn sidled closer, though he made no attempt to take the gun from me by force. His voice dropped to a barely audible murmur.

"Give me the gun. It is hardly your only weapon, and it isn't even your most fearsome one."

I blinked at him in surprise. Just when I thought I had him all figured out, he'd go and surprise me like this. He was talking about my mortality spell, and instead of blurting it out and revealing my secret to the Queen, he was taking pains to keep it between us. I was sure it was for his own benefit somehow, rather than for mine, but I was grateful anyway. I also knew that once again, he was right. So I flicked the safety back on and forced my cramped fingers to release their stranglehold on the gun. Then I handed the gun to Arawn butt-first, and I was left with no defenses save the one I doubted I'd be willing to use.

chapter twenty-one

As soon as the gun left my hand, I braced myself for an attack, feeling naked and helpless without it. Titania looked at me like I was a cockroach she wanted to stomp, but she didn't try to call magic and she didn't give the Erlking permission to take me. Either she was being honorable, or I had awakened a kernel of doubt in her with my accusations. I didn't much care which.

"Show me your proof," she commanded.

"First, we have to figure out how far away from a mortal object I have to be before it goes poof."

Titania's brows drew together ever so slightly, and I realized she might not be familiar with the mortal version of modern English.

"Before it disappears," I clarified.

"This resembles more an escape plan than proof of my son's guilt," she said.

I rolled my eyes at her. "Yeah, because I came bursting into your bedroom in an attempt to escape. If I wanted to escape, I wouldn't be here." I could tell she didn't appreciate my sarcasm, but I didn't have it in me to apologize. Maybe this wasn't an appropriate way to speak to the Queen of the Seelie Court, but I'd been through too much to stress about etiquette.

"There are about ten thousand Knights and a couple of trolls outside your door," I continued, since she didn't look convinced by my reasonable argument, "and you're worried I'm going to try to escape from under their noses?"

"They did not stop you from entering."

Arawn held out his hand again. "Give me the brooch. If you don't have that, I think we can all feel secure that you will not try to escape."

I wanted to hand over the brooch even less than I'd wanted to hand over the gun, but it wasn't like I had a lot of options. If Titania decided she didn't want to hear what I had to say, she could condemn me in a heartbeat and there'd be nothing I could do to prevent it.

To my shame, my hand was shaking when I laid the brooch in Arawn's palm. One by one, Titania was stripping away my defenses, and I was letting her. But what choice did I have?

"I believe you are telling the truth," Arawn said as he took the brooch. "As long as you are telling the truth, you have nothing to fear."

I met his gaze for a moment, surprised by this hint of humanity. He was a stone-cold killer, a skilled manipulator, and if not exactly a liar, then at least a deceiver. But he was the closest thing I had to a friend right now, and wasn't that a sorry state of affairs?

I looked away quickly and started unfastening my watch. "So, um, I'm going to put this on the far side of the room." I held up the watch for Titania to see. "Then I'm going to back away until whatever happens to mortal stuff when there's no Faeriewalker around happens."

I waited for Titania's approval before moving, because I suspected she had an itchy magical trigger finger. She pursed her lips like she wasn't happy with this idea, but nodded curtly.

"Proceed."

There was no furniture in the room except for the huge bed, and like in the hallway, there was a carpet of white rose petals. They looked for all the world like they were loose, fresh from the flower and scattered willy-nilly. And yet when I stepped, they didn't move, nor did they look crushed. Maybe they were just a pretty illusion, although considering the rose-scented air, I thought they were probably real.

Titania shadowed my movements, and I felt her eyes on me. The sensation made me shiver, and my skin prickled with goose bumps. Not the magic-induced kind, but the creeped-out kind. I set the watch carefully on the floor, then began backing away.

I started to sweat when I was about halfway across the room. The watch was still there, and I couldn't help worrying that something was going to go wrong. I knew I had to be "close" for my Faeriewalker magic to work, but I had no idea just how close "close" was. I suspected Titania wouldn't have much patience with me, and I stared at my watch, willing it to hurry up and disappear.

When my back bumped up against the door to the room, I felt sure that Titania would declare my time was up. The watch was still there, a brown, faux-croco stripe in the rose-petal carpet.

"I guess I have to go outside the room," I said, wishing my voice didn't sound so tentative.

"Arawn will accompany you," Titania replied, not looking away from the watch.

Like she needed more security than she already had. Though come to think of it, I wouldn't mind having Arawn nearby if I had to walk past those trolls. He, at least, was the devil I knew.

He opened the door for me, then stepped out and said something I couldn't hear to the Knights and trolls on guard. I hoped it was something like "Don't attack the girl who's about to come out the door."

Taking a deep breath for courage, I backed over the threshold. The guards had to be surprised to see me, considering they hadn't seen me go in, but a quick glance to each side showed me they were paying no attention to me, no doubt thanks to Arawn's warning.

The door frame quickly blocked my view of the watch, but I could see Titania staring at it, so I knew it was still there. I was about three steps into the hallway when Titania jumped a little, then looked over her shoulder at me.

"It is gone," she said.

Fighting an insane desire to flee down the hallway away from the dangerous Faerie Queen, I forced myself back into the bedroom, Arawn following close behind.

"All right," I said. "Now let's bring Elizabeth here. I'll put another item from the mortal world down, and then I'll back away as she stays in the room. If she's not a Faeriewalker, the item will disappear when I'm three steps out. If she *is* a Faeriewalker, it won't go anywhere."

Titania nodded, then strode to the door. I guess she didn't mind having her guards see her in her almost completely see-through wrap.

"I will have the girl Elizabeth brought here," she announced as she yanked open the door.

"How sure are you that this Elizabeth is the Faeriewalker?" Arawn asked me in an undertone.

I chewed my lip. I'd felt pretty sure until he'd asked. But really, I was basing my theory on little more than a guess. There had been a lot of servants in that dining room when the bomb went off, and it was possible one of the others had been in Henry's entourage and hadn't stuck out in my mind. Elizabeth *looked* like a full-blooded Fae, beautiful and perfect, but genetics are sometimes fickle.

"Sure enough to stake my life on it, I guess," I answered, my voice a little quavery.

He put a hand on my shoulder and squeezed. "You are probably right. The Faeriewalker must have a very powerful Fae parent, and I can't help noticing the link between the names Henry and Elizabeth."

I didn't at first know what he was talking about, but it didn't take me a long time to figure it out, not when I was so aware of how much the Fae lived in the past. The first Queen Elizabeth had been the daughter of Henry VIII. Come to think of it, she'd been famous for being a redhead as well.

"So you think Elizabeth is Prince Henry's daughter," I said.

"Likely. Assuming she is the Faeriewalker."

Damn. I thought I had it bad with my parental issues, but I couldn't imagine having Henry as a father. He treated her badly even for a servant, much less for a daughter. And here I was, turning her over to save my own hide.

I shoved the guilt aside as best I could. I wasn't doing this just for myself. I was doing it for my dad, and Ethan, and Kimber, and Keane, and Finn. I still hated it, still wished I could have thought of another way to prove my innocence, but there didn't seem to be one.

Titania came back into the room, bringing with her the arctic chill of her displeasure. I wished she'd put some clothes on, but perhaps the Fae didn't have the same modesty issues as humans. She seemed quite unconscious of her state of undress. The Erlking, I noticed from his occasional appreciative glances, was much more aware of it than she was.

Soon, there was a commotion out in the hall, and I tensed up, my imagination telling me it was the Queen's guards coming to seize me. I stared at the door with what I felt sure were scared eyes, and when someone knocked, I was so tense I jumped.

"Enter," the Queen beckoned. I hadn't seen her move, but somehow she had changed out of the gauzy wrap and into an elaborate white and gold kimono-like gown, and her hair was gathered in a loose but elegant chignon at the back of her head.

The door opened, and Henry burst in, dressed in his usual flashy doublet and leggings. Behind him, a Knight entered, dragging Elizabeth by the arm. She had obviously been in bed when the Knights had come for her. Her hair was disheveled from sleep, and it looked like she'd dressed in a frantic rush, her skirts dragging on the floor behind her because she'd skipped the bustle. I supposed she was lucky the Knights had allowed her time to dress at all. Tears streaked her face, and guilt hammered at me harder than ever.

Henry came to an abrupt halt when he saw me standing there beside the Erlking. I thought I saw a hint of fear in his eyes, but maybe that was just what I wanted to see.

"What is the meaning of this?" he demanded of his mother. "Why have my quarters been raided and my servant dragged from her bed?"

If Henry had nothing to hide, I doubted he would have been able to muster much outrage over the seizure of one of his servants. It wasn't like he had a warm and caring relationship with them.

"Forgive the intrusion, my son," Titania said in a voice that clearly conveyed she didn't like his tone. "I had no intention of disrupting your evening and want only to question this child."

She gestured at Elizabeth, who looked like she was about to faint from terror. The girl gave me a pleading look, but though I'd helped her against the Green Lady, I couldn't help her against this. I prayed that Titania would take pity on her and realize that her son was the one to blame.

Henry dialed down the outrage. I guess he saw that Titania didn't appreciate it. When he spoke again, he managed to sound calm and only mildly curious.

"Why should you need to question a servant girl? She is no one."

My dad had told me that Henry lacked the wit and subtlety he needed to be a star player in Court politics, and it seemed he was right. His protests, even when so toned down, were as good as him screaming, "I have something to hide!" Of course, he *did* have something to hide, so he probably felt pretty trapped.

Titania arched one brow. "If she is, as you say, no one, then this will take but a moment." She turned to me. "Put your mortal item in its place."

I unzipped my backpack, looking for something that definitely didn't belong in Faerie. The first thing I came upon was my camera, but I was reluctant to part with it.

"How about this?" the Erlking suggested, holding up my gun. "I have no plans to give it back to you, and as soon as I leave your presence it will be gone anyway."

I nodded. The gun had outlived its usefulness. The Erlking walked to the other end of the room, putting the gun on the floor approximately where my watch had been.

"Bring her closer," Titania ordered her Knight, who yanked Elizabeth forward, practically pulling her off her feet.

Henry was still trying to play it calm, but he wasn't doing a very good job of it. His facial expression might have been bland, but every muscle in his body looked coiled and tight. I didn't need to see the gun disappear to be sure that I was right, but Titania would need the concrete proof.

The Knight shoved Elizabeth down to her knees while still keeping hold of her arm. She gave a little cry of pain, quickly stifled.

"There is no reason to be brutal with the poor child," Arawn said, stepping forward and getting up into the Knight's face. "She isn't going anywhere."

The Knight paled and let go of Elizabeth's arm, taking a hasty step back. Even one of the Queen's Knights knew better than to mess with the Erlking.

My stomach twisted as I realized the Erlking was already beginning his campaign to seduce Elizabeth, coming to her rescue, showing her kindness when no one else would. She was a miserable, broken creature, and even younger than me. What were the chances she could resist Arawn's charms? He certainly had them, when he wanted to. Somehow, I was going to have to find a way to warn her of her danger.

But I was getting ahead of myself. I still had to prove she was a Faeriewalker. And once I did, Titania might turn her over to the Erlking anyway.

"This is a trick," Henry said. "That is not truly a mortal weapon. It is merely an illusion, and Seamus has arranged this."

I might have blurted an outraged response, except Titania's laugh surprised me into silence. Henry's cheeks reddened, and his eyes flashed with anger. And a hint of fear, I was sure of it.

"Seamus is a clever and subtle man," Titania said, "but I'm sure he could have found a simpler way than this to strike at you if he wished." She stalked closer to him, the coldness of her gaze now directed at him rather than me. "You seem strangely reluctant to see this test carried out, my son. Almost as though you already know this child is a Faeriewalker. Perhaps I begin to understand why you were so opposed to my decision to invite Seamus's daughter to Court."

Henry shook his head. "You cannot possibly think that of me! I am merely concerned that this is a trick."

Titania's smile was almost wry. "And that I am too weak-minded to see through such a trick?"

That shut him up, at least momentarily. His hand rubbed nervously over his hip, and I wondered if he had a weapon concealed somewhere in his doublet.

Titania turned to me and nodded. I took that as my cue to leave the room, so I made my way hastily to the door. I had to go around Henry to get there, and I didn't like that one bit. He'd stopped rubbing his hip, and I saw no sign of a weapon in his hand, but that didn't mean there *wasn't* one.

The only thing that kept me moving forward was the conviction that Henry didn't dare kill me in front of all these people, especially when that would make him look guiltier than ever. I let out a breath I hadn't even realized I was holding when I made it past him without incident and walked through the door out into the hall. I made a point of walking past where I'd stood when the watch disappeared, just to make it doubly obvious that the gun was still there.

"Now the child," Titania said.

The Knight who'd dragged Elizabeth into the room cast a brief, worried look at Arawn before reaching for her again. Arawn stopped him with a forbidding glare.

"I will escort her," Arawn said, and when Titania didn't object, the Knight backed off.

Elizabeth still looked terrified, but Arawn bent and said something to her I couldn't hear. She sniffled and nodded, then allowed him to help her to her feet.

"Just look at her!" Henry said, and now he sounded downright desperate. "Does she look like a half-breed? You can plainly see mortal blood in that one." He gestured contemptuously at me. "But Elizabeth is entirely Fae. You may check for glamour if you'd like."

"How kind of you to allow me such a privilege," Titania said acidly. "Looks can be deceiving, and I will not rely on them to tell me whether the child is a Faeriewalker or not. Arawn, please take her out of the room."

Arawn bowed, then put a hand lightly on Elizabeth's back and guided her toward the door. She looked even tinier and more vulnerable next to him. She wiped tears from her face as she walked, but her cheeks were still blotchy and her eyes red and swollen. I had to fight another surge of guilt.

I forced my eyes away from Elizabeth's pitiful figure and watched Titania instead. The Queen was facing away from the door, watching the gun. Henry was looking back and forth between her and the gun, no doubt trying to figure out how to salvage the situation.

When Titania suddenly whirled on Henry with a snarl, I knew the gun had disappeared. And then Henry did what any trapped animal would do: he attacked.

chapter twenty-two

I'd been right all along. Henry *did* have a concealed weapon. He must have known the moment the Knights had come for Elizabeth that he was in deep trouble.

No one had time to react. By the time I saw the glint of metal in Henry's hand and tried to shout a warning, the gun had already fired.

A giant fist punched me in the shoulder, the impact so brutal I fell backward onto the carpet of rose petals. Elizabeth screamed, and Arawn tried to shield her with his body, but even the Erlking wasn't fast enough to intercept a bullet. The gun boomed again, and Elizabeth's scream turned to a shriek as blood suddenly spotted the front of her dress. Her eyes went wide with shock, and she sank to her knees.

I touched my shaking hand to my shoulder, and it came away wet with blood.

"Nobody move!" Henry yelled.

My vision swam, and I felt like the room was bucking beneath me. Maybe that was just the footsteps of the Knights and trolls as they reacted to Henry's surprise attack. Magic filled the air, making it hard to breathe.

"Anyone casts a spell, and she's dead!" Henry barked. I had to blink a few times to clear my vision enough to see that he'd put the gun to Titania's head. "And trust me, I can shoot faster than you can get the Faeriewalkers out of range."

Oh, a dispassionate voice in my head murmured. *That's why he shot us. To keep us from running away and making the gun go poof.* I wondered how many other mortal weapons he had smuggled into Faerie with Elizabeth's help.

I forced myself up into a sitting position. I thought for a minute I was going to pass out. Blood ran hotly down my chest, and my right arm didn't want to move. I was weak and nauseous, but it didn't hurt much at all. I'd read enough books to figure that wasn't a good sign, but I was thankful not to have to feel it.

Elizabeth was in worse shape than me. Henry's shot had hit me in the shoulder, but he'd hit her in the chest. She was lying on her back, spatters of her blood making the white rose petals look red. Her chest was moving with her breaths, but she was unconscious, and far too pale. Maybe Henry had intended to kill her—he only needed one of us alive and in the vicinity to keep the gun operational—or maybe he'd been aiming for her shoulder, too, and had missed. He probably didn't have much practice with mortal weapons. Either way, I knew she was in dire trouble.

The Knights and the trolls had frozen in place with the threat to their Queen. I'd have doubted Henry would shoot his own mother, except he'd obviously had no compunction about shooting his daughter.

Arawn spared a withering look for the Knights who had brought Elizabeth to Titania's room. "You didn't think to check him for mortal weapons before you brought him into the Queen's presence with a suspected Faeriewalker at his side and a charge of treason looming over his head?" He shook his head in disgust, then turned to Henry.

"You are aware she is not *my* Queen," Arawn said to Henry. He spoke in a normal tone of voice, as if nothing out of the ordinary were happening.

"And therefore this is none of your business," Henry responded. "I'm sure you and my mother have some agreements you'd prefer not to lose, so you would prefer not to see the throne change hands. I suggest you stay out of the way."

Arawn shrugged. "Very well. But you've gone through a great deal of trouble to make sure you have a Faeriewalker at your disposal. I assure you, your daughter would make a more tractable servant than Dana, so please allow me to heal the child's injury before she expires."

I crawled over to Elizabeth and took her hand in mine. I didn't know if she could feel it, but after giving her up as I had, I had to give her whatever comfort I could. Her eyelashes fluttered briefly at my touch, but she didn't open her eyes.

"You may heal her," Henry said, "but make no attempt to move her or the other Faeriewalker."

Arawn nodded, then moved slowly to Elizabeth's other side, keeping a wary eye on Henry as he did so. Not that Henry's gun could do him any damage, but perhaps he actually cared what happened to Titania. He had been in her bed, after all.

"Now, Mother," Henry said, "we must put this unfortunate misunderstanding behind us. To that end, you will accept a geis not to harm me nor cause any other person to harm me. We will then peacefully go our separate ways."

Arawn looked at me across Elizabeth's body, as he put his hand over the bloody wound.

"You have to kill him, Dana," he murmured, his voice so soft I almost didn't hear him over the thudding of my heart.

I blinked stupidly at him, my mind feeling all blurry as the first hints of pain worked their way into my consciousness. "Huh?"

"You're the only one who can," Arawn continued, not looking at me anymore. He was trying hard to make sure Henry didn't realize he was talking to me. "The Sidhe are hard to kill, remember? The Knights would need multiple spells to destroy him, and he will kill Titania as soon as the first is released. *You* need only one."

Elizabeth made a soft, whimpering sound, and I squeezed her hand harder. I'd seen the Erlking heal a bullet wound before, and it hadn't looked like much fun for the healee.

He was joking, right?

"Do you agree to my geis?" Henry asked the queen.

Titania stood tall and proud, her expression devoid of anything resembling human emotion. Her son had betrayed her and was even now threatening her life, but she looked neither hurt nor scared nor angry. I'd seen statues that conveyed more emotion than the Faerie Queen did right now.

"If she agrees," Arawn continued, "he'll get away with it. With almost killing Elaine, with framing you, with abusing his child and then shooting her."

The pain in my shoulder had become a steady throb, but I thought it wasn't bleeding quite so much anymore. Elizabeth's back arched, and her hand nearly crushed mine as a cry tore from her throat. With a shudder, she went limp, and the Erlking moved his hand away from the wound, holding a squashed bullet between his fingers.

I shivered, suddenly cold. I hoped that meant I was chilled by the Erlking's suggestion, not that I was in the process of bleeding out.

"It is agreed," Titania said. I knew that wasn't good, but my head was foggy enough that for a moment, I forgot why.

"Dana!" Arawn said in an urgent hiss. "You haven't much time."

I blinked, swaying and wondering if it would be okay if I lay down. "*You* kill him," I mumbled. "You're not part of her Court, so you're not covered by the agreement."

"But I would need Titania's permission to kill him, and the geis will not allow her to give it to me."

Oh. That sucked.

"Guess he's getting away with it," I said, because there was no way I was going to kill someone in cold blood. Even assuming I was able to gather enough magic to cast my spell before I passed out.

There was already plenty of magic in the air, though thanks to the gun at Titania's head, no one dared unleash it, but I felt a surge as she accepted the geis Henry forced on her.

I thought it was all over now, that Henry would lower the gun and leave the building and then I could allow myself to collapse. But he wasn't finished. The gun was still at the Queen's head.

"I am going to leave the palace now," he said. "And I'm taking the Faeriewalkers with me. Both of them. Agree that you will make no attempt to stop me."

Uh-oh. That couldn't be good. Not for me, and not for Elizabeth.

"Do it now," the Erlking urged me. "If you leave the palace with him, you will be in no shape to defend yourself later."

"I'm in no shape to defend myself *now*," I said. At least, I think that's what I said. My words were slurring, my vision swimming

Arawn reached over and grabbed my shoulder, his hand coming down right over the bullet wound. And suddenly, I had no trouble whatsoever feeling the pain.

I couldn't suppress a scream.

"Take your hands off my property!" Henry shouted, and Arawn sat back on his heels and wiped his hands on his pants.

"I was merely removing the bullet," he said mildly.

"Don't touch her again. She is mine."

"Or at least will be, if Her Majesty agrees to your terms," the Erlking corrected, and I knew his words were directed more at me than at Henry.

My wounded shoulder was still throbbing, but my head was a

little clearer, and I no longer thought I would pass out any moment.

"Help me," Elizabeth said, and I realized I was still holding her hand. She was conscious, but that was about the best I could say about her condition. Her cheeks were almost as pale as the rose petals. And there was a glassy look in her eyes, like she was on the verge of shock. "Don't let him take me again. Please. I'd rather die."

She couldn't have understood exactly what the Erlking was asking me to do. There were only a handful of people who knew I could do magic at all, and only the Erlking and Ethan knew about my deadly spell. But she *did* understand that I somehow had the power to kill Henry, and she desperately wanted me to do it.

The terror on Elizabeth's face was more than I could bear.

There was a roaring sound in my ears, so loud I couldn't hear whatever Henry and Titania said next. I could, however, feel the swell of magic, and I knew that Titania had agreed to let Henry take both me and Elizabeth. Henry lowered the gun, a self-satisfied smile on his face. Then he strode through the doorway, between the two furious-looking trolls, and headed toward us.

If it had been just myself I was defending, I probably would have hesitated, maybe long enough to make self-defense impossible. But through our clasped hands, I could feel Elizabeth trembling as she cowered on the floor, curled almost into fetal position. And I knew I couldn't let Henry take her. Not again.

The roaring in my ears drowned out the sound, but I felt the vibration in my head as I started to hum under my breath. The air was already thick with magic. It didn't appear as if the Knights had lowered their guard one iota, despite knowing they couldn't hurt Henry. The magic prickled over my skin and made breathing hard, and I wasn't sure whether it was responding to my call, or if it was just a residual effect of all the Knights' magic.

I watched Henry approach as I continued to hum. I couldn't be sure the magic was paying attention to me, and that was probably a good thing. As long as I couldn't tell where the magic was coming from, no one else could, either, and they couldn't stop me.

Henry met my glare with a spark of gloating malice. He'd disliked me before he'd even met me, just because I was my father's daughter. And now he thought he was getting to hurt me and my father by making me his helpless prisoner.

I waited until he was only a couple of steps away before I released my shrill high note, sending the magic at him in a barely controlled rush.

The magic slammed into Henry's chest, lifting him off his feet. His eyes widened in shock and fear, and he let out a shriek as the magic propelled him away from me, back through the door into Titania's room. He almost bowled into Titania herself, but she sidestepped neatly and avoided his flailing arms as he tried to grab on to her. He was flying straight for the far wall, but just before he slammed into it, there was a strange popping sound, and Henry just . . . disappeared.

His empty clothes fell to the floor.

chapter twenty-three

The hall fell completely silent, everyone staring in shock and confusion at the pile of clothes that had once been Prince Henry. Everyone except Arawn, of course, who wasn't surprised by what had happened and was stroking Elizabeth's hair as she quietly cried.

Titania, still showing no emotion, walked slowly toward Henry's clothes. When she reached them, she gave them a little nudge with her foot, as if she wasn't sure that Henry wasn't still there. Then she knelt beside them and ran her hand over the rich velvet fabric, the gesture almost tender, like she was brushing the hair out of a child's face.

I sat very still on the floor, hugging myself and tucking my hands under my arms to hide their trembling.

I'd just killed a person. No, Henry's wasn't the first death I was at least partially responsible for. I had used my terrible spell against Aunt Grace, but it wasn't my spell that killed her, at least not directly. And though I'd hated her, I hadn't actually been *trying* to kill her. But I'd known Henry would die when I cast my spell on him. I was a murderer.

"Killing someone in self-defense is not a crime," Arawn said, his voice seeming to echo through the hall. I didn't know if he was talking to me, or to Titania. Maybe both.

Titania rose to her feet slowly, moving like an old lady. Her expression was still tightly controlled, but I got the feeling she was holding on to that control by a thread. I also got the feeling it would be bad news for everyone around her if she lost that control. There was a palpable tension in the air, and it wasn't just because of the shock of Henry's death. Her eyes locked on me, and the ancient power in her gaze held me trapped as she stepped away from Henry's body—well, Henry's clothes—and came toward me.

My instinct for self-preservation suggested I start humming again, but I resisted the urge. Threatening the Queen didn't seem like such a hot idea after I'd just killed her son. I'm sure she'd been plenty mad at him after what he'd done, but I knew from experience that it was hard to stop loving family, even when they screwed up.

"What did you do to my son?" Titania asked, her voice as icy as it had ever been.

I licked my lips nervously. "I, um, made him mortal, I think. I'm sorry, but I couldn't let him take me. Or Elizabeth." Inspiration hit me, though I might have been confusing inspiration with desperation. "Elizabeth is your granddaughter. You saw how he treated her: like a piece of property, one he didn't have to take good care of. He shot her, and if Arawn hadn't spoken up, Henry would have been just as happy to let her die. Never mind what you think about me, but did you really want him leaving here with her as his prisoner? Again?"

I couldn't tell from looking at her whether my argument was having any effect or not. Poker players everywhere would envy her lack of expression.

"I should have you executed," she said, and one of the trolls eagerly stepped forward. Volunteering for the job, I guess.

"She has committed no crime," Arawn said. I wasn't sure why he was defending me, but I wasn't about to complain. I seemed to be very good at annoying the Fae. I didn't want to annoy Titania while she was deciding whether to execute me, so I was happy to let Arawn do the talking.

"She killed my son."

"In self-defense. And after he had shot her and your granddaughter and held a mortal weapon to your head. Surely you can't blame her for that."

"Henry would never have resorted to such drastic methods had she not forced him into it."

It didn't sound like Titania was much for forgiving and forgetting. Maybe I should start calling magic after all. Only now everyone was aware I could do it, and I suspected I'd be dead before the first note left my lips. Henry's magic might have protected him from being killed by one deadly spell—except for mine—but I didn't have the same luxury.

"He sired a Faeriewalker, Titania," Arawn said with what sounded like a hint of exasperation in his voice. "Sired her and then kept her secret from everyone, including you. You can't imagine his motives for doing that were pure."

Titania considered that for a long, painful moment. Then she turned to Elizabeth, and her voice softened.

"Where is your mother, child?" she asked.

Elizabeth still looked like she was one wrong move away from fainting in terror, but she managed to answer. "He killed her," she said, sounding even younger than she was. "He came to Avalon about three years ago and he visited my mother." Her eyes welled with tears. "She was so happy that I would finally have a chance to meet my father. But when he found out about me . . ." Her voice trailed off.

"What happened when he found out about you?" Titania

prompted. Considering how cold and terrifying she was capable of being, I had to admit I was impressed by how gently she spoke to Elizabeth.

"He killed her," Elizabeth whispered. "He killed her and took me away. Then he brought me to Faerie."

Titania looked appalled. "That cannot be," she said, but it didn't sound like she believed her own words.

"Dana did you a favor," Arawn said. "Let her go, and be consoled that you have gained a granddaughter."

"I will think on it," Titania responded.

A Fae serving woman stepped through the fake wall and into the hallway. She didn't look surprised by what she saw, so I guessed she'd been summoned somehow. Titania beckoned the woman forward, putting a hand on Elizabeth's shoulder.

"Take this child to a healer, that we might be certain her wounds have been properly tended," Titania said. "And have Henry's suite emptied and redecorated for her."

Elizabeth's eyes widened and her mouth dropped open. Titania smiled at her, that smile thawing the ice in her eyes. There might even have been a hint of kindness in her face, though kindness and Faerie Queens didn't seem to go together.

"You are my granddaughter, and both of your parents are dead. I will care for you as your father ought to have cared for you from the day you were born."

"C-can I go back to Avalon?" Elizabeth asked wistfully.

Titania stroked her hair, the touch both gentle and possessive. "Someday, perhaps."

Someday when Elizabeth had been thoroughly trained to be Titania's lapdog, she meant. It appeared her philosophy about Faeriewalkers was that they should be allowed the privilege of living as long as they made themselves useful. It remained to be seen whether killing Henry had made me useful or condemned me.

The servant led Elizabeth away.

"You come with me," Titania said to me with a wave of her hand, then headed toward her room.

I followed reluctantly, wishing she'd just make up her mind about me one way or the other. I wanted out of here, out of the Sunne Palace and out of Faerie. Arawn took a step to follow, but Titania turned to him and shook her head.

"You, I did not invite," she said. "Not this time."

Arawn grinned at her. "And you think that will stop me? I have a vested interest in Dana's well-being."

The reminder brought heat to my cheeks, especially when Titania's sharp glance my way told me she knew exactly what the Erlking was talking about. I reminded myself that I hadn't done anything wrong when I'd agreed to give the Erlking my virginity. It was the only way I could save Ethan, and I never planned to make good on my part of the deal, even though the cost to me was going to get heavier and heavier as time went by.

Titania looked at me. "Arawn is a most dangerous ally," she said.

"Don't worry," I told her. "I won't do anything stupid with him."

Arawn laughed softly. "She is a stubborn little thing, our Faeriewalker."

I glared up at him, but that didn't do much to dispel his amusement. I wondered if he still believed there was a chance in hell I was going to sleep with him someday. He'd claimed once that he thought time would whittle away my resistance, but that was before I knew what all the consequences would be.

That led me to thinking about Elizabeth again. Here was another female Faeriewalker—one who was apparently a virgin, or Henry wouldn't have offered her to the Green Lady—who would be more vulnerable to him. And neither Titania, nor any other member of her Court, could warn Elizabeth about Arawn's ulterior motives.

No, I was the only one who could, and it made me wonder if I'd outlived my usefulness to him.

Of course, he had argued with Titania to save my life. But his scheming and machinations were so complex I rarely figured out exactly what he was up to until it was way too late.

Titania made a face of polite skepticism, but didn't say anything. This time when Arawn made to follow us back into her room, she didn't protest.

I blinked in surprise when I walked through the doorway into a completely different room from the one we'd been in before. The bed was gone, as was the carpet of rose petals. The floor was now covered in apple-green grass, trimmed short like on a golf course, and the furniture consisted of three chairs, unlike any I'd ever seen before. They sprouted from the ground, complete with gnarled roots, their glossy-smooth trunks forming scooped-out seats adorned with fluffy cushions that looked suspiciously like moss. There were three of them, arranged in a triangle and facing one another, but one of them was adorned with white climbing roses that filled the room with their scent.

Titania took a seat on the rose-covered chair, gesturing me and Arawn into the other two. Both chairs were large enough for Arawn to sit comfortably, which meant that my chair made me feel small and vulnerable. Which, come to think of it, I was, considering I was in the presence of two of the most powerful people in Faerie.

Titania sat rigidly straight in her chair, looking very queenly in her fancy embroidered gown and with her steely eyes. Arawn was considerably more relaxed, almost sprawled in his chair, and there was a twinkle in his eye that said he expected to enjoy whatever was coming next.

"I have heard that the people of Avalon are used to being more frank and straightforward than we of the Courts," Titania began.

"An understatement," Arawn interrupted with a chuckle.

Titania flashed him a look of annoyance that didn't bother him in the least, but she didn't allow him to distract her for long. "I will therefore attempt to be frank and straightforward."

Oh, goody.

"My inclination is to order your execution," she said, and the pit of my stomach dropped out. I could have done without the whole frank-and-straightforward thing if this was what she meant. "You have killed my son. Not without reason, I know, but it is still a crime punishable by death."

My heart hammered somewhere up around my throat, and my skin was all clammy. I hadn't exactly thought I was home free, but I had thought the scales were tipping in my favor. Apparently, I'd been wrong.

"But that would be the *excuse* for putting you to death," Arawn said, "not the *reason* for it."

Titania gave him another dirty look, her face far more expressive now than it had been before.

Arawn shrugged. "By the time you got through your 'frank and straightforward' explanation, Dana would have been so frightened and confused she'd have no idea what you were saying. I've spent enough time in Avalon to speak like a native, as it were."

She obviously didn't like it. I wasn't sure *I* much liked it, either.

"The *reason* for it," Arawn continued, "is that you are a threat. Even more of a threat than Titania originally realized."

Because of the spell, he meant. The spell he'd urged me to cast. The spell he'd known would show Titania just how dangerous I was capable of being.

It was stupid to feel betrayed by the Erlking, but I couldn't help it. I knew how false his charms were, but I fell for them every damn time.

"You could kill the Queen, or any of her people, without a single weapon at hand," the Erlking said, as if he hadn't made his point already. "That makes you the most dangerous Faeriewalker ever born."

I must have looked as terrified as I felt, because Titania shushed the Erlking and spoke softly, like she'd spoken to Elizabeth.

"It doesn't have to be that way," she said. "All you need do to prove you are not a danger to us is to swear allegiance to the Seelie Court."

The jaws of the trap snapped shut around my ankle.

chapter twenty-four

My father had once told me that because I was the daughter of a Seelie Fae, I was automatically considered part of the Seelie Court. But having other people assume I was a member of the Seelie Court was not the same as *being* a member of the Seelie Court. I wasn't bound by any oaths, and Titania had no right to order me around. But if I swore allegiance to the Court . . .

I glanced at the Erlking, who wasn't quite smirking, but who definitely had a hint of knowing triumph in his eyes. I understood exactly why he liked where this was going. If I swore allegiance to the Seelie Court, then I'd also be bound by his agreement with Titania not to tell anyone that if a virgin gave herself to him of her own free will, he could steal her powers, and even her life. The geis around this agreement was so strong that my father hadn't been able to give me even an oblique warning about it. Which meant there would be no one who could warn Elizabeth that her new "friend" had ulterior motives.

I shook my head at him, my hands clenched into fists in my lap. "I fall for your tricks every time," I said bitterly. "You'd think I'd know better by now."

"There was no trick," he said. "Not this time. You were the only one who could kill Henry, and if you didn't do it, both you and Elizabeth would have suffered."

"And you didn't give a thought to how it might benefit you when you pushed me into doing it, right?"

He shrugged his massive shoulders. "I won't claim I was unaware of the advantages. But that isn't why I did it. I am not the monster you like to think me."

"Yeah, you're a candidate for sainthood."

As usual, he laughed at my sarcasm, but the laughter faded quickly. "Have you ever considered that once Titania gave me permission to hunt you, I could have bound you to the Wild Hunt and forced you to take me out into the mortal world whenever I wished?"

"Oh, and that's not what you were trying to do when you had Ethan try to kidnap me in the middle of the night?"

He gave me a condescending look. "Think about it a minute, Dana." His expression turned wry. "And assume I am not stupid."

That was one thing I was sure he was not.

No, he wasn't stupid at all. So why on earth had he used Ethan to try to capture me? Thanks to the mark on my shoulder, Arawn could find me wherever I was, and if he and his Wild Hunt found me, there would be nothing I could do to escape them. If Arawn hadn't tried to use Ethan, I wouldn't even have known he was hunting me. Not until it was too late, at least.

And then there was the *way* he'd had Ethan try to capture me. Ethan had said he'd fought the orders as best he could, making as much noise as possible so that Keane and Kimber would wake up and stop him. But surely the Erlking knew better than to allow any wiggle room in his orders. He could have ordered Ethan to sneak me quietly out of camp, maybe even knock me unconscious so I couldn't fight him, and Ethan would have had to do it.

"But why?" I asked, totally bewildered. Every time I thought I had the Erlking figured out, he'd do something to prove I was completely wrong.

"Had such an opportunity presented itself to me in the early days, when I did not yet know you," he said, "I would have taken it. I still want very badly to hunt in the mortal world, and if I could persuade or coerce you into taking me, I would. But I would not see you destroyed in the process. Being bound to my Hunt would destroy your special spark. And remember that mortals who are bound to the Hunt cannot survive it for long. Your Fae blood would preserve your life for several years, maybe even a decade, but you are too mortal to survive it indefinitely."

I rubbed my eyes, exhausted and headachy from all the stress and the constant intrigue. I was pretty sure he was telling the truth about not wanting to bind me to the Hunt, but I wasn't sure his reasons were anything so benevolent. After all, he still had hopes that I would give him my virginity, and that he could claim my Faeriewalker powers as his own. If he did that, he'd have access to the mortal world anytime he wanted, not just for as long as my body could survive the rigors of the Hunt. Reasons within reasons within reasons, all tangled together and confusing.

"Whatever," I mumbled with a shake of my head. Maybe he'd set me up, or maybe he hadn't. In the end, it didn't much matter.

I wrenched my gaze away from the Erlking and faced Titania instead. "You realize that if I am a member of the Seelie Court, I can't warn Elizabeth about him."

"Don't forget that Connor is still a member of my Hunt," the Erlking reminded me.

I flinched, because I had kinda forgotten about Connor. When I'd first learned the Erlking's secret, he'd promised me that if I told anyone, he'd make Connor pay for it. I couldn't say I actually *knew* my brother, so maybe I was protecting someone who didn't deserve protecting. But Connor was Fae, and therefore immortal, and the suffering the Erlking could inflict on him if he wished to . . .

"It will be my responsibility to protect my granddaughter," Titania said. "She is not the only girlchild I have had to keep from Arawn's influence."

Something about her tone of voice chilled me, though I couldn't say just what. But I knew the most foolproof way to protect Elizabeth from Arawn without actually telling her the truth was to make sure she didn't stay a virgin very long.

Was Titania that cold? That ruthless? I wished like hell my dad were here so I could ask him. I was in way, way over my head. I'd thought I'd had some clue about what Fae politics and intrigue were like, but it was worse even than I'd imagined. Maybe saving Elizabeth from Henry's clutches wasn't going to turn out to be such a good thing after all.

"Come now," Titania said. "You are a natural child of the Seelie Court. It is only fitting that you take your proper place. Swear allegiance, and we can put all of this unpleasantness behind us."

It was a no-brainer, right? Join the Seelie Court and live, or refuse to join and die. But if there was one thing I'd learned through hard experience, it was that nothing about the Fae was simple.

"I want to talk to my dad before I decide," I said.

"You already know what your father would advise," Titania said. There was an edge of impatience in her voice. She probably wasn't used to people not doing exactly what she told them to, when she told them to do it.

My dad would tell me I had no choice. But then my dad had also believed I had no choice but to give up on Ethan once the Erlking had captured him. I didn't like the deal I'd made with the Erlking, but the fact remained that if I had it to do over again, I'd do the same thing. I could never have let Ethan be enslaved to the Wild Hunt, not when I could save him.

My instincts—or over-the-top paranoia, take your pick—were telling me that if I agreed to the Faerie Queen's deal, I'd be as much a slave as Ethan had been. I wanted to live, but not like that. Maybe I was being stubborn, or immature, or just basically stupid, but I'd walked into one trap too many, and I wasn't willing to walk into another.

When Henry had been coming for me, the magic had come to my call faster than ever before. I'd had the element of surprise on my side, but then I figured I'd probably have it now, too. Titania was too sure of herself to think I'd put up more than a token resistance. I was just a scared kid, after all. But I was a scared kid who was sick to death of being manipulated and pushed around. I might be in a room with two of the most powerful people in Faerie, but thanks to my unusual magic, *I* was one of the most powerful people in Faerie, too. And it was time to prove it.

I rubbed my lips with my thumb, pretending I was thinking it over while I hummed so quietly the sound was no more than a faint vibration in my throat.

The magic had no trouble hearing me, and suddenly the room prickled with its energy. Titania gasped and leapt to her feet, though Arawn only raised his eyebrows. He'd said once that my spell might not work against him because he wasn't Sidhe, so maybe he wasn't all that worried. Then again, the Bogles hadn't been Sidhe, either.

"I'm not planning to cast anything," I told Titania, then hummed again to make sure the magic didn't lose interest. "Just reminding you that I can. I don't want to join the Seelie Court. I just want to go home and be a normal teenager." Hah! Like that was ever going to happen!

I hummed a little more. "If you're worried about how dangerous I am because of my magic, then I'll let you put a geis on me not to use it except in self-defense. Like the deal Arawn has with the government of Avalon about not attacking its citizens."

Titania was practically trembling with fury, and if she hadn't been an out-and-out enemy before, she sure as hell was now.

"I'm not threatening you," I said. "I called magic because I was afraid to say no to you without some way to defend myself when you've made it clear you're going to kill me if I don't agree."

That wasn't entirely true. Yes, having the magic primed and at the ready might discourage anyone from trying to kill me, but my decision to call it had been based more on anger than fear. But Titania didn't have to know that.

My words didn't seem to appease her much. In fact, I could have sworn her eyes were going to start glowing red any moment.

"Titania, my dear," the Erlking drawled. "I suggest you refrain from doing anything rash. If there's one thing I've learned about Dana over the course of our acquaintance, it's that she will defend those she cares about with single-minded ferocity. Harming her father or her friends would be . . . inadvisable."

My heart stuttered, and my voice faltered. I hadn't even thought about what Titania might do to her helpless captives if she was pissed off at me but couldn't hurt me. Anger had stolen some of my common sense, and if Arawn hadn't spoken up, I might not have recognized the threat until too late.

I recovered my composure quickly, before the magic could seep away. My hum was pretty tuneless, but it was enough to keep the magic swirling around me.

"Give us all safe passage back to Avalon," I said. "Me, and my father, and Ethan, and Keane, and Kimber, and Finn. And Elizabeth!" The last was an unexpected addition, but hell, after what I'd put her through, I figured I might as well include her. "You do that, and I'll accept the geis never to attack anyone of the Seelie Court with my magic unless they attack me first."

Titania dropped back into her seat. She'd put on her courtly mask again, her emotions hidden beneath the surface, but I knew she was still seething. She tapped her fingers on the arm of her chair as she thought. I kept humming, though it was hard to keep it up when the magic made the air so thin.

Titania seemed to think about it forever before she finally came to a decision. She made one more try to recruit me, though it seemed a bit halfhearted.

"If you swear allegiance to the Seelie Court, it will not only make peace between you and my people, it will also protect you from my counterpart of the Unseelie Court. Mab has wanted to eliminate you from the first moment she learned of your existence, but she would not dare to act against a member of my Court."

"I bet if she knew what I could do, she wouldn't be so hot to make an enemy of me," I countered. Arawn laughed at that, though Titania looked very much unamused. "So do we have a deal, or don't we?"

"You may not take Elizabeth," Titania said. "She is my kinswoman, and therefore mine to protect."

"You mean control."

"You may not have her," she repeated. "I will grant safe passage for you and the others, but she remains here with me."

I'd have liked to have helped Elizabeth, but I could tell Titania wouldn't budge. Plus, she was right. Elizabeth was her granddaughter, and I was just going to have to hope she'd take better care of her than Henry had.

I shivered, wondering if I had thought of everything, whether I'd left any kind of devastating loophole open that would get me or the others hurt. But I couldn't think of anything, and the constant press of the magic was starting to make my vision go blurry around the edges.

"I guess we have a deal then," I said, standing up and holding my hand out for her to shake.

She looked at my hand like it was a dog turd and she didn't want to touch it. Out of the corner of my eye, I saw Arawn finally rise from his chair. He pulled a knife out of his boot and handed it hilt-first to Titania.

"Don't get jumpy," he told me when I took a hasty step away. "The deal must be sealed with blood." He grinned at me. "I don't think either one of you would like to seal it with a kiss."

Oh, hell no! When I'd made my deal with Arawn, we'd sealed it with a kiss and the magic had made me so out of control I'd practically been ready to tear my clothes off and do him on the spot. I was *so* not going there with Titania, even though Arawn had warned me that a deal sealed in blood involved a fair amount of pain.

I finally stopped humming, because I was going to pass out if I didn't. I half-expected Titania to plunge the Erlking's knife into my chest, but instead she grabbed my wrist in a bone-crushing grip and then slashed my palm.

The pain was a shock to my system, and I let out a strangled cry that wasn't quite a scream. She had cut me so deep I could see a hint of bone, and I couldn't suppress the tears that sprang to my eyes. She made a much shallower cut to her own palm, then pressed our bleeding wounds together as magic slammed into us both.

This time, I did scream. I'd thought the wound hurt *before* the magic enhanced it. It was all I could do to stay conscious while Titania repeated the terms of our deal. Even though her wound wasn't as deep, she had to be hurting, too, but you couldn't tell by her face or voice. She was once again the cool, emotionless Queen of Faerie, while I was sobbing like a little girl.

Somehow, I managed to stammer out my own part of the agreement before my vision went black and the pain abruptly stopped.

chapter twenty-five

I woke up lying flat on my back on the grassy floor, my head pillowed in Arawn's lap. At first, I was groggy enough not to be quite sure what was going on, but when my mind cleared, I hastily sat up.

Too hastily, my swimming head told me, and I had to close my eyes until the world steadied around me and I didn't feel quite so much like barfing.

When I opened my eyes again, I saw Arawn had moved away and was now sitting with his back propped against the base of one of the chairs, one long leg stretched out in front of him, the other bent. He was watching me, but he didn't say anything, for which I was grateful. I needed a little time to gather my wits before I would be capable of conversation.

I shuddered as I remembered why I had been lying unconscious on the floor. There was a lot of blood on my pants, though whether from the bullet wound or the slice in my palm, I wasn't sure. I turned my hand over and looked at my palm, but someone—either Titania, or more likely Arawn—had healed the bone-deep cut until there was nothing left of it but a thin red line.

"All your wounds are healed," Arawn said quietly, like he was trying not to startle a frightened animal.

I nodded, still not trusting my voice. I glanced around the room and saw that Titania was gone, which was probably a good thing. The less she and I saw of one another, the more likely I'd survive to adulthood.

It took a while for the implications of the Erlking's words to sink in. *All* your wounds are healed, he'd said. Meaning the burn, too?

"The mark would have finished repairing itself in another day or two," he said, answering my unspoken question. "I merely sped it along."

"So Ethan's face will heal, too?" I asked, and discovered my voice was hoarse and my throat raw. How much had I screamed? I didn't want to know.

He nodded. "When Titania releases him, I will fix his mark as well. I'm sure he will be more pleasing to your eye without a suppurating wound on his face."

"And coincidentally, he'll be a lot easier for you to control."

"Maybe, maybe not."

I frowned at him. "What's *that* supposed to mean?"

"I have a proposition for you."

I quickly scrambled to my feet, and although dizziness threatened to swamp me again, I gritted my teeth and fought through it. "Oh, no!" I snapped, taking a step back from him. "No more of your propositions!"

He laughed and stayed seated. I was severely tempted to call the magic back. The Erlking was an independent power, not a member of the Seelie Court, which meant he wasn't covered under my agreement with Titania.

"I think you'll want to hear this proposition," he said.

No, I didn't exactly want to hear it. But I wasn't sure I could afford *not* to hear it. Damn him!

The Erlking must have sensed my capitulation, though I didn't say anything. Keeping a careful eye on me—if I didn't know better,

I might almost think he was afraid of me—he rose to his feet. I had to practically crane my neck to meet his eyes.

"I've come to know you rather well over the course of our acquaintance," he said in that deep, rumbly voice of his.

Way too well, in my opinion. Half the time I swore he could predict my actions before I had a clue what I was going to do.

"I once thought I could persuade you to fulfill our agreement over time, but now I'm not so sure."

"But you can't go back on our agreement, right?" I asked in alarm.

He patted the air with his hand in a calming gesture. "No, no, that's not where I'm going with this."

I'd have let out a breath of relief if I didn't suspect that wherever he *was* going with this was going to be worse.

"You have obviously become very protective of Elizabeth," he continued.

Yeah, I was so protective of her that I'd given her up. Twice.

"You did not accept Titania's proposal that you pledge allegiance to the Seelie Court, and therefore you are free to warn Elizabeth about me."

I'd been trying not to think about that, but of course I never seemed to be able to avoid unpleasantness for long.

"I haven't forgotten you hold Connor hostage," I said, staring at the floor in hopes that Arawn wouldn't read anything in my face. Because I was going to have to make a choice between protecting Elizabeth and protecting Connor, and I wasn't sure what choice I'd end up making. Connor was my brother, but Elizabeth had already been through so much in her short life. I felt so sorry for her I could almost taste it.

"But perhaps that isn't enough to persuade you to hold your tongue," the Erlking said.

So much for trying to hide what I was thinking.

"Besides," he said, his voice gentling, "Connor has been a member of my Hunt for many centuries. As I've tried to tell you, I'm not the monster you think I am. I can like and dislike people just as anyone else can, and I like Connor. I would very much prefer not to be forced to hurt him for something that is not his fault. I will do it if you force my hand, but I don't wish to. Do you understand?"

I was too exhausted to manage much of a glare, but I did the best I could. "Yeah, I get it. It would hurt you as much as it would hurt him, blah, blah, blah."

Arawn's lips twitched like he was suppressing a smile. "My proposal is this: I will unconditionally release Ethan from the Hunt and from my service. I will remove my mark from him, and it will be like his capture never happened."

Suddenly, my knees felt all weak and wobbly again, and I hurried to sit in one of the chairs before I collapsed. "Would that mean . . . ?" I couldn't even speak the words, almost afraid of the answer.

"It means Ethan would no longer be my hostage. It means I could no longer bind him to my Hunt should you bestow your virginity upon another."

To be freed from my agreement with the Erlking . . . My mind could barely encompass what that would mean.

In the weeks since I'd made my devil's bargain, I'd tried to resign myself to a truly depressing future. I would never be able to have sex without losing Ethan to the Wild Hunt, and even if he and I broke up someday, I'd never have been willing to sacrifice him like that. I'd tried to convince myself that I could stand the idea of dying a virgin, that I could still have a good life even if I could never hope to get married or have kids or even have anything resembling a normal relationship with a guy. I hadn't had any success fooling myself.

"You're too strong-willed for me to believe you will ever give yourself to me," the Erlking said. "There seems little point in keeping our agreement intact."

Even in my shocky and exhausted state of mind, it wasn't hard to guess what the catch was. "You mean now that you know there's another Faeriewalker you can prey on. One who's more likely to give you what you want."

"Indeed. In return for Ethan's release, you will accept a geis that will prevent you from revealing my secret."

"So I can gain my freedom, but only if I make no attempt to warn Elizabeth away from you." I felt tears of anger and frustration building in my eyes and fought to keep them from falling.

He nodded. His eyes looked almost kind, but it was a total lie. "One of the hardest lessons to learn in life is that you cannot save everyone. I think that lesson is *particularly* hard for you."

A part of me knew he was right, but I refused to give up without a fight. I hummed a note. The magic came to my call, but it felt sluggish, and the room spun around me. The Erlking didn't look even mildly alarmed.

"Magic takes its toll," he said, "and you've used a lot of it today."

"I bet I can manage one more spell," I panted, though I wasn't so sure. I barely had hold of any magic at all right now, and I suspected it took rather a lot to cast my special spell.

The Erlking sat down, completely relaxed despite what he'd seen my magic do earlier. "I honestly don't think your spell will work on me."

Like he would tell me if he thought it would.

His brow creased in thought, and he hesitated as if trying to pick his words carefully. "I was not born," he said. "I have no parents, no memories of childhood, no memories of being anything other than what I am now. There's a reason I'm immortal, and I think it may be that I'm not exactly alive in the first place. I am a force of nature, or a construct of magic, or an integral element of Faerie. But I am not something that can be killed."

I let the magic go, but only because my whole body was shaking with the strain of trying to hold even a thimbleful of it. The Erl-king sounded sincere, and maybe he really believed what he was saying. But I certainly wouldn't put it past him to be making this up to discourage me from casting my spell. As far as I could tell, he'd never outright lied to me, but that didn't mean he *couldn't*.

"You have saved your friends and you have saved your father, against all odds," he said. "Be content with that. Let Titania shoulder the burden of protecting Elizabeth. Titania and I have danced this dance before many times. Sometimes I win, sometimes she does. But in any case, you do not leave the child undefended if you look out for your own best interests for once."

I hate giving up. Maybe I'm just a naturally contrary person, but I always feel like there's a solution to every problem if only I dig deep enough. But I was tired of digging. Tired, period.

"What about Connor?" I asked. Part of my current agreement with the Erlking was that he'd let Connor go if and when I actually fulfilled my part.

"Do you honestly mean to suggest that one day you would have done what was necessary to free him?"

I sighed, my shoulders slumping. "No." My voice was little more than a defeated whisper.

"He has been bound to me, to the Wild Hunt, for most of his life. I'm not certain how he would have fared had you managed to free him. Let him be."

"And your mark? Will you get it off of me?"

He shook his head. "You have amply demonstrated your power, and it's true that when word reaches Mab of what you can do, she might hesitate to attack you. But she might not. She is more capricious than Titania. You can still use my mark to summon me, should you ever need me. Even if we void our agreement, I am still your ally." His face broke into a smile. "Whether you want me as one or not."

I made an undignified snorting sound.

The Erlking pulled his knife out of his boot. Titania must have given it back to him after she finished slicing me open with it. I really wasn't looking forward to another blood oath.

"We can seal our new bargain with a kiss, if you'd prefer," the Erlking said, but not like he thought I'd go for it.

I shook my head and held out my hand, wincing in anticipation. "Let's just get this over with."

chapter twenty-six

By the time I'd finished swearing my new oath with the Erlking, I was so exhausted it was all I could do to stay conscious. My legs refused to hold me up, and the Erlking ended up carrying me to the bedroom I'd shared so briefly with Kimber when we'd first arrived at the palace. We seemed to make it there in about ten seconds, which made me suspect I'd lost consciousness along the way, and the moment he laid me on the bed, sleep dragged at me so hard I couldn't resist. The last thing I remembered was the Erlking sitting on the edge of the bed and prying off my filth-encrusted shoes.

My internal clock told me it was at least several hours later, if not a whole day or more, when I next woke up. My head felt about three feet thick, and my mouth tasted like something had crawled in there and died. My eyes were all crusty with sleep when I blinked them open.

Sunlight was pouring in the windows, confirming my guess that I'd been out for a long time. I tried a tentative stretch, which every muscle in my body objected to. I still felt like I could sleep another week, but as my brain cells began to wake up one by one and I started remembering everything that had happened, sleep seemed like a less likely option.

Licking my lips, trying to get the bad taste out of my mouth, I propped myself up on my elbows and looked around. Tears stung my eyes when I saw Kimber curled up on a poofy chair, her nose buried in an ancient-looking book that probably weighed as much as I did. She was so absorbed in the book she didn't even notice me moving.

"I see you're doing a little light reading," I croaked, then cleared my throat as Kimber jumped and squealed, the book sliding off her lap and hitting the floor with a thump.

She put her hand to her chest and took a deep breath. "You scared the crap out of me!" she scolded.

Leave it to Kimber to get all absorbed in a book that looked like it had been printed in the 1800s. Yeah, looks could be deceiving in Faerie, but Kimber was enough of a brainiac that she read stuff like Shakespeare for pleasure.

"Sorry," I said insincerely. "Go ahead and finish your book. I'll just sit here quietly and wait." To demonstrate my determination, I pushed myself up into a sitting position, and found the effort left me panting. I also noticed for the first time that someone had cleaned me up and put a flannel nightshirt on me. Oh, God, I hoped it hadn't been the Erlking! I remembered him taking off my shoes.

"Take it easy," Kimber said, and I blinked in surprise to find her sitting on the edge of my bed. She'd been clear across the room last time I looked.

"How did you get here so fast?" I muttered, and I sounded incoherent even to my own ears.

"You're having a kind of magic hangover," Kimber explained. "You'll be sleeping and spacing out a lot for the next day or so. You must have used a buttload of magic. I've never seen anyone have it this bad. Not even Ethan when he's showboated himself into exhaustion."

I rubbed my crusty eyes, wondering how much Kimber knew

about what had happened. Did she know I'd killed Henry? And *how* I'd killed him?

"Are you all right?" I asked her, because I wasn't sure I wanted to know the answers to my other questions.

"In the state you're in, you're asking *me* if *I'm* all right?"

"Well, I had some pretty major doubts when you were captured and hauled back here!"

She made a face. "Sorry. Right. I'm fine. Everyone's fine. They weren't exactly nice to us, but they didn't hurt us or anything. We were just locked up for a while is all."

"Does 'everyone' include my dad and Finn?"

"Yeah, they're fine, too." There was something just slightly false in her tone, and it gave me a chill.

"Tell me the truth!" I demanded.

"Well, aren't you the cranky patient?"

"Please, Kimber. Tell me what's going on."

"They're fine," she said, sounding more convincing this time. "They had a rough time of it while we were gone, but they're fine now."

I swallowed hard, trying not to imagine just what kind of "rough time" they'd been having. I might have hoped Titania would be at least a little attached to my dad and might not want to hurt him. After all, they'd been together more than a century, and they had a kid. But the fact that she'd been sleeping with the Erlking told me just how sentimental she was.

"You know coming after us when you could have used the brooch to get away was probably one of the stupidest moves in the history of mankind," Kimber said. "You might want to avoid your dad for the next year or two until he's had a chance to calm down."

Great. I'd come back and saved everyone, and my dad was mad at me for it. Not that I was surprised, mind you. I think it's in the parental rule book somewhere that you have to get mad at your kids if they do something dangerous, even if it's the right thing to do and everything turns out well in the end.

"I couldn't just run away and leave you all behind," I said. "I couldn't have lived with that. Maybe coming back was stupid, but I'd do it again in a heartbeat." And I refused to feel bad about it.

Kimber winced. "I suggest you not say that to your dad. Or to Finn. Or to the boys, for that matter."

"But my saying it doesn't bother *you*?" I had a feeling that wasn't a good thing, and the look on Kimber's face confirmed it.

"We'll talk when you're all better."

I didn't like the sound of that. "Kimber—"

"Don't!" she snapped. "We're not doing this now." She sounded really angry, but her eyes were kind of shiny, like she was about to cry.

I guess that answered my question about whether she'd forgiven me. Every secret I'd kept, I'd kept with good reason. At least, what I'd thought was a good reason at the time. Looking back, I wasn't so sure.

"Can I at least say I'm sorry?" I asked.

"You don't actually believe words will make it better, do you?"

No, I didn't. I'd told too many lies for my words to have much meaning. I wanted to point out that my coming back to the palace after she and the others were captured spoke louder than any words, but I didn't. Tears burned my eyes. Maybe I saved my friends' lives, but that didn't make me any less of a screw-up. I wasn't good friend material, not when I was biologically incapable of trust and honesty.

Kimber was the only real friend I'd ever had, the only one I'd had more than the most superficial relationship with. The thought that I might lose her friendship, that I might already have lost it, hurt more than the bullet wound and the bone-deep gash on my palm combined.

My throat ached and my nose got all stuffy as I fought to contain tears. I was always reluctant to cry in front of anyone. My mom cried at the drop of a hat, using her tears as a tool to get sympathy whenever she'd done something stupid or irresponsible. She cried so that you'd rush in with reassurances and tell her everything was going to be all right, so that you'd somehow end up apologizing for being mad at her when *she* was the one who'd been in the wrong. I was *not* going to be like that.

I looked into Kimber's stony face, saw how she sat with her arms crossed over her chest in what I knew was a defensive posture, and realized I was doing it again. Hiding things from her, then justifying myself with reasoning that couldn't withstand close examination.

Was I really trying to put on a "brave" face and pretend that losing Kimber's friendship wouldn't hurt me? Was that the message I wanted to send her? Was that what she deserved?

I let the tears fall, and once they started, I couldn't get them to stop. Too much had happened, and I'd been putting on the brave face for too long. I'd hurt my best friend. I'd killed a man. And I'd abandoned Elizabeth when I could have helped her. Each decision had felt like the right one at the time, but I was far from sure now. These weren't the kinds of decisions I should be having to make, not at my age! My decisions shouldn't determine who lived and who died, who was protected and who was thrown to the wolves. My most earth-shattering decision right now should be which colleges to apply to in the fall, not whether letting my best friend in on a secret might get me or her killed.

Kimber sighed and gave me a hug. That made me cry even harder. This was exactly why I hadn't wanted to let myself cry in the first place. I didn't want to manipulate Kimber into forgiving me.

"I-I'm sorry," I choked out through my tight throat, meaning I was sorry I was sniveling all over her, but I couldn't get a deep enough breath to say the whole thing.

"I know," she said softly, still hugging me. "I'm sorry, too. I can't even imagine going through everything you've been through." She was a far better friend than I deserved.

Eventually, the tears began to dry up and Kimber let go of me. She didn't leave, though, instead sitting quietly on the bed beside me, waiting for the hiccuping to finish. I felt even more tired now than I had when I'd first woken up, the crying jag stealing the last of my energy. I think I even did one of those magic-hangover space-outs somewhere along the way, because my face went from being damp with tears to bone-dry in the blink of an eye.

"You still need a lot of rest," Kimber said, her voice startling me out of yet another daze.

I blinked and shook my head. "I'm fine," I said automatically, despite how heavy my eyelids felt. I didn't want to just blubber all over Kimber's shoulder and then take a nap.

"Go to sleep," Kimber ordered. "I'll still be here when you wake up."

"Really?" I asked, managing to sound hopeful and skeptical all at once.

She snorted. "You don't think I'm letting you off that easy, do you? You've got lots more gut-spilling to do, and you can't do it in the state you're in. So sleep, already."

My eyes slid shut despite my best efforts to keep them open.

Kimber was wrong. She *wasn't* still there when I woke up.

I awakened to the unfamiliar feel of an arm wrapped around my waist and a warm body snuggled up against my back. I went from sound asleep to wide awake in the space between heartbeats, my breath catching in my lungs.

I knew without having to look that it was Ethan. Maybe it was just a natural guess—who else would be cuddled up on the bed with me?—or maybe there was something about the feel or the scent of him that gave him away. Whatever it was, I was lying in bed with him, his whole body pressed up against mine, and the sensation was both exhilarating and terrifying.

I held absolutely still, not wanting the moment to end. As long as we lay still and quiet, there were no complications, and I could just enjoy the warmth and comfort of his body. If he knew I was awake, he might go and ruin things by giving me his version of the lecture on why I shouldn't have come back.

I wondered why he was in my room and Kimber was gone. I imagined my dad was insisting I be under twenty-four-hour guard, but I wouldn't have thought Ethan would get a shift. There was no way my dad would trust Ethan that far. He was the proverbial fox guarding the henhouse.

Ethan shifted behind me, pressing closer, nuzzling my neck. "I know you're awake," he murmured against my skin, and the feel of his lips made me break out in goose bumps.

So much for lying still and quiet.

"What are you doing here?" I asked, then wanted to bop myself for it. It was pretty obvious what he was doing as he brushed light kisses all the way up the side of my neck. I wanted to rephrase the question in a way that made sense, but my thoughts were too scrambled.

The hand at my waist slipped under the edge of my nightshirt, touching the sensitive skin of my lower belly. Cue more goose bumps. And I had to remind myself to breathe.

"You freed me," Ethan whispered right in my ear as he worked his hand farther up under the night shirt.

Right, I remembered in a flash. I'd made a new deal with the Erlking, and so Ethan and I were free to . . .

But surely he didn't mean to take advantage of that freedom *now*. I was still recuperating. And I wasn't ready to go from doing nothing but some heavy kissing to going all the way.

Ethan's hand stilled on my stomach. "Don't tell me you think I'm such an asshole that I'm planning to jump you here in your sickbed."

I let out a breath I hadn't realized I was holding. Guess my trust issues were showing again. Then again, Ethan was a teenaged boy, and I knew he'd earned his reputation as a player fair and square.

I squirmed around so I could face him. He was as gorgeous as he'd been the first time I'd met him, the blue stag gone from his face, along with any sign of the hideous burn. His eyes weren't the same, were older and wiser and more serious, but at least he was free. I reached up and touched his face where the mark had been, marveling at the softness of his skin.

"When I wake up and find you in my bed with your hand up my shirt, you can't blame me for making certain assumptions," I said tartly.

Ethan grinned at me. "I didn't put my hand up your shirt until after you were awake," he reminded me, and I couldn't stifle a bit of a laugh as I rolled my eyes at him.

"A technicality."

His grin faded as he leaned down to brush a soft kiss on my lips, pulling back quickly before either of us could catch fire. "I know my reputation," he said. "And I know I earned it. Once upon a time, I probably *would* have tried to take advantage of the situation. But I'm not that guy anymore."

Maybe I was veering too far to the other end of the trust-o-meter, but I believed him. "So putting your hand up my shirt isn't taking advantage?" I asked, but I smiled to let him know I was teasing.

"All depends where that hand ends up, doesn't it?"

Right now, it rested right at the bottom of my rib cage, the thumb stroking idly back and forth. The touch was hot and soothing all at once.

"So what are you doing here, really?" I asked. "I can't believe my dad or any of the rest of the crew would leave you alone in a bedroom with me."

He made an exaggerated face of innocence. "I can't imagine why not."

"Ethan . . ."

"Kimber was here to watch over you," he said. "I threatened to do something unpleasant to Keane if she didn't give us some alone time. She threatened to do something even more unpleasant to me if I didn't behave like a gentleman." He shuddered theatrically. "You won't tell her about the hand-up-the-shirt thing, will you? Because I think we'll both end up missing the parts she removes with a rusty spoon if she finds out."

I laughed and blushed at the same time. "Your secret's safe with me."

To show his appreciation of my restraint, he bent down and kissed me until all my thoughts and fears retreated.

I don't remember falling asleep again, but I must have, because when I next opened my eyes, it was dark out and Kimber was back on guard duty. She was reading another huge tome—its binding green instead of red, so I knew it was a different book—this time sitting on the bed beside me with her back propped up against the wall. I tried to be quiet about it as I sat up and yawned, not wanting to startle her as I'd done earlier.

I felt better. I was stiff and achy from too much time in bed, but my mind felt a whole lot clearer. My stomach rumbled loudly, reminding me that it had been at least twenty-four hours since I'd last eaten.

Kimber put her book aside. "Sleeping Beauty awakens," she said.

I responded with an unladylike snort. I didn't want to know what I looked like right now, but I figured I was more likely to break mirrors than win over Prince Charming. I rubbed at my gritty eyes and tried a tentative stretch. I really wished the Fae had coffee, because I sure could have used some.

"How are you feeling?" Kimber asked.

"Alive." That was the best I could say about my condition at the moment.

"Oh, good. I wasn't looking forward to dragging your corpse down to the caravan in the morning."

"Huh?"

"We're leaving. First thing in the morning, whether you're up to it or not. I'm not quite sure if Titania kicked us out, or if your dad just decided it was time to go. Strangely, people don't seem to want a one-woman killing machine around."

Well, that answered the question of whether my friends knew what I did to Henry. I guess if I were an immortal Fae, I wouldn't want to be around someone like me, either.

"Your dad hired some locals to provide horses and supplies," Kimber continued. "We don't get a royal escort this time."

I grimaced. "Considering what happened the last time we had a royal escort, I'd say that's a good thing."

"Couldn't agree more. Now get out of bed and get washed up and dressed. You need to stuff some food down your gullet and regain some strength. After that, your dad wants to talk to you." Her grin was almost evil. "I think you're grounded until the sun explodes."

I had a feeling that once we got back to Avalon, I was going to be spending a lot of time in my safe house. That would get old fast, I knew, but right now, I'd have liked nothing better than to be curled up in my own bed.

"There's no place like home," I murmured under my breath, and wished for some ruby slippers.

My knees almost buckled when I got out of the bed. Kimber

reached out to steady me, but my knees firmed up before I did a face-plant.

"Wow," I said. "I'm worse off than I thought." And tomorrow, I got to go horseback riding. Oh, joy.

"You'll feel better after you've eaten. The magic hangover is hitting you extra hard because you're half-starved."

My stomach roared in agreement, but I wasn't quite ready to get moving yet. Kimber was acting like her normal self, but I couldn't help wondering if she was just being nice to me until I got better.

"So, um, are you still speaking to me?" I asked.

She crossed her arms over her chest and narrowed her eyes at me. "Yeah, I'm still speaking to you. I'm going to be speaking to you *a lot* over the next few days."

She looked angry and implacable, and I knew her words were meant to be something like a threat. But I had to fight off a smile anyway. I'd happily listen to as many stern lectures as she wanted to give, as long as she stayed my friend.

chapter twenty-seven

I avoided going to see my dad for as long as I could. I mean, yeah, I wanted to see him, wanted to assure myself with my own two eyes that he was okay. Facing his anger was a whole other question.

I followed Kimber's directions to a little sitting room where every horizontal surface that wasn't a seat was covered with bowls of fruit, or pastries, or bread. There was also a vast selection of different teas, and a steaming pitcher of water. Even not being a tea fan, I made myself a cup, wanting some liquid to wash the food down with.

While my tea was steeping, I put together a plate of the most recognizable of the fruits along with a thick slice of bread and some kind of turnover. When I sat down on one of the chairs with my plate on my lap and reached for my tea, I saw that the water pitcher was still filled to the brim and steaming.

Magic water. I'd never seen that trick in Avalon. Then again, in Avalon we had electricity and water mains.

My stomach wasn't up for a big meal, but I ate as much as I could before heading back toward the suite of rooms where we were staying. My hands were clammy when I stood in front of my dad's door and tried to get myself to knock.

It wasn't that I was afraid of my dad. I knew he'd never hurt me.

But aside from the fact that I'd taken what he was sure to think were unacceptable risks in coming back to the palace, he had now learned a whole lot of secrets I'd been keeping. Things I should have confided in him, just as I should have confided in Kimber. And let's not even talk about the fact that I'd killed someone. Someone my dad hated, but still . . .

Maybe knowing about my secret spell, my dad would be afraid of me. The thought made the hunk of bread in my stomach feel like a lump of lead. Even the Erlking had been unsettled when he'd learned what I could do, but I wasn't sure I could stand it if my dad suddenly looked at me as if I were something dangerous.

I guess I wasn't completely silent, because as I stood hesitating, trying to find the guts to knock, the door swung open.

My dad was dressed in what was, for him, casual clothes: wool slacks with a button-down oxford shirt. A kink in the leather of his belt showed that he'd had to go down a notch to make it tight enough, and the shirt looked almost baggy on him. I felt my lower lip start to quiver as I thought about how terrible an ordeal he must have been through to lose that much weight in so little time.

Dad pulled me over the threshold and into a hug before I had time to get too maudlin. I hugged him back and tried not to notice that I could feel his ribs.

"I was afraid I'd lost you," my dad said, his voice all husky like he was about to cry himself. "I was so sure bringing you here was the right thing to do, and I almost got you killed."

I hated hearing the pain in his voice. I'd have preferred he yell at me, like I'd expected him to. Of course, I was sure the yelling would come eventually. Not that he ever really *yelled*. Yelling was too undignified. But he could give the softest whisper the same bite as other people could give a full-throttle bellow.

"You had no way of knowing," I said, surprised that he was still hugging me. Effusive displays of emotion were not his thing.

"I *should* have known. I should never have risked you."

"Dad, I'm all right. And you're smart and all, but I don't see how you could be expected to know Henry had a Faeriewalker daughter and wanted to eliminate the competition."

He finally released me from the hug, though he kept his hand on my shoulder as if afraid I'd disappear if he didn't hold on.

"He told me you'd been caught," Dad said, his eyes haunted. "He told me they were torturing you for information and there was nothing I could do to save you. I knew he was probably lying, but I couldn't be sure . . ."

I assumed "he" was Henry. Somewhere along the line, I'd lost all hint of guilt about killing him. The idea that I'd killed a person still gave me the shivers, but I was glad Henry was dead, and knew that if I had it all to do over again, I'd do the same thing. If there was anyone who needed killing, Henry was it.

"I'm all right, Dad," I said, though he could see that for himself. "I'm actually more worried about you and Finn. You've lost so much weight . . ." I hadn't seen Finn yet, although Kimber had assured me he was okay.

Dad sighed, finally letting go of me and moving to a pair of chairs facing an empty fireplace. I followed and sat down, though I watched his face carefully. He's usually really good at hiding his feelings, but he wasn't doing such a good job of it today. That told me more than I wanted to know about what he'd been through.

"It was an ordeal," he admitted, his eyes saying "ordeal" was too mild a term. "I won't insult you by lying about it." Was there a hint of reproach in those words? "But I'm not going to give you the details, so don't ask. We will both recover fully, and that's all you need to know. You can pester Finn about it tomorrow when we leave, but right now, you have a whole lot of explaining to do."

And just like that, my dad was back to being himself again, giving me that stern paternal face he had perfected. Usually, I'd either dig in my heels when he looked at me like that, or I'd start feeling guilty, but today I was just glad he was alive and well. And I knew that however mad he might be at me for the chances I had taken, he could never make me genuinely sorry for it.

Epilogue

Thanks to my dad's skillful use of the standing stones, it took us only three days of easy travel to reach the Avalon border. Titania had offered to send a couple of her Knights with us for security, but my dad had declined the offer. No, I wasn't what you'd call completely safe. Despite his nasty personality, Henry surely had friends who would hate me forever for killing him, and we had no way of knowing if Mab still wanted me dead or not.

"The extra security would be nice," my dad told me, "but I suspect the Knights would be there more as spies than protectors, and I'd rather do without."

When he put it that way, I couldn't help but agree. Besides, the six of us all by ourselves could travel at a quicker pace than we could if we had another handful of Knights—and their supplies—with us.

That last terrible day in the woods seemed to have changed something between Ethan and Keane. Not that they suddenly liked each other or anything—they still bickered enough to make themselves truly annoying—but I no longer got the feeling they might burst into violence at any moment. Even when Kimber and Keane weren't as sneaky about stealing kisses as they thought.

When I saw how Keane looked at her when she wasn't looking, I stopped worrying that he was using her to get to Ethan. Maybe it had started out that way, but it was definitely more than that now.

Everyone was still pretty mad at me for all the secrets I'd kept, particularly Kimber. But I got the feeling it was the kind of mad that would fade away in time. I'd come close to completely destroying our friendship, and I knew it. I couldn't swear I'd never keep a secret from her again—after all, I *was* still keeping a secret, enforced by the Erlking's geis—but I was going to make every effort to be as open with her as humanly possible.

You might think now that I had an arrangement with Titania, my dad would finally ease up on some of the paranoid security measures he'd been taking to keep me protected. Like maybe he would let me live with him in his real, normal house instead of keeping me entombed in my underground safe house. Or that he might decide I no longer needed a bodyguard twenty-four/seven. If you think that, you don't know my dad.

Sure, I'm in a much safer position than I was before my trip to Faerie. Before going to Faerie, we'd thought both Queens wanted me dead. Maybe Mab still does, but even if Titania might prefer I be dead, she isn't going to try to arrange it. I pointed out to my dad that everyone now knew how dangerous I was in my own right. At which point my dad pointed out that now that people know about my spell, they'll be much more able to avoid it. I'll still always be vulnerable to the surprise attack, or to overwhelming numbers.

Dad has a point, but I can't help wondering if maybe some of the security stuff is just a way of keeping me from being alone with Ethan. There are times when Dad treats me like he thinks of me as a responsible adult, but as soon as Ethan enters the picture, I become a little girl again. Dad won't forbid me from seeing Ethan, no matter how little he approves, but he's going to make damn sure the two of us never have enough privacy for things to go too far.

(Dad's definition of "too far" being anything past first base, as far as I can tell.) Apparently now that I no longer have my agreement with the Erlking forcing me to chastity, my dad is convinced I'll turn into a sex-crazed teen and let Ethan get away with anything he damn well pleases.

I'd never admit it out loud, but in some ways, I'm glad for my dad's overprotectiveness. I love Ethan, and I love knowing that I'm no longer under the Erkling's thumb. I love knowing that when I'm ready, we can go all the way. But I know I'm not ready yet, and as long as my dad doesn't give us alone time, I don't have to tell Ethan that.

I'm trying to be more trusting these days, I really am. But it's not so easy to change who I am at my core. I tell myself that Ethan would be just fine with waiting until I'm ready, and most of the time I actually believe it. But there's a part of me that fears if I tell him no, he'll start pushing. Or worse, that he'll dump me. If this thing between us is ever going to go to the next level, I'm going to have to face that fear eventually. But for the time being, I'm perfectly happy to let my dad's rules and regulations make it a moot point.

Which brings me to my mom.

I wish I could say I returned home to Avalon to find my mom a changed woman, sober and vowing to stay that way. I wish I could say that our tempestuous parting had finally broken through the walls of denial and shown her that her drinking didn't only hurt her, it hurt me as well. I wish that fearing she would lose me were enough to give her the will to get her life under control.

Unfortunately, I can't say any of those things. My mom was living in an apartment my dad had rented for her, seeing as she was too flat broke to afford anything on her own. Dad took me to see her on the very day we made it back from Avalon, but she didn't answer when we rang the doorbell. Dad wasn't overly concerned with her right to privacy, so he used his magic to coax the lock open and let us in.

We found my mom on the floor in the bathroom. Taking a shower when you're too drunk to stand up can be hazardous to your health. My mom had apparently tripped over the edge of the tub trying to get out and had broken her hip. She'd been lying there just over twenty-four hours when my dad and I found her. I shudder to think what might have happened if we'd stayed in Faerie a day or two longer. I don't think anyone would have found her until too late, and I couldn't thank my dad enough for deciding to go in even though she hadn't answered the door.

Thanks to the magic of the Fae healers, Mom's broken hip was little more than an inconvenience, one they could mend in a few hours. The alcohol poisoning was another matter, something the Fae healers couldn't treat, which meant Mom got to spend some quality time in the hospital.

On the day Dad and I brought her in, she was in and out of consciousness, but even when she was conscious, she wasn't what you'd call coherent. I spent several hours by her bedside, crying when she was unconscious, then trying to put on a brave face when she woke up. I needn't have bothered with the brave face—she didn't remember anything between one period of wakefulness and the next, though I wasn't sure if that was because of the lingering effects of alcohol or because of whatever drugs the doctors were feeding through her IV. Dad eventually coaxed me out of the hospital, and I spent the night at his house for the first time since I'd moved into my safe house.

Needless to say, this wasn't the kind of homecoming I'd had in mind.

When I went to visit Mom in the hospital again the next day, it was to find her awake and, if not alert, at least coherent. Dad stepped out of the room when he saw that Mom was awake, giving me some private time alone with her. I wasn't sure whether to be grateful or panicked.

She looked terrible, of course. Her skin was unusually pale, her hair greasy and lank, her eyes sunken. She still had an IV in her arm, but at least she didn't have an oxygen tube in her nose. Everything about this was my worst nightmare come true. And the worst part was that she'd done this to *herself.*

I hugged myself as I stared at her pale and sickly face, but there was no sting in my eyes, no tightening of my throat. Just a hollow, hopeless feeling in the middle of my chest. I might have thought that she'd feel bad about what she'd done to herself while I was gone, that she might be embarrassed by it or even downright ashamed. I expected her to avoid eye contact and look guilty, but instead, her face lit up when she saw me and she gave a little cry of joy.

"Dana! You're back!" She reached out her arms to me, expecting me to rush into them and hug her. Apparently, she had no memory of having seen me the day before. The happy flush in her cheeks made her look almost healthy, but I didn't go to her. I should have been glad she was alive—and somewhere deep inside, I know I was—but I was in too much pain to acknowledge it.

"I don't understand, Mom," I said, shaking my head. "How can you do this to yourself? Don't you care that you almost *died*?"

She blinked at me as if she couldn't possibly imagine what I was talking about, her arms slowly sinking as she realized I wasn't going to let her hug me. "I broke a bone, honey. That's not the same as almost dying. And I'm fine now." She tried another bright smile, but I still kept my distance.

"If Dad and I had been in Faerie any longer, you'd be dead," I said. "All because you couldn't stay off the booze for just a couple of weeks."

She dismissed that argument with a wave. "Don't be overdramatic. I fell in the shower. It happens to people all the time. I'll just have to get one of those rubber bath mats."

My jaw dropped as I realized what she was implying. "So you think that was just some kind of random accident? Something that could have happened to anybody?"

She frowned at me. "Of course, honey. It was clumsy and stupid of me, but—"

"Mom, you were drunk out of your mind. So drunk you couldn't even walk. *That's* why you fell. All the rubber mats in the world wouldn't have helped you."

"I was not drunk," she said with a look of offended dignity.

Oh. My. God. In the face of all this, she was *still* going to deny she had a drinking problem? "If you weren't drunk, then why was there an empty bottle of gin in the bathroom?"

"I'd had a drink or two," she said dismissively, "but that doesn't mean I was drunk. I just needed to unwind a little."

"Because everyone knows casual drinkers often take bottles of booze into the bathroom with them."

"Enough, Dana. I don't have to explain myself to you."

I seriously considered grabbing the first breakable object I could get my hands on and throwing it across the room. "You're in the hospital for alcohol poisoning," I said through gritted teeth. "You were unconscious or hallucinating most of the day yesterday. The doctor said you had a blood alcohol level of point-two-one percent when we brought you in. And you're going to lie there and tell me it was all just an innocent little accident, something that could have happened to anyone. Is that it?"

No matter how deeply in denial she was, I can't possibly believe she didn't know she had a problem. But no amount of insurmountable evidence was going to budge her. I wanted to strangle her. I wanted to hug her. I wanted to beg and plead and cry. I wanted to force her into rehab, or get her declared incompetent again and back under my father's care.

I didn't do any of those things. When my mom merely lay in her hospital bed in mulish silence, my shoulders slumped, and I thought that maybe, just maybe, it was time for me to accept the inevitable: my mom wasn't going to quit drinking until it killed her. And there was nothing I could do but sit there and watch it happen.

I was in a foul mood when I left my mom's room, angry and scared and on the verge of tears. My dad wasn't standing guard outside the door, as I'd expected. The waiting room was only a few yards down the hall, but I was still pleasantly surprised that he'd given me that much freedom. Maybe he'd stepped back from full red alert for once. I took a few deep breaths to get my emotions under control, then headed to the waiting room.

But it wasn't my dad I found sitting in that waiting room. It was Kimber, Keane, and Ethan. I stood there in openmouthed shock, so surprised to see them I didn't know what to say. There was a moment of somewhat awkward silence before Kimber stepped forward, smiling gently.

"Your dad thought you could use some company," she explained. "We're not supposed to leave the hospital, and you have to call him to come pick you up when you're ready to go, but we can maybe hang out in the cafeteria for a while. I don't know about you, but I could go for a nice spot of tea."

I probably made my "ugh, tea" face, because Ethan suddenly put in, "Or coffee. I'm sure they have some coffee down there, though I can't promise it's any good."

Keane frowned. "I thought girls were supposed to eat ice cream when they're feeling blue."

"You're right," Ethan agreed, then mimicked Keane's mock-puzzled look. "Or is it chocolate?"

Kimber laughed and rolled her eyes, hooking my elbow with hers and nudging me down the hall toward the elevators. "You can have mocha ice cream and get all the good stuff at once," she told me. "I'll have that spot of tea, and the boys can have whatever it is manly-men consider comfort food. Hot dogs? Beef jerky?"

"Pizza," I suggested with a tentative smile. "I think boys eat pizza with lots of greasy meat products like sausage on top."

"Hey!" Ethan protested. "Don't disrespect my sausage!"

Keane gave a snort of laughter. "But your sausage is always up to no good."

Ethan's eyes narrowed dangerously, and I thought for a moment the truce was over. Then he shook off whatever annoyance he was feeling. "Shall I make another crude sausage joke that might offend the girls, or should I just let it go?" His cheeks colored as he recognized how his words could be twisted in the context of this conversation. "Er, that is—"

We all laughed before he could finish backpedaling.

My friends' intervention didn't stop with their visit to the hospital. A couple of days later, Kimber dragged me to an Alateen meeting, which she'd found through a little Internet research. Sitting around talking to other teens with alcoholic family members isn't exactly easy for me. I've been keeping that particular dark secret so long that it's hard for me to open up. But since Kimber dragged me to that first meeting, I've been going once a week. Sometimes Kimber comes with me for moral support, sometimes Ethan does. I still grumble about going, but I have to admit, it helps to know I'm not alone. It helps even more that my friends are so accepting and willing to help.

I'm hearing the message more and more that I can't save my mom from herself. It's the same thing the Erlking told me when I wanted to save Elizabeth. *You can't save everyone,* his voice sometimes whispers in my head. Maybe he's right. Maybe they're *all* right. But every time I halfway decide to give up, I remember that I managed to save Ethan from the Erlking's clutches when *everyone* told me it couldn't be done.

I am not going to give up on my mom. They say that where there's a will, there's a way. Well, I have one hell of a strong will. And even if it turns out there really *is* no way, I know I'll survive. I'm not alone anymore. I've got my dad, and Ethan, and my friends. Before I'd come to Avalon, I couldn't have conceived of leaning on anyone, of asking anyone for help. Doing so will probably never come easy for me. But now I know I *can* do it, and it *does* help. And that makes all the difference in the world.